By Lilith Saintcrow

Dante Valentine novels
Working for the Devil
Dead Man Rising
The Devil's Right Hand
Saint City Sinners
To Hell and Back

Dante Valentine (omnibus)

Jill Kismet novels
Night Shift
Hunter's Prayer
Redemption Alley
Flesh Circus
Heaven's Spite
Angel Town

Bannon and Clare novels
The Iron Wyrm Affair

THE IRON WYRM AFFAIR

Bannon & Clare: Book One

LILITH SAINTCROW

orbit

www.orbitbooks.net

ORBIT

First published in Great Britain in 2012 by Orbit

A CIP catalogue record for this book
is available from the British Library.

ISBN 978-0-356-50092-8

Typeset in Times by Palimpsest Book Production Limited,
Falkirk, Stirlingshire
Printed and bound in Great Britain by
Clays Ltd, St Ives plc

Papers used by Orbit are from well-managed forests
and other responsible sources.

MIX
Paper from
responsible sources
FSC® C104740

Orbit
An imprint of
Little, Brown Book Group
100 Victoria Embankment
London EC4Y 0DY

An Hachette UK Company
www.hachette.co.uk

www.orbitbooks.net

For those who serve in shadow

Acknowledgements

Thanks are due to the long list of the Usual Suspects: Miriam and Devi, for believing in my crazed little stories; my children for understanding why I hunch over typing for long periods of time; Mel for gently keeping me sane; Christa and Sixten for love and coffee. Thanks are also due to Lee Jackson for his love of Victoriana, and to Susan Barnes (soon to be a Usual Suspect) for putting up with me. And finally, as always, once again I will thank you, my Readers, in the way we both like best. Sit back, relax, and let me tell you a story . . .

Prelude

A Promise of Diversion

When the young dark-haired woman stepped into his parlour, Archibald Clare was only mildly intrigued. Her companion was of more immediate interest, a tall man in a close-fitting velvet jacket, moving with a grace that bespoke some experience with physical mayhem. The way he carried himself, lightly and easily, with a clean economy of movement – not to mention the way his eyes roved in controlled arcs – all but shouted danger. He was hatless, too, and wore curious boots.

The chain of deduction led Clare in an extraordinary direction, and he cast another glance at the woman to verify it.

Yes. Of no more than middle height, and slight, she was in very dark green. Fine cloth, a trifle antiquated, though the sleeves were close as fashion now dictated, and her bonnet perched just so on brown curls, its brim small enough that it would not interfere with her side vision. However, her skirts were divided, her boots serviceable instead of decorative – though of just as fine a quality as the man's – and her jewellery was eccentric, to say the least. Emerald drops worth a fortune at her ears, and the necklace was an amber cabochon large enough to be a baleful eye. Two rings on gloved hands, one with a dull unprecious black stone and the other a star sapphire a royal family might have envied.

The man had a lean face to match the rest of him, strange yellow eyes, and tidy dark hair still dewed with crystal droplets from the light rain falling over Londinium tonight. The moisture, however, did not cling to her. One more piece of evidence, and Clare did not much like where it led.

He set the viola and its bow down, nudging aside a stack of paper with careful precision, and waited for the opening gambit. As he had suspected, *she* spoke.

"Good evening, sir. You are Dr Archibald Clare. Distinguished author of *The Art and Science of Observation*." She paused. Aristocratic nose, firm mouth, very decided for such a childlike face. "Bachelor. And very-recently-unregistered mentath."

"Sorceress." Clare steepled his fingers under his very long, very sensitive nose. Her toilette favoured musk, of course, for a brunette. Still, the scent was not common, and it held an edge of something acrid that should have been troublesome instead of strangely pleasing. "And a Shield. I would invite you to sit, but I hardly think you will."

A slight smile; her chin lifted. She did not give her name, as if she expected him to suspect it. Her curls, if they were not natural, were very close. There was a slight bit of untidiness to them – some recent exertion, perhaps? "Since there is no seat available, *sir*, I am to take that as one of your deductions?"

Even the hassock had a pile of papers and books stacked terrifyingly high. He had been researching, of course. The intersections between musical scale and the behaviour of certain tiny animals. It was the intervals, perhaps. Each note held its own space. He was seeking to determine which set of spaces would make the insects (and later, other things) possibly—

Clare waved one pale, long-fingered hand. Emotion was threatening, prickling at his throat. With a certain rational annoyance he labelled it as *fear*, and dismissed it. There was very little chance she meant him harm. The man was a larger question, but if *she* meant him no harm, the man certainly did not. "If you like. Speak quickly, I am occupied."

She cast one eloquent glance over the room. If not for the efforts of the landlady, Mrs Ginn, dirty dishes would have been stacked on every horizontal surface. As it was, his quarters were cluttered with a full set of alembics and burners, glass jars of various substances, shallow dishes for knocking his pipe clean. The tabac smoke blunted the damned sensitivity in his nose just enough, and he wished for his pipe. The acridity in her scent was becoming more marked, and very definitely not unpleasant.

The room's disorder even threatened the grate, the mantel above it groaning under a weight of books and handwritten journals stacked every which way.

The sorceress, finishing her unhurried investigation, next examined him from tip to toe. He was in his dressing gown, and his pipe had long since grown cold. His feet were in the rubbed-bare slippers, and if it had not been past the hour of reasonable entertaining he might have been vaguely uncomfortable at the idea of a lady seeing him in such disrepair. Red-eyed, his hair mussed, and unshaven, he was in no condition to receive company.

He was, in fact, the picture of a mentath about to implode from boredom. If she knew some of the circumstances behind his recent ill luck, she would guess he was closer to imploding and fusing his faculties into unworkable porridge than was advisable, comfortable . . . or even sane.

Yet if she knew the circumstances behind his ill luck, would she look so calm? He did not know nearly enough yet. Frustration tickled behind his eyes, the sensation of pounding and seething inside the cup of his skull easing a fraction as he considered the possibilities of her arrival.

Her gloved hand rose, and she held up a card. It was dun-coloured, and before she tossed it – a passionless, accurate flick of her fingers that snapped it through intervening space neat as you please, as if she dealt faro – he had already deduced and verified its provenance.

He plucked it out of the air. "I am called to the service of the

Crown. You are to hold my leash. It is, of course, urgent. Does it have to do with an art professor?" For it had been some time since he had crossed wits with Dr Vance, and *that* would distract him most handily. The man was a deuced wonderful adversary.

His sally was only worth a raised eyebrow. She must have practised that look in the mirror; her features were strangely childlike, and the effect of the very adult expression was . . . odd. "No. It *is* urgent, and Mikal will stand guard while you . . . dress. I shall be in the hansom outside. You have ten minutes, sir."

With that, she turned on her heel. Her skirts made a low, sweet sound, and the man was already holding the door. She glanced up, those wide dark eyes flashing once, and a ghost of a smile touched her soft mouth.

Interesting. Clare added that to the chain of deduction. He only hoped this problem would last more than a night and provide him further relief. If the young Queen or one of the ministers had sent a summons card, it promised to be very diverting indeed.

It was a delight to have something unknown, but within guessing reach. He sniffed the card. A faint trace of musk, but no violet-water. Not the Queen personally, then. He had not thought it likely – why would Her Majesty trouble herself with *him*? It was a faint joy to find he was correct.

His faculties were, evidently, not porridge *yet*.

The ink was correct as well, just the faintest bitter astringent note as he inhaled deeply. The crest on the front was absolutely genuine, and the handwriting on the back was firm and masculine, not to mention familiar. *Why, it's Cedric.*

In other words, the Chancellor of the Exchequer, Lord Grayson. The Prime Minister was new and inexperienced, since the Queen had banished her lady mother's creatures from her Cabinet, and Grayson had survived with, no doubt, some measure of cunning or because someone thought him incompetent enough to do no harm. Having been at Yton with the man, Clare was inclined to lean towards the former.

And dear old Cedric had exerted his influence so Clare was merely unregistered and not facing imprisonment, a mercy that had teeth. Even more interesting.

Miss Emma Bannon is our representative. Please use haste, and discretion.

Emma Bannon. Clare had never heard the name before, but then a sorceress would not wish her name bruited about overmuch. Just as a mentath, registered or no, would not. So he made a special note of it, adding everything about the woman to the mental drawer that bore her name. She would not take a carved nameplate. No, Miss Bannon's plate would be yellowed parchment, with dragonsblood ink tracing out the letters of her name in a clear, feminine hand.

The man's drawer was featureless blank metal, burnished to a high gloss. He waited by the open door. Cleared his throat, a low rumble. Meant to hurry Clare along, no doubt.

Clare opened one eye, just a sliver. "There are nine and a quarter minutes left. Do *not* make unnecessary noise, sir."

The man – a sorceress's Shield, meant to guard against physical danger while the sorceress dealt with more arcane perils – remained silent, but his mouth firmed. He did not look amused.

Mikal. His colour was too dark and his features too aquiline to be properly Britannic. Perhaps Tinkerfolk? Or even from the Indus?

For the moment, he decided, the man's drawer could remain metal. He did not know enough about him. It would have to do. One thing was certain: if the sorceress had left one of her Shields with him, she was standing guard against some more than mundane threat outside. Which meant the problem he was about to address was most likely fiendishly complex, extraordinarily important, and worth more than a day or two of his busy brain's feverish working.

Thank God. The relief was palpable.

Clare shot to his feet and began packing.

Chapter One

A Pleasant Evening Ride

Emma Bannon, Sorceress Prime and servant to Britannia's current incarnation, mentally ran through every foul word that would never cross the lips of a lady. She timed them to the clockhorse's steady jogtrot, and her awareness dilated. The simmering cauldron of the streets was just as it always was; there was no breath of ill intent.

Of course, there had not been earlier, either, when she had been a quarter-hour too late to save the *other* unregistered mentath. It was only one of the many things about this situation seemingly designed to try her often considerable patience.

Mikal would be taking the rooftop road, running while she sat at ease in a hired carriage. It was the knowledge that while he did so he could forget some things that eased her conscience, though not completely.

Still, he was a Shield. He would not consent to share a carriage with her unless he was certain of her safety. And there was not room enough to manoeuvre in a two-person conveyance, should he require it.

She was heartily sick of hired carts. Her own carriages were *far* more comfortable, but this matter required discretion. Having it shouted to the heavens that she was alert to the pattern under these occurrences might not precisely frighten her opponents, but it would become more difficult to attack them from an unexpected quarter. Which was, she had to admit, her preferred method.

Even a Prime can benefit from guile, Llew had often remarked. And of course, she would think of him. She seemed constitutionally incapable of leaving well enough alone, and *that* irritated her as well.

Beside her, Clare dozed. He was a very thin man, with a long, mournful face; his gloves were darned but his waistcoat was of fine cloth, though it had seen better days. His eyes were blue, and they glittered feverishly under half-closed lids. An unregistered mentath would find it difficult to secure proper employment, and by the looks of his quarters, Clare had been suffering from boredom for several weeks, desperately seeking a series of experiments to exercise his active brain.

Mentath was like sorcerous talent. If not trained, and *used*, it turned on its bearer.

At least he had found time to shave, and he had brought two bags. One, no doubt, held linens. God alone knew what was in the second. Perhaps she should apply deduction to the problem, as if she did not have several others crowding her attention at the moment.

Chief among said problems were the murderers, who had so far eluded her efforts. Queen Victrix was young, and just recently freed from the confines of her domineering mother's sway. Her new Consort, Alberich, was a moderating influence – but he did not have enough power at Court just yet to be an effective shield for Britannia's incarnation.

The ruling spirit was old, and wise, but Her vessels . . . well, they were not indestructible.

And that, Emma told herself sternly, *is as far as we shall go with such a train of thought.* She found herself rubbing the sardonyx on her left middle finger, polishing it with her opposite thumb. Even through her thin gloves, the stone prickled hotly. Her posture did not change, but her awareness contracted. She felt for the source of the disturbance, flashing through and discarding a number of fine invisible threads.

Blast and bother. Other words, less polite, rose as well. Her pulse and respiration did not change, but she tasted a faint tang of adrenalin before sorcerous training clamped tight on such functions to free her from some of flesh's more . . . distracting . . . reactions.

"I say, whatever is the matter?" Archibald Clare's blue eyes were wide open now, and he looked interested. Almost, dare she think it, intrigued. It did nothing for his long, almost ugly features. His cloth was serviceable, though hardly elegant – one could infer that a mentath had other priorities than fashion, even if he had an eye for quality and the means to purchase such. But at least he was cleaner than he had been, and had arrived in the hansom in nine and a half minutes precisely. Now they were on Sarpesson Street, threading through amusement-seekers and those whom a little rain would not deter from their nightly appointments.

The disturbance peaked, and a not-quite-seen starburst of gunpowder igniting flashed through the ordered lattices of her consciousness.

The clockhorse screamed as his reins were jerked, and the hansom yawed alarmingly. Archibald Clare's hand dashed for the door handle, but Emma was already moving. Her arms closed around the tall, fragile man, and she shouted a Word that exploded the cab away from them both. Shards and splinters, driven outwards, peppered the street surface. The glass of the cab's tiny windows broke with a high, sweet tinkle, grinding into crystalline dust.

Shouts. Screams. Pounding footsteps. Emma struggled upright, shaking her skirts with numb hands. The horse had gone avast, rearing and plunging, throwing tiny metal slivers and dribs of oil as well as stray crackling sparks of sorcery, but the traces were tangled and it stood little chance of running loose. The driver was gone, and she snapped a quick glance at the overhanging rooftops before the unhealthy canine shapes resolved out of thinning rain, slinking low as gaslamp gleam painted their slick, heaving sides.

Sootdogs. Oh, how unpleasant. The one that had leapt on the hansom's roof had most likely taken the driver, and Emma cursed aloud now as it landed with a thump, its shining hide running with vapour.

"*Most* unusual!" Archibald Clare yelled. He had gained his feet as well, and his eyes were alight now. The mournfulness had vanished. He had also produced a queerly barrelled pistol, which would be of *no* use against the dog-shaped sorcerous things now gathering. "*Quite* diverting!"

The star sapphire on her right third finger warmed. A globe-shield shimmered into being, and to the roil of smouldering wood, gunpowder and fear was added another scent: the smoke-gloss of sorcery. One of the sootdogs leapt, crashing into the shield, and the shock sent Emma to her knees, holding grimly. Both her hands were outstretched now, and her tongue occupied in chanting.

Sarpesson Street was neither deserted nor crowded at this late hour. The people gathering to watch the outcome of a hansom crash pushed against those onlookers alert enough to note that something entirely different was occurring, and the resultant chaos was merely noise to be shunted aside as her concentration narrowed.

Where is Mikal?

She had no time to wonder further. The sootdogs hunched and wove closer, snarling. Their packed-cinder sides heaved and black tongues lolled between obsidian-chip teeth; they could strip a large adult male to bone in under a minute. There were the onlookers to think of as well, and Clare behind and to her right, laughing as he sighted down the odd little pistol's chunky nose. Only he was not pointing it at the dogs, thank God. He was aiming for the rooftop.

You idiot. The chant filled her mouth. She could spare no words to tell him not to fire, that Mikal was—

The lead dog crashed against the shield. Emma's body jerked

as the impact tore through her, but she held steady, the sapphire now a ringing blue flame. Her voice rose, a clear contralto, and she assayed the difficult rill of notes that would split her focus and make another Major Work possible.

That was part of what made a Prime – the ability to concentrate completely on multiple channellings of ætheric force. One's capacity could not be infinite, just like the charge of force carried and renewed every Tideturn.

But one did not need infinite capacity. *One needs only slightly more capacity than the problem at hand calls for*, as her third-form Sophological Studies professor had often intoned.

Mikal arrived.

His dark green coat fluttered as he landed in the midst of the dogs, a Shield's fury glimmering to Sight, bright spatters and spangles invisible to normal vision. The sorcery-made things cringed, snapping; his blades tore through their insubstantial hides. The charmsilver laid along the knives' flats, as well as the will to strike, would be of far more use than Mr Clare's pistol.

Which spoke, behind her, the ball tearing through the shield from a direction the protection wasn't meant to hold. The fabric of the shield collapsed, and Emma had just enough time to deflect the backlash, tearing a hole in the brick-faced fabric of the street and exploding the clockhorse into gobbets of metal and rags of flesh, before one of the dogs turned with stomach-churning speed and launched itself at her – and the man she had been charged to protect.

She shrieked another Word through the chant's descant, her hand snapping out again, fingers contorted in a gesture definitely *not* acceptable in polite company. The ray of ætheric force smashed through brick dust, destroying even more of the road's surface, and crunched into the sootdog.

Emma bolted to her feet, snapping her hand back, and the line of force followed as the dog crumpled, whining and shattering into fragments. She could not hold the forcewhip for very long, but if more of the dogs came—

The last one died under Mikal's flashing knives. He muttered something in his native tongue, whirled on his heel, and stalked toward his Prima. That normally meant the battle was finished.

Yet Emma's mind was not eased. She half turned, chant dying on her lips and her gaze roving, searching. Heard the mutter of the crowd, dangerously frightened. Sorcerous force pulsed and bled from her fingers, a fountain of crimson sparks popping against the rainy air. For a moment the mood of the crowd threatened to distract her, but she closed it away and concentrated, seeking the source of the disturbance.

Sorcerous traces glowed, faint and fading, as the man who had fired the initial shot – most likely to mark them for the dogs – fled. He had some sort of defence laid on him, meant to keep him from a sorcerer's notice.

Perhaps from a sorcerer, but not from a Prime. Not from me, oh no. The dead see all. Her Discipline was of the Black, and it was moments like these when she would be glad of its practicality – if she could spare the attention.

Time spun outwards, dilating, as she followed him over rooftops and down into a stinking alley, refuse piled high on each side, running with the taste of fear and blood in his mouth. Something had injured him.

Mikal? But then why did he not kill the man—

The world jolted underneath her, a stunning blow to her shoulder, a great spiked roil of pain through her chest. Mikal screamed, but she was breathless. Sorcerous force spilled free, uncontained, and other screams rose.

She could possibly injure someone.

Emma came back to herself, clutching at her shoulder. Hot blood welled between her fingers, and the green silk would be ruined. Not to mention her gloves.

At least they had shot her, and not the mentath.

Oh, damn. The pain crested again, became a giant animal with its teeth in her flesh.

Mikal caught her. His mouth moved soundlessly, and Emma

sought with desperate fury to contain the force thundering through her. Backlash could cause yet more damage, to the street and to onlookers, if she let it loose.

A Prime's uncontrolled force was nothing to be trifled with.

It was the traditional function of a Shield to handle such overflow, but if he had only wounded the fellow on the roof she could not trust that he was not part of—

"*Let it GO!*" Mikal roared, and the ætheric bonds between them flamed into painful life. She fought it, seeking to contain what she could, and her skull exploded with pain.

She knew no more.

Chapter Two

Dreadful Aesthetics

This part of Whitehall was full of heavy graceless furniture, all the more shocking for the quality of its materials. Clare was no great arbiter of taste – fashion was largely useless frippery, unless it fuelled the deductions he could make about his fellow man – but he thought Miss Bannon would wince internally at the clutter here. One did not have to follow fashion to have a decent set of aesthetics.

So much of aesthetics was merely pain avoidance for those with any sensibilities.

Lord Cedric Grayson, the current Chancellor of the Exchequer, let out a heavy sigh, lowering his wide bulk into an overstuffed leather chair, perhaps custom-commissioned for his size. He had always been large and ruddy, and good dinners at his clubs had long ago begun to blur his outlines. Clare lifted his glass goblet, carefully. He did not like sherry even at the best of times.

Still, this was . . . *intriguing*.

"So far, you are the only mentath we've recovered." Grayson's great grizzled head dropped a trifle, as if he did not believe it himself. "Miss Bannon is extraordinary."

"She is also severely wounded." Clare sniffed slightly. And *cheap* sherry, as well, when Cedric could afford far better. It was obscene. But then, Grayson had always been a false economiser, even at Yton. *Penny wise, pound foolish*, as Mrs Ginn would sniff. "So. Someone is killing mentaths."

"Yes. Mostly registered ones, so far." The Chancellor's wide horseface was pale, and his greying hair slightly mussed from the pressure of a wig. It was late for them to be in Chambers, but if someone was stalking and killing registered mentaths, the entire Cabinet would be having a royal fit.

In more ways than one. Her Majesty's mentaths, rigorously trained and schooled at public expense, were extraordinarily useful in many areas of the Empire. *Britannia rests on the backs of sorcery and genius*, the saying went, and it was largely true. From calculating interest and odds to deducing and anticipating economic fluctuations, not to mention the ability to see the patterns behind military tactics, a mentath's work was varied and quite useful.

A *registered* mentath could take his pick of clients and cases. One unstable enough to be unregistered was less lucky. "Since I am not one of that august company at this date, perhaps I was not meant to be assassinated." Clare set the glass down and steepled his fingers. "I am not altogether certain I was the target of *this* attempt, either."

"Dear God, man." Grayson was wise enough not to ask what Clare based his statement on. This, in Clare's opinion, raised him above average intelligence. Of course, Grayson had not achieved his present position by being *completely* thickheaded, even if he was at heart a penny-pinching little pettifogger. "You're not suggesting Miss Bannon was the target?"

Clare's fingers moved, tapping against each other restlessly, precisely once. "I am *uncertain*. The attack was sorcerous *and* physical." For a moment his faculties strained at the corners of his memory of events.

He supposed he was lucky. Another mentath, confronted with the illogic of sorcery, might retreat into a comforting abstract structure, a dream of rationality meant to keep irrationality out. Fortunately, Archibald Clare was willing to admit to illogic – if only so far as the oddities of a complex structure he did not understand *yet*.

A mentath could not, strictly speaking, go mad. But he could *retreat*, and that retreat would make him unstable, rob him of experiential data and send him careening down a path of irrelevance and increasing isolation. The end of that road was a comfortable room in a well-appointed madhouse, if one was registered – and the poorhouse if one was not.

"If war is declared on sorcerers too . . ." Grayson shook his heavy, sweating head. Clear drops stood out on his forehead, and he gazed at Clare's sherry glass. His bloodshot blue eyes blinked once, sadly. "Her Majesty is most vexed."

Another pair of extraordinarily interesting statements. "Perhaps you should start at the beginning. We have some time while Miss Bannon is treated."

"It is exceedingly difficult to keep Miss Bannon down for any length of time." Grayson rubbed at his face with one meaty paw. "At any moment she will come stalking through that door in high dudgeon. Suffice to say there have been four of Her Majesty's registered geniuses recently lost to foul play."

"Four? How interesting." Clare settled more deeply into his chair, steepling his fingers before his long nose.

Grayson took a bracing gulp of sherry. "Interesting? *Disturbing* is the proper word. Tomlinson was the first to come to Miss Bannon's attention, found dead without a scratch in his parlour. Apoplexy was suspected; the attending forensic sorcerer had all but declared it. Miss Bannon had been summoned, as Crown representative, since Tomlinson had some rather ticklish matters to do research for, cryptography or the like. Well, Miss Bannon arrived, took one look at the mess, and accused the original sorcerer of incompetence, saying he had smeared traces and she could not rule out a bit of nastiness instead of disease. There was a scene."

"Indeed," Clare murmured. He found that exceedingly easy to believe. Miss Bannon did not seem the manner of woman to forgive incompetence of any stripe.

"Then there was Masters the Elder, and Peter Smythe on Rockway – Smythe had just arrived from Indus, a rather ticklish situation resolved there, I'm told. The most current is Throckmorton. Masters was shot on Picksadowne, Smythe stabbed in an alley off Nightmarket, and Throckmorton, poor chap, burned to death at his Grace Street address."

"And . . .?" Clare controlled his impatience. Why did they give him information so *slowly*?

"Miss Bannon found the fire at Throckmorton's sorcerous in origin. She is convinced the cases are connected. After Masters's misfortune, at Miss Bannon's insistence sorcerers were hastily sent to stand guard over every registered mentath. Smythe's sorcerer has disappeared. Throckmorton's . . . well, you'll see."

This was proving more and more diverting. Clare's eyebrow rose. "I will?"

"He's in Bedlam. No doubt you will wish to examine him."

"No doubt." The obvious question, however, was one he was interested in Grayson answering. "Why was I brought here? There must be other unregistereds eager for the chance to work."

"Well, you have been quite useful in Her Majesty's service. There's no doubt of that." Grayson paused, delicately. "There *is* the little matter of your registration. Not that I blamed you for it, quite a rum deal, that. Bring this matter to a satisfactory close, and . . . who can say?"

Ah. There was the sweet in the poison. Clare considered this. "I gather Miss Bannon is just as insubordinate and intransigent as myself. And just as expendable in this current situation." He did not think Miss Bannon would be *expendable*, precisely.

But he did wish to see Cedric's reaction.

Grayson actually had the grace to flush. And cough. He kept glancing at Clare's sherry as if he longed to take a draught himself.

I thought he was more enamoured of port. Perhaps his tastes have changed. Clare shelved the idea, warmed to his theme. "Furthermore, the *registered* mentaths have been whisked to safety or are presumably at great risk, so time is of the essence and the need desperate – otherwise I would *still* be rotting at home, given the nature of my . . . mistakes. I further gather there have been corresponding deaths among those, like myself, so unfortunate as to be *unregistered* for one reason or another."

Grayson's flush deepened. Clare admitted he was enjoying himself. No, that was not quite correct. He was enjoying himself *immensely*. "How many?" he enquired.

"Well. That is, ahem." Grayson cleared his throat. "Let me be frank, Archibald."

Now the game truly begins. Clare brought all his faculties to bear, his concentration narrowing. "Please do be, Cedric."

"You are the only remaining unregistered mentath-class genius remaining alive in Londinium. The others . . . their bodies were savaged. Certain parts are . . . missing."

Archibald's fingers tightened, pressing against each other. "Ah." *Most interesting indeed.*

Chapter Three

Theory and Practice

Her eyes opened slowly, and out of the candlelit gloom Mikal's face appeared. His mouth was set. For a single vertiginous instant memory rose to choke her; she was convinced she was in the round room under Crawford's country estate, the walls dripping wet stone and her head aching, the Shield murmuring *Easy, Prima, he shall not harm you again.* The slumped, torn rag of the body in the corner, the sorcerer who had been her gaoler throttled to death and mutilated; the smell of death and the restraints at her wrists easing as Mikal worked them loose.

Emma's heart leapt into her throat and commenced pounding with most unbecoming intensity.

She returned to the present with a violent start, disarranging the damp handkerchief on her forehead; a draught of violet and lavender scent unsettled her stomach even further. Mikal's hands descended on her shoulders; he pushed her back on to the divan. "Lie still." It was amazing, how he could speak through tight-clenched teeth. "The mentath is with Lord Grayson, he is safe enough. *You*, on the other hand, took a lead ball to the shoulder."

It mattered little. If she was still alive and Mikal was alive *and* conscious, her shoulder was a small problem already solved. Furthermore, she was *not* trapped in the small room that featured in her nightmares.

The relief was, as usual, indescribable. A mere month ago she had emerged from that stone-walled room, the torn and rotting bodies of her former Shields strewn in the hall like so much rubbish, and had not wept. Even after her nightmares, she did not.

The tears would not come. And *that*, she reminded herself, was what truly made her Prime. The capacity to split her focus was only a symptom.

"Was that what it was?" She peeled the handkerchief from her forehead. It was one of her own, and doused with *vitae*. That accounted for the violet-lavender. Her stomach twisted again.

"I drained the overflow. And attended to your wound." His eyes gleamed in the dimness. "I would counsel you not to move too quickly. You will likely ignore me."

She crushed the scrap of linen and lace in her palm. Her dress jacket was undone, her camisole sticky with sweat and blood; her loosely laced corset was still abominably tight, and the tingle of a limited healing-sorcery itched in her shoulder. This was one of the dusty, forgotten rooms of Whitehall, full of whispers it did not do to listen overmuch to. The furniture was exceedingly awful, though modern, and she immediately guessed this was part of Grayson's offices. The dimness was a balm to her sensitised eyes.

"I cannot protect you," Mikal continued. Under his colouring, he was remarkably pale. None of the blood or gunpowder had tainted his clothes, but a pall of almost visible smoke cloaked him. Or perhaps it was his anger. "You would do better to cast me off."

Not this argument again. "If you were not in a Prime's service, you would be executed in less than a day. In case you have forgotten that small detail, Mikal."

A half-shrug, his shoulder lifting and dropping. "You do not trust me."

She could hardly argue with the truth. *If you throttled one sorcerer you swore to protect, another would be a small matter, would it not?* "I have little reason to distrust you." The lie tasted of brass, and she suddenly longed for a glass of decent wine and an exceedingly sensational and frivolous novel, read in the comfort of her own bed.

Mikal grimaced slightly. He settled back on the stool placed precisely by the divan, glanced at the door. A Shield's awareness, marking the exit though he had never forgotten it. "I murdered my last sorcerer with my bare hands, Prima. You are not stupid enough to forget."

Hence, you must be lying, Emma, and I know it. But, as always, it was left unsaid.

So she chose truth. "I might have murdered him myself, had you not." She held out the handkerchief. "Here. *Vitae* unsettles me a little, I fear."

"There was no rum." A slight, pained smile. He took the linen, calloused but sensitive fingers brushing hers.

An unwilling smile touched her lips as well. "We make do with what we have. Now let us have no more of this *cast off* business. We have other matters to attend to."

His chin set. When he scowled, or practised his stubborn look, he was almost ugly. He did not have a pretty face.

Then why did his expression make her heart leap so indiscreetly?

Emma pushed herself gingerly up, tilted her chin down to examine her shoulder. Under the shredded green silk and the torn and stained bit of her camisole showing, pale unmarked skin moved. The tingle-itch of healing had settled more deeply, flesh and bone protesting as it was forced to knit. *Well. That was instructive.*

"I am sorry. I took the ones on the east side of the street; then there were the dogs. That particular threat was the most critical."

She nodded. Her hair had come loose, her bonnet was missing, and the silk was ruined. Now would come her admission of mistrust, and his . . . possible hurt. Or did he care so much what she thought?

Why *she* cared about a Shield's tender pride was beyond her. The Shields were to protect a Prime from physical threats and bleed off backlash, nothing more.

Come now. In theory, yes. In practice, no. All we care about is practice, correct? We have not achieved our position by being impractical. And yes, that is a royal "we", isn't it, Emma?

One day, that nasty little voice in her head might swallow its tongue and poison itself. Until it did, however, she was forced to endure its infuriating habit of being correct, as well as its habit of being singularly unhelpful.

She eased her legs off the divan, skirts bunching and sliding. A moment's work had them assembled correctly. She'd bled down the front of her dress, splashes and streaks caught in the material, her hems torn and singed. The edges of her petticoats draggled, also singed. Her boots were spattered with mud and spots of blood, but still serviceable.

Anger was pointless. Anger over some stained cloth was doubly so. She swallowed it with an effort, turned her attention to other things. "The man who fired the initial shot – most probably to mark us – had a protection. I lost him in an alley, but we shall find the trail after we visit Bedlam."

"The mentath seemed to have some ideas. No doubt he will have more after visiting Grayson."

Always assuming we can believe a single word spilling from the Lord Chancellor's forked tongue. Her dislike of the Chancellor was unreasoning; he was a servant of Britannia just as she was.

Still, she did not have to enjoy his company. After all, Crawford had been a servant too. A treacherous one, but a servant nonetheless.

Mikal was indirectly reminding her of the mentath's capacity as a resource, with a Shield's infinite tact. She nodded, patting at her hair. A few quick movements, pins sliding in, and she had the mess reasonably under control. *Bloody hell. I liked that bonnet, too.* "I am sending Grayson an itemised bill for *every* dress ruined in this affair." She gained her feet in a lunge, swayed, and sat back down on the divan. Hard.

Mikal's eyes glinted, yellowish in the dimness. He did not have to say *I told you so.* He merely steadied her, carefully keeping the *vitae*-soaked handkerchief away. "You look lovely."

Heat rose on the surface of her throat, stained her cheeks. "You prefer the dishevelled, then?"

"Better dishevelled than dead, Prima. If you are careful, I believe you may stand now."

He was correct once more, damn him. As usual. Her legs trembled, but they held her. Mikal rose too, hovering, his hand near her elbow.

"I shall manage quite well, thank you." Emma exhaled sharply, frustration copper-bright to Sight cloaking her before she pushed it down and away. It was merely another weakness training would overcome. "Let us collect the mentath, then. I am loath to lose him now."

"Emma." Mikal caught her arm. "Did you think I had deliberately left the one who shot you?"

His mouth shaping her Christian name was a small victory, one she decided not to celebrate even internally. *The thought crossed my mind, Mikal.* "I was too busy to think such things. Come, leave that rag and let us find our mentath."

He did not turn loose of her. Instead, he held her arm – perhaps to steady her, perhaps for some other reason. Emma pulled against his fingers, silk slipping on her bruised arm.

"You need another Shield. *More* Shields." Said calmly, matter-of-fact. "A half-dozen at least. A full complement would be better."

I had four, Mikal. They died protecting me. "I *need* you to burn that *vitae*-infested rag and accompany me to wherever Grayson is filling that mentath's head with useless supposition," she snapped. "If you are *unhappy* with my service, Shield, then by all means remove yourself from my *aegis* and present yourself to the Collegia for extermination."

He turned pale. Such a thing did not seem possible, given his colouring. "I would that you had at least a single Shield you could trust, instead of losing precious time to backlash sickness because you will not let me perform my function."

Oddly, it stung. Perhaps because he was correct. Again. "We have no time for this argument." The divan groaned slightly; she could have sliced ice with the words. Emma took a firmer hold on her temper. It was her besetting sin, that temper. "When this mystery is solved, we shall approach the question of whether *I decide* to take the responsibility of another Shield or three, or twenty, *in addition* to my current intransigent Indus princeling. We will make a fine meal for our enemies, yours no less than mine, should we continue in this manner. Now *shut up* and rid me of that handkerchief, Mikal. I shall find Lord Grayson and Mr Clare, and I expect you to accompany me."

She tore her arm from his grasp, set out for the door. Her skirts rustled oddly, and the floor was moving most strangely beneath her boots.

The amber *prie-dieu*, dangling at her breastbone from a silver chain, turned into a spot of warmth. There was enough force stored in it for two strong minor Works, a multiplicity of Words, or merely to keep her upright until dawn's Tideturn renewed the world's sorcerous energies. Her sardonyx was drained, and should there be more unpleasantness in store tonight . . . well.

It did not matter. The best thing was to go from one task to the next, as quickly and thoroughly as possible.

There was a *fsssh!* and a pop behind her as Mikal called flame into being. The skin between her shoulder blades roughened instinctively. He was armed, and—

It was ridiculous. If he wished her death, he had many opportunities on a daily basis to gratify that urge. She was stupid to waste time and energy fretting about it.

Unless that is part of the plan, Emma. How long would you

wait, for a vengeance? And you cannot credit any reason he might give you for how he became your Shield.

Yet had Mikal not betrayed his sworn oath to the sorcerer who had almost killed her, she would be dead, and all this academic.

She twisted the crystal doorknob and stepped into the hall. The dead clustered here, diaphanous grey scarves of ill intent or mere confusion, soaking into the walls. Lamplight – Whitehall was now fitted with gas – ran wetly over every surface, and she heard voices not too far away. One, no doubt, was the mentath. Who had dealt with a sorcerous attack with far more presence of mind than she would ever have expected from a logic machine trapped in ailing flesh.

"Emma." Mikal, from the darkened room behind her. "I wish you could trust me."

She did not dignify it with a response, sweeping away. *Oh, Mikal. So do I.*

Chapter Four

In One Fashion or Another

The door was swept unceremoniously open, and Grayson visibly flinched. Clare was gratified to find his nerves were still steady. Besides, he had heard the determined tap of female footsteps, dainty little bootheels crackling with authority, and deduced Miss Bannon was in a fine mood.

Her sandalwood curls were caught up and repinned, but she was hatless and her dress was sadly the worse for wear. Smoke and fury hung on her in almost visible veils, and she was dead pale. Her dark eyes burned rather like coals, and Clare had no doubt that any obstacle in her way had been toppled, uprooted or simply crushed.

Green silk flopped uneasily at the shoulder, a scrap of under-clothing tantalisingly visible, but there was no sign of a wound. Just pale, unmarked skin, and the amber cabochon glowing in a most peculiar manner.

Grayson gained his feet in a walrus lunge. He had turned an alarming shade of floury yeastiness, but most people did when confronted with an angry sorcerer. "Miss Bannon. *Very* glad to see you on your feet, indeed! I was just bringing Clare here—"

She gave him a single cutting glance, and short shrift. "Filling his head with nonsense, no doubt. We are dealing with conspiracy of the blackest hue, Lord Grayson, and I am afraid I may tarry no longer. Mr Clare, are you disposed to linger, or would you accompany me? Whitehall should be relatively safe, but I confess your talents may be of some use in the hunt before me."

Clare was only too glad to leave the mediocre sherry. He set it down, untasted. "I would be most honoured to accompany you, Miss Bannon. Lord Grayson has informed me of the deaths of several mentaths and the unfortunate circumstances surrounding Mr Throckmorton's erstwhile guard. I gather we are bound for Bedlam?"

"In one fashion or another." But a corner of her lips twitched. "You do your profession justice, Mr Clare. I trust you were not injured?"

"Not at all, thanks to your efforts." Clare recovered his hat, glanced at his bags. "Will I be needing linens, Miss Bannon, or may I leave them as superfluous weight?"

Now she was certainly amused, a steely smile instead of a single lip-twitch, at odds with her childlike face. With that spark in her dark eyes, Miss Bannon would be counted attractive, if not downright striking. "I believe linens may be procured with little difficulty anywhere in the Empire we are likely to arrive, Mr Clare. You may have those sent to my house in Mayefair; I believe they shall arrive promptly."

"Very well. Cedric, I do trust you'll send these along for me? My very favourite waistcoat is in that bag. We shall return when we've sorted out this mess, or when we require some aid. Good to see you, old boy." Clare offered his hand, and noted with some mild amusement that Cedric's palm was sweating.

He didn't blame the man.

Mentaths were not overtly feared the way sorcerers were. Dispassionate logic was easier to swallow than sorcery's flagrant violations of what the general populace took to be *normal*. Logic was easily hidden, and most mentaths were discreet by nature. There were exceptions, of course, but none of them as notable as the least of sorcery's odd children.

"God and Her Majesty be with you," Cedric managed. "Miss Bannon, are you quite certain you do not—"

"I require nothing else at the moment, sir. Thank you, God and Her Majesty." She turned on one dainty heel and strode away, ragged skirts flapping. Clare arranged his features in something resembling composure, fetched the small black bag containing his working notables, and hurried out of the door.

His legs were much longer, but Miss Bannon had a surprisingly energetic stride. He arrived at her side halfway down the corridor. "I know better than to take Lord Grayson's suppositions as anything but, Miss Bannon."

Miss Bannon's chin was set. She seemed none the worse for wear, despite her ruined clothing. "You were at school with him, were you not?"

Was that a deduction? He decided not to ask. "At Yton."

"Was he an insufferable, blind-headed prig then, too?"

Clare strangled a laugh by sheer force of will. *Quite diverting.* He made a *tsk-tsk* sound, settling into her speed. The dusky hall would take them to the Gallery; she perhaps meant them to come out through the Bell Gate and from there to find another hansom. "Impolitic, Miss Bannon."

"I do not play *politics*, Mr Clare."

I think you are a deadly player when you lower yourself to do so, miss. "Politics play, even if *you* do not. If you have no care for your own career, think of mine. Grayson dangled the renewal of my registration before me. Why, do you suppose, did he do so?"

"He does not expect you to live long enough to claim such a prize." Her tone suggested she found the idea insulting and likely all at once. "How did you lose your registration, if I may ask?"

For a moment, irrationality threatened to blind him. "I killed a man," he said, evenly enough. "Unfortunately, it was the *wrong* man. A mentath cannot afford to do such a thing." *Even if the beast needed killing.*

Even if I do not regret it.

"Hm." Her pace did not slacken, but her heels did not jab the wooden floor with such hurtful little crackles. "In that, Mr Clare, mentaths and sorcerers are akin. You kill one tiny little Peer of the Realm, and suddenly your career is gone. It is a great relief to me that I have no career to lose."

"Indeed? Then why are you—" The question was ridiculous, but he wished to gauge her response. When she slanted him a very amused, dark-eyed glance, he nodded internally. "Ah. I see. You are as expendable as I have become."

Her reply gave him much to think on. "In the service of Britannia, Mr Clare, *all* are expendable. Come."

Chapter Five

An Insoluble Puzzle

"I cannot understand why it is often so difficult to find a hansom," she muttered, as she reclaimed her hand from Mikal's.

"I have applied logic to the question." Clare's tone was thoughtful. He shook his top hat, removed a speck of dust from the brim, and replaced it on his head with a decided motion. "And, to be honest, I have never arrived at a satisfactory answer."

The driver, his own battered stuff hat set at a rakish angle and his rotund body wrapped against the chill, cracked his whip over the heaving, coppery back of his clockwork horse, and hooves clattered away down the dark street. Tiny sparks of stray sorcery winked out in their wake. Gasflame flickered, wan light hardly licking the surface of the cobblestones, not daring to penetrate the crevices between.

"At least we were not attacked during this short voyage," Clare continued. "I must confess I am relieved."

Are you? For I am not. An enemy resourceful and practised, not to mention financed well enough to send sootdogs and hired thugs, was likely to have an idea of the finitude of even a Prime's power. The Tideturn of dawn was distressingly far away, and even that flood of sorcerous energy would not stave off the effects of fatigue and hunger.

Worry about such an event when it becomes critical, Emma. Before then, simply do what must be done. She straightened her back. For Bethlehem Hospital crouched before them, a long pile of brick and stone shimmering with misery.

The very bricks of Bedlam were warped, but had nevertheless been carried from the old site in Bishop's Gate two decades ago with the Regent's false economy. Sorcerers had warned against reusing the building materials, but it had done little good.

The sprawling monstrosity, its cupola leering at the sky and running with golden charter-charms, took up a considerable space – physical as well as psychic layers accreted for a good two hundred years since the insane had begun to be "treated" rather than merely confined or executed. In the near distance, the smoke of the Black Wark rose, the kernel of Southwark with its cinderfall and pall of incessant gloomy smoke.

Emma swallowed drily, and Mikal's hand closed over her shoulder. She stepped away. Any Shield would not like a sorcerer setting foot in this place.

Of course, Mikal was not *any* Shield, any more than she was *any* sorceress. There was a time when a sorceress of her Discipline would have been executed as soon as certain proclivities and talents began to show, whether she was Prime or merely witch. A man whose Discipline lay in the Black, rather than the White or Grey, had less to fear.

Men always had less to fear.

Emma raised her chin. Gaslamp glow picked out screaming faces swirling in the brick wall, and for a moment it was difficult to separate the audible howls from the silent ones. It sounded a merry night in Bedlam, cries and screams from the depths of the building muffled by stone, a seashell roar of discontent. The ætheric protections set on the place resounded, a discordance of smashed violins and overstressed stones.

Her *prie-dieu* warmed further against her chest. It would have to be enough.

She set off for the postern, her heels clicking against cobbles.

Her skirt was ragged, and its hem was torn. She must look a sight. Irritation flashed through her and away.

Clare fell into step beside her. "Why is a sorcerer in Bedlam, may I ask? Was there no other sanatorium?"

Her jaw was set so tightly she almost had difficulty replying. "Not with a fully drawn Greater Circle free, no. Llewellyn is no witch or Adept. He is – *was* Prime; even mad or broken he is not likely to be amenable to containment."

"Ah. *Was* Prime?"

Will I have to teach him the classes of sorcerer? "Sanity is a prerequisite for carrying the title. However disputable one considers the term when applied to a sorcerer." *And he is a peer; he cannot be thrown in a common prison.* For a moment her skin chilled, and Mikal was close enough that she could feel the heat from him. She knew without looking that his mouth would be set tight in disapproval. So was her own.

"I see." Clare absorbed this. "Miss Bannon?"

For the love of Heaven, will you not be quiet? "Yes, Mr Clare?"

"Is it advisable to enter through the side door?"

For a man who functioned by logic and deduction, he certainly seemed thick. "The main entrance is closed and locked at dusk. I do not relish the idea of wasting time waiting for the head warden to be called from his *divertissements*. Also, the more unremarked we can be, the better."

"I hardly think we will pass unremarked."

A sharp retort died on Emma's tongue. Perhaps he was simply making conversation, seeking to set her at her ease. Or he wished to find out if she was as empty-headed, as most men, even fleshly logic engines, considered women to be. "Llewellyn is being held near this door."

"I see."

Do you? I fear you do not. The outside guard was half-asleep, propped in the doorway at the top of a short flight of uneven stairs. Heavily bearded and reeking of gin, he blinked as the trio approached, and by the time Emma had set foot on the first step, bracing herself, his eyes had widened to the size of poached eggs and he had straightened, pulling at the high-collared broadcloth of his uniform coat. "Visitin' hours is one to three—"

Mikal was suddenly *there*, shoving him against the wall and making a swift movement. The *ulp* the man made was lost in the sound of the double blow to chin and paunch. Mikal's fingers flicked, subtracting the ring of heavy iron keys from the broad leather belt. There was a gleam of sharp metal, and the sliced belt thudded to the top step. The man slumped; Mikal lowered him fairly gently.

Clare's eyebrows nested in his hairline. "Is this really necessary?"

Paused on the second step, Emma strangled a flare of impatience. *You are an irritant, mentath.* "If Mikal is doing it, yes."

Mikal already had the correct key selected and inserted into the postern door. "The man reeks of gin," he remarked. "He was disposed to be troublesome. Petty authority." His lip curled, disdain clearly visible in the set of his shoulders as well. "He will not remember us."

"Let us hope as much." Clare did not sound convinced.

The door opened with a small groan; Mikal glanced inside. He nodded, once, and Emma continued up the stairs.

They plunged into Bedlam's grey confusion. Gaslamps hissed down the long hall, and she braced herself. For a moment the walls rippled, the entire hungry, semi-sentient pile of stone resonating as it took notice of what she was.

The Endor! The Endor is here! A mouthless, windless whisper, unheard by living ears, brushed against the surfaces of her skin and clothing. Grey smokelike figures crowded close, their sighs rising in volume as they sensed she could hear them. Ghostly fingers brushed her, slipping over the smooth, hard shell of a Prime's will; Mikal half turned and caught her arm. At the Shield's touch, the entire hallway clicked back into place with a sub-audible thump.

Another of a Shield's functions – an anchor. The more ætheric force a sorcerer could carry, the more danger of being lost on the currents the rest of humanity could not feel.

"Miss Bannon?" Clare, with a faint touch of concern. "You've gone quite white."

"Quite well," she murmured. Found her usual crisp tone again. "I am quite well, thank you. Mikal? Llewellyn is down the hall to the right. Fifth door, I believe."

"He will not be happy to see us," Mikal observed, but his grip was bruising-hard.

No, he did not like his Prima setting foot in this place. She was a fool to mistrust him. A traitorous warmth bloomed in her belly, was sternly shelved. And yet, how long before he decided she was as expendable as Crawford had evidently been?

Now is not the time for that thought. "We are not visiting him for tea." She followed his pressure on her arm. Surely it was not weakness to feel grateful. Entering Bedlam by herself would be . . . uncomfortable. "All the same, Mikal . . ." *Be prepared, for I am exhausted. And more than that, Llewellyn would like nothing better than to injure us both.*

"Say no more." He slanted her a deadly unamused glance, his mouth a thin straight line. Shortened his stride to match hers, while the mentath trailed in their wake. The corridor was stone-floored and reeked of pain and filth. At least it was swept, and the barred iron doors to either side merely vibrated uneasily. The place had quieted, at least physically, only faint echoes of faraway moans piercing the hush.

Other senses were not nearly so easily lulled. She folded her free hand over Mikal's, ignoring his second, slightly startled glance. The added contact helped shunt aside the screaming rush of whispered agony roaring through the hall, lifting strands of her hair on an unphysical breeze.

"Something's amiss." She was barely aware of speaking. "Badly amiss."

Mikal slowed, tense and alert. Their footsteps echoed. "I suppose it would do no good to ask you to—"

Retreat? In the service of the Queen? I hardly think so. "No good at all, my Shield."

"Miss Bannon?" Clare had caught up, and offered his arm on her other side. "May I be of assistance?"

It was a curious gesture, but one she appreciated. She loosed her grip on Mikal's hand and took Clare's arm as well. After all, she was a lady now. No matter how often she had the urge to repeat blue words. "Thank you, Mr Clare. This place is . . . distressing, to any sorcerer."

The hallway swayed under her feet, but Mikal's arm was steady, and so was Clare's. The misery of this place was dark wine against her palate, stroking against her will with a cat's-tongue rasp.

"Fifth door." Mikal's tone suggested he was extraordinarily alert. His arm was tense, muscle standing out under her fingers, and he slowed. "Mentath. The key is on a hook, just there."

"Ah. Yes." The mentath's long face pinched together, a change from its usual bright interest. Faint distaste swirled from him, a powdery blue to Sight, and Emma's *prie-dieu* sparked. It was taking more force than she liked to insulate herself from the dead crowding these halls, and the despair locked in the fabric of the building was troubling as well.

If Llewellyn Gwynnfud, Lord Sellwyth, had any sanity remaining, this place might well rob him of it.

The door was locked and barred, rivulets of golden charm and charter symbols sliding down its scarred iron surface. Clare peered through the observation slit, studiously avoiding touching it. He blinked, absorbing whatever vista the slit presented for a long moment. "Miss Bannon? Is it safe to unlock the door?"

"The charm and charter won't harm you, Mr Clare." Her voice came from very far away, but it carried all its usual briskness. *Thank Heaven for that.* "Its only function is to *contain*."

"Very well, then." He settled back on his heels and inserted the clumsy key into the lock. He even lifted the iron bar out of its brackets and set it aside, handling the bulk with startling ease for such a lean man. "I should warn you, it appears the patient is awake and expecting us."

"Well, good." Asperity tinted her tone. "I would hate to have to disturb a gentleman's slumber. Or question his corpse."

The air quivered as Clare gingerly folded his hand around the door handle; he pulled and it slid open with little trouble, well oiled. The charter symbols runnelled uneasily, but Mikal exhaled very softly and they calmed.

Llewellyn was indeed awake.

The stone cube was comfortless, and chill. A straw pallet was tossed in one corner, but it would do no good to a man trapped inside ætheric containment in the middle of the floor. Charm and charter wandered golden over the walls, and Emma blinked. *Most odd. Most exceedingly odd – who closed him in here? Old work, very old.*

The sorcerer sat in the exact centre of the Circle, its blue lines shifting over stone flagstones. He was shockingly dirty, as if he had rubbed filth into his own garments – the remains of an opera suit, draggled with dirt and torn in interesting places. His face was streaked with grime, and it was difficult to ascertain his features for a moment. They smeared like ink on wet paper, but perhaps it was only her vision blurring with fatigue.

Mikal's arm tightened. She knew what he was thinking – *Where are his Shields?*

She had seen no profit in informing him that the Shields had been found disembowelled. Which was, if one thought about it, the only way to cause enough damage to keep a Shield truly incapable of combat for long enough to kill him.

"Good evening, Llewellyn." *I sound quite calm. Very well, that.*

For he needed precious little of an opening to rob her of her composure.

His head lifted, strings of decaying blond hair twining with a life of their own, mixing with a grey Gwynnfud would have been infuriated with. With no charm to keep the colour its usual parchment pale, and none of the enhancements he favoured, he looked much less prepossessing than usual.

His long fingers spasmed, twisting together, and a glimmer of charm appeared on them. She tensed, and so did the Circle, its blue lines cavorting in intricate knots. It ran over the floor in wet streaks, and something about it was not as it should be, either.

"Emma." The word echoed through shifting veils of sorcerous interference. He *sounded* sane, at least. Terribly, calmly sane. Which was perhaps the worst that could befall them.

For while Emma Bannon was certain she could handle a sorcerer gripped in madness, a sane and mocking Llewellyn was another matter entirely.

Her grip on Mikal's arm loosened. If there was an event here, he had to be free to fight. Her chin lifted as she examined the Circle's work, storing away the odd peculiarities of personality visible in the strands. A sorcerer's memory was trained just as ruthlessly as her ability; in some cases, even more. And this was work she had not seen before. "Rather bad accommodations, I'm afraid. Are you well?"

His laugh came from the bottom of a dark well. Veils of sorcery shifted, keeping a Prime's force contained. His will, even broken or twisted, would fight any containment laid upon it; a Prime did not take a bridle well, if at all. Hence the hardening of the air, alive with ætheric force, blurring his outlines as if he sat behind a screen.

"I'm locked in a cell in Bedlam, Emma. Obviously I am not *well*." His dark eyes glimmered through the strings of hair. "And I have not even a change of linen. Barbarians."

Your household should have bribed someone to bring such things to you. Her wariness increased, if that were possible. "If you will waste my time, Lord Sellwyth, I shall go elsewhere."

It was a gamble, of course. It could prick his pride, and he might well refuse to say anything now. It could also trigger whatever unpleasantness was waiting around the corner, making the charm and charter react oddly. She was passing familiar with most native-Britannium sorcerers' work; sorcery always carried the stamp of its channel. But this was . . . odd.

And, as she had suspected, the thing Llewellyn feared most was the loss of his audience. "I would not want to waste *your* time, dear Bannon." He made the words a sing-song, rolling his head on his shoulders. Strings of hair crawled against each other and the cloth of his coat with bloated little whispers as sorcery crackled. "Especially when you've brought a snake-charmer and a lapdog with you."

Fortunately, Clare had enough presence of mind to hold his peace. Mikal almost twitched, restlessly, and Llewellyn's smile widened. "How long will it be before he strangles you, just like he did Crawford? And you, Emma. Queen and Country, how *boring*. Wouldn't you like some *real* power?"

How very unlike you to be so direct. Emma's concentration narrowed. "Throckmorton, Llewellyn. Your charge. You undertook to guard him at Britannia's request; he is dead, your Shields are dead, and you are . . . here. Whatever could have happened?" Precise, drily astonished, for all the world like a professor mocking a slightly dim student. Llewellyn hated that tone, especially when it was delivered by a woman.

His face contorted for a bare moment. The sorcerous interference intensified, streaks of shimmering painting the outside of a perfect, invisible globe as a Prime's will reflexively sought to break its cage. "Mentath," he whispered. "*That's* a mentath; some fool's let you get your hands on one. *Stupid*—"

Get my hands on— But the physical structure of Bedlam tolled once, a giant bell shivering as a hammerstroke echoed through the lattices of probability, and something hit her from the side, driving her down.

Chapter Six

Reflexes and Temper

It was a most interesting conversation, layers of inference and deduction ticking below the conscious surface of Clare's faculties, and he wondered briefly just when the sorcerer trapped in the Circle had ceased to be Miss Bannon's lover. Well, at least they had most certainly been intimate at one time, and sorcery's children had far different standards than the common crowd, but still, quite interesting. And from the sound of it, Miss Bannon had broken the attachment, yet there was no lingering of regret in her.

Clare's wonderings were interrupted by an odd scent. *Brimstone, perhaps?* And a faint low scraping, like a match swept across a strikeplate. The space inside the circle rippled, oddly, becoming no more than a painted screen for a bare moment.

He leapt, knocking Miss Bannon down. A moment of excruciating heat kissed the back of his coat. Then he was rolling, a confusion of shadows flickering as someone hurtled over him, deadly silent with flashing blades. Stink of wet, smoking wool, Miss Bannon struggling to her feet, the amber suddenly a glowing yellow star in the dimness as she snapped two words. Her hands flung themselves out, white birds, slim fingers fluttering. There was a crack, and a sudden showering smell of wet salt.

"Mikal?" Bannon, breathless in the sudden quiet.

"Here." The single word was so grim Clare tensed.

"The mentath—"

"Well enough." Clare finished shrugging out of his jacket. The wool was smoking, a dull, unpleasant fume. "Well. *That* was entertaining."

"Quick reflexes." The other man bent down, offering his hand. "For one of your kind."

He means it as a compliment. "And your own reflexes?"

The sorceress murmered. Thin threads of smoke traced up from her dress. The yellow-eyed man glanced at her. "Not quick enough, apparently. No—" He caught Clare's shoulder. "Do not approach her just now."

The sorceress's jaw worked, and for a moment Clare had the uneasy feeling of lightning about to strike – a raising of fine hairs on his arms and neck, his glands responding to some feral current.

He decided she was indeed not to be approached. "That must have been heard. We shall have guards here in a moment, and explanations to be made."

For there was a large smoking hole in the wall, odd twisted writing scored around its edges. Bedlam had sorcerous protections, but this did not seem to be one of them responding to Miss Bannon. Of course, Clare admitted, he could not be certain. But Miss Bannon would have no doubt alerted him, would she not?

The Shield's next words placed all doubt aside.

"A cunning trap, and well laid. We shall indeed be going." Mikal's lean face set itself, lines bracketing his mouth. "But my Prima has a temper, mentath. Wait just a moment."

The sorceress, indeed, was trembling. She stared at the hole in the wall to the next cell's blackness, her lips now moving soundlessly. The writing scored around the edges of the hole burned with sullen foxfire.

Clare cast a nervous glance at the steel-framed door. Grayson had indeed had worthless suppositions, but not as useless as Miss Bannon had supposed. One or two of them were quite reasonable, given the Chancellor's knowledge of events. And the encircled sorcerer's words had been most peculiar indeed.

But *this* was something altogether different. And troubling. "Does Miss Bannon have enemies?"

Mikal's profile vaguely reminded Clare of a classical statue. The Shield leaned forward, weight on the balls of his feet and his long coat oddly pristine. His attention was focused on the woman, whose trembling had spread into the air around her. Rather like the heat haze above a fire, air almost solid and shimmering as something invisible stroked it.

"She is *Prime*," the Shield said, quietly, as if that should be explanation enough. "And she does not suffer fools gladly."

"Well, I could see that." Clare stamped on his jacket once or twice more, to make certain it would not combust, and picked it up. Shook it out, shrugged into it. His hat had flown away; he found it in the ruins of the straw pallet. He glanced through the hole in the wall as he did so, but the uncertain light permitted no disclosing of its secrets. It was an oubliette; it might as well have been a painted-black circle. "Miss Bannon? Miss Bannon. If you please, we should be going now."

The yellow-eyed man inhaled sharply, but when Clare glanced up, he saw the sorceress had regained her composure. She clutched at her shoulder as if it had been re-injured, and red sparks revolved in her dilated pupils for a moment before winking out.

"You're quite right." Curiously husky. "My thanks, Mr Clare. Mikal, let us be gone from here at once."

"The sorcerer—" Clare did not relish the thought of giving her the news, but it had to be said.

For nothing remained of Llewellyn Gwynnfud but a rag of flesh and charred, twisting bone splinters, still trapped inside the circle of blue flame and heavy, rippling shifting.

"Appears dead, of course." She inhaled sharply and sagged,

and the yellow-eyed man apparently judged her temper safe enough, for he stepped forward and took her arm again. As soon as he did, Bannon swayed further, the tension leaving her. "And good riddance. Though I suspect he did not think they would deal with him in quite this manner."

They? "Which manner would that be?" Clare enquired, as Mikal ushered the sorceress to the door and glanced out into the hall.

"As bait." Miss Bannon's tone was passing grim. "Now they know *I* am at their heels, and in no uncertain fashion. Mikal?"

He all but dragged her along. "I hear footsteps. Out the same way we entered, and step lightly."

Miss Bannon, however, swayed drunkenly, her chestnut hair slipping free of pins. "I . . . I cannot . . ."

Her eyes rolled up, their whites glaring, and she went completely limp. The Shield did not pause, simply swept her up in his arms and cast a grim glance at Clare. "She has exhausted herself."

"Quite," Clare agreed as he followed, out into the hall. Bedlam was alive with screams and moans, a ship rocking on a storm sea of lunacy. "How long has she been baying at foxes in this manner?"

"Since before dawn yesterday; no sleep and very little food. Before that, a week's worth of work."

Clare jammed his hat more firmly on to his head. "That does not surprise me. Where are we bound?"

"For home." And the man would say no more.

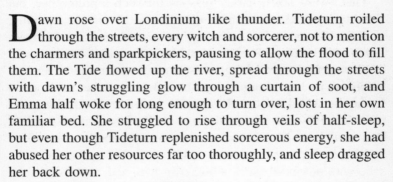

Chapter Seven

Breakfast in Mayefair

Dawn rose over Londinium like thunder. Tideturn roiled through the streets, every witch and sorcerer, not to mention the charmers and sparkpickers, pausing to allow the flood to fill them. The Tide flowed up the river, spread through the streets with dawn's struggling glow through a curtain of soot, and Emma half woke for long enough to turn over, lost in her own familiar bed. She struggled to rise through veils of half-sleep, but even though Tideturn replenished sorcerous energy, she had abused her other resources far too thoroughly, and sleep dragged her back down.

When her eyes would finally open, she was greeted by her own room, dimly lit, the blue velvet curtains tightly drawn and the ormolu clock on the mantel ticking away to itself. A softly shimmering ball of witchlight hung caged in silver over her vanity, brightening as she pushed herself up on her elbows and yawned.

Sensing her return to consciousness, the room quivered. She made a gesture, fingers fluttering, and the drapes slowly pulled back, the charm on them singing a low humming note of satisfaction. Filmy grey Londinium light spilled through the window. The house resonated, its mistress awake, and she heard footsteps in the hall.

"*Bonjour!*" Severine trilled, sweeping the door open. Her plump face opened wide in a sunny smile, and her starched cap was shockingly white. "*Chocolat et croissant pour ma fille.*" Her skirts swept the royal-blue carpeting, and her eyes danced with good humour. The indenture collar rested against her throat, a soft foxfire gleam, the powdery surface of the metal lovingly polished.

One could tell a great deal about a servant from the state of their collar. And an indenture provided a degree of status; it meant References and certain legal rights. Most sorcerers above Master level could and did engage *only* indentureds; it was a question of safety and loyalty.

There were other, darker reasons for such a preference, but Emma preferred not to think upon them. Not in the morning, at least. She stretched, wincing as several muscles twinged. "*Bonjour*, Severine. Has your goddaughter had her baby yet?"

"Not yet, not yet." Fragrant steam rose from the silver tray balanced in her plump paws, and behind Severine trooped Catherine and Isobel, lady's maids both scrubbed clean and cheerful. The scar tracing down Isobel's face was responding very well to the new fleshstitching treatment, and Emma nodded as they both dropped a curtsy. "*Monsieur le bouclier* is in the salle with our guest. Such a breakfast they had, too! Cook shall have to send out for more ham."

"I leave that in Cook's capable hands." Emma yawned again and slid free of the bed. Everything on her ached, and her hair felt stiff with grime. "Isobel, my dear, draw me a bath. Catherine, something dowdy today, I am going through dresses at an alarming rate."

"The green silk's fair done for, mum." Catherine's fair freckled face pinched in on itself as soon as she'd spoken, her collar glowing as well. She often flinched at the end of a sentence, despite the indenture here being relatively easy. Or at least, Emma thought it should be regarded as comparatively easy. Mistreated underlings stood a higher chance of being disloyal underlings even with the insurance of a collar; she had seen enough of indenture to know *that*.

Catherine had come to her Without Reference, and Severine had much protested indenturing a girl who had no papers. Finch had been against the notion too.

But they were not the mistress at 34½ Brooke Street. Catherine's doglike fidelity and skill with a needle – she was a sempstress of no mean ability, so much that Emma suspected her of a limited needle-charmer's talent, though not enough sorcery to make it illegal to indenture her – not to mention her untiring capacity for work, had proven said mistress right in this instance.

Had she been proven wrong, she was more than capable of punishing the transgressor in her own fashion.

Severine busied herself at the tiny table near the window, fussing until everything was just so. "You are pale, *madame*. You work too hard. Come, the *chocolat* is hot. And the croissants fresh! Very fresh."

"Just a moment, *cher* Severine." Emma stretched again, luxuriously, as Catherine disappeared into the dress-house and Isobel's humming started up in the bath room over a cascade of falling water. The girl was always singing something or another. Today it was a tune much heard on Picksdowne, a country girl bemoaning faithless love and a city gent. It was vaguely improper, but Isobel was a good girl. She and Catherine reworked and shared Emma's cast-off dresses, though not the burnt and battered ones, and more than once they had performed last-minute miracles when Emma's wardrobe required such.

To be a servant of Britannia of Emma Bannon's stripe could – and sometimes did – require going with little to no notice from a filthy back alley in Whitchapel or Seven Dials to a Grosvenor Square ball.

Both environments had their dangers, certainly. There were others in the service of the ruling spirit much as Emma was, but she eschewed any contact with them. Murky secret societies were, in her opinion, only to be infiltrated. Besides, there was certain latitude granted her as a soloist, so to speak.

And not so incidentally, even other sorcerers would feel trepidation at the prospect of dealing with a woman who was both Prime and of a Black branch of Discipline. Even if she kept her *exact* branch a fairly close secret, she would be hard pressed to pass as even one of the Grey, let alone the White. For one thing, she was too bloody practical.

And for another, she did not mind the blood and screaming as a proper woman should.

Emma touched the obsidian globe on her nightstand. The globe's surface, chased with silver in fluid charter symbols, rippled and trembled like water. Her fingers stroked, soothing, and the house vibrated again. Every ætheriel protection on her home was clear and tight, a Prime's will and ætheric force coursing in channels laid through physical substance, tied swiftly and efficiently with complex invisible knots, and all as it should be.

The novels stacked around the obsidian globe were all exceedingly improper and sensational, and she smiled ruefully at them. *When this is all over, I'll lie abed and read for a week.*

She had been making herself that promise for months. There was always a fresh crisis brewing. The Prince Consort was inexperienced and the Queen was still young, even though she *was* Britannia, and there was no shortage of intrigue. Victrix's lady mother had only recently been prised from her daughter's tender back, her influence slowly leaching away from the young Queen, who had not proved amenable to being ruled by Dearest Mum (as she was irreverently but very quietly called) after all.

If not for a dedicated few interested in serving Queen Victrix rather than her mother . . . well, who could say? Britannia would reign, no doubt, long after her current incarnation fell prey to old age, and after Emma's long life as a Prime was finished as well.

Still, it did not mean she could neglect her duty.

Queen and Country, how boring. Wouldn't you like some real power? And Llewellyn's parting words – Emma did, indeed, have her hands on a mentath.

No doubt Mr Clare would have some ideas. She had a few of her own, including where to start the next day's unravelling of this tangled web. But for the moment, she shrugged into her robe and settled at the small table, and Severine clucked over her while she had her morning *chocolat*. In short order she was finished, the day's gown was chosen, and the luxury of hot water was not nearly savoured enough before she was in her dressing room, being loosely corseted and encased in a high-collared almost drab brown velvet, her hair chafed dry and lovingly pinned up by Isobel's quick fingers, a little parfum dabbed behind her ears and her jewel cases opened, plundered, and put away. Catherine retreated to the bath room and Isobel to the bedroom, to set both to rights before the chambermaids came along to clean.

Thus fortified, and her thoughts somewhat rearranged, she checked herself in the large mirror over her white-painted vanity and frowned slightly. Slightly dowdy, yes. But at least if *this* dress were ruined, she would not feel so bad. "Severine. Do have Catherine report to Mr Finch on the frocks I've had damaged in the past week, and ask Finch to prepare a bill, itemized, for each. And for the ones I will no doubt ruin in the near future."

"*Oui, madame.*" Severine clasped her plump hands, standing near the door. "Cook will want to know the menu—"

"I'll be leaving the menu in your and Cook's hands for the upcoming week. Mr Finch should know I am not receiving for the time being, as well."

"*Oui, madame.*" Severine's cheeks had turned pale. When the menu was left to her and Cook it was always acceptable – but still, the housekeeper was terrified of a misstep, as well as breathless with fear for her mistress.

Severine's last indenture had not been pleasant. Emma had learned it was best not to reassure her overmuch; such coddling only made her more nervous. Like mastering a high-strung unAltered horse, it was best to be firm and brisk, but gentle.

"And please do have Finch secure more linens for our guest, and find him a suitable valet among the footmen. I rather think Mr Clare may be stopping with us for a while."

The salle was long and drenched with sunlight as well as the directionless glow of witchballs caged in filigreed aluminium, the floor mellow wood occasionally covered with rough mats supposed to make a fall during Mikal's daily practice less dangerous. Of course, the idea of Mikal *falling* was preposterous. Rather, the mats were a gesture.

Or they were for the infrequent times when she had company capable of sparring with a Shield. Like today.

Well, perhaps *capable* was too generous a term. For Mikal moved almost gently, deflecting the mentath's flurry of blows. Clare was not untrained, but to an eye used to the Collegia's classes of practising Shield candidates he appeared slow and graceless. Still, he was sweating, stripped to the waist, and surprisingly muscular. Emma folded her arms, watching Mikal as he gave ground, pivoting neatly and pulling the mentath off balance. A single strike, and Clare doubled up, losing most of his air. Mikal wore an odd little smile, one that meant he was enjoying himself.

Emma took notice of her unladylike posture, and clasped her gloved hands before her. The sardonyx ring prickled, and she had kept the amber prie-dieu, freshly glowing with a charge of sorcerous power from Tideturn. Today, though, the earrings were long jet daggers, and the cameo at her throat could hold a great deal of charge. Two more rings – one ruby, another a thick dull golden band – completed today's set. She was as prepared as it was possible to be.

He will not like this. She waited patiently, watching Mikal's smile deepen a trifle as Clare levered himself up from the mats.

"You do *not* have to look so bloody entertained, sir," Clare panted.

"My apologies." Mikal's grin widened. "Another round? You are quite agile, mentath."

Clare waved the compliment away. "No, no. I fear I am done. And Miss Bannon has made her appearance."

Oh, so you remarked my absence, did you? "Gentlemen." She accepted Mikal's traditional bow and Clare's slightly less formal movement with a nod. "Did you sleep well, Mr Clare?"

He flushed, all the way up to the roots of his sandy hair. "Quite well, thank you. And you, Miss Bannon?"

"I am well enough, thank you. I shall be gone for the day, hunting some rather interesting loose ends of this conspiracy. Here is the safest place for you, Mr Clare, and with Mikal to watch over you—"

"Prima." Just the one word, but Mikal's face was a thunder-cloud.

"Do not interrupt, Shield." She let the sentence carry its own warning. "Your charge is to protect the mentath. It appears mentaths are central to this series of events; therefore, he shall be as safe as I may make him while I hunt in other quarters. I shall hopefully return in time for dinner – Mr Clare, we dine a trifle early, I do hope that won't inconvenience you?"

"My digestion agrees with the notion." But his long, sweat-greased face had returned to mournfulness, and he shrugged into a threadbare shirt, folding down the turnover collar precisely. "However, Miss Bannon, I am not at all certain that I am the only target of the attacks we have endured so far. Last night—"

There are other reasons for me keeping you mewed here, thank you. "These foxes now know I am at their heels. My barouche is making deceptive rounds today, and I shall slip about largely unseen." She loosed her fingers with an effort, ignoring Mikal's tension, a powder-bloom of deep bruiselike colour visible to Sight. "I assure you, Mr Clare, I am *quite* capable of performing the duty Her Majesty has assigned me – namely, protecting a mentath, and ferreting out the source of this unpleasantness." Her shoulders ached; she relaxed them with an effort. "My staff has been set to procuring you fresh linens – yours have arrived from the Chancellor's care, and been laundered – and providing you with a valet, since you may be my guest for some small length of time. Would you be so kind as to accept Mr Finch's questions on those matters, once you have refreshed yourself?"

"Delighted to." The look on his face shouted that he would be anything but. Still, he did not waste time. He simply shook hands with Mikal and left the salle. Of course, he would think her terribly unfeminine.

Let him. His opinion matters little; his continued existence is what I am to protect. She held Mikal's gaze as the salle door closed with a decisive snick, and the Shield's cheekbones were flushed with ugly colour under their copper.

Fighting did not make him blush so.

"You will guard the mentath." Even, level, her tone nevertheless paled the sunlight coming through the long upper windows. The witchballs shuddered, one of them spitting a few blue sparks.

"My Prima." His jaw set. A fine thin tremor ran through him as her will hardened, the link between them painfully taut.

My Prima. As in, it is my duty to guard you. "He is in more danger than I am. And I have my reasons, Mikal."

A small, restless movement. If he dared, she almost thought he would *argue* with her.

And that could not be allowed.

"Good." She touched her skirts, her reticule brushing against velvet. The bonnet she'd chosen was far worse than dowdy, but at least she would feel no sting if it was lost or damaged, and it did not interfere with her peripheral vision. "Until dinner, then."

And there she would have left it, but for his stubbornness.

"Emma." Tight-clipped, her name, forced from his throat. "Please."

Sorcerous force flared through her. He fought it, but she was Prime, and her will forced his knees to bend. When he was in a Shield's abeyance, kneeling with his hands resting loose against his thighs, head bowed and almost every muscle locked, she let out a soft sound between her teeth.

"I am *Prime*." The words turned to gall, scorching her throat. "I am not some hedge-charmer to be ordered about. I *allow* you a great deal, Mikal, but I will not abide disobedience. You will guard the mentath." *The threat of you strangling me as well is not enough to make me tolerate an order from a Shield. Not nearly enough at all.*

The struggle went out of him. He slumped inside the cage of her will. "Yes," he murmured.

"Yes . . .?"

"Yes, my Prima."

It was a wonder he did not hate her. Of course, he very well might. But as long as he was desirous of continued survival, they were allied. Hatred mattered little in such an alliance.

Or so I tell myself. Until he finds a better treaty to sign, and then? Who knows? "Good." She turned, skirts swishing, and set off for the door. Her will slackened, but Mikal did not move.

"Emma." Softly, now.

She did not halt.

"Be careful." A little more loudly than he had to, making the salle's bright air tremble, dust swirling softly. "I would not care to lose you."

Sudden self-loathing bit under her breastbone. It was a familiar feeling. "I have no intention of being lost, Mikal. Thank you." *I should not have done this. Forgive me.* The words trembled just on the edge of her tongue, but she swallowed them, and left him behind in the sunlit salle.

Chapter Eight

You Will Do, Sir

The sorceress's house was odd indeed. It was a good address – Mayefair was a *very* respectable part of Londinium, and Miss Bannon was of course comfortable. Rare indeed was the sorcerer with bad business sense, though most of them affected a high disdain for such matters. To be in trade carried its own shame, sometimes worse than the stigma of sorcery.

The house seemed far larger than its exterior would have given one to surmise, and he did not like that illogical notion at all. It caused him some discomfort until he consigned it to his mental drawer of complex problems judged worthy of further investigation at some later date, if at all.

The suite he had been shown to by the cadaverous Finch – tall, thin, marks of childhood malnutrition around his jaw and evident in his bowed legs, dressed in dusty black but with his indenture collar lovingly polished – was furnished spare, dark, and heavy, but the fume of scorched dust told him hurried cleaning charms had been applied just prior to his residence. Dark wainscoting, leather and wine-red upholstery, but the bed was fresh and its linen crisp. Fire crackled merrily on the grate, and he was gratified to see that during his morning's exercise newspapers and periodicals had been brought, stacked neatly on the huge desk. Plenty of paper had been provided as well, and a complete set of *Encyclopaedie Britannicus*, in fifty-eight volumes, was arranged on the bookshelf, along with two dictionaries and a chemist's arrangement of reference works.

Miss Bannon must have given orders. It would do to keep his faculties occupied for a short while.

The servants were proud, but they spared no effort. Each one had a burnished indenture collar, and they were an odd assortment. Finch, for example, spoke with a laborious upper-crust wheeze, but Clare's trained ear caught traces of a youth spent mouthing Whitchapel's slur and slang. The man's musculature was wasted, but several of his mannerisms led Clare to the conclusion that Finch was familiar with the ungraceful dance of a knife fight or two in the darkness of a forgotten alley.

Then there was the pair of chambermaids – one with long chestnut ripples pulled tightly back, all elbows and angles in her brushed black gown, the other a short, plump, fair Irish colleen – who descended on his room to put it to rights a few moments after he pulled the bell-rope upon awakening. And the housekeeper, a round merry-eyed Frenchwoman with an atrocious Picardie accent, who had fussed him into a Delft-and-cream breakfast room and *tsk*ed over him.

The chambermaids both flinched at odd moments, and the housekeeper compulsively straightened everything she could lay her hands upon, tweaking with deft fingers. Yet they did not seem precisely *afraid*; Clare's sensitive nose caught no acrid note of fresh fear. The food, of course, was superlative, for all that Miss Bannon made no appearance until mid-morning in the salle.

And what an appearance that had been.

The man Mikal was still a puzzle. Clare settled in a chair next to the fire and lit his pipe, puffing thoughtfully. He was ready to turn his entire attention to the problem of the Shield, but there was a tap at the door.

A pleasure foregone was enough to irritate him at the moment. "Enter!"

The door opened and the Shield appeared, his yellow eyes flaming and his entire body stiff. "I hesitate to disturb——" he began, but Clare brightened and waved him further into the room.

"Come in, come in! You will do for a half-hour at least. Is Miss Bannon gone?"

"I saw her to the door." The man's jaw set, and Clare deduced he was most unhappy with this turn of events. It was, from what he could remember, not at all usual for a sorcerer, especially a powerful Prime, to set foot outside without a Shield or three, or more.

Of course, what Clare knew of sorcery was little more than the average man would. It did not do to think too much on the illogical feats such people were capable of performing. On the other hand, a surface study of such things would have armed him with enough to make workable deductions about Miss Bannon's character.

Let us test the waters. "No doubt you can tell me her true motivation in leaving the pair of us mewed here." He took a mouthful of smoke, tasted it speculatively, and almost smiled at the sensation. Mentaths did not feel as others did; logic was the pleasure they moved towards, and irrationality or illogic the pain they retreated from. Emotions were to be subdued, harnessed, accounted for and set on the shelf of deduction.

Privately, Clare had decided that few mentaths were completely emotionless. They simply did not account fully for Feeling, it being easier to see the occlusion in a subject's gaze than in their own. It was simply another variable to guard against, watch for, and marvel at the infinite variety of.

"She thinks to protect you." The Shield lowered himself into the chair across the fire, sat bolt upright, his hands resting on his knees. His long grey coat, buttoned all the way to the neck, did nothing to hide the muscle underneath. Outside the window, Londinium continued its morning roil under a blue spring sky lensed with coal-smoke fog. Shafts of smoke and steam rose; the note of copper from the Themis told Clare there would be clouds by afternoon and fog tonight. "Since the Queen, via Lord Grayson, consigned you to her care."

"Fetching concern," Clare murmured, puffing on his pipe, his eyes half lidding. The mournfulness of his features was accentuated by this manoeuvre. "Tell me, Mr Mikal—"

"Just Mikal." The man's chin lifted slightly.

Aha. Jealous of our pride, are we? "Mr Just Mikal, how many Shields does a sorcerer of Miss Bannon's stature – that is to say, a Prime – normally employ?"

Mikal considered this. His short hair was mussed, as if he had run his hands through it. When he visibly decided the information could do no harm, he finally responded. "A half-dozen is the normal minimum, but my Prima keeps her own counsel and does as she pleases. She had four Shields some time ago, and . . . well. It is a dangerous occupation."

"Four Shields. Before you?"

"Yes." Mikal's face visibly closed. Clare could almost hear the snap. Most interesting.

"And she has been chasing this conspiracy . . ."

"Three days. Sir. Since she was called to examine a mentath's body *in situ*—"

"That would be Tomlinson, I take it. The first to die."

"The first she was called to examine." Those yellow eyes glittered. Their colour seemed much more pronounced now, as the Shield gave Clare his attention.

Very good. You are not stupid, nor do you assume much. "Your lady suspects there must be more."

"She has not seen fit to share her thoughts with me."

Well. This is a pleasant game. "We will get exactly nowhere should you continue being obstreperous."

"Or should you continue seeking to bait me."

An extraordinary hypothesis presented itself. Clare held his silence for a long moment, puffing at his pipe. Hooves and wheels rumbled outside through the city's arteries, an ever-present muted Londinium song. "You do not trust me."

A single shrug.

"It has occurred to you – or perhaps to Miss Bannon – that a mentath, or more than one, may be involved in this conspiracy not just as a victim, but as a conspirator."

Another shrug.

Well. You are even less stupid than I initially supposed. "May we at least for the moment proceed under the assumption that I am not, supported by the evidence that I have been almost murdered in the past twenty-four hours?"

A grudging nod.

Well, that's half the distance to Noncastel. "Many thanks, sir. So. Start at the beginning, and tell me what occurred from the moment our dear sorceress was called from her usual work – which no doubt involved driving herself to exhaustion – to the scene."

Mikal gazed at him for a long moment. Thoughts moved behind that yellow gaze, and the planes of his face took on a sharper cast. "My Prima was called to a house at Elnor Cross; she arrived to find the body of a mentath and fading marks of sorcery. The attending forensic sorcerer had blurred several traces and my Prima was in a fine mood—"

"No, no." Clare waved his pipe. Sweet smoke drifted, taking angular shapes as if it sensed the tension radiating from the other man. His colouring was not nearly dark enough to be Tinkerfolk, Clare decided. Indus, most likely, but the shape of his cheekbones was . . . odd. "The *house*, first. Precisely where is it located? Give me the street address and the number of rooms, then describe to me which room the body was in. Then you will give me the name of the sorcerer, and *only then* proceed to our Bannon's arrival and what transpired then."

Mikal blinked. "You wish for a Recall, then?"

How very interesting. "A Recall?"

"A sorcerer may need to use a Shield's eyes. There are two ways of doing so, a Glove and a Recall. We are trained to observe and offer only what we have observed. That is Recall."

The fascinating question of just what a "Glove" consisted of could occupy him another time, Clare decided. "Very well, then. May I question you during the process, or must I save my questions for afterwards?"

A single economical movement. "Save them. You do not know how to question properly."

I doubt you would teach me to do so, sir. Clare puffed on his pipe again. The tobacco was fine, and for a moment he considered a fraction of coja to sharpen his faculties. Discarded the notion – for if he paused, he suspected Mikal might think better of this offer. "Very well. Proceed when you are ready, sir, and I shall pay most close attention."

Tomlinson was found slumped in a heavy armchair, his dressing jacket unwrinkled, no visible sign of foul play. It seemed a routine case of apoplexy – not common in mentaths, but also not unheard of, the logical patterns of the brain snarling and melting, stewing in irrationality. Tomlinson, however, was busy amid several cases that should have kept his faculties sufficiently exercised.

The attending Master Sorcerer, a certain Hugh Devon, seemed surprised when Miss Emma Bannon made her appearance as the Crown's representative. He seemed even more surprised when she took him to task for smearing the delicate ætheric traceries rumbling and resonating inside the room: "Bumbling like an idiot; now we cannot rule out foul play!"

At which point Mr Devon turned apoplectic-red himself, sputtered, and one of his Shields – a tall, lean blond man – stepped forward. Mikal had merely watched. Miss Bannon had arched one elegant eyebrow. "Leave." Just the one word, but it cut through the other sorcerer's sizzling and transformed the air in the overcushioned sitting room to ice.

Devon and his pair of Shields quit the room, and once they did, Mikal watched as his Prima stalked to the bookcase and pulled free three redrope folders, of the sort solicitors and barristers used. She checked them, one eye on Tomlinson's stocky corpse, and suddenly fixed her own Shield with a searching gaze. "He is without his slippers, Mikal."

She was correct. A pair of tattered woollen socks clasped the mentath's limp feet.

"And I cannot even question his shade, for that fool Devon has tangled everything beyond repair. Come, Mikal. We must examine the room and then seek out the Chancellor; there is something odd afoot."

Masters the Elder, shot on Picksadowne Street between numbers 14 and 15½; there were no witnesses to speak of. Certainly there were onlookers, but none would swear to a description of the shooter. In that part of town, that was very little mystery. The mystery lay in what on earth Masters was doing there, and why he was shot three times – once to the heart, and two bullets shattering his skull. Which meant his shade could not be questioned either, Miss Bannon noted aloud to her Shield.

Very interesting indeed.

Smythe was stabbed near Nightmarket, just before Tideturn. Again, onlookers but no witnesses, and by the time Miss Bannon had arrived his body had been picked clean – and the ætheric traces were smudged as well. It could have been by the pickers; rare was the corpseduster who wished to be found guilty of such a thing.

The sorcerer set to watch Smythe, a certain Mr Newberry, was nowhere to be found. Miss Bannon had commanded Mikal to stand guard over the body and disappeared into the nearby alley, emerging startlingly pale. She did not grant him leave to view the alley for himself, but he did see bodies carried forth from it when help arrived.

He could not swear they were Shields, yet . . .

Throckmorton's house was still blazing when they arrived. Miss Bannon had quelled the fire with surprising difficulty, sorcery fuelling the twisting flames and fighting her control. A crimson salamander, its forked tongue flickering white-hot, had launched itself at Mikal's Prima, and he had killed it. Its ashes, treated with vitae, *glowed blue, proving it had been controlled. Which made the fire sorcerous in origin, and the entire chain of events began to take on a disturbing cast. Throckmorton's corpse was corkscrewed and charred, flesh hanging in ribbons. Either the salamander had been feasting on his remains, or he had been tortured before his death.*

Or both. The heat-shattered skull and cooked brain meant his shade could not be questioned either, and that *put the sorceress in a fine mood as well.*

The Prime who was to be watching the unfortunate Throckmorton, Llewellyn Gwynnfud, was found causing a scene in a Whitchapel brothel, gibbering and Shieldless, and transported to Bedlam by a contingent of nervous hieromancers. And then the first dead unregistered mentaths were found, their bodies terribly mutilated, and Miss Emma Bannon's temper had passed beyond uncertain to downright combative.

She had begun, it seemed, to take something personally.

"Most interesting." Clare relit his pipe. "And did Miss Bannon also search Throckmorton's house?"

"Thoroughly. What little was left of it."

Mutilated if unregistered. How unpleasant. His skin briefly chilled, and he set the thought aside. There were other questions to answer first. "And . . . you will pardon my asking, but what is Miss Bannon's Discipline? Every sorcerer has a Discipline, correct?"

Mikal nodded. His straight-backed posture was the same, but his face had eased slightly. "Yes."

"And Miss Bannon's is . . ."

Mikal's mouth turned into a thin straight line.

Do not insult my intelligence. "Oh come now, man. If I had not guessed her to be one of the Black, I would have to be thick indeed. A sorcerer does not so cavalierly mention questioning shades unless their Discipline overlaps with the Black, correct?"

It was not so outré a guess. Sorcerers were not overly social, but Miss Bannon seemed standoffish even by their standards. She behaved as a woman who was accustomed to having others fear her, and Cedric Grayson had turned pale and sweating. The three branches of sorcery were supposedly all equal, but whispers swirled about the Grey, and swirled even further about the Black. Nothing concrete, certainly . . . but *something* could be inferred even from rumour.

Another small, grudging nod from the Shield.

Clare had to restrain a sigh. "I am not one of the callow multitudes, Mr Mikal. Logic dictates that the service of Britannia's incarnation must hold those the common man perceives to be dangerous. Miss Bannon may be exceeding dangerous, but she is not an ogress, and she does not represent a danger to *me*. I ask about her Discipline only to clarify a point or two to myself and to found my chain of deduction on solid—"

"She is of the Black." Mikal propelled himself to his feet. "There. You know now, mentath. Tread carefully. *She is my Prima*. If you threaten her, I shall find ways to make you regret it."

Threaten her? Clare lowered his pipe. "Who was Crawford?" The name was common, but something nagged at his memory. A recent scandal, perhaps?

The colour drained from Mikal's face, leaving him ashen under the copper. His eyes lit, venomous yellow irises glowing. One hand twitched, a subtle movement.

Clare tensed. He was no match for the Shield, but the sorceress's orders were for Clare to be unharmed.

At least, he *assumed* those were her orders. The threat of some dire consequence that would leave Clare physically unmarked was not to be taken lightly.

"Crawford." The ghost of an accent tinted the word. "He was the first man I killed for her." Mikal's tongue darted out, wetted his thin lips. "He was not – and shall not be – the last."

And with that, the Shield stalked across the room, swept the door open, and stepped into the hall. He would stand guard there, probably the better to keep his temper.

Dead, then. This requires thought. Clare puffed on his pipe. A slight smile played about his mouth. A very successful chain of deduction, far more data than he'd had before, and much was now clearer about Mikal the Shield.

What an extraordinarily diverting morning this was proving to be.

Chapter Nine

The Abortionist

Tideturn had laid smoking gossamer fabric over the traces of the ætheric protection on last night's luckily escaped assassin. Emma clasped her hands before her, lowering her head as she concentrated, invisible threads singing as she handled them so, so delicately. There was joy to be found in the complexity of such an operation, her touch deft and quick.

Like the scales on a butterfly's wings, the imprint of a sorcerer's work on the fabric of the visible world fluttered. Her memory swallowed the pattern whole, comparing it to the thick ætheric tangles laid over Llewellyn Gwynnfud last night.

There was no overlap. Well, it was hardly a surprise that more than one sorcerer was involved in this.

The climax of last night's events bothered her, though. She should have been able to guess the irregularities in the charm and charter symbols would act so vigorously, and perhaps taken steps to keep Llewellyn alive for further questioning.

But you did not, Emma. Was it because the thought of him dead did not distress you at all? It is rather a relief, isn't it? Come now, be honest.

Well, if she had to be *absolutely* honest, she would have preferred snuffing Llewellyn's candle herself. Yet another unfeminine trait. Or was the desire to be thorough and tidy so unlady-like? Llew had been a loose end.

He had almost certainly suspected what had happened in Crawford's round room, and further suspected that Emma would be vulnerable. He was far too dangerous to possess knowledge of a weakness of that magnitude.

It is well that he is dead, and we have business with the living. She returned to herself, shaking her head slightly. The alley was piled with refuse, and if not for the air-clearing charm every Londinium sorcerer with any talent learned early and used religiously, it would be easily ripe enough to turn her stomach. The cobbles underfoot were coated with slick foulness, and she edged forward cautiously.

There. She caught sight of a gleam – a copper disc and a broken ribbon, tossed aside as soon as it was used. *Oh, you idiot, whoever you are. Bless your stupidity, for you have given me an opening.*

Here in the sunlight, without a single Shield, she would have to use all appropriate caution. She picked her way over the slimy stones, keeping her breathing even with an effort. Sarpesson Street was quieter at this hour, but traffic still rumbled past, whipcracks and clockwork sparks echoing oddly in the alley's choked confines.

He came down there, *triggered the protection, flung it away. Hard to see in the dark, and hoping the refuse would cover it. Then . . . where would he go?*

She bent, her stays digging briefly even though she was only loosely corseted – there was fashion and there was idiocy, and while she was vain enough to love the former, she was not willing to indulge the latter. A stray shaft of weak sunlight pierced the alley's roof, buildings sloping together alarmingly overhead, and even that was enough to jab at her sensitised eyes.

Blast and bother. She tweezed the ribbon carefully between gloved fingers and slowly straightened, holding the protection disc stiff-armed away from her body as it glowed dully. The charm had been well made, even though its physical matrix was flimsy and disposable. It was at the very least the work of a Master Sorcerer, and as she examined it more closely, Emma realised it was familiar.

She breathed a term a respectable lady would faint upon hearing, then cast a squinting glance over her shoulder as if someone might witness her lapse. No, the alley was deserted. So why the sudden sense of being observed, lifting the fine hairs on her nape and tingling down her spine under the drab brown velvet?

Proceed very carefully indeed, Emma. He is bound to guess you will show up at his door, unless you are dead.

And Konstantin Serafimovitch Gippius would not trust a rumour of Emma Bannon's demise until he could see her mutilated body.

Perhaps not even then.

Even this early in the day, Whitchapel seethed with a crush of stinking humanity – ragpickers, pickpockets, loiterers, day labourers, streetmerchants, hevvymancers and drays, public houses doing a brisk trade in cups of gin and tankers of beer, washerwomen and ragged drabs, stray sparks and flicks of charm and sorcery crackling along the filthy street. Pawnbrokers' coloured signs flashed with catchcharms, their infrequent windows glowing with lightfinger wards and their doors reinforced. Clockhorses strained and whinnied, shouts and cries echoed, and the entire squeezing, throbbing mass teemed not only with the living but the vaporous dead. Ragged children darted through the crowd; at the corner of Dray Street and Sephrin a cart carrying a load of barrels lay sideways, a man lying groaning, half crushed under one side and the onlookers jostling to get a better view as a gang of labourers – not a hevvymancer in sight – struggled to heave the cart away. Clockwork horses screamed, their gears grating and sorcerous energy spilling dangerously uncontrolled.

It would have taken mere moments to restore some order, but any disturbance of the æther here would warn her quarry.

The carter will be dead within a quarter-hour anyway, she told herself sternly as she threaded through the crowd, the cameo at her throat warming as thin filaments of glamour turned her into anything other than a respectable woman sliding into Whitchapel. *The greater good of all demands I do not become distracted here.*

Still, the screams and moans rang in her ears as she turned on Thrawl, slowing as a press of human flesh choked about her. A pickmancer's nimble fingers brushed for her skirt pocket, but her sardonyx ring sparked and the touch was hurriedly drawn back. A raddled drab, her ruined face turned up to the morning light and runnelled with decaying powder, sang nonsense in a cracked unlovely alto, while a mob of flashboys whooped near the low sooty entrance of the Cross and Spaulders, their draggled finery sparking slightly with sartorial charms. Alterations gleamed – any flashboy worth the name would have an amendment, the more visible the better. One had a blackened clockwork hand that spat sparks from its hooked fingers, another a green-glass eye rolling in an exposed, bony socket. Cheap work, that, but this was Whitchapel.

Everything was cheap here. Including human life.

Already the sky was hazed – not nearly enough; the light speared through her skull. This would be so much *easier* after dusk.

It would be easier for Gippius too. So Emma blinked furiously, did *not* lift her handkerchief to her nose, and kept the subtle threads of glamour blending together. Some few of the slightly sorcerous on the street glanced at her once or twice, but she was Prime and they were merely sparks. They would not see what she truly was unless she willed it.

A venous network of alleys had grown around Thrawl, slumping tenements festooned with sagging laundry hung on lines despite the coal dust, refuse packed into corners. Children

screamed and ran about, playing some game that made sense
only to them, the slurring drawl of the Eastron End already
evident in their joyous accents. Malnourished but agile, they
were more problematic than the adults – sometimes a child's
gaze would pierce a glamour where even an Adept's could not.

She found the rat's nest of alleyways she was looking for,
and plunged into welcome gloom. Some doors hung ajar,
shadows flitting through them; a colourless vapour of gin and
hopelessness rose. A baby cried, wheedling and insistent, somewhere in the depths of a building. A man crouched on a low
step in front of a battered, dispirited wooden door. Muffled cries
were heard from inside, and the man's eyes followed Emma's
shadow as he peeled his nails with a short, wicked knife, taking
care to palm the filthy clippings up to his mouth as an insurance
against charming.

At the far end of the alley the abortionist's door, studded with
iron nails, grimaced. Emma braced herself and strode for it, her
boots slipping a little against the crust coating the alley floor.
No wonder Gippius had sunk into this quarter of the city – few
constables would brave this hole.

Few sorcerers would, even.

Invisible strings quivered under the surface of the visible.
The cameo warmed at her throat, and the ætheric protections in
Gippius's walls resonated slightly.

That is not a good sign. The door had no knob; she simply
focused – and stepped through, a shivering curtain of glamour
sparking and fizzing as her will shunted the river of charm and
charter aside.

Gippius was quick and deadly, but he was not native. In his
country, she would be the sorcerous stranger, and the resultant
struggle might have had a different outcome. As it was, she
flung out a hand, the Cossack who did a Shield's duty for
Konstantin stumbled back into a mound of clothing waiting for
the ragpickers, and Emma's other gloved hand made a curious
tracing motion as she spoke a minor Word. Witchlight flared,

and Konstantin Gippius stumbled back, clutching at his throat. A single line of chant, low and vicious, poured from Emma's mouth, a fierce hurtful thrill of sorcery spilling through her, and the Cossack shrieked as ætheric bonds snapped into place over him.

The chant faded into the humming of live sorcery. Emma climbed to her feet, brushing off her dress. The Cossack's shriek was cut short on a gurgle; she grimaced and made certain her bonnet was straight. The huge glass jars filling every shelf chattered and clattered together, the abominations inside twitching as dark, pudgy Gippius thrashed on the trash-strewn floor. He was turning a most amazing shade of purple.

"Behave yourself," she said sternly, and flicked her fingers, releasing the silencing.

Gippius's throat swelled with sound. Sorcery flashed towards her; she batted the venomous yellow darting coils aside and tightened her gloved fist, humming a low sustained note. The silencing clamped down again, the cameo a spot of scorch against her chest. "I said *behave yourself*, Gippius! Or I shall choke you to death and go a-traipsing through your house for what I wish."

Spluttering, the Russian thrashed. His boots drummed the floor. When she judged she had perhaps expressed her seriousness in terms he could comprehend, she fractionally loosened her hold once again.

The abominations in the jars moved too, slopping their baths of amber solution against dusty glass. Tiny piping cries echoed, their large heads and tiny malformed bodies twitching. Metal clinked – some of them had been Altered. Gippius's science was inefficient, and disgusting as well.

It is a very good thing I have a strong stomach. Emma eyed Gippius as he lay quiescent, glaring balefully. Greasy black hair hung in strings, sawdust from his rolling about griming the curls. A crimson spark lit in the backs of his pupils, but quickly dimmed and was extinguished as his face grew more and more plummy.

She eased the constriction, in increments. It took a good long while for his tortured gasps to even out, and the Cossack moaned to one side. Emma spent the time eyeing the jar-living abominations, examining the filthy curtain drawn to mark the entrance to Gippius's surgery, the low sullen light of malformed witchballs sparking orange as they bobbed in cheap lantern-cages. The stove in the corner glowed sullenly as well, and the large pot bubbling atop it reeked of cabbage.

When she judged it safe enough, and further judged she had Konstantin's entire attention, she drew the protection disc and its broken ribbon from her skirt pocket.

"Now," she said quietly, for it did not do to shout if there was no need, "I am about to question you, Konstantin Serafimovitch. If you do not have proper answers – or if I even *suspect* any impropriety such as dishonesty in your answers – first I will kill your Cossack. If you continue to be remiss, I shall shatter all your jars. If you are *still* remiss, I shall be forced to make things very unpleasant for your *corpus*." She paused, let him absorb this. "And I do not have to cease when you expire, either."

Now he was moaning as well. The counterpoint of male agony was almost musical.

She began working her gloves off, finger by finger, though her flesh crawled at the thought of touching anything in this hole with bare flesh. "Now. Let us start with this protection charm."

Chapter Ten

Tea and Data

Newspaper clippings scattered over the table, turned this way and that as he tested connections between them. Two volumes of the *Encylopaedie* stood open as well, a further three stacked on the chair, and he paced between the fireplace and the window. More papers, covered with his cramped handwriting, fluttered as he passed the table. The desk was snowed under with a drift of notes and more volumes.

Occasionally he stopped, running his hands through thinning hair. His pipe had long since gone out.

"The connections," he muttered, several times. "I *must* have more data!"

He had endured the visit from Mr Finch, interrupting his research with idiocy about linens and a valet, and further endured the measuring-charms and queries of the footman chosen to do valet duty. His freshly laundered linens, sent by an obliging Grayson, had been delivered and stowed away. Then, thankfully, they had left him in peace – what peace there was, for he was beginning to be sorely pressed.

The door resounded under a series of knocks, and when it opened, the Shield took in the explosion of paper and Clare's pacing. "Tea," he said, the single word as colourless as it was possible for a syllable to be. His mouth turned down at the corners, and he was actually grey under his copper hue. "In the conservatory."

"*That's not where she takes her tea!*" Clare cried, turning in a jerky half-circle. "I know that much! I am engaged on deducing much more. But there's one piece, *one critical piece* – or maybe more than one. I cannot tell. I must have more data!"

Mikal's features betrayed no surprise. Just that grey, set monotone. "My Prima takes her tea in her study, but you are a guest, and the conservatory is made avail—"

Clare halted, staring at him. "My God, man, you look *dreadful*."

The Shield's head dipped, a fractional nod. "Thank you. Tea, mentath. Come along."

"Why do you—" Clare stopped short. His head cocked, the chain of deduction enfolding. "Surely you are not so worried for Miss Bannon's safety that you—"

"Tea," Mikal repeated, and retreated into the hall, pulling the door to but not latching it. Which effectively halted the conversation, though only until Clare could exit his suite.

Unfortunately the Shield had taken that into account, and was at the other end of the hall before Clare could gather himself. He led Clare through the house, always just at the end of a hall or at the bottom of stairs, and did not slacken the pace until Clare stepped into the largish conservatory's pearly glow. A thin dusting of rain streaked the glass walls, rippling panes held in filigreed wrought-iron, charter symbols falling through the metal like golden oil. The day had turned grey-haze, but the collection of potted plants and small, ruthlessly pruned larger bushes – orange, lemon, lime, false lime, rosemary, bay laurel, and the like – still drank in the light greedily. The north end was given to straggling, rank, baneful plants – rue, pennyroyal, nightshade, wolfsbane, nettle, hadthorn, and more. East and west held common herbs – feverfew, a few mint species, chamomile, costmary and other culinary and common-charm plants. The south end was given to exotics – a tomato plant, green unripe fruit hanging on charter-charm-reinforced green stems, orchids Clare could not name, a small planter of fiery scarlet tulips, a dwarf rose whose petals were a velvety purple very close to black. Each was covered by a crystalline dome of sorcery, ringing with thin, gentle sounds when the atmosphere inside stirred the leaves – a quite pleasant sound, like faraway bells.

To properly examine every plant would take perhaps an hour and a half. Here was another unexpected richness. It was not the sort of room Clare would expect to find Miss Bannon in, and his estimation of her character went through a sharp change as a result. Which led him down several interesting and troubling roads all at once.

The furniture was white-painted wicker, the chairs cushioned with rich blue velvet. A snow-white cloth trimmed in scallops of blue lace covered the tabletop, the service was burnished to within an inch of its silvery life, and a full tea was arranged on three tiers, the shimmer of a keeping charm visible over it. The air was alive with sorcery.

Mikal prowled near the northern end of the sunroom, pacing, his boots soundless on the mellow-glowing, satiny wooden floor. The light picked out red highlights in his dark hair, stroked the nap of his velvet coat, and made his colour even more sickly.

The housekeeper, her black crêpe rustling, hovered over the table bobbing a tiny curtsey. Her cap was placed so precisely he half expected it to bow as well. Her round face lit with genuine pleasure, and not a single lock of dark hair was out of place. Her indenture collar glowed. "*Bonjour, Monsieur Clare!* Tea is generally mine, *madame* prefers it so. Shall I pour for you?"

He could very well pour for himself. But here was another opportunity for deduction and questioning. "I would be delighted, Madame Noyon. Please, join me. It seems Mr Mikal doesn't care for tea."

"He never does. *Madame* would make him sit, but he is not likely to now." Her plump nervous hands moved, and Clare laid a private bet with himself about which chair she would prefer him in.

"How often does Miss Bannon leave him behind to fret, then?"

That earned him a solemn French glance. Her collar flashed, and her daggered jet earrings swung. "*Monsieur.*" Sudden, icy politeness. She indicated the chair he had chosen, and at least his instincts were not off.

"Very well. I am only concerned for Miss Bannon's safety, Madame Noyon."

"Well." Slightly mollified, she began the ritual of tea with an ease that spoke of long practice. She made an abortive movement for the milk, and he deduced Miss Bannon habitually took some, and was often otherwise occupied while Madame Noyon poured. Some of the savouries appeared to be favoured by his absent hostess, too. "You have no need to fear, *monsieur.* Our *madame* is the finest sorcerer in Londinium. When she says a thing is to be done, *pouf!* It is done."

Touching faith. He added a few more links to the chain of deduction. "She rescued you, did she not?"

"*Ma foi,* she rescued us all! Lemon?"

"No, thank you. Rescued you all?"

"Finch, he was thief. Catherine, she was Without Reference, as you *Anglais* say. Wilbur in the stables, he was—"

Mikal was suddenly across the table, yellow eyes glowing. "Enough. The domestics are no interest of yours, mentath."

Madame Noyon gasped, her hand to her mouth. The tea service rattled slightly, the table underneath it responding to a feral current.

"You could sit and have tea," Clare returned, mildly enough. "The more I know, Mr Mikal, the more help I am to your mistress. A mentath is useless without data."

"You are worse than useless anyway." The Shield's graven face had lost even more colour. "If she is harmed while I am forced to sit—"

"*Monseiur le bouclie.*" Madame Noyon tapped the teapot with the lemon knife. "You are in very bad manners. Monsieur Clare is our guest, and *madame* left instructions. You sit, or pace, but do not loaf about table like vulture!"

Clare watched as the Shield's face congested, suffusing with a ghastly flush before the man turned on his booted heel and glided away towards the north end. The rain intensified, spattering glass and iron, the charter symbols sending up small wisps of fog as cold water touched them.

Madame Noyon swallowed, audibly. Her fingers trembled slightly before she firmed her mouth and put on a bright expression. "*Madame* returns soon, *monsieur*. Eat, eat. You are thin like Mr Finch, you must eat."

Clare certainly intended to. His landlady's teas were nowhere near as grand, and only a fool would let his digestion be troubled.

Yet he pushed his chair back and rose. He approached the north end of the conservatory, his hands clasped behind his back and the slap of rain intensifying again. Rivulets slid their cold fingers over the glass.

"Mr Mikal." He hoped his tone was not overly familiar – or overly distant. Dealing with this messiness was so *difficult*. "I beg your pardon, sir. I do not intend to be a burden, and my intent in questioning about Miss Bannon is purely so I may assist her in whatever way necessary, to the best of my ability. I may be useless, and own no sorcery, but I am striving to become *less* useless, and I very much crave your assistance in that endeavour."

Mikal had come to a stop, his head down, staring at a thornspiked, venomous-looking plant in a low earthenware pot. His shoulders hunched, as if expecting a blow, but straightened just as swiftly.

Clare retreated to the tea table. But halfway through his second scone, Mikal dropped into the chair across from him. Madame Noyon's eyebrows nested in her hairline, but she poured for him too. The Shield's face did not ease and his colour did not return. He was still grey as the rain.

But he drank his tea, staring up over Clare's head at an infinitely receding point, and Clare was hard pressed not to feel . . .

. . . well, extremely pleased.

Chapter Eleven

Unpleasantness is Not Over

I must reach home. The bright blood welling beneath her gloved hand clasped to her ribs splattered her skirt, and she was no doubt leaving a trail a mile wide. Ætheric strings quivered; the effort to mislead the parties searching for her consumed most of her waning strength. *Why is there never a hansom?*

She could barely hail one as it was, bleeding so badly. Not to mention a respectable driver might not stop, even if her glamour held. Another fiery pang rolled through her as the æther twisted, a screaming rush of air almost touching her disarranged curls, and for a moment the effort of blurring what an onlooker would see almost failed. Fresh hot claret slid between her fingers.

If not for her corset stays, she might well have been a dead woman. They had turned the knife a fraction, slowing it, and the man attacking her had died of a burst of raw shrieking sorcerous power. Konstantin had not lied; he had given her all the information she could reasonably suppose he had. But those who had engaged the services of one of the actual rooftop assassins – Charles Knigsbury was at least one of his names, a flashboy who had procured the protection from the abortionist on his own account – had also thought to ensure said assassin would not open his lips to one Emma Bannon.

Or indeed, to anyone.

The sorcery she had used on the small, rat-faced flashboy still stinking of gunpowder and terror had triggered a larger explosion of hurtful magic; Knigsbury's body had literally shredded itself to pieces, and a fine cloud of mist-boiled blood had coated the inside of his stinking Dorset Alley doss. The resultant ætheric confusion had allowed her to slip away, but moments later she had felt the passage of an invisible bird of prey, and deduced the flashboy was bait of a different sort.

Well, I did think to spring a trap or two today. An unsteady, hitching noise escaped her; she reached out blindly and braced herself against a soot-laden brick wall. It looked vaguely familiar, a corner she saw almost every day, albeit usually through a carriage window. The rain intensified, threading through her glamour with tiny cold trickles, and she was well on her way to looking like a drowned cat.

A drowned, *bleeding* cat. Her knees buckled.

Emma, this will not do. Stand up! The snap of command was not hers. For a moment she was in the girls' dormer at the Collegia again, her hair shorn and her skin smarting from the scrubbing, an orphan among the bigger girls who knew what to do and where to go – and how to bully the newcomer. And Prima Grinaud, the high magistrix of the younger classes, wasp-waisted and severe in her black watered silk, snapping sharply whenever Emma cried. *Stop that noise. Collegia sorceresses do not snivel.*

And little Emma had learned. Unfortunately, all that learning now seemed likely to pour out on to a filthy Londinium street.

No, not filthy. There's the hedge. I am nearly home. Instead of brick, her free hand scraped the laurel hedge, washed with rain and glowing green even through the assault of smoke. Was it smoke? It certainly clouded her vision, but she smelled nothing but the familiar wet stone and Londinium coal stink.

And the sharp-sweet copper tang of blood.

No, it wasn't smoke. Her sensitive eyes were merely failing her. It had been so bright earlier, even through the lowering clouds; her head hurt, a spike of pain through her temples. The gate quivered, iron resonating with distress; for a moment she was unable to remember the peculiar ætheric half-twist that would calm the restive guardian work wedded to metal and stone.

Either that, or she was clutching the wrong gate. But no, she blinked hazily several times and looked up as another wave of sorcery slid past her, ruffling her hair and almost, almost catching the edge of her skirts. When they found the blood trail—

I am home. Numerals made of powdery silver metal danced, charter symbols racing over their surface in golden crackles: *34½*, a sweeter set of digits she had never seen. The high-arched gate trembled until she calmed it and found the breath to hum a simple descant.

Or she tried to. It took her a long while of sipping in air suddenly treacle-thick.

Finally she managed it. The gate shuddered and unlatched, one half sliding inward; veils of ætheric energy parted just as the next wave of sorcerously fuelled seeking tore past, arrowing unerringly for her as she tipped herself forward. It nipped at her heels, the sympathetic ætheric string from her own blood yanking, seeking to drag her backwards into the street.

But she was safely inside her own gate, the defences on her sanctum snapping shut, and Emma Bannon went to her knees on the wet, pretty front walk, lilac hedges snapping and thrashing as the house recognised her and filled with distress. Rain pattered down; she went over sideways, her hand still clamped to the wound. Another hot gush of blood; she heard running feet and exclamations, and she struggled against the grey cotton cocoon closing around her.

Thank goodness this dress was already ugly, she thought.

And, *I must live. I* must.

I know too much to die now.

Chapter Twelve

Our First Dinner

Normally, Clare supposed, a woman half-dead of the application of a knife to her lung – discovered covered in blood and water at her own front door, no less – would be put abed for weeks. Certainly she would not appear, pale as milk and with one half of her childlike, almost pretty face bruised, at her dinner table in fresh dark green silk with *very* close sleeves and divided skirts, brushed boots, the cameo still caught at her throat and a new pair of earrings – sapphires in heavy silver – dangling with each turn of her head. Her ringlets were re-arranged as well, and though she did not wear a bonnet, he was fairly certain one lay in waiting, probably in Madame Noyon's capable care.

It was no great trick to deduce that Miss Bannon's day was far from over.

The Shield, his jaw set so hard it looked fit to crack his strong white teeth, hovered behind her thronelike chair at the head of a long mahogany table, its legs of massive carved gryphonshape shifting restlessly. Against the Prompeian red of the draperies and the bronze walls, Mikal's olive velvet and yellow eyes were aesthetically displeasing but not altogether inappropriate. He was no longer grey, but boiling with tightly controlled fury.

At least, *fury* was the word Clare thought applicable. It could have been *rage*. *Anger* was altogether too pale a term for the vibrating, incandescent wrath leaking from his every pore.

Clare viewed his cream of asparagus soup with a discerning eye, tasted it, and discovered it was superlative. *That* was no surprise; Miss Bannon did not stint and Cook, like Madame Noyon, appeared to be French. The sideboard was massive but not overpowering; the large greenery in its Chinois-style pots was carefully charmed and rustled pleasingly. The folding screens were marvels of restraint, and he wished for the chance to examine them more closely. The epergne was *also* a marvel of restraint, its height managing to look graceful and lacy instead of massively overdone.

Of course, a sorcerer lived as flagrantly as he could, but Miss Bannon's discriminations appeared to be more in the realm of actual taste and quality, instead of fad and wild freakishness. The silver was of fineness, though plain, the linens snow-white.

He cleared his throat. "I take it your day was successful, Miss Bannon?"

"Quite." She was hoarse, and she flinched slightly as she reached for her water glass. As if her side pained her. "In fact, Mr Clare, I wish to put some questions to you."

Oh, I'm certain you do. "I have some questions as well. Shall we interrogate each other over dinner? You are likely to have some entertainment planned for the evening."

"If by *entertainment* you mean conspiracy-hunting and unpleasantness, as a matter of fact, yes." The circles under her eyes matched the bruising on her face; she winced again as she set her glass down. "I do beg your pardon. I hope my state does not interfere with your digestion."

"Madam, almost nothing interferes with my digestion. It is a great advantage to being a mentath." He savoured a mouthful of soup. "Here is an observation. There is a group of mentaths. Some are killed for one reason. Others are killed for a separate – but connected – reason, and mutilated in some fashion. Smythe had just returned from Indus, as Grayson commented. It makes little sense to think he was involved, unless—"

"Smythe was not in Indus." Miss Bannon's gaze flashed. Did she look amused? Perhaps. "That is where Grayson was *told* he had gone. In reality, he was in Kent, at a country house owned by the Crown."

"Ah." Clare's eyelids lowered. He savoured another spoonful. "You had various and sundry reasons for leaving me mewed in your house with your Shield, then, not merely my safety."

The barest flash of surprise crossed her bruised face. It looked as if someone had struck her violently, and also tried to throttle her. The marks were fading, her skin rippling a little as the ancient symbols of charter surfaced and dove beneath the paleness. Healing sorcery.

If he had not had such excellent digestion, the sight might have turned his stomach. Besides, it was ridiculous to let such a thing interfere with one's repast.

"I did," she admitted. "Though you must admit you are safest here, and—"

"Oh, tell him," Mikal snarled. "You cannot trust me, so you wander out into Londinium and find yourself a knife to fall on."

Clare was hard put to restrain a flash of most unbecoming glee at the rich new vistas of deduction *that* remark opened.

"If you will not let me eat my dinner in peace, Shield, you may wait in the hall." But Miss Bannon did not sound sharp. Only weary.

The Shield leaned over her shoulder. "What if you had died, Prima? What then?"

"Then I would be spared this most unwelcome display at the table." Miss Bannon gazed steadily at Clare. "My apologies, sir. My Shield forgets himself."

"I do not *forget*." Mikal planted himself solidly, folding his arms. The high carved back of Miss Bannon's chair did nothing to blunt the force of the ire coming from him. "Such is my curse."

"Should you truly wish a curse, Mikal, continue in this manner." Miss Bannon sampled her soup. Finch appeared, his thin arms bearing a tray with decanters; he busied himself at the sideboard. The footmen came and went, serving with clockwork precision and muffled feet. One of them was missing his left smallest finger, quite an oddity. "Mr Clare. Tomlinson and Smythe were given different . . . pieces, as it were, of a puzzle. They seemed to be very near to a solution in their respective ways. Masters and Throckmorton were apparently given parts of those separate puzzle pieces, and—"

You are telling me a carefully chosen tale, which probably bears only kissing relation to the truth. "I have the idea, thank you. What were they researching?" *And why were the unregistered mentaths mutilated? You avoid that subject with much alacrity, Miss Bannon.*

"If I were at liberty to disclose that, Mr Clare . . ." She needed say no more.

"Very well." He turned his attention to the soup, momentarily, while deductions assumed a different shape inside his skull. "That rather materially changes things. You are aware of the nature of this puzzle; Lord Grayson is now too. Which means the Chancellor is suspected, or your orders are from another quarter, or—"

"Or I am a part of the conspiracy, keeping you alive for my own nefarious reasons. Mr Finch? I require rum. Shocking at dinner, but my nerves rather demand it. Mikal, either *sit down* at the place laid for you, or go out into the hall. I will *not* have this behaviour at dinner."

"I prefer to wait upon you, my Prima." It was a shock to see a grown man so mulishly defiant, like a child expecting a spanking.

"Then you may wait in the hall." The dishes rattled, the table shifted slightly, and the plants whispered under their charm domes. Clare applied himself more fully to his soup.

The Shield pulled out the chair to Miss Bannon's left – the

right was reserved for Clare – and a servant hurried forward. Finch brought a carafe and a small crystal glass, poured something Clare's sensitive nose verified was indeed rum, and Miss Bannon quaffed it smoothly, as if such an operation was habitual.

Some colour came back into her face – natural colour, not the garishness of bruising. "Thank you, Finch. I shall relate to you the most interesting portions of my day, Mr Clare, since your digestion is so sound, and you shall analyse what I tell you."

"Very well." Clare settled in his chair. The gryphon-carved table legs chose to still themselves, which was a decided improvement. What she told him now would be as close to the truth as she could risk.

She wasted little time. "Last night a single one of our attackers escaped. I meant to trace his whereabouts after we visited Bedlam, but it was not possible. However, had I not waited for daylight, today's events might have gone in a very different direction. In any case, I found our attacker had received a protection from a certain sorcerer I am familiar with. I visited said sorcerer's domicile in Whitchapel and received the information that the man – a flashboy, if you are familiar with the term?"

"A man of the lower classes. One who has been Altered. Specifically, a type of petty criminal who takes it as a point of pride." Such men were dangerous. If the Alteration did not make them unstable, the crime they were steeped in would do so. Their tempers were notoriously nasty, and by all accounts extraordinarily short.

And Miss Bannon had ventured alone into the sink of filth, danger and corruption that was Whitchapel. *Most* intriguing.

"Precisely." Miss Bannon gave a nod of approval, drained another small glass of rum, and the roast chicken was brought in. "I received the information that our flashboy had arrived, requested a protection, paid, and left."

"Exactly how much did he pay?"

"Two gold sovereigns, a guinea, and fivepence. One rather gets the idea he was pressed for time, and that he had so much as a mark of faith from his employer."

"It being Whitchapel," Clare observed, "the fivepence was no gratuity."

"No, the sorcerer squeezed for every farthing the flashboy was willing to part with. In any case, I found the flashboy's doss and persuaded him to give *some* information before he attacked me. I defended myself – *I* did not kill him – and in the process, a truly terrible amount of sorcery was triggered on him." She eyed Clare speculatively, and her colour was indeed better. She set to the roast chicken with a will, and Clare copied her example. "It was old sorcery, the same practitioner as last night's event in Bedlam. Our flashboy was no sorcerer, so it . . . the force tore him apart. It was intended to not only do so but also incapacitate any sorcerous visitor so his employer could discover any meddling in his business."

"His?"

"I find it extraordinarily unlikely this is a woman, sir."

Clare was inclined to agree, but Mikal could apparently stand it no longer. The Shield stared at the chicken on his plate, the potato balls drenched in golden butter, the scattered parsley, as if it were a mass of writhing snakes. "*Injured* you? Stabbed you in the lung, and—"

"Do *not* interrupt, Mikal." A line had appeared between Miss Bannon's arched eyebrows. "I am sure Mr Clare is aware of the extent of my injuries. So, mentath, your analysis, if you please."

Clare sampled a potato ball. *Most excellent*. "I have been reading the papers today. Your hospitality is wonderful, Miss Bannon. The *Encyclopaedie* was also useful, though I may need some other texts—"

She waved a hand, her rings sparkling. Fire opals this time, two of them set in heavy bronze and surrounded by what appeared to be tiny uncut diamonds. "Merely inform Mr Finch of your requirements. Analysis, please."

"You will not like it."

"That does not detract from its validity."

"You are a very managing female, Miss Bannon."

Thus ensued a very long silence as Clare's utensils made tiny noises against his plate. The ham arrived and was dealt with, a dish of *haricots verts* in a sauce full of lemony tang as well. No oysters, but he did not feel stinted.

It took until the sherbet for him to notice the uncomfortable quality of the silence. At least, a normal person might have called it uncomfortable. It was heavy, cold, and almost . . . reptilian. The gryphons carved into the table legs shifted, the table's surface completely level and the fluid motion underneath almost enough to unseat even *his* stomach.

The illogic of it bothered him. A table should not move so.

"My analysis—" he began.

"Is that I am a 'managing female'?" Miss Bannon enquired, almost sweetly. The tone alarmed him, and he diverted his attention from the exquisite bone-china sherbet dish.

He was right to be alarmed, for he noted Mikal had tensed. The Shield's head was up, and he stared at the sorceress with the leashed expectation of a bloodhound. The sorceress, her curls falling forward, toyed with a small silver spoon, tracing patterns through melting lemon sherbet.

Aha. We have found a chink in your armour, Sorceress Prime. "Is that you know far more than you are telling me, and hence your invitation to analyse is a trap. I shall at the very best look like an idiot, and at the worst waste precious time."

"Indeed." She settled back in her chair, and the sherbet was whisked away. So was Mikal's, untouched. "Excuse me. I have preparations to make before I leave the house again. Enjoy your coffee, Mr Clare." She rose, and Mikal all but leapt upright as well.

"I do hope I shall be able to accompany you?" Clare pushed his chair back and gained his feet. "Now that you have satisfied yourself that I am not part of this conspiracy?"

"I have not satisfied myself on that account, sir. But you may accompany me." She glanced once at Mikal. "I wish you precisely where I may watch you. We shall leave in a half-hour."

Chapter Thirteen

Britannia's Worst

Emma spent most of that half-hour roaming her study as the swelling on her face retreated, running her fingers along leather-clad spines and attempting to clear her mind. The skull on her desk creaked each time she passed, bone-dust rising and settling along its grinning curves. Mikal, by now well acquainted with this ritual, stood by the door, his hands crossed in a Shield's habitual pose.

Scraps covered with her handwriting scattered across the desk as well, different charm and charter symbols, experiments, notes and drawings arranged in a system no other person would be able to decipher. A globe of malachite on a brass Atlas's straining shoulders spun lazily, a small scraping sound under the rustle of her skirts. The long black drapes moved slightly as well, and witchglobes in heavy bronze cages sputtered, almost sparking and giving out a low bloody light that *precisely* matched her feelings at the moment.

The little sounds only underscored Mikal's silence. She finally halted next to the high-backed, severe leather chairs before the fireplace. Gripped the back of one, her fingers turning white. Her chest ached, so she squeezed harder. Healing sorcery could only do so much, and Mikal's facility with it was not infinite, though certainly not inconsiderable either.

The map of the Empire over the fireplace, etched on brass and framed in Ceylon ebony, glowed with soft golden reflections, showing the passage of sunlight over the Empire's dominions. The sun indeed never set; Britannia's sway was wide.

But even *she* was not infinite, or invulnerable.

Emma stared, stiffening her knees, and for a moment she considered retreating behind her walls and doing no more. God knew she had paid enough, over and over, for every scrap she had received.

But that would be treachery of a different sort, wouldn't it. To simply leave the Queen without a sorceress willing to do the worst.

And there was her regrettable pride, raising its head. There might be Primes more powerful than Emma Bannon, and a few more socially acceptable, and perhaps even one or two as loyal. Yet there was no Prime who would sink to the depths *she* would in service to the current holder of Britannia's essence.

Who was, after all, merely a girl who had been thrust on to the throne, and fought with surprising skill and ferocity to free herself from those who would use her.

Is that why I find myself so inclined to settle in this harness? Emma half turned, uncramping her hand with an effort. The Shield's gaze met hers.

What could she say? "Before I left . . . that was unjustified, Mikal. My temper is . . . uncertain."

A single nod. Perhaps an acceptance of the apology, perhaps simply affirmation of his hearing it.

Proud to the end, her Shield. At least the past month had taught her *that*. And today's events had been rather a slap of cold water. Since the Crawford . . . affair, she had been simply focused on her service to Britannia. As if working herself into a rag of bone and nervous ætheric force would somehow give her an answer.

There may not be another time to ask. "Mikal?"

"Prima."

"Why did you do . . . what you did?" *And what is the assurance that you will not violate your Shield oath again, if you judge me as you judged* him? *Or did you? I do not know enough to guess at the music that moves you.*

Perhaps I should ask Mr Clare to deduce its measures. For a moment, she thought of explaining to a mentath how she had been trapped in chains and a Major Circle not of her devising, close to having her sorcery torn out of her by the roots, and what she had heard as Mikal's fingers closed around Crawford's throat. The crackling of little bones, the awful choking noises mixing with her own panicked, ineffectual cries.

To be so helpless was enough to drive a Prime to the edge of sanity. Or past. And Emma wondered if she had been quite sane since the experience.

Perhaps Mikal chose to misunderstand her question. "It was a choice between service to another Prime or death." Calm, matter-of-fact, his expression set and unyielding. "You said it yourself, Prima. They would kill me if I were not in service to a sorcerer who could protect me, and you are the only one willing to do so."

At least that you have found. What was the danger of continuing thus? She braced herself, and took the next logical step. "You may, if you choose, leave my service and stay in my house as a sanctuary. The Collegia will censure me, but at least you will still be alive." *And I will not have to wonder when you will find me lacking and squeeze the life out of me.*

"No."

Well, at least she had made him express a preference. "Very well. You may decide otherwise at any—"

"No." His eyes flamed. She wondered, not for the first time, how much of what she suspected of his bloodline was true. "Do not ask again, Prima."

Very well. I shall simply be on guard. As I have been. And look how satisfactorily that *has proceeded.* Still, he had not turned on her yet. "You will need to be fully armed tonight."

The crimson light made him an ochre statue, except for the gleams of his eyes. "I am."

"Already?" She sounded mocking, she supposed.

"I do not take it lightly when *my* Prima is stabbed in the lung."

Your *Prima. Did you feel so proprietary of* your *Prime, lo that scant month ago?* "I returned, did I not?"

"Barely, Emma. Shall we continue this conversation, or would you like to bring me to my knees again and save time?"

I apologised, Mikal. "You say that as if you do not enjoy it." Sharp, a prick for his temper, no less regrettable than her own.

He chose not to give battle, for once. "No more or less than you do, Prima. Shall I ask where we are bound tonight? Tideturn is close. No more than a quarter-hour."

I am aware of that. She glanced at the softly ticking grand-father clock, its face showing the different hours of the day in jewelled simulacra of the Ages of Man. Sorcery bubbled in its depths, its wheels and cogs and springs measuring each second of eternity. Given proper care, the works would continue even when the thick oak casing, sheathed in chasing metal, turned to dust. The dealer had sworn it was from an alchemyst's labora-tory, hinting that so august a personage as von Tachel had owned it at one time. Exceedingly unlikely . . . but still, Emma liked it, and the jewelled simulacra were a reminder.

Especially the dirty labourer at noon, lifting his mug of foaming beer to blackened lips, and the drab pleading with the gentleman at eleven.

The massive dragon's head carved above the face, its eyes glowing with soft sorcery, held its jaws in a constant, silent roar. *Time*, it said, *is a gaping maw like mine. You have escaped the worst.*

And she had, even before Miles Crawford had so neatly trapped her. But for an accident of fate, she could have ended as a drab herself, in the very slums she had been hunting through this afternoon.

"Southwark," she heard herself say. "We are visiting Mehitabel."

She had the satisfaction of seeing her Shield pale before she swept past him and through her study doors.

Chapter Fourteen

The Wark and the Werks

Clare offered his hand, but the sorceress put no weight on it as she climbed into the hansom, her petticoats oddly soundless.

"All the same, my good man, one shouldn't have to throw oneself into the street to attract a driver's attention." Clare looked back at the house – it appeared dark, closed up for the night, the gates to the front walk locked by invisible hands.

"I stops for my fares, I does." The driver's gin-blossomed nose and cheeks all but glowed in the ruddiness of dusk. The sun was sinking quickly, and the fog was rising. A regular Londinium pea-souper, creeping up the Themis. "You won't find no one else willin t'take you half-crost that bridge, no sir. Not Southwark, this close to Turn. Right lucky you are."

"Very lucky indeed, especially since we're paying double fare." The man was no use for deductive purposes; he was a cockerel Cockney with a war wound to his left leg, reeking of gin and married to a Stepney woman who tied the traditional ribbon in his buttonhole.

"Mr Clare." The sorceress leaned forward. Her swelling and bruising had gone down remarkably, and a crease of annoyance lingered on her forehead. "Cease arguing with the man and get *into* the carriage."

He complied, the door banged shut, and the heaving brass flanks of the clockhorse crackled under the whip. *Altered horse and Altered flashboy,* his brain whispered. *There is no connection, do be reasonable.*

He was uneasy. It was the gryphons at the table, of course. Irrationality bothered him as it would bother *any* mentath. That was all.

No, it is not. You haven't enough information. Simply be patient. It was hard to be patient, he acknowledged, when Miss Bannon so assiduously avoided the subject of the mutilations of unregistered mentaths.

That hit a trifle close to home, so to speak.

Mikal had disappeared, though Clare suspected further trouble would bring his reappearance. The Shield no longer looked grey and drawn, though grim enough, and the sorceress was still pale, wincing slightly when she had to move in certain ways. The wound could very easily have proved deadly.

I did not kill him, she had hurriedly said, as if he would suspect such a thing. The mental drawer bearing Miss Bannon's name had turned into a large bureau with several nooks and crannies. She was doing far more to keep his faculties exercised than the conspiracy.

Which was beginning to take on some troubling characteristics in its own right, to be sure.

The hansom jolted, Miss Bannon swayed into him, and Clare murmured an apology. "Close quarters."

"Indeed." She was rather alarmingly white, her curls swinging. "Mr Clare, I have not been entirely open with you."

"Of course. You are not entirely open with anyone, Miss Bannon. You have learned not to be."

"Another deduction."

"Have you read my monograph, madam? Deduction is my life. Any mentath's, really, but mine *especially*." He permitted himself a sardonic raise of the eyebrows, glanced at her, and was gratified to find a slight smile. "I deduce you are more irritated with your own ill luck than with me *or* your Shield. I deduce you were an orphan, and your early life taught you the value of luxury. I *further* deduce this 'conspiracy' is actually a disagreement over a certain item mentaths have been engaged in—"

"Wait." She cocked her head, lifting one gloved hand, and shivered. Clare consulted his pocket watch.

Tideturn.

Charter symbols, glowing gold, crawled over her skin. Her jewellery boiled with sparks, the cameo becoming a miniature lamp, filling the cab's interior with soft light. Clare watched, fascinated, as the charter symbols dove into her flesh, stray sorcery dust puffing from the folds of her dress and winking out of existence in mid-air. Fresh charter-charm marks appeared, a river of runic writing coating her.

Miss Bannon exhaled, sharply, and the lights faded. She shook her fingers, and sparks popped. One of the clockhorses neighed, and the cab jolted. "Much better," she muttered, and turned her dark eyes on Clare. There was no trace of the horrific bruising on her face and throat, and she did not flinch at another jolt. "You were saying. A certain item?"

"A certain item mentaths have been engaged in building, but in parts, so none of them knows the whole." He tucked his watch away, carefully. Fresh linens of exceeding quality had magically appeared for him, and a permanent measuring charm had been applied to him and his clothes. The valet was, at least, dexterous and did not seek to engage him in superfluous conversation.

Miss Bannon's hospitality was proving itself legendary in stature.

"Hm." Neither affirming nor denying.

"An item Lord Grayson was deliberately kept somewhat unaware of." *Or you hope he is unaware.* "Which means you have been involved with these mentaths for longer than they have been dying, and your orders come from another quarter indeed."

"And who do you suppose could *order* me about, sir?" The cab lurched; she lifted her chin, but relaxed immediately. Clare's stomach somersaulted, perhaps expecting a repeat of last night's games.

"I have noted the royal seal on several items in your excellent library, which I availed myself of just before we left, and the statue of Britannia in your entry hall is of solid silver, as well as stamped with the royal imprimatur. No doubt you offered some great service and were given a token – but even if you had not been, you would have continued to serve. Your utterance of *God and Her Majesty* is sincere. And, one suspects, heartfelt."

Her lips pursed. Her hands clasped together, lying decorously well bred in her lap. Despite the likely chill of the evening, she wore no shawl. She was hatless as well, despite his guess to the contrary. She perhaps expected an unpleasant event during which a bonnet would be a hindrance.

He did not find this a soothing observation.

Silence stretched between them, broken only by the clopping of metal-reinforced hooves and the driver's half-muffled cheerful catcalls as they turned south. Other hackney drivers responded, and the crowded streets around them were a low mumbling surf-roar. Just after Tideturn the city was a freshly yeasted, bubbling mass, especially near the Themis.

"Let us suppose you are to be trusted." Miss Bannon peered through the window, watching the crowd whirl past. "What then?"

"Why then, Miss Bannon, we discover who has been killing sorcerers and mentaths, uncover the missing pieces of this item, learn who among Her Majesty's subjects is treacherous enough to wish to steal this item and presumably use it against Britannia's current incarnation, and—"

"Be home in time for tea?"

It took him by surprise, and his wheezing laugh did as well. He sobered almost instantly as the hansom slowed, swimming against the tide at the northern edge of the Iron Bridge. "One hopes."

"Indeed. Then let us proceed with this understanding, Mr Clare: I am responsible for your safety, and I do not forgive disobedience or incompetence. You are relatively competent; may I trust you not to question?"

An exceedingly *managing female.* "Until further notice, Miss Bannon, you may. Provided your requests fall within the compass of my ability."

"Fair enough. We are at the Bridge; no doubt our driver will be stopping soon. You are a gentleman, but pray do not precede me from the carriage. You are far more vulnerable than I."

A sharp bite of irritation flashed through him. He shelved it with difficulty. "Very well."

"Thank you." Primly, she gathered herself, and as if in response, the hansom halted.

Queen's Bridge – otherwise known as the Southwark or the Iron, to balance the Stone Bridge as one of Londinium's arteries – loomed in twilight, fog shrouding both of its massive ends. Black iron gleamed wetly, the Themis rippling with gold under its arches as Tideturn spilled and eddied back to sea. It was perhaps the ugliest bridge in Londinium, and the charter symbols cast into its long span crawled with touches of vermilion. Some said the Bridges kept the Themis under control, binding the ancient, hungry demigod sleeping in the river's depths.

Most illogical. Still, the cold iron was superstitiously comforting.

At the Bridge's southern end, the Wark sent up columns of dense smoke underlit with crimson, the unsleeping foundries audible even at this distance. Cinders fell like Twelfthnight snow there, and the bridge thrummed unpleasantly underfoot.

"'Tis as far as I go, worships." The driver was pale under his gin-touched cheeks. "The Black Wark's unsteady tonight. Feel it in the Bridge, you can."

Mikal had appeared at Miss Bannon's elbow, yellow eyes taking a last gleam from the Themis. He murmured to the sorceress, who nodded once, sharply, her earrings swinging. "Give him a further half-crown, Shield. He's done well. Mr Clare, come with me."

"Thank you. Good man." Clare dusted his hat. The Wark's cinders would perhaps ruin it. "Off you go, then. Mind you," he remarked to the sorceress, "I am still no closer to discovering why a hansom can be so bloody difficult to find."

Mikal tossed a coin, the flick of his fingers invisible in the uncertain light. The cabbie, however, plucked the half-crown from the air, and the coin vanished. He tipped his hat at the sorceress and winked before lifting the reins.

"Conspiracy." Miss Bannon watched as the hansom negotiated a tight turn, the clockhorse's Altered hooves clipping the bridge's surface. Stray sparks of sorcery winked out in its wake. The whip cracked, and their driver made good his escape.

"That could be so." Clare's dinner was not sitting so excellently at the moment. He put his shoulders back, seeking to ease the discomfort.

The middle of the Bridge was deserted. On either end, Londinium teemed; Queen Street's terminus on to Upper Themis was crowded with warehouses and sloping tenements. Lights winked among them, gasflame and the pallid gleams of the occasional witchglobe. On the other end, Southwark's bloody glow made a low, unhappy noise.

Miss Bannon did not relax until the hansom was out of sight, vanished on to Upper Themis Road. Even then, the tension in her only abated; it did not cease. "Safe enough," she murmured. "Come, Mr Clare. Listen closely while we walk."

He offered his arm. Stray cinders fluttered, a grey curtain.

"We are about to enter Southwark." She did not lean on him, though she rested a gloved hand delicately and correctly in the crook of his elbow. Mikal stepped away, turning smartly, and trailed on Miss Bannon's other side.

"Obviously."

"Do not interrupt. Once we step off the Bridge, no matter

how important, do not speak without express permission from me. The . . . lady we are visiting is eccentric, and much of the Black Wark is full of her ears. She is also *exceedingly* dangerous."

"If she is dangerous enough to cause you this concern, Miss Bannon, rest assured I shall follow your instructions precisely. Who is she?"

"Her name is Mehitabel." Miss Bannon's jaw was set, and she looked pale. "Mehitabel the Black."

"What a curious name. Tell me, Miss Bannon, should one fear her?"

Her childlike face with its aristocratic nose was solemn, and she gave him one very small, tight-mouthed smile. "You are sane, Mr Clare. That means *yes*."

The heart of Southwark was the Black Wark, grey and red. Grey from the piled cinders the shuffling ashwalkers pushed along with their long flat brooms, the wagons loaded with the stuff taken to the soap factories grumbling along on traditional wooden wheels. Red from the glow of the foundries, red for the beating heart under the Wark's crazyquilt of streets and jumbled alleys. The gaslamps here corroded swiftly from the cinderfall; yellow fog sent thin tendrils questing along the cobbles. The low red glow made the fog flinch, hugging corners and pooling in darker spots.

Between Blackfriar and Londinium Bridges, the Iron Bridge stood and the Themis was dark, great fingers combing its silk as the foundries drank and sent their products forth. Metalwork, mechanisterum used for Alteration, the huge warehouses for the making of clockhorses on the near side of High Borough, close to the Leather Market. Blackfriar, Londinium Bridge, Great Dover-Borough High-Wellington and Great Surrey to the west and east, Greenwitch at the south; these were the confines of the Black Wark. Some said those streets had powerful enchantments buried underneath, wedded to rails of pure silver, keeping the Wark contained. Whispers told of workshops in the Wark where workers so Altered as to be merely metal skeletons grinned and leapt, or streets faced in dark metallic clockwork that *changed* when the fog grew thick and the cinderfall was particularly intense.

The Wark's natives were Altered young. Immigrants, mostly Eirean, poured in to work at the foundries and warehouses, living twenty or more to a stinking room while gleaming delicate clockworks and massive metalwork were shipped out clean and sparkling on each tide.

If a gentleman went into the Wark, he hired Altered guides, native flashboys working in groups of a half-dozen or more who mostly took it as a point of rough pride to guard their employers. The Wark's flashboys were feared even in the Eastron End's worst slums, and rumour had it they were often contracted for shady work even a Thugee from darkest Indus would flinch at.

At the end of the Iron Bridge, Mikal stepped forward, and the veil of cinderfall parted.

"Passage a pence apiece!" a rough voice croaked. "Threepee for your worships!"

A bridgekeeper appeared in a circle of gaslamp glow, cinders shaking from the brim of his hat. Round and wrapped in odds and ends; metal gleamed as his Alterations came into view – a lobster claw instead of a left hand, soot-crusted metal gleaming in odd scraped-bare spots, and a glass eye lit with venomous yellow, like the fog. He moved oddly, lurching, and Clare's interest sharpened.

He has been Altered even more thoroughly than that. Look, there. Wheels. He has wheels instead of feet. They were not quality Alterations, either. Rough edges and clicking cogs caked with grease and cinders, no smoothly gleaming surfaces.

Clare held his tongue with difficulty.

"Mikal." The sorceress did not break stride, drawing him on.

"Ye'll be wanting guides, worships, specially after Tideturn." The bridgekeeper chuckled. "And wit a laddle too!"

Movement in the shadows. Clare stiffened, but Miss Bannon

simply tilted her head. "I require no *guide*, Carthamus, and you should polish that eye of yours. Give your dogs the signal to withdraw, or you'll lose a goodly portion of them to my temper."

Mikal's hand flicked. Three pennies chimed on the cobbled street, almost lost in a drift of cinders. The Shield stepped back, almost mincingly, and the bridgekeeper cursed.

"Watch your tongue," Miss Bannon snapped, and her fingers clamped on Clare's arm with surprising strength. "This way."

"There are quite a few of them." Mikal, hushed and low.

"Oh, I should think so. She's expecting me."

They plunged into the Wark, Clare's senses quivering-alert, and he almost wished he had chosen to remain in Mayefair.

Chapter Fifteen

Steelstruck Teeth

The jackals gathered the instant they stepped off the Bridge, and Emma didn't bother hailing one of the footcabs. Mikal was tense, his footsteps following hers and the scent of his readiness gunpowder-sharp, a different crimson than the low foundry glow. To Sight, the Wark was full of sharp-edged runic shapes trembling on the edge of the visible, an alien charter language wearing at the warp and weft of Londinium's ancient sorcery. The cinders whispered in toothless, burning voices, and she wished she had brought a veil. Sparks lifted lazily into the fog, the Wark still resonating from Tideturn like a giant bell shivering long after its vibration voice has dropped below the audible.

The taste of sorcery here was metallic, and there was so much interference it was almost a relief to feel Clare's arm solid and real under her hand. Mikal could not anchor her – he would be far more occupied if any of the jackal flashboys took it into their heads to make trouble for the trespassers.

What a time to wish for more Shields. The thought was there and gone in a flash; she had other matters to attend to.

The cinderfall changed direction, flakes of ash spinning though there was no wind. Londinium's fog kept creeping, sliding its fingers into the cracks, and was forced back by the intelligence in the Wark's red glow.

A sharp right, staying well away from the dark, toothless-gaping alleys; she set their course and decided to approach the Blackwerks from the north. It made sense, and the less time she spent in the Wark with a mentath at her sleeve, the better.

He was already looking decidedly green. She supposed she should have mentioned that the sorcery within the Wark's confines, not only illogical but *alien*, might discommode him.

Scuttling things moved in the shadows, clinking sharp edges dragged over cobbles and through filth. Whispers, gleams of eyes from the towering roofs. A small foundry opened on their right; glowing metal poured from one giant cauldron to another, sparks flying as the workers inside became cutpaper shadows. Tiny, paired gleams peering through grates and clustering in the alleys told her the rats were out in force, their sleek sides heaving and their naked tails leaving opalescent slug-sheens behind.

She had to prod Clare. He was slowing down, craning his head to take everything in. He would be straining to make sense of the cinderfall's eddies and flows, the light not behaving as it should, the little slithering scrapes in the darkness.

"Merely observe," she whispered, as if he was a Shield trainee and she was responsible for teaching him to Glove. "Do not analyse."

He gave her a wide-eyed look that qualified as shocked.

It would likely not fool the Black Lady. They turned with Park Street's sharp bend, and it was not her imagination – the gaslamps were dimming. The cinderfall was a curtain, sweeping closer. The tiny paired gleams slid free of the alleymouths, drawing closer as the cinders smoothed over their wet-gleaming flanks.

Oh, for Heaven's sake. She breathed a most impolite term, glanced at Mikal, and snapped her free hand out, fingers twisting as a half-measure of chant pulled its way free of her lips, sliding bloody and whole into the thick darkness.

Clear silver light flamed. A sorcerous circle smoked into being around them, familiar charter symbols flashing and twisting through the cinderfall, and the rats scattered. They were Altered too, clockworks spinning in their hindquarters, grease splashing from the gears and their little diamond claws skritching against the cobbles.

"*Enough!*" she snapped, and the gaslamps flared back into guttering light. Londinium's fog writhed, its tendrils thickening. "I am not to be trifled with, Mehitabel!"

All motion ceased for a moment, the cinders arrested in their slow whirling motion and sparkling in mid-air. The light faded, a witchball popping into being and hovering behind Emma, dimming slightly as her attention turned from it. And as she expected, when the world hitched forward and time began again, there was a flashboy just at the edge of her sphere of normalcy, his top hat cocked and his moth-eaten purple velvet jacket carefully brushed. His right hand was a marvel of Alteration, black metal that looked almost exactly like the appendage he had been born with, and the metallic patterns etched on his ageless-young face were familiar.

He was high in Mehitabel's favour, and would probably continue to be so for a long while yet. At least while his reflexes were good and his cruelty pleased her.

"Ladyname." He grinned, his teeth steel chips. That right hand flexed with a dry, oily sound, and Mikal stepped forward. Just one step, but it was enough. The flashboy gave him a brief glance, then addressed Emma again. "Ye use Ladyname. Billybong o'ye, laddle."

"She knows my name as well," Emma replied crisply. "I am on *business,* Dodgerboy. Bound for the Blackwerks, and I do not appreciate this nonsense."

"Guide ye, and for no fiddle e'en." The flashboy turned, the nails pounded into his boot heels striking a single crimson spark from a garbage-slick cobble. "Ladyname be specting."

She permitted herself a single, unamused chuckle. "Well, I would hardly dare call upon her otherwise. Lead on, Dodgerboy, and mind yourself. I suspect the Lady would hate to lose you."

"Oh, aye. 'M flash-quick. Pop yer farthings a' three paces,

leave cammie rag for the wisps." He waved his un-Altered hand, a flash of grimy pale skin.

Emma squeezed Clare's arm again. The witchball brightened. "He means he could pick your pockets clean at three paces and leave your handkerchief for lesser thieves. It is most likely no boast, so Mikal will cut off his fingers – *all* of them – should he approach us. Let us be along, I have other business to transact tonight."

The flashboy glanced once at Clare. "Deefer, that 'un?"

She tapped her foot, the gesture losing something under her skirts but still, she hoped, expressing her displeasure. "He is not deaf, *or* dumb, not that it is your *business*. Do we move along, or do I set your hair on fire and visit your mistress while in a bad mood?"

He gave no reply, just showed his steel-struck teeth again. For a moment Emma imagined those teeth meeting in flesh, blood squirting free and griming the bright metal, and quelled a shudder.

She had seen Mehitabel's flashboys feeding, once.

But Dodgerboy set off, and once Mikal nodded, his jaw set in a grim line, she propelled Clare along with the simple expedient of pulling on his arm, and they walked further into the Wark, followed by a bobbing silver globe of witchlight.

Two steps later, she noticed Mikal had disappeared.

Good.

Chapter Sixteen

Not You, Too

The Blackwerks rose, spines of black metal corkscrewed with heat and stress. Clare's skull felt tight, confining. There was simply too much illogic here. The cinders, for one thing – there was no way the fires of the Wark could produce this much matter. Yet it had to come from *somewhere*. And the rats – something so small should not be Altered. Their eyes glowed viciously, and they scuttled with quick, oily movements.

The young Altered boy walked ahead of them, whistling, hands stuffed deep in his pockets. Every once in a while he performed a curious little hop-skip, but to no rhythm Clare could discern. Miss Bannon's tension communicated itself through her grip on his arm. If this was a promenade, it was one through a Hellish underworld where every angle was subtly skewed.

As soon as the thought arrived, the squeezing of his skull ceased. He began seeking to catalogue the precise measurement in degrees of every angle, calculating the inconsistencies and attempting to apply a theory to them. It was difficult mental work, and he was faintly aware of sweat springing up on his brow, but the relief of having a task was immense.

A pair of huge spiny gates, their tops tortured by unimaginable heat, stood ajar. Ash piled high on either side, drifting against a gap-toothed brick wall. A painted tin sign proclaimed

Blackwerks, and the Altered boy minced through the gates, turning and giving a deep bow. "Enter, w'ships, Ladyname be bless'd. Step right inna the Werks." Two stamps of his left foot, his boot heel ringing against cracked cobbles, and he danced back into an orange glow.

The cavern of the Werks rose, its entire front open and exhaling a burning draught. Machinery twisted inside, cauldrons tipping and pouring substances he did not care to think too deeply on. Wheels ticked, their toothed edges meshing with others, huge soot-blackened chains shivering, clashing, or stretched taut. The cinderfall intensified here, Clare was glad of his hat. Somehow the falling matter avoided Miss Bannon, and the witchlight behind them made everything in the circle of its glow keep to its proper proportions. He wondered what effort it cost Miss Bannon to keep that sphere of normalcy steady, and decided not to ask.

A slim figure resolved out of the heatglare, gliding forward. *What is this?*

It was a woman. Or perhaps it had been once. Long swaying black bombazine skirts, stiff with ash, smooth black metal skin, an explosion of ash-grey horsehair held back with jet-dangling pins. Its arms were marvels of Alteration, metal bones and hands of fine delicate clockwork opening and closing as it – *she* rolled forward. The face was also blank metal and clockwork, the nose merely sinus caverns; the eyes were hen's-egg rubies lit from within by feral intelligence.

Miss Bannon squeezed his arm again, warningly. Clare stared.

The thing's mouth – or the aperture serving it as a mouth – moved. *"Prima."* The voice held a rush and crackle of flame, and the skirts shuddered as whatever contraption was underneath them encountered an irregularity in the flooring.

That dress was fashionable a decade ago. He caught sight of a reading-glass dangling from a thin metal chain, hiding in the skirts. *Does this thing read? How long ago was it human? Does it have any flesh left?*

"Mehitabel." Miss Bannon nodded, once. "I have come for what I left."

A rasp-clanking screech rose from the thing's chest. It took Clare a moment to recognise that rusted, painful sound for what it was.

Laughter.

The hideous noise cut off sharply, and the boy who had led them here stepped back nervously, like an unAltered horse scenting the metal and blood of the pens. The thing called Mehitabel turned its head, servomotors in the neck ratcheting with dry terrible grace. The wretched imitation of a human movement made Clare's dinner writhe.

Perhaps my digestion is not as sound as it could be, he noted, and found himself clutching at Miss Bannon's hand on his arm. Patting slightly, as if she were startled and he meant to soothe. His throat was tight.

Emotion. Cease this.

But his feelings did not listen.

"Oh, Mehitabel." Miss Bannon sounded, of all things, saddened. "Not you too."

"*You do not know your enemies, sorceressss.*" Rust showered from the thing's elbow joints as it lifted its arms. Its mouth widened, a spark of glowing-coal red dilating far back in its throat. Miss Bannon stepped forward, disengaging herself from Clare with a practised twist of her hand, and the witchlight intensified behind them, casting a frail screen of clear silver light against the venomous crimson of the Werks. Machinery shuddered and crashed as Mehitabel's body jerked, and Miss Bannon yelled an anatomical term Clare had never thought a lady would be conversant with.

The crashing ceased. Mehitabel's metal body froze, in stasis.

"I may not know my enemies," Miss Bannon said softly, her hands held out in a curious contorted gesture, fingers interlaced. "But I am *Prime*, little wyrm, and you are only here on sufferance."

The metal thing shuddered. There was a flicker of motion, and Clare's blurted warning was lost in a draught of scalding air. Mikal was suddenly *there*, smacking aside Dodgerboy's hand with contemptuous ease, the slender gleam of a knife flying in a high arc to vanish into the ash outside. The Shield made another swift motion, almost as an afterthought, and the Altered boy flew backwards, vanishing into a haze of red light and confused, whirling cinders.

"*Sufferance?*" A low, thick burping chuckle rode the rush of hot stinking air out of the Werks. The voice was terrible, a dry-scaled monstrous thing approximating human words over the groaning of metal and crackling of flame, the sibilants laden with toxic dust. "*Oh, I think not, monkeychild. You are in* my *home now.*"

The witchlight blazed, sharp silver brilliance. "Mikal." Miss Bannon's voice cut through the thing's laughter. "Take him. And *run.*"

The descant scorched her throat, her focus splitting as the great twisting metal thing fought her hold. Her left hand cramped, burning as she held the rope of intent, the force clamped over Mehitabel's simulacrum fraying at the edges. She had to choose – the trueform or the metal echo, layers of the physical and ætheric vibrating as sorcery spread in rayed patterns, the Wark quivering as she forced its sorcery to her will.

I will pay for this later. A Greater Word rose within the fabric of the chant, weaving itself between the syllables. It settled on the metal form, which buckled and curled like paper in a fire.

A massive wrecked scream rose from Mehitabel's unseen trueform. *That must sting.*

But it freed Emma to bring her focus back to a single object, white-hot sorcerous force running through her veins. The Blackwerks seethed with running feet, shouts. Mehitabel's flash-boys and the antlike workers who crawled through the heat-shimmering cavern began to appear, flickering unsteadily through the cinderfall.

Emma's hands shot out, sorcery crackling between them. She *squeezed*, smoke rising from her rings and the scorched material of her gloves, and Mehitabel shrieked again. The flashboys froze, workers dropping where they stood. The chant died away now that Emma had her grip.

"I can crush flesh just as easily," she called, the words slicing through snap-crackling flame and shuddering metallic clanking. The simulacrum's face continued melting, runnels of liquid iron sliding down, its unfashionable dress a torch. "Even *your* flesh. Where is it, *Me-hi-ta-beh-ru-la gu'rush Me-hi-lwa*?" The foreign syllables punctured tortured air; Emma's throat scorched and her eyes watering as she accented each in its proper place.

Hours of study and careful tortuous work had suddenly returned its investment. Mehitabel had obviously never guessed that Emma might uncover her truename, much less *use* it.

A wyrm would never forget, let alone forgive such a thing.

The Blackwerks . . . stopped.

Sparks and cinders hung in mid-air. The burning simulacrum was a painting, flames caught in mid-twist, its face terribly ruined.

A huge, narrow head, triple-crowned and triple-tongued, rose from a crucible of molten metal, snaking forward on a flexible, black-scaled neck. The eyes were jewels of flame, matching the now-cracked rubies of the simulacrum, and leathery wings spread through the cinderfall, their bladed edges cutting through individual flecks and sparks held in stasis.

The tongues flickered, smoke wreathing the wyrm's long body in curiously lethargic veils. Mehitabel held the Werks out of Time's slipstream, her wings ruffling as they combed slumbering air. The heat was immense, awesome, the cup of metal holding the lower half of her body bubbling with thick tearing sounds. She turned her head sideways, one ruby eye glinting, but Emma leaned back, fingers burning, the thin fine leash of her will cutting across the dragon's snout.

They are the children of Time, her teacher had intoned long ago. *They are of the Powers, and their elders sleep. We should be glad of that slumber, for if* those *wyrms awakened they would shake this isle – and plenty more – from their backs, and the Age of Flame would return.*

Mehitabel's head jerked back and she glared, one clawed forelimb sinking into the edge of the crucible and digging in with another tortured sound. The tongues flickered. "*You* are dead."

"Not yet, wyrm." Emma set her boots more firmly. "Where is it?"

"It isss not here." Heat lapped Mehitabel's sides, her flexible ribs heaving bellows-like.

"*Where is it?*" Emma's hands clenched, pressure enfolding the wyrm. She bore down. The sensation was different from the crunch-crushing of metal – slippery and armoured, giving resiliently and struggling to escape. The dragon could make another simulacrum, but its trueform was also vulnerable – especially to an angry sorceress who knew its name.

That was also what it meant to be Prime – to pronounce a name of such power without your tongue scorching and your eyes melting in hot runnels down your cheeks. Some were of the opinion that only a Prime's overweening pride shielded him from such agony. Others said it was the size of the ætheric charge Primes were able to carry. None had solved the riddle, and Emma's own research was inconclusive at best.

Had Mikal taken the mentath away? She hoped so. This much concentrated sorcery was dangerous, and what she was about to do with it doubly so. And they had a chance to escape Mehitabel's flashboys and the other dangers of the Wark *now*, while she held the wyrm captive.

The dragon hissed, lowering its head. Its teeth were slashes of obsidian, each one with a thin line of crimson at its glassy heart. "One came and relieved me of the burden. Shake in terror, little monkey—"

Emma's fists jerked. Mehitabel howled, a gush of rancid

oily-hot breath pushing Emma's hair back, wringing scalding tears free to paint her cheeks, snapping her skirts. When the wyrm was done making noise, Emma released the pressure. But only slightly, her concentration narrowing to a single white-hot point.

"Names, Mehitabel. Who came, and for whom?"

"I will kill you for thiss. You will *dieeeee*—" The word spiralled up into a glassine screech.

Her own voice, a knife through something hot and brittle. "*Names*, Mehitabel! Truenames! Or we learn the look of your insides, ironwyrm!" The force of Tideturn would start to fail her soon. The cameo was a spot of molten heat at her throat, and her rings glowed, finally scorching away the last of the kidskin on her fingers. The fire opals, shimmering charter symbols rising through their depths, popped sparks that hung restlessly for too long before dropping with languid grace.

Mehitabel gasped. *No flame without air*, Emma recited inwardly, and another chant filled her throat. This one was low and dark, a single syllable of the language of Unmaking, and before she had finished the first measure the dragon was thrashing against her hold as its ruddy glow dimmed.

When the dragon was limp but still burning, a sullen ember, Emma halted. "Names." She sounded strange even to herself, harsh and brutal. "Truenames. Now."

"Llewellyn," Mehitabel hissed. "Llewellyn Gwynnfud."

This does not surprise me. "Who else?"

"One of our—"

Oh, you are not about to play a riddling game with me. "Name, Mehitabel. Truename."

"A fat man, and sstupid. Graysson was the only name he gave—"

A chill knifed through her, her sweat turning to clammy ice. "Who *else*?"

"An Old One." Mehitabel chuckled. The sound was a scream of tortured iron. "*Him* you will not ssorcer so eassily, monkey-bitch."

The chant rose again. Her focus was slipping. Holding even a young wyrm was difficult, and she still had to escape the Wark. The silver witchlight behind her blazed, her shadow cut of black paper on the fine, soft ankle-deep ashfall.

Mehitabel thrashed, gasping soundlessly. Molten metal slopped against the crucible's sides. "*Who?*" Emma demanded again, when the dragon had quieted. There was precious little time left. Her arms trembled, and did her legs. A crystalline drop of sweat traced down her cheek; her hair was damp. Hot beads of blood welled between her clenched, smoking fingers, soaking into the shredded remains of her gloves.

"*Vortisss,*" Mehitabel hissed. "*Vortiss cruca esssth.*"

That's not a name. But Emma's hold slipped for a single heartbeat; Mehitabel slid free –

– and arrowed straight for her tormentor, head snaking, wings shedding globules of molten metal, jaws held wide.

Chapter Seventeen

It Discommodes Me

One moment the sorceress stood, slim and composed, between Clare and the abominable metal thing. There was a curious sensation, as if a thunderstorm threatened, the fine hairs all over his body standing up and a queer weightless vertigo filling him. Mikal was a shadow flicker in his peripheral vision, there and gone in less than a flash.

Then, confusion. The shock knocked him to the ground, foul heat showering over him in a gush of rank oily sweat. His hat went flying, and he had the pepperbox pistol free as soon as his head cleared, searching for somewhat to use the weapon upon.

The reptilian thing thrashed as Mikal leapt aside, his blades painting vermilion streaks through gouts of falling ash. The cavern was full of motion, tattered flashboys with gleaming Alterations seething like ants, the workers – scarecrow figures in shapeless grey smocks and draggling frocks, dull-eyed and vacant – crawling forward with odd jerky grace. The only still point was the sorceress, flung face-down in a drift of ash like a doll. Cinders gathered on her limp, bleeding hands, her gloves scorched and tattered, flesh flayed almost to bone.

Clare made it to her in a scrabbling scramble, as the reptilian thing gave out a choked terrible sound and Mikal's blades flashed again.

She was astonishingly light. Clare slid an arm under her, the ash smoking along his jacket sleeve. She coughed, her eyes welling with tears that streaked the soot on her face, and he congratulated himself. At least she would not suffocate.

A flashboy in a scarlet jacket leapt. Clare's arm jerked, the pepperbox pistol's first barrel spoke, but the crack of it was lost in massive, ear-grinding noise. The flashboy folded down, his Alteration – an arm that was no longer an arm, but a scythe of bone and iron – sending up one last bloody gleam before he fell into ash and the rest hesitated, uncertain, their eyes shining with pinpricks of mad red intelligence.

Just like the rats. Shudders worked through Clare's frame, but he ignored them. *Three shots left, then we shall be forced to improvise.* A thud rocked the entire Blackwerks, molten metal splashing in high scorching arcs, and he found himself dragging the sorceress's limp form towards the entrance, where a draught of cooler air poured the snowflake cinders into the Werks' maw. An instinctive move, the body seeking to protect itself, but that was acceptable because logic tallied with it, and—

The sorceress woke, her dark eyes snapping open and her ribs expanding as she drew in a long, gasping breath. Another massive crash shook the Werks. The cameo, askew at Miss Bannon's throat, filled with silvery radiance.

Mikal shouted, a wordless challenge, and Miss Bannon blinked. She stared up at Clare, her gaze so blank and terrible he wondered if she recognised him at all. A pin tumbled from her hair, losing itself in thick ash.

Her lips shaped a word under the noise. He had no trouble deciphering it.

Mikal?

Tension invaded her. She scrambled to her feet, and Clare did as well, though the ground quaked. The mob of flashboys and workers was now pressing close, streaming through the twisted machinery, intent on the sorceress – and by extension, on Clare himself.

This will become quite unpleasant very quickly. As if it was not already unpleasant *enough.*

The Shield shouted again, and the wyrm made a sound like half-molten metal tearing and bubbling. The sorceress threw out her hands, fingers flashing in a complicated gesture that ended in a contorted fashion Clare recognised as a faintly obscene gesture more suited to a hevvy or a dockmancer than a lady of quality.

Miss Bannon was becoming more and more interesting.

Sorcery crackled, a rain of crimson sparks bleeding from her pale fingertips, and the sorceress *leaned* as if pulling a heavy weight, her body arched and a word bursting free of her lips. Blood spattered from her flayed hands; Clare winced, his throat tightening with something suspiciously like fear, raising the pistol. Two more shots. Perhaps its menace would keep the gathering crowd back.

He needn't have bothered. For Miss Bannon moved, flinging her arms, her skirts swaying, and the long, black-scaled body of the wyrm was tossed aside like a wet sheet, directly into the crowd of flashboys and workers.

The Shield moved smoothly back, his curious glove-soled boots shuffling lightly through accumulating ashfall, and glanced back at them. His yellow irises glowed, and his lean face was bright with a fierce, devouring joy.

Shouts, screams, the wyrm's cheated howl. Mikal reached them, nodded once, ash crowning his dark hair and that terrible happiness glowing through his entire body. Miss Bannon turned, smartly, and her bloody hands were full of a low reddish light, somehow cleaner than the Wark's glow.

The light pooled between her fingers, and she cast it at the floor. Smoke roiled, puffing up, and Clare understood they were to flee.

His lungs were afire and his ribs seized with a giant gripping stitch. Clare wheezed, leaning against the alley's wall, desperately seeking to regain his breath. The ashfall had intensified, a soft warm killing snow. At least they would not freeze to death here, but suffocation was a real danger.

Mikal examined the sorceress's hands, his fingers tapping and plucking while charter-symbols bled from his flesh to hers. Clare did not wish to observe the way her rent flesh was closing, in violation of physical laws. He also did not wish to observe Miss Bannon's pinched, wan little face. The silvery witchlight had vanished, and so had most of the sphere of normalcy; every angle was off by a random number of degrees and the falling cinders obeyed no law that he could find, except the law of downward motion. Among these annoyances, the least was Miss Bannon's face.

"That is all I can do." The joy had left Mikal's lean features. His coat was torn and the ash in his hair turned him prematurely grey.

"We must escape the Wark." Miss Bannon closed her dark eyes, leaning wearily against the same wall propping Clare up. "*She* will have her eyes about soon."

"Which route?" Mikal did not let go of her hands, examining her palms critically. The cuts had been deep and were still flushed and angry-looking, despite the soft foxfire glow of charter sorcery stitching the flesh together.

"West." Bruised circles stood out underneath Miss Bannon's eyes. Her skirts were tattered, and there was a smudge of ash on her cheek. Still, most of the falling cinders avoided her; the grit clinging to her hair was perhaps from lying face-down on the Blackwerks floor. "Borough or Newington. Probably the former; but both pass by the gaols, and that is not *her* purview. At least, not while Ethes is present."

"Very well." The Shield finally let her blood-masked hands drop. "We shall not be free of pursuit for long."

"Oh, I know." A curl fell in her face; she wrinkled her proud nose. "The mentath?"

"Well enough." Mikal didn't even spare Clare a glance. "Do you need—"

"No, Mikal. Thank you." She finally opened her eyes. "Mr Clare. Thank you, as well."

His breathing had finally eased somewhat, and the stitch was slowly retreating. "Most . . . diverting." The pressure behind his eyes mounted another notch as he sought to find some pattern in the random angles, or the spinning flakes of ashfall. "Though I would very much like to exit this district, Miss Bannon. It . . . discommodes me."

"You have survived your first encounter with a dragon. They affect the orderly progression of Time most strongly, and the illogic you are seeing is a result of *her* presence." Bannon shuddered. "I will not take either of you to task for not fleeing when I gave the word."

"Good." Clare swallowed, hard. An illogic so strong it could affect Time itself? The very notion caused an uncomfortable sensation within the cage of his ribs. *I could live quite comfortably for the rest of my days without another such experience.* Still, having an explanation for the warping and strangeness helped. "For I believe we did very well indeed."

Mikal's head tilted. "Feet," he said, softly. "Small, and large."

"Newington it is." Miss Bannon straightened. The remnants of her gloves fluttered as she plucked gingerly at her torn skirts. "Come along, gentlemen. There is no time to waste."

The streets of the Black Wark trembled slightly, like a small animal. The buildings stood blank-faced, no light in any of the infrequent, often broken windows, their holes stuffed with various fabrics and papers to keep the elements at bay. Warehouses leaned against each other, slumping dispiritedly under the caustic unsnow. The roofs were steeply pitched, and the only sound was the kiss-landing of cinders or the sudden whispering slide of ash off a roof edge, landing with a soft plop on the street. The gaslamps here were infrequent, wan, sickly circles of orange glow pulled close about their stems.

Clare blinked away ash and followed the swish of Bannon's ragged skirts. He fixed his eyes on the draggled hem, cloth behaving very much as cloth should. A certain relief at the sight loosened the tightness inside his ribs and the iron band around his temples.

"How far?" Miss Bannon whispered.

"Three streets, I think." Mikal's footsteps were soundless. "The rats. Dodger, possibly. I do not think I killed him. Perhaps one or two others."

"She expected me to move in a different direction." Miss Bannon sounded thoughtful. "Which one, I wonder."

"Passing close to Horsemonger is also dangerous. Not to mention Queensbench." Mikal, soft and equally thoughtful. *Well,* Clare thought. *He obviously respects her ability. That is most heartening.*

"Ethes is no trouble, and Captain Gall even less. But I see your point." Miss Bannon halted. "Mr Clare? Are you well?"

It was becoming more difficult to draw breath. "Well enough. Damnable atmosphere here."

"Oh, good heavens." She half turned, snapped her fingers, and muttered a word he could not decipher. Immediately, the ash shook itself free of his hair, whirling away, and he no longer felt as if he were breathing through a damp woollen blanket. "Better?"

"Quite." He stared at her boot toes, peeping at him from her ragged hem. If he concentrated on those, on how they rested against ankle-thick ash that behaved as ash should near them, he could ignore the rest for a short while.

A soft, scraping sound. Metal, drawn from a sheath. "Go." Mikal, tense now.

"Take the mentath, I shall delay—"

"No." The Shield thought little of this notion. "They come to kill, my Prima. Take care near the prison; I shall be close."

"Mikal – oh, *bloody* hell."

Clare might have raised his eyebrows to hear such language from a woman, but he was too busy studying her boots. He could infer much from the way she stood, toes pointed slightly outward, the fractional favouring of her right foot meaning she was right-handed. *She must dance well, and lightly. And she can move very softly if she wishes. Best to remember that.*

Her toes were whisked away as she turned, and her hand crept into the crook of his elbow. She tugged him along, and Clare allowed himself to be led.

A low, grinding noise had begun, but Clare felt absolutely no desire to look up.

"I did not think it would affect you this badly. Come, Mr Clare. It shall be better very rapidly; the closer we are to the gaols, the less stray sorcery there is about to trouble you."

"Jolly good." His skull squeezed everything inside it, pressure building again. Every random angle he had measured since stepping into the Wark's confines, every calculation of the speed and drift of cinders falling, refused to snap together into a pattern. What *was* that hideous grinding noise? It could not be his teeth, for all that his jaw was clenched tight.

"Do *not* look up," Miss Bannon said softly, hurrying him along. Their steps were muffled in the ash, now above ankle-high. How often did they clear the streets here? It had to be frequently, else anything living would choke to death.

The terrible grating continued, and Miss Bannon muttered another highly colourful term. A hot, rank breath poured past them, tugging at Clare's coat and hat, flapping the sorceress's skirts. He did not raise his eyes, but his reasoning leapt ahead. *The street. The street is moving.* He could *imagine* it, from the ripples pouring through the field of cracked and rutted cobbles, walls receding and others pushed forward as the Wark reshaped itself. Miss Bannon exhaled quickly, a short sharp puff. "Tricksome," she muttered. "Very tricksome."

His stomach revolved. His digestion was not its usual capable self. But as they hurried on, Miss Bannon's boots now clicking faintly instead of muffled in ash, it settled remarkably. She was humming, a queer atonal melody looping on itself, and Clare found that the sound covered up the grinding tolerably well. It did not cover the choked cry from their left, or the rushing skitter of tiny metallic rodent feet. Miss Bannon's grip on him tightened, but whether that was for his comfort or her own, he could not guess.

The composition of the ash underfoot changed, slick and greasy instead of fine and dry, and Miss Bannon's humming grew strained. The grinding suddenly ceased to their left; the sorceress lunged forward, dragging Clare along. A subliminal *snap* echoed through Clare's entire body, the iron bands constricting his chest loosening slightly. He dared to glance up, and the grey bulk of Queensbench Gaol shimmered with pinpricks of light. The prison's massive gate yawned, the gibbet in the small square before it crawling with blood-coloured charter charms. Their pace quickened, ashfall turning to hard hail-stinging pellets. A sharp turn to the left, and he understood by the sudden close rumble of traffic that they were skirting a thoroughfare. Darkness pressed close, gaslights muffled, and they plunged into a maze of debtors' tenements. Another cry sounded to their right, ending with a clash of steel.

Mikal. The Shield was doing his best to hold back their pursuers. But the shadows were alive with tiny crimson eyes now, and small twitching metallic noses.

It was a dreadful time, he reflected, to wish Miss Bannon had more of Mikal's type about. "Miss Bannon?" Clare whispered, as their pace quickened still more.

"What?" Her tone could in no way be described as *patient*.

"I rather believe we should run."

Chapter Eighteen

We Use You Dreadfully

Emma had rarely been so glad to see Londinium's yellow fog tonguing the surface of buildings and swallowing carriages. Clare stumbled, blinking, as they emerged on Greenwitch Road, gaslamps hissing cheerfully to greet them. Behind them, the Wark boiled, stray cinders popping and sizzling as they pressed against the street's boundary. Traffic had moved away from this side of Greenwitch, but the crowd very pointedly did *not* look to see what might have been ejected from the ashfall.

The mentath stumbled again, went heavily to his knees, and proceeded to retch. Emma clamped a hand to her side, the freshly healed stab wound unhappy at rough treatment. Her corset, loose as it was, still cut intolerably. She shook her hair, spitting a clearing charm between her teeth, not caring if she would need the energy later. The dross of the Wark fell away in veils, grey matter shushing as the charm crackled it loose.

It would take more than a minor sorcery to get the burnt-metal tang of Southwark out of her mouth, though.

A clockrat spilled over the rim of the street, scuttling weakly as it fought the constraints of normal time. Emma's hand jabbed forward, the golden ring gleaming – but Mikal appeared. A quick hard stamp, a scream of tortured metal, and a puff of vile-smelling crimson smoke; and the rat was merely a twisted scrap of metal and moth-eaten fur. The Shield's eyes glowed furiously, and specks of blood and other fluids dewed his filthy coat. He looked little the worse for wear, despite being covered in Wark-ash.

She shuddered. Clare retched again, feelingly. "A *range*!" he choked. "From thirty-three to eighty-nine per cent! It can only be explained in a *range*!"

Dear God, is he seeking to analyse Mehitabel? Or the rats? "Clare." She coughed, caught her breath. *I think we may have survived. Perhaps.* "Clare, cease. There are other problems requiring your attention."

"Prima." Mikal's hand on her shoulder, his fingers iron clamps. "*Emma.*"

She swayed, but only slightly. "You've done well." *Well? More like "magnificently". One Shield, a small army of Mehitabel's flashboys, the rats – I cannot understand how we are not all dead.*

Either she had hurt the ironwyrm far more than she thought possible or likely, or Mehitabel had expected Emma to flee in a different direction – perhaps north, the way they had entered the Wark. Or – most chilling, but a prospect that must be considered – Mehitabel the Black *let* them go for some wyrm-twisting reason, even though Emma had used her truename.

"Easy hunting." Mikal's mouth twisted up at one corner, a fey grimace. The ash gave him an old man's hair, caught in his eyebrows, drifting on his shoulders. "Her troops are clumsy, and loud, and had to check every dark corner."

"*What* problems?" Clare managed, through another retch. "Never. *Never* again."

"Oh, we shall brave the Wark again, if duty demands it." Emma let out a shaky breath. The idea of going home, throwing her corset into the grate, and watching it burn was extraordinarily satisfying. "But not tonight. At the moment, Mr Clare, we are on Greenwitch, and I wish you to help me find a hansom."

"Oh, excellent," Clare moaned. "Wonderful. What the deuce for?"

"To ride in, master of deduction." Her tone was more tart than she intended. "We have news to deliver."

It was past midnight, and the stable smelled of hay and dry oily flanks. Restless movement in the capacious stalls, half-opened eyes, the perches overhead full of a rustling stillness.

The gryphons were nervous. Iridescent plumage ruffled, spike feathers mantling; sharp amber or obsidian beaks clacked once or twice, breaking the quiet. Tawny or coal-dark flanks rippled with muscle, claws flexing in the darkness. Emma stood very still, carefully in the middle of the central passage, her skirts pulled close. Mikal was so near she could feel the heat of him.

Clare peered over one stall door, his eyes wide. "Fascinating," he breathed. "Head under wing. Indeed. The musculature is wonderful. *Wonderful*."

The gryphon stable was long and high, dim but not completely dark. Britannia's proud steeds took sleepy notice, ruffling as they scented a Prime.

Of all the meats gryphons preferred, they adored sorcery-seasoned best.

Mikal's hand rested on Emma's shoulder, a welcome weight. A door at the far end opened, quietly, skirts rustling on a breath of golden rose scent, overlaid with violet-water. Emma stiffened. Clare did not straighten, leaning over the stall's door like a child peering into a sweetshop.

"Mr Clare," the sorceress whispered. "*Do* stop that, sir. They are dangerous."

"Indeed they are." A female voice, high and young, but with the stamp of absolute authority on each syllable. "No, my friend, do not courtesy. We know you must be uncomfortable here."

Emma sank down into a curtsey anyway, glad she had applied cleaning charms to all three of them. Mikal's hand remained on her shoulder, and Clare hopped down from the stall door, hurriedly doffing his hat. "And who do we have the pleasure of— Dear God!" He lurched forward into a bow. "Your Majesty!"

Alexandrina Victrix, the new Queen and Britannia's current incarnation, pushed back her capacious sable-velvet hood. Her wide blue eyes danced merrily, but her mouth turned down at the corners. "Is this a mentath?"

"Yes, Your Majesty." Emma forced her legs to straighten. "One of the few remaining in Londinium, Mr Archibald Clare."

"Your Majesty." Clare had turned decidedly pink around his cheekbones, though the sorceress doubted any eyes but hers would see it.

Emma's mouth wanted to twitch, but the business at hand dispelled any amusement. "I bring grave news for Britannia."

"Since when do you not? You are Our stormcrow; We shall have Dulcie make you a mantle of black feathers." The Queen's young face could not stay solemn for long, but a shadow moved behind her eyes. "We jest. Do not think yourself undervalued."

"I would not presume," Emma replied, a trifle stiffly. "Your Majesty . . . I have failed you. The core is missing."

The young woman was silent for a few moments, her dark hair – braided in twin loops over her ears, but slightly dishevelled, as if she had been called from sleep – glinting in the dimness. Even so, pearls hung from her tender ears, and a simple strand of pearls clasped her slim throat. The shadow in her eyes grew, and her young face changed by a crucial fraction. "Missing?"

"I left it with Mehitabel." Emma's chin held itself firmly high. "It was taken with her consent. She gave me names."

"The dragons are involved? Most interesting." The Queen tapped her lips with a slim white finger; under the cloak her red robe was patterned with gold-thread fleur-de-lis. The shadow of age and experience passed more clearly over her face, features changing and blurring like clay under water. The signet on her left hand flashed, its single charter symbol fluorescing briefly before returning to quiescence. "This was Our miscalculation, Prima. The Black Mistress has been true to her word before; it is . . . disconcerting to find she is no longer. What names were you given?"

Some very uncomfortable ones. "I almost fear to say."

"Fear? You?" The Queen's laugh echoed, an ageless ripple of amusement. "Unlikely. You wish more proof, and to finish this matter to your own satisfaction, if not Ours."

Emma almost winced. Britannia was old, and wise. The spirit of rule had seen many such as her come and go. She was the power of Empire; was a Prime, in the end, was merely a human servant. "She mentioned the Chancellor of the Exchequer, and Llewellyn Gwynnfud, Lord Sellwyth. And another name. *Vortis.*"

Feathers whispered like a wheatfield under summer wind as the gryphons took notice. Lambent eyes opened, lit with phosphorescent dust. Mikal's fingers tightened, a silent bolstering.

Yet a still small voice inside her whispered that Mehitabel's flashboys had not chased them nearly enough. And Llewellyn, of course. *How long will it be before he strangles you, as he did Crawford?*

"That name is . . . not well known to Us. But known enough." Deep lines etched themselves on the Queen's soft cheeks. The fine hairs on Emma's arms and legs and nape rose, tingling as if she stood in the path of a Greater Work or even the unloosing of a Discipline. The gryphons stirred again, and a blue spark danced in the Queen's pupils as the power that was Britannia woke further and peered out of her chosen vessel. "And the Chancellor, you say? Grayson?"

"A wyrm's word—" Emma began, hurriedly, but the Queen's finger twitched and she swallowed the remainder of the sentence.

"If he be innocent, he hath nothing to fear from thee, Prima. Thy judgement shall be thorough, but above all *unerring.*" The blue spark brightened, widening until it filled the Queen's dilated pupils.

A not-so-subtle reminder. Emma's mouth was dry. She had, indeed, lied to Victrix about Crawford, and by extension, she had lied to Britannia. The ruling spirit of Empire had either chosen to believe Emma's version of events in the round stone room, or – more likely – she guessed at the truth and reserved her judgement because Emma was useful. "I am uneasy, Your Majesty. Too much is unknown."

Britannia retreated like Tideturn along the Themis, a rushing weight felt more than heard. The Queen blinked, pulling her cloak closer. "Then you shall uncover it. And the mentath . . ."

"Yesmum?" Clare drew himself up very straight indeed, his long, lanky frame poker-stiff. "Your Majesty?"

The Queen actually smiled, becoming a girl again. "Is he trustworthy, Prima?"

I am the wrong person to ask, my Queen. I do not even trust myself. "I think so. Certainly he faced the ironwyrm with much presence of mind."

"Then tell him everything. We cannot finish this without a mentath; it would seem Britannia is favoured in these as well as in sorceresses." Victrix paused. "And Emma . . ."

Her pulse sought to quicken; training pressed down upon Emma's traitorous body. "Yes, Your Majesty?"

"Be careful. If the Chancellor is involved, Britannia's protection may . . . wear thin, and Alberich Our Consort is not overfond of sorcerers. Do you understand?"

Britannia rules, but we cannot move openly against a Chancellor of the Exchequer without compromising the Cabinet. Your lady mother would love to intrude another of her creatures to said Cabinet, and your Consort is not only low of influence but also dislikes sorcerers with an almost religious passion. So it is quiet, and deadly, and everything must be kept as smooth as possible. "Quite, Your Majesty."

And, not so incidentally, if any part of this becomes a scandal, I will be the one to feel its sting.

"We use you dreadfully." The Queen stepped back, a heavy rustle of velvet, and the gryphons murmured, a susurrus of sharp-edged feathers.

"I am Britannia's subject." Stiffly, she sank into another curtsey. "I am to be used."

"I wish . . ." But the Queen shook her dark head, her braids swinging, and was gone. The open door let in a draught of garden-scented night, tinged with the violet-water she favoured, and closed softly.

Clare's mouth was suspiciously ajar. "That was the *Queen*." He sounded stunned.

Indeed it was. "We are wont to meet here, when occasion calls for it." And God help her, but did she not sound proud? That pride, another of her besetting sins.

"Little sorceress." A rush of feathers ruffling; the voice was gravel-deep and quiet, but full of hurtful edges. An amber beak slid over the closest stall door, and Emma's knees turned suspiciously weak.

The eyes were deep darkness ringed with gold, an eagle's stare in a head larger than her own torso. Feathered with ink-black, the powerful neck vanished into the stall's dimness, and Mikal was somehow before her, his shoulders blocking the view of the gryphon as it clacked its beak once, a sound like lacquered blocks of dense wood slamming together.

"Close enough, skycousin," Mikal said mildly.

"Merely a mouthful." The gryphon laughed. "But I am not so hungry tonight, even for magic. Listen."

Clare stepped forward, as if fascinated, staring at the gryphon's left forelimb, which had crept up to the stall door and closed around the thick wood, burnished obsidian claws sinking in. "Fabulous musculature," he muttered, and the gryphon clacked its beak again. It looked . . . amused, its eyes twin cruel glints.

"Mr Clare." A horrified whisper; Emma's throat was dry. "They are *carnivores*."

"They look well fed." The mentath cocked his head, and his lean face was alight with something suspiciously close to joy. "Yes, that beak is definitely from a bird of prey."

"Enough." The gryphon's head turned sidelong; he fixed Emma with one bright eye. "Sorceress. We know Vortis of old." The claws tightened. "You go wyrm-hunting, then."

It was the gryphons' ancient alliance with Britannia that had held the island stable, as the Age of Flame strangled on its own ash and the dragons returned to slumber. Or so it was told, and any study of the beasts was hazardous enough that very few sorcerers would attempt it. Emma stared at the creature's beak – its sharp edges, the flickering of dim light over the deep-pitted nostrils. How the creatures spoke without lips fit for such an operation was a mystery indeed; gryphons were not dissected after their deaths.

No, they *ate* their own. She suppressed a shudder, grateful for Mikal's presence between her and the creature. "Perhaps. A wyrm's word is a castle built on sand."

"Or air." The proud head lowered in a terrifying approximation of a nod. "You should have more Shields, sorceress."

"I have as many as I require at the moment." *The ironwyrm would have had me, but for Mikal. And yet.*

"We are many, and you are a tempting morsel." A laugh like boulders grinding. "But we are sleepy, too. You should go now."

I think so. For she noted the subtle tension in the beast's forelimb, raven feathers shading into blue-black fur. "Thank you. Mr Clare, do come along."

"A whole new area of study—" Clare, his sharp blue eyes positively feverish, stepped closer to the gryphon's claw.

Mikal lunged forward. The wood of the stall door groaned, splintering, and the Shield yanked Clare back, tearing his already worse-for-wear frock coat. The gryphon's claw closed on empty air, and the beast chuckled.

"Enough," Mikal said, pleasantly. "Stand near my Prima." He did not take his eyes from the beast. "That was unwise, skycousin."

"He is a mere nibble anyway, and unseasoned." The gryphon's eyes half lidded. "No matter. Take them and go, *Nágah*. Safe winds."

"Fair flying." Mikal stepped back. "Prima?"

"This way, Mr Clare." She made her hands unclench, grabbed the mentath's sleeve. "And do not pass too closely to the stalls."

Clare did not reply. But he did not demur, either. When they finally eased free of the stable's northern door and into the close-melting fog scraping the surface of the road and Greens Park beyond, Emma found she was trembling.

Chapter Nineteen

For My Tender Person

Greens Park was utterly deserted, yellow fog turning impenetrable black in places, licking the lawns and tangled trees. This close to the Palace, the shadows were free of thieves and thugs. Such would not be the case in other Londinium parklands.

They walked a fair distance to reach Picksdowne, Clare muttering to himself about musculature for a good deal of the way. It was absolutely *fascinating*, and he found himself wondering what discoveries one could make if a gryphon corpse happened to appear in one's workshop. He knew little of the beasts save that they were the only animals fit to draw Britannia's carriage; their riders were highly trained officers, and there had been corps of gryphon-riders used as sky cavalry in the battles with the damned Corsican—

Beside him, Miss Bannon cleared her throat. She was occupied in seeking to restore the ragged mass of her gloves.

"Oh yes." He had almost forgotten her presence, so intrigued was he by the glimpse of a new unknown. One that obeyed patterns, one that helped the hideous memory of Southwark recede. "There are things you no doubt wish to tell me, Miss Bannon."

"Indeed." Was there a catch in her voice? On her other side, the Shield stepped lightly, a trifle closer than was perhaps his habit.

The gryphons had severely shaken Miss Bannon. She was paper-pale, and her fingers nervously scrubbed themselves together while she sought to straighten her gloves. Still, she pressed onward over the gravelled walk, and her pace did not slacken. "What do you know of Masters the Elder? And Throckmorton?"

"Nothing more than their names: mentaths are acquainted with their peers only so far. I can surmise a great deal, Miss Bannon, but it is as the analysis you invited me to provide: a trap. Perhaps you should simply enlighten me."

The amount of shaky grievance she could fit into a simple sigh was immense. "Perhaps I should. In any case, the Queen commanded—"

"And she is not here to enforce said command."

A palpable hit, for she stiffened slightly before forging onwards, crisply and politely. "Pray do not insult me so, sir. Masters the Elder was engaged in building a core. Throckmorton had made a number of significant breakthroughs, and he and Smythe were brought together despite the danger. Certain advances were made."

Maddeningly, she ceased her explanation there – or perhaps not maddeningly, for his faculties leapt ahead, devoured this new problem, and his nerves sustained another rather unpleasant shock, adding to the night's already long list of unpleasantnesses.

"A core? Dear lady, you cannot possibly . . ." What was that cold feeling down his back? His jacket was ripped, certainly, but this was akin to dread. He noted the feeling, sought to put it aside.

It would not go.

"Throckmorton and Smythe, with Masters's core, achieved the impossible." She halted, but perhaps that was only because his feet had nailed themselves to the walk. Londinium's fog pressed close, and the Shield's gaze rested on his sorceress, yellow eyes lambent in the darkness. "A transmitting, stable, and powerful logic engine."

The fog had perhaps stolen all the air from the park. Clare stepped back, gravel grinding under his much-abused boots. He stared at the sorceress, who could have no possible idea what she was saying. He actually *goggled* at her, his jaw suspiciously loose.

"Such an engine . . ." He wetted his lips, continued. "Such an engine is not impossible. Theoretically, mind you. Extraordinarily difficult and never successfully—"

"I am *fully* aware it has never been done before. I am no mentath, but I have certain talents as a facilitator and organiser; much scientific work for the Queen can be and is done quietly. I am responsible for arranging such things. The mentaths who have been lately killed were all, in one fashion or another, involved in the making of said engine. The others . . . well. I am of the opinion many were murdered because of a particular note Throckmorton made of the peculiar nature of logic engines. They require a mentath to utilise them."

"Well, yes." Clare shivered. He was not cold. An ordinary person seeking to run a logic engine would be turned into a brain-melted automaton, injured beyond repair by the amplification. Lovelace had been the first to survive the wiring to a very weak engine; several geniuses had assumed that if a *woman* could endure it, a man's brain – even a non-mentath's – would have little difficulty.

The resultant casualties had been thought-provoking, the scandal immense. Some said the scandal had contributed to Lovelace's early death; others blamed the inefficiency of the engine – Babbage's work, true, but perhaps not up to the standards one would have wanted. There was, in particular, one scathing little paper written by Somerville, vindicating her pupil at Babbage's expense. Rare female mentaths were now required to be registered with the Crown as a result of the affair, and were wards of the Court until their marriages.

He heard his own voice, strangely strong and clear. "A . . . transmitting logic engine. Transmitting, I presume, to receiving engines. The amplification could save the trouble of murdering whatever mentath would wire himself to such a thing." *And the unregistered mentaths were mutilated.* He could not shake himself of the exceedingly unpleasant thought.

"Tests were made, at the country house in Surrey. It performed spectacularly well, from what the assembled reported. The engine is useless without Masters's core; I took the precaution of transporting the core to the Wark, where Mehitabel had agreed to hold it. Imagine my surprise when Masters and Smythe both turned up dead – they were not even supposed to be *in* Londinium. The engine has disappeared. Now it appears the core has disappeared as well." She paused. "Her Majesty is worried."

As well she should be. Dear God. "I presume you share her concern," he muttered, numbly.

"Oh, I do. The Chancellor, your Yton friend, may be involved. Llewellyn might have been a part of the conspiracy – for all I know, he may have killed Throckmorton himself. And yet several things do not make sense. The work was theoretical; a logic engine is valuable, yes, but all signs point towards the conspirators having *some* defined use for it already."

". . . It does. They do, rather." He was, he thought, beginning to recover from the shock somewhat.

"I suspect a military application." Patiently, as if she expected some further reaction from him.

Clare blinked. "I should think so."

"The question becomes, then, *which* military. You see the difficulty." Her hands still worked at each other, at odds with her calm, logical tone. The fire opals in her rings glowed dully, foxfire gleams.

"Britannia has many enemies. Any one of whom would not hesitate to use such an engine . . ." *But for what precisely?* "Even if there is not a military application *yet*, the consequences in manufacturing alone could be tremendous. And even in Alteration." His dinner, had any of it been left, might have tried for an escape at the last thought. "The unregistered mentaths. Their bodies were somehow savaged?"

"Certain pieces were missing, Alteration is not out of the question. I do not know enough yet." Emma Bannon's dark eyes glittered. "But now, Mr Clare, it is war. I will brook no treachery or threat to Britannia's vessel."

"Admirable of you," Clare muttered. "No wonder you locked me up in your house." *Keeping me safe, certainly. And any mentath is suspect. There is precious little* I *would not do to lay my hands on such an engine. The research possibilities . . . simply staggering.*

But it would not do to voice *that* particular thought.

"You may become extraordinarily *necessary*, Mr Clare." She finally stopped twisting at the ragged remains of her gloves. "If not, you are at the least useful. But in any event, you must be protected."

"I cannot quibble with *that* sentiment."

"Consequently, we are about to pay a visit." She dropped her hands, but her gaze was still level and quite disconcerting. It took Clare a few moments to discover why, exactly, he perceived such discomfort.

A woman should not look so . . . determined. "To gain some further variety of protection for my tender person?" He was only halfway flippant. Still, it gave him a chance to gather himself. The irrational feelings were highly uncomfortable, and he longed for some quiet to restore his nerves.

"Precisely. While we walk, occupy those admirable faculties of yours with the question of how you will uncover the whereabouts of a core and a transmitting logic engine. My methods have produced little of value at great cost, and I am needed to solve another riddle."

He found he could walk again. The Park was deadly still, but Londinium growled in the distance like a wild beast, and the

Palace was a faint smear of indistinct light behind the boiling-thick fog. If Miss Bannon took another four steps, she might well be lost to his sight entirely, so he hurried after her, his torn jacket flapping. "And what riddle would that be, Miss Bannon?"

"The riddle of a dragon, sir. Come along."

Arrowing north and west from St Giles, Totthame lay under a dense blanket of boiling yellow. The shops were closed tight against the choking fog – except for some of the brokers, low-glowing brass-caged witchballs barely visible above their doors and a flashboy or two often lounging on the step to keep the metal from disappearing. Side doors leading to individual closets for the gentler sellers to haggle privately were closed and bolted at this hour, but furtive movements could be seen in the shadows about them.

The swaybacked, dull-flanked clockhorse didn't even swish its ragged tail as they disembarked. The cab driver, swathed to his nose in oddments, was no trouble either, hiding Alterations from his misspent youth as a flashboy. Clare decided him as a Sussex youngblood come to Londinium to make good and only now as a man wishing he'd stayed where he was born. So much was obvious from the style of his dress and the broad accent in which he grunted the bare minimum necessary to secure their custom and give his price. Mikal appeared out of nowhere again and paid the man before they were allowed to alight, and Miss Bannon, still sunk in the profound silence she had spent the entire ride in, set off for the far side of Totthame with a quick light stride.

Mikal, silent as well, followed in her wake, glancing back at Clare as he hurried to keep up. The fog cringed away from her, curling in beseeching fingers. She was making directly for a broker's door, and the flashboys lounging there – one slim dark youth with half his face covered in a sheath of shining metal, the other just as dark but stocky, with gleaming tentacles where his left hand should be – elbowed each other. The thin one sniggered, and opened his mouth to address her.

Mikal's stride lengthened, but whatever the flashboys saw on Miss Bannon's face cut their ribaldry short. They hopped aside, the stocky one awkwardly, and the sorceress sailed past them, a slender yacht passing between battleships.

"Wise of you," Clare mumbled, and hopped up the biscuit-coloured stone step. The tentacle Alterations rasped drily against each other, scaled metal letting fall a single venomous-golden drop of oil, splattering on blue breeches. The stocky flashboy breathed a curse.

Inside, an exhaled fug of sweet tabac smoke, dust, paper, and the breath of mouldering merchandise piled in mountains enclosed them. Carpenter's tools beached themselves against the front of the shop; a pile of larger leather tack sat mouldering under hanging bridles and hacks. A cloud of handkerchiefs foamed over a long counter in front of the side door that would lead to the closets where the shy would seek to trade their wares.

Miss Bannon turned in a complete circle, her hands become fists and the sapphires dangling from her ears flaming.

"Twistneedle!" she called, and a mound of cloth moved near the back of the narrow shop. The shelves groaned with odds and ends – china, metal, clothing, a pair of duelling pistols in a long, dusty glass cabinet, a tangle of cheap paste jewellery and slightly less cheap snuffboxes threatening to swallow the gleaming barrels. Patterns formed with lightning speed, Clare's brain seizing on the sudden sensory overload and categorising, deducing, sorting puzzle pieces with incredible rapidity.

For the first time that long night, he was comforted.

"Don't *shout*, woman." A thready, reedy, irritable voice. More puffs of tabac smoke rose from the rear of the store. "I'm an old man. I needs my rest."

"Do not anger me, then. Ludovico. I want him."

"Oh, so many do. So many do." A wide, froggish face over a striped muffler rose peevishly from what Clare had taken to be a soulless mound of piled clothing in bundles; a polished brass earring gleamed. The round little man pushed aside a froth of calico petticoats and grinned widely, showing rotten stump-teeth. The pipe in his soft, round brown hand fumed extravagantly, while rings gleamed on the thick fingers. One was even a real diamond, Clare noted. "What will you give, miss? I don't hand out nothing for free, not even to those I fancy."

"Mikal." Deadly quiet.

The Shield glided forward, and the frog-man cowered, raising both plump hands. "None o' that! He's upstairs. Sleepin', most like."

Clare placed the accent – this man had probably never ventured more than a half-mile from Totthame in his life. Deduction ticked along under the surface of every item piled inside the narrow cavern. He wondered why he had never visited a pawnbroker's before – a single shop could keep him occupied for weeks. And with every deduction, Southwark retreated, more distant and dreamlike.

A movement behind a clutch of hanging frock coats in different colours, a slight twitching. *There's a door behind there,* Clare realised in a flash, but it was Mikal who moved, slapping aside the flung knife, its blade a blur in the smoke, burying itself in a pile of waistcoats tumbling off three narrow wooden shelves.

Some of the waistcoats still had traces of blood marring the fabric. Not just a pawner's, then. Clare's skin chilled.

A corpsepicker's shop.

"Ah." Miss Bannon sounded amused. "*There* you are."

"Call off your snake-charmer, *signora*." The frock coats twitched again. "I have the more knives, I use them, eh?"

Naples, Clare thought. *No more than twenty-six. And more afraid of the Shield than the sorceress.*

Interesting.

"He gets in rather a temper when you fling knives at me, *Signor* Valentinelli." Miss Bannon did not move; Mikal was now threading his way between two mounds of bundled, ticketed clothing. "I am not certain I should calm him."

The invisible voice let loose a torrent of abuse in gutter Italian, but Miss Bannon simply nodded and picked her way to the pile of waistcoats. Her mouth set itself firmly as she retrieved the flung knife, and Mikal halted before the hanging coats, tense and ready.

The cursing ceased. "Is there money, then?"

Miss Bannon straightened. "Haven't I always paid well for your services, *signor*? Be a dear and put a kettle on, I could do with a cup after the night I've had."

A sleek dark head appeared, pushing through the frock coats with a slightly reptilian movement. The face was still coarsely handsome, but ravaged with pox scars and bad living, and the close-set dark eyes flicked over the entire pawnshop. "What is it? Knife, *pistole*, garrotte?"

Neapolitan indeed. Clare placed the accent to his satisfaction. Miss Bannon was proving to have extraordinary acquaintances indeed.

"Maybe none, maybe all and more." Miss Bannon now sounded amused. "I bring you a chance to injure yourself in new and interesting ways. Do you really wish to discuss it here?"

Valentinelli let out a hoarse sound approximating a laugh. "Come up then. But keep *il serpente* away. He make me nervous."

"Poor Ludo, *nervous*. Mikal, keep a close eye on him." Miss Bannon held the knife away from her skirts, delicately, and shook a stray curl out of her face. "We would hate to have him faint."

The Neapolitan's face screwed itself up into a mask of dislike and disappeared, with a creak of leather hinges. Mikal pushed the frock coats aside, and Miss Bannon motioned Clare forward.

"Come, Mr Clare. *Signor* Valentinelli is to be your guardian angel."

Chapter Twenty

More If I Die

Ludovico's room was just the same: a monk's cell, narrow and dark, holding only a single cot and a small leather trunk, a guttering candle throwing dancing shadows over the peeling plaster. Mikal checked it with a glance and nodded them inside. She took the opportunity to hand him the flung knife; he made it disappear with no discernible flicker of expression.

The Neapolitan promptly threw himself down on the cot, eyeing Emma speculatively. He was a quick little man, the efficiency of his movements lacking any sort of grace and bespeaking a great deal of comfort with physical violence. Sleek dark hair, those dark, close-set eyes in the scar-ravaged face – childhood smallpox had been vicious to him. Stretching his arms over his head and yawning, he settled his shoulders more comfortably. He looked like a hevvy, shirt and braces worn but stout, his trousers rough and his boots dusty.

The opening move was hers. "Not even a cup of tea. Your hospitality suffers, *signor*."

"You are here after hours, *signora*."

"You keep no hours. Do *not* annoy me. This is the man you'll be guarding."

Ludovico scratched along his ribs, tucking his other arm under his head. "Why? What's he done?"

"That is no concern of yours. You're to keep his skin whole while I'm occupied with other things." She paused as Mikal tensed slightly, the candleflame flinching and righting itself. "You may have to kill a sorcerer or two to do so."

The effect was immediate, and gratifying. Valentinelli sat straight up, eyes narrowing, and a dull-bladed stiletto appeared in his left hand. He spun it over his knuckles, and Emma did not miss Mikal's own hand twitching slightly.

It was a high compliment from her Shield.

"Why you no have more of *him* to watch *il bambino*, eh?" He jabbed a finger at Mikal, still spinning the knife over his knuckles, catching the hilt as it rocketed past. The grime under his short-bitten fingernails, black half-moons, matched the crease in his neck.

She forced herself not to swallow drily. "That is not your concern. Shall I go elsewhere, *signor*?"

"At this time of night? And Valentinelli is the best. I protect from *il Diavolo* himself; you pay me. In gold."

"In guineas, yes." The smile fixed to her face wasn't pleasant, Emma suspected, but it covered a set grimace of almost distaste. "Since you are a gentleman."

He jabbed forked fingers at her and hissed. "Not even for gold do I let a woman mock me, *strega*."

She gathered her patience once more. "I am not mocking, *assassino*. For the last time, shall I seek elsewhere?"

A supremely indifferent shrug. "I take the job. Twenty guinea, more if I die."

"Very well." She did not miss the way he blinked at her readiness to take his first price. It was bad form not to haggle, but she had no patience for his tender feelings at this point. "Bring yourself to me, *signor*. You'll be bound for this."

"Ai, you're serious." He heaved himself off the bed and paced towards her, graceless but silent. "What he do, you want him alive this bad?"

"Again, none of your concern." Emma held her ground,

suddenly very aware of the space between her and the Neapolitan. Mikal's eyes flamed in the dimness, matching the candle's glow. "Mr Clare, please come here."

The mentath stared at Valentinelli in the uncertain light, his eyes half closed. His colour was much better, and he seemed to have recovered from the shock of the Wark quite nicely. "You," he said, suddenly, "had a wife at one time, sir."

Valentinelli halted. Emma could have cursed the mentath roundly.

"She die," the Neapolitan said. "What, you a *strego*? Or you *inquisitore*?"

"Neither." Clare's eyelids drooped a bit more. "Your accent is really wonderful. There's something, though—"

"*Mr* Clare." Emma stepped forward and plucked the black-bladed stiletto from Ludo's filthy fingers. "Do stop carrying on, and come here. You know what to do, Ludovico."

"If he is *inquisitore*—" His voice rose, losing for a moment the soft singing of Calabria and becoming more clipped, more educated, and generally more dangerous.

"He is *not* one of the holy running dogs, *do* be reasonable! He's simply a mentath. Give me your hand, Mr Clare."

"I don't know what you mean by *simply* a—" Damn the man, he sounded *irritated*. Emma grabbed his hand, the knife flickered, and he actually *yelped* at the bite of the blade. "What are you *doing*?"

Ensuring your survival despite your thickheadedness. "You are an execrable nuisance, sir. Your hand, Valentinelli."

Mikal drifted closer. Ludovico glanced at the Shield, his jaw set and his grimy fingers working as if he felt a neck under them. A trickle of sweat traced down Emma's spine, cool and distinct.

"Mentath? *Mentale*? Ah." He smelled of leather and male, a sharp underbite of grappa and sour sweat. "I forgive him, then." His cupped palm was strangely clean, given the condition of his nails. But then, she had seen him in many different lights, and this was only one of them.

Her breath caught, her pulse threatening to gallop before she invoked iron control. The man unsettled her.

More precisely, he reminded her of certain childhood things. Things best left in the recesses of memory, uncalled and unmissed.

"Most civil of you," she murmured, and the knife bit again. A bleeding slash on the Neapolitan's palm matched on the mentath's, she pressed their hands together. Ludovico had done this before, but Clare resisted; she was forced to glare at him and make a sharp *tsk*ing noise.

When their palms were clasped together, the copper tang of hot blood reaching her sensitive nose, she closed her eyes, her own fingers a white cage around theirs. "*S*——!" she breathed.

It was a Greater Word of Binding, and even more of Tideturn's charge trickled free of her flesh, sliding into the two men and licking hungrily at the scant blood. She flicked her hands back, like a hedge conjuror flapping a handkerchief, and a brief gunpowder flash painted the peeling walls.

She swayed, and Mikal was there, as usual, bracing her. His jaw was set; Emma wondered just what her own face was expressing.

"There." She found, to her relief, that she could still speak in a businesslike manner. "'Tis done. Present yourself at my door no later than Tideturn next, Valentinelli, and afterwards Mr Clare shall not stir one step without you."

"How long?" The Neapolitan examined his palm – smooth, unbroken skin, criss-crossed by thin faint lines where other bindings had been sworn. He arched one sleek eyebrow, and his white teeth showed as his lip lifted.

"You have other pressing appointments, I take it? As long as it is necessary, Ludovico. Until I take the binding off. You'd best hope nothing happens to me, too." Even the candleflame stung her suddenly sensitive eyes. They squeezed shut with no prompting on her part, tears rising reflexively.

"Home?" Mikal pulled her away, and she made no demur.

"Yes. Home. Come along, Mr Clare."

"Yes, well." Clare cleared his throat. "Archibald Clare. Mentath. How do you do."

She prised one eyelid open enough to see Clare offering his hand to the Neapolitan.

"Ludovico Valentinelli. Murderer and thief. Your servant, sir." Those dark eyes had lit with something very much like amusement.

"Murd—" Clare audibly thought better of finishing the word. "Well. Very interesting. A pleasure. I shall accompany Miss Bannon to her home, then, and wait for our next meeting."

"Do that. And be careful with *la signora*; be a shame to lose her pretty face. Give me my knife, *strega*."

"Oh no." Her fingers tightened on the leather-wrapped hilt. *The blade's sensitised now; it could cut that binding I just laid on you. Try again, bandit.* "That wouldn't do at all, Ludo. Mikal shall leave you the one you flung at me, though. Pleasant dreams."

There was a sharp meaty sound as Ludovico's knife thudded into the wall aross the room, and Mikal's lip curled. The Neapolitan's curses followed them out of the door, but she could tell he was intrigued.

Good.

The hectic strength sustaining her after dancing with Mehitabel had largely deserted its post by the time they reached Mayefair. In any case, she could not search for more answers until morning and a visit to the Collegia. The darkened foyer was a balm, the house sleepily taking notice of her return. The rooms would be ready, since the servants were well accustomed to her appearing and disappearing at odd hours.

Emma could wish that it was not quite so routine. "I suggest you take some rest, Mr Clare." She could finally occupy herself in stripping the remains of her gloves from her aching hands.

The mentath was remarkably spry. "Oh, indubitably. I shall

no doubt sleep well. You have some interesting friends, Miss Bannon."

I have few "friends", Mr Clare. "Valentinelli is not a friend. He is more . . . a non-enemy. I amuse him, he is reliable. Especially once he is hedged with a blood oath."

"Yes, well, I am not at all certain I like the idea of a filthy Italian bleeding on me." Clare actually *sniffed*. "But if you say he is capable, Miss Bannon, I shall take you at your word. I shall expect him at dawn or shortly after."

She gave up on her gloves and leaned into Mikal's hand on her arm. "Breakfast will be shortly after Tideturn. I presume your agile faculties are even now turning over the question of how and where to—"

"Oh yes. In fact, I have tomorrow's investigation planned."

Her conscience pinched, but she was, blessedly, too tired to care. "Good." She took an experimental step toward the stairs; Mikal moved with her. The Shield's frustration and annoyance was bright lemon yellow to Sight; her temples throbbed as it communicated to her.

"Miss Bannon?"

For the love of Heaven, what now? "Yes?"

"You have suddenly decided this Valentinelli is sufficient protection for my fragile person. Either you have a high faith in his capabilities, or—"

Or I shall dangle you in the water and see which fish rises. You do well to suspect me, sir. "I have become a much larger threat to these conspirators than you, Mr Clare. And by now, they are informed of it. You may take some comfort, at least, in that."

Wisely, perhaps, Clare left it at that. Emma set herself to climbing the stairs and navigating halls. Her skirts dragged, the Wark's ash still clung to her despite carefully applied cleaning-charms, and her Shield was about to explode.

He had the grace to keep himself quiet until the door to her dressing room opened, and she moved as if to free herself from his grasp. Her bed had rarely seemed so welcoming.

"Emma." Quietly.

Please. Not now. But he had apparently decided that yes, now was the time for a discussion.

"A dragon, Emma."

One of the Timeless, albeit a young wyrm. "Yes." She fixed her gaze on the shadowed bulk of one wardrobe, the dressing room's interior faintly glowing from the pale grey carpet and the plain silk hangings. "You should have taken the mentath and fled."

"Leaving you to Mehitabel." A single shake of his dark head, one she felt through his hand on her arm. "You should not ask such things of me."

"What should I ask of you, then? I am very tired, Mikal."

"A *dragon*, Emma."

You are repeating yourself. "I am fully aware of what transpired at the Blackwerks. The ironwyrm had orders to kill me. Those orders could only have come from another of the Timeless; a dragon would not care to obey a sorcerer, even to kill another of our ilk." She stared at the wardrobe. "And Britannia herself warns me that if Grayson is in league with the wyrms, her protection may not be enough. They are dangerous, and her compact with them is old and fragile. To them, we are merely temporary guests, and our Empire a wisp of cloud."

"Then why should they care if . . ." It struck him. He stiffened, his fingers clamping her flesh. "Ah."

"Someone has *made* them care for this piece of mechanisterum, Mikal. I must find out precisely who and neutralise the threat they represent to Britannia, or even the possible military uses of a logic engine will be beside the point. I am extraordinarily fatigued. You may retire."

He still did not let go. "What if I have no wish to retire?"

"Then you may dance in the conservatory or paint in the kitchen for all I care. Turn loose."

He did, but when she paced unsteadily into her dressing room he followed, closing the door with a faint but definite *snick*.

Every piece of jewellery on her tired body was dark and dead spent. She was barely upright, and if he sought to free himself of the shackle of duty to another sorcerer, there was no better time. She halted, swaying unsteadily, in a square of moonlight from the glass panels set in the ceiling, charter symbols sliding sleepily over them in constellation patterns.

And she waited.

His breath touched her hair. The closeness was too comforting; she shut her eyes and thought of Ludovico's filthy fingernails, the healthy animal smell of him, alcohol and exertion. Mikal was perfumed only with soot and the familiar tang of sorcery, a faint hint of maleness underneath.

It was useless. The pointless urge, once more, rose in her throat. This time she did not bar it. "Thrent," she whispered. "Jourdain. Harry. Namal."

"They betrayed you." Intimate, the touch of air against her ear. She shivered, swaying again, but he didn't touch her. "That was why they died."

Tall, dark Thrent. Small, blond, agile Jourdain. Harry with his smile, Namal with his gravity.

"They did not betray me. *He* killed them." The last name. She licked her dry, smoke-tarnished lips, said it to rob it of power: "Miles Crawford."

"He hurt you." So soft. "So he died. And *they* allowed themselves to be taken by surprise; their betrayal was in their carelessness. I would have murdered them myself for it, if *he* had not."

They eliminated the rest of his *Shields while Crawford sprang his trap on me. It was my fault, of course. I judged myself too highly.* "Very comforting." But her breath caught. He leaned a little closer, the almost-touch paradoxically, exquisitely more intimate than his fingertips could ever hope to be.

"You know what I am." A mere breath.

I am not certain at all. "I have my suspicions."

And there was the *other* reason to mistrust him. For there

were certain troubling things she had observed in her Shield, and if her suspicions were correct, the ease with which he had throttled Crawford was a dire sign indeed.

"Easy enough to prove."

"What if I prefer them to remain suspicions?" Her voice did not sound like her own. It lacked utterly the bite Emma was accustomed to putting behind each word.

"You cannot abide mysteries, Prima. It is," he finally touched her, warm fingers sliding under the half-awry mass of her hair, stroking her nape, "a small weakness."

That you have no idea of my other weaknesses is a very good thing. She raised her chin, pushed her shoulders back, and stepped firmly away from Mikal's hand. "Thank you, Shield. You may retire."

His hand fell to his side. "Do you wish me to sleep at your door like a dog?"

Would you? How charming. Her shoes were filthy; she had tracked cinderfall and God alone knew what else into the house. The maids would have a time of it in the morning. Another dress ruined, too, and sending a bill to Grayson was not likely to gain her any remuneration.

And unless she wished to ring a bell and wake someone to help her undress, Mikal would. It was, after all, part of a Shield's function to act as valet – or lady's maid, as the case may be.

"D—n your eyes." Unladylike, yes. But her flesh crawled, and her temper had worn thin.

"Is that a yes or a no?" He even sounded *amused*, blast him to the seventh Hell of Tripurnis.

Her only answer was to tack for her bedroom. Her bedraggled skirts were lead blankets, her bloomers chafed, and she would have had a special demise planned for her corset, had she not been so utterly exhausted. Let him do as he pleased. She was far too tired to care.

Or so she tried to tell herself, as she heard his footsteps behind her.

Chapter Twenty-One

Becoming Acquainted

Tideturn came slightly after dawn, filling the city with humming expectancy. The fog had not lifted, and there was no steady rain to keep it in check, just a few flirting spatters every now and again. The city smelled venomous, an odour that penetrated even Miss Bannon's sorcerously sealed dominion.

Despite that, breakfast was, as Clare had come to expect, superlative. The only dimming of his enjoyment came from the presence of the pox-scarred Neapolitan, who strolled in with great familiarity and proceeded to show terrible manners. The man's nails were no longer caked with filth, and he had somewhere found a respectable black wool waistcoat and a flashboy's watch chain, as well as a stickpin with a small, vile purple gem of no worth whatsoever. His high-collar shirt was of fine quality, but he still looked almost like a carter uneasy with high company. It was, the mentath decided, a carefully chosen façade.

Valentinelli's boots had belonged to a gentleman once, and Clare found himself engaging in unsupported speculation about how they had found their way to the Neapolitan's clumping feet.

The man *could*, Clare thought, walk lightly as a cat. He was choosing not to, stamping around the exquisite Delft-and-cream breakfast room. The soothing jacquard of the blinds was probably wasted on the assassin, who gave the room a single glance

– rather as a general would take in the terrain – and grunted at Clare, before loading a plate with all manner of provender and leering at one of the maids. Who simply ignored him with a toss of her honeybrown head.

Clare took this to mean she had some prior experience of the man.

Very interesting indeed.

Valentinelli filled his mouth with sausage, crammed in an egg, and chewed with great relish. He slurped his tea, wiping his fingers on the fine waistcoat – all the while standing between two potted palms whose charmed crystal cover-globes sang a wandering, tinkling melody. Clare studied him for a few more moments, sipping his tea meditatively and nibbling at kippers on toast. The furniture here was surprisingly light and ladylike. From the size of the two small tables, Miss Bannon usually breakfasted alone.

Madame Noyon had left him to it after pouring tea; most likely she was attending to Miss Bannon's morning toilette and the business of running the house according to her employer's wishes. The breakfast table was of pale ash wood, its legs carved with water lilies and its cloth stunning white; the breakfast plate was delicate silver and stamped with a swan under a lightning bolt. Very Greque of the woman, indeed.

Clare crunched the last of his kippers and toast, washed it down with heavily lemoned tea, and decided to hazard a throw.

"I say, *signor*. You have quite the noble carriage."

The Neapolitan gave him one swift, evil glance. He took another huge bite of sausage, let his mouth fall open while chewing. His scarred cheeks had turned pale.

Clare dabbed at his lips with a napkin. "It is *marvellously* interesting that you are not a natural at rudeness. You were trained in fine manners. Your habit of performing the exact opposite of those manners gives you away."

A flush touched the Neapolitan's neck. Clare smiled inwardly. It was so *satisfying* to deduce correctly.

"A Campanian nobleman? Your accent, which you take pains to disguise, is too refined for anything else. But you left your homeland young, *signor*. You have adopted the English method of slurping tea, and you wear the watch chain as a costume piece instead of as a true hevvy or a carter would. And though you are no doubt very good with a dagger, it is the rapier that is your true love. Yours is an old house, where such things are still a mark of honour."

The Neapolitan grunted. His muscle-corded shoulders were tense.

Clare was actually— Was he? Yes. He was *enjoying* himself. The man presented a solvable puzzle, not without its dangers but well worth a morning's diversion.

"Very well then, keep your secrets." He considered another cup of tea, tapping his toe lightly. "This morning we shall go a-visiting. A friend of mine, or rather a close acquaintance. His is a respectable address; you may find yourself bored."

The Neapolitan swallowed a wad of insulted provender. When he spoke, it was in the tones of a wearied upper-class Exfall student, complete with precisely paced crispness on the long vowels. "If you keep talking, *sir*, I shan't be bored at all. Disgusted, perhaps, but not bored." No trace of Italy marred the words – the mimicry was near perfect. He grimaced, his tongue showing flecks of chewed sausage and crumbs of fried egg as he stuck it out as far as possible.

At that moment the door opened, and Miss Bannon appeared. There were faint smudges under her dark eyes, and she cocked her head as Clare rose hastily.

"Good morning. I see you two are becoming acquainted." Today it was dark blue wool, a travelling dress. The jewellery was plain, too – another cameo at her throat, four plain silver bands on her left hand and a sapphire on her right ring finger, her earrings long jet drops that would have been vulgar had she been wearing mourning. A brooch of twisted fluid silver alive with golden charter-charms completed the *ensemble*, and her hatpins dangled short strings of twinkling blue beads. The hat itself, small, blue, and exquisitely expensive, sat at a jaunty angle on her dark curls. It was *not* a bonnet, and he was obliquely gladdened to see so. Aesthetically, this was far more pleasing.

"I am gratified to see you well, Miss Bannon. Good morning."

The Neapolitan merely made a chuffing sound and buried his snout in more food.

"You seem to have disturbed Signor Valentinelli. Ludovico, *do* please come and sit down." She moved across the room, betraying no stiffness or injury, but she winced slightly as she sank into a Delft-cushioned chair opposite Clare, who lowered himself back down and eyed the teapot.

Mikal appeared, tidy dark hair and a fresh high-collared coat of the same dark green velvet, his glove-boots soundless as he nodded at Clare and began filling a plate.

Valentinelli glowered at the sorceress, swallowing another mass. "When you take the blood oath off, *strega*, I kill him." The Italian was back, singing under the surface of his words. Strengthening morning light fell pearly and pale across his scars, picking out the fresh grease stains on his waistcoat.

Miss Bannon examined him for a long moment, her hands motionless on the carved chair arms. "That would distress me," she remarked, mildly enough. The charter symbols cascading over the glass panels in the ceiling shivered, wheeling apart and coming together in new patterns. A brief rattle of rain touched them, steaming off immediately, leaving streaks of dust.

"Maybe I let him live. For you." The Neapolitan let out a resounding belch.

"Your magnanimousness fills me with gratitude." Miss Bannon accepted a plate of fruit and toast from Mikal. There was a small, very fresh and livid bruise on the side of her neck, low near the delicate arch of her collarbone, and Clare's eyebrows almost raised. It was extraordinarily uncomfortable to see such a thing.

Well. She is sorceress, and may do as she pleases, but still.

The Shield was the same, impenetrable. But his fingers brushed her shoulder as he turned away from serving her breakfast, and his yellow eyes were a trifle sleepy-lidded. Clare's estimation of their relationship twisted sideways a few crucial degrees. His organ of Remembrance, having had time to search through dusty vaults and cellars, served up something quite interesting.

The scandal surrounding Miles Crawford, Duke of Embraith and Sorcerer Prime, had been only glancingly mentioned by a former employer. Clare had simply stored the details and moved on, uninterested but unable to let any information leave his grasp unmarked. The Duke had been caught embezzling from the Crown, or some such; there were whispers of some *bad form*, which could mean anything from wiping his nose incorrectly at his club to the pleasures of Sodom. There had been no breath of sorcery surrounding his demise, which Clare had found a trifle odd at the time, but it did not warrant his attention. Sorcery was not a matter he found of great interest, and he had been . . . busy.

That had been the last time he crossed wits with Dr Vance, and the memory was pleasing and bitter at once. The pleasure of such an opponent and the bitterness of being outfoxed that once warred with each other most improperly.

Miss Bannon *tsk*ed at Valentinelli. "Must you behave in this manner? Mr Clare, I trust you slept well."

"As well as can be expected. There is a great deal to do today."

A small nod, very graceful. "Certainly. Mikal?"

The Shield poured his sorceress a cup of tea. As soon as he had delivered it, he produced a sheaf of papers. He handed them silently to Clare, gave the Neapolitan a single scorching look, and turned away to fill his own plate. His breakfast was just as hearty as Valentinelli's, but he managed it with infinitely more grace. For one thing, he sat to Miss Bannon's left side and used the silver.

"My, what is this?" The notations were interesting; Clare

scanned three pages and grew increasingly still, the breakfast room receding as he concentrated. All thoughts of Vance and old scandal fled. "Dear God."

"Indeed. That should aid your investigations – and I do not need to remark on the trust implied by even the simple admission of my possession of such papers."

"Working notes – these are Smythe's, I take it?"

Another nod, as she sipped tea with exquisite care. "I could not find Throckmorton's. There was very little left of his residence. There are also a few pages of Masters's notes on the bottom – they may be of some use as well."

"Undoubtedly. Thank you, Miss Bannon. This will aid my investigations immensely."

"There is one more thing." Her left-hand fingers flicked, the silver rings glinting dully, and a small crystalline pendant on a fine metal chain swung. It glowed even in the weak sunlight, a confection of silver wire and some colourless solid substance he could not immediately identify. "You shall wear this. If you are in dire need, I will be alerted, and I will offer what assistance I can at a distance, and furthermore make every effort to reach you. There is likely to be a great deal of annoyance involved in your investigations."

"I say. Is that an actual Bocannon's Nut?" Clare accepted the pendant, and Miss Bannon nodded before buttering her toast.

"With a few improvements, yes. They are time-consuming to create, and they can be broken, so do be careful."

Valentinelli pulled the last chair away from the small round table, dragging it along the carpet. He dropped into it, crushing the cushion, and banged his plate down on Miss Bannon's right. "Why you give him that, eh? I tell you I take care of him."

"Nevertheless." Miss Bannon's childlike face was unwontedly grave instead of simply set. "You may have occasion to thank me for it before this affair is finished. Do you recall the second time I made use of your services?"

The Neapolitan actually turned cheese-pale, his pockmarked

cheeks singularly unattractive as the blood drained away. "*Ci. Incubo, e la giovana signorina. E il sangue.* I remember."

"This is likely to be much worse." Miss Bannon applied herself to her toast and fruit, delicately conveying an apricot slice to her decided little mouth. "You may now leave the house at any time, Mr Clare, and return as you please. There is a brougham engaged and waiting at the front gate; you have the use of it all day." A final nod, the curls massed over her ears bouncing. "I suggest you do not loiter."

The driver was a broad-faced, pleasant man much exercised by the prospect of a full day's beneficent hire, and his maroon brougham was clean and well ordered. The clockhorses were freshly oiled and springy; the whip cracked smartly, and Valentinelli was suddenly businesslike. The sneering uncouth mask fell away, and what rose to replace it was a calm, unblinking, almost feline stillness.

The Neapolitan proved somewhat less terrible as a travelling companion. Clare had exited Miss Bannon's house with a shambling carter. Now he sat beside a dangerous man. He held his tongue, his attention divided between Valentinelli's immobility and the fog-choked, yellow-glowing street outside the window.

Sigmund Baerbarth's lodging in Clarney Greens was up two flights of stairs, the rooms spacious and well appointed but appallingly old-fashioned. The Bavarian kept them, antiquated as they were, because his workshop was situated directly behind the Queen Anne building holding his lodgings, in a long blue structure that had once been some manner of factory.

There was no chalked circle on the low wooden door inside the draughty building, so Clare tapped twice and entered. Valentinelli muttered a curse, shoving past him to peer at the tangled interior. A horrific noise was coming from the depths of the building, but that was normal enough. The Neapolitan finally nodded, curling a lip at Clare in lieu of simply saying it was safe to enter.

Shafts of sunlight pierced the dusty cavern, hulks of gutted machinery rising on either side. Metal gleamed, cogwheels as tall as Clare's leg or watchmaker-tiny, bits of oiled leather and horsehair, struts and spars, carapaces and wheels in unholy profusion.

"Sig!" Clare called. "I say, Sigmund! Put the kettle on, you've visitors!"

A clanking rumble was the only reply. A mass of metal jerked, shuddering, and Clare watched as it heaved three times, oily steam sputtering from overworked valves. The shape suddenly made sense as he saw insectile legs with high, black-oiled joints. The body, slung below and between them, twitched and shivered. Atop the metal beast's back, a short pudgy figure held on with grim determination, his arm rising and a monstrous black spanner rising with it. The man brought his arm down decidedly, a massive clanging resounded, and the pile of metal slumped, wheezing clouds of vile-smelling green steam.

The rotund man kept beating at the iron back, making a terrific noise, until it finally splayed on the sawdust-scattered floor, bleeding dark grease and panting scorched steam. A rich basso profundo voice rose, rumbling through quite a few scatological terms Clare might have blushed at had they been in Queen's English.

"Sig!" he called again. "Good show, I say! You've almost got that working."

"Eh?" Sigmund's seamed bald head jerked up, the leather-and-brass goggles clamped to his face making his eyes into swimming poached eggs. "Archibald? *Guten Tag,* man! *Wer ist das?*"

"Name's Valentinelli, he's my insurance. Bit of trouble, old man. I need your advice."

"Very good!" The Bavarian dropped the spanner with a clatter and hopped down, sawdust puffing from his boots. He wore a machinist's apron, and when he freed himself from the goggles one could see watery brown eyes under bushy iron-grey brows.

His moustache was magnificent, if a trifle singed, and his side whiskers were vast – to make up for his egg-bald head, since he was a vain man. "Come, I make you tea. And there is wurst! Cheese and your foul kippers, too. Come, come." He pumped Clare's hand with abandon, grabbed Valentinelli's and did the same. "You are small and thin. Italian, *ja*? No matter, you eat too. Baerbarth is not proud."

The Neapolitan gave a wolfish grin. "Neither is Valentinelli, *signor. Ciao.*"

"*Ja, ja*, come. This way, this way—"

He led them between stacks of machinery, into a section of smaller metal carcasses. The light came from gaslamps and high dusty windows, weakly struggling to penetrate the corners, glinting off sharp edges.

Four easy chairs crouched in front of a coal grate; a massive pigeonhole desk loaded with papers and smaller cogwheels and gears hunched to one side. This portion of the old factory was better lit and warmer, and a hanging rack constructed of scrap metal above the desk held loops of wurst links and a gigantic wheel of cheese in a net bag. The kettle near the grate was hot, and in short order a second breakfast was prepared. Valentinelli and Baerbarth set to with a will, while Clare contented himself with terrible, harsh tea cut with almost turned milk.

"Now." Sigmund's eyes gleamed with interest. "Tell me, Herr Clare. What is problem?"

There was nothing for it but to leap in, however indirectly. "I need Prussian capacitors."

Sigmund shrugged, chewing meditatively at a wurst as thick as his burly wrist. He was only a genius; his faculties were not quite mentath quality and he had failed the notoriously difficult Wurzburg Examinations twice. For all that, he was generous, loyal, and honest to a fault. If not for the efforts of his landlady McAllister and his sometimes assistant Chompton – a thin, half-feral lad with a near-miraculous affinity for clockhorse gears – he would probably have been cheated out of every farthing long ago.

"Capacitors." The great gleaming head nodded. "Prussians? Gone. Gentlemen bought mine month ago; none to be had, love or money. I could find you Davinports or some French ones, feh!" His face balled itself up to show his feelings on such a matter. To Sig, German mechanisterum was the apotheosis of the art, English was serviceable, and the French altogether too delicate and fancy to be considered proper mechanisterum at all. "But no, *mein Herr*, no Prussians. Not even my Becker haf them."

Ah, so the trail is not as cold as I feared. "Now that is very odd." Clare's nose sank into his teacup. His habitual chair was a wide broken-in leather monstrosity, smelling slightly sharpish with rot like everything in the factory. Valentinelli's head made a quick catlike movement, enquiring, as he perched on a wooden stool next to the grate – Chompton's usual spot. "And where is young Chompers today?"

"He is picking river-shore, like good boy. Back before Tide, I tell him, but he grunt and wave his arms. Young men!" He rolled his weak, blinking eyes. "I find you Prussians, but it take time."

"That's quite all right. I have another question, my friend—"

"Of course. You would like wurst, eh? Or cheese? Bread is good, I just scrape mould off. More tea?"

"No thank you. Sig, old man, how would one trace a certain shipment of Prussian capacitors? *Without* drawing attention to oneself?"

The Bavarian grinned widely. One of his front teeth was discoloured; he had a positive horror of toothcharmers. "Aha! Now is revealed!"

No, but I would like you to think so. "Indeed. And?"

Sigmund sank back in his faded blue armchair, blowsy pink cabbage roses blooming horrifically over its surface like spreading fungus. It squeaked as he settled his squat frame more firmly. "Difficult. Very difficult."

"But not impossible." The tea was almost undrinkable, but

at least it was strong. One could always do with a spot more to help a situation settle the proper way. "And if anyone can, Sig . . ."

"Archie. Is difficult, this thing you ask, *ja*?" Suddenly very grave, Sigmund took another mouthful of wurst and chewed. Like a cow, he thought best while ruminating.

A thin thread of unease touched Clare's nape. He glanced at the stool by the grate.

Valentinelli had vanished.

Chapter Twenty-Two

They Are Not Exercised Enough

The dark green curricle was fast and light, especially with Mikal at the reins and the matched clockwork bays high-stepping. A trifle flashy, not quite the *thing* for a lady, but one had only to look at the witchballs spitting in their gilded cages, swinging from the swan-neck leaf springs, and the dash-charm sparking with crimson as it deflected mud and flung stones from the passenger, to know it was not just a lady but one of sorcery's odd children being driven by a nonchalant Shield through a press of Londinium traffic rather startlingly resembling the seventh circle of Hell.

The curricle took a hard left, cutting through a sea of humanity. Shouts and curses rose. Emma paid no attention. Her eyes shut, she leaned back in her seat, fine invisible threads flashing one by one through her receptive consciousness as she held herself still. One gloved hand held tight to the loop of leather on her left, her fingers almost numb. Mikal shifted his weight, the clockhorses so matched their drumming hoofbeats sounded like one creature, Londinium's chill fogday breath teasing at her veil. Even the strongest air-clearing charm could not make the great dozing beast of the city smell better than foul on days like this, when one of Dr Bell's jars had descended over everything from St Paul's Road to the Oval, and beyond. The night's fog crouched well past daybreak, peering in windows, fingering pedestrians, cloaking whole streets with blank billowing hangings of thick yellow vapour. Some, especially the ditch-charmers and hedgerow conjurors, swore Londinium altered itself behind the fog. Outside the Black Wark, the Well, Whitchapel's Sink or Mile End – or some other odd pockets – few believed them.

Still, those sorcery touched did not laugh at the notion. At least, not overloud, and certainly never overlong.

The avenues widened as they travelled north and west toward Regent's Park. Traffic thinned through Marylbone, taking the great sweep of Portland Place past terraced Georgian houses standing proud-shouldered, sparkling with wards and charms. Precious few were sorcerer's houses – no, the unsorcerous fashionable paid for defences, the flashier the better.

A sorcerer's defences were generally likely to be less visible and more deadly.

Mikal made a short, sharp sound, shifting again, and the horses leapt forward. Pelting up the Place was certainly one way to make a statement, and she did not wonder why he had chosen this particular route. She was to be as ostentatious as possible today, so her quarry would focus on her as the larger threat – and hopefully not notice Clare's poking about overmuch.

If they noticed *too* much, well, Valentinelli was the best protection she could provide, next to her own self. Ludovico might have made a fine Shield, if he'd been moulded earlier. He would have needed a light touch, though, and *that* was something very few sorcerers possessed.

Whoever rose to the bait of a mentath and an assassin would be interesting indeed. There was an art to preparing a hook without losing either hook or bait, and she intended to do so today.

The bay clockhorses, every inch of them gleaming now, ran like foam on crashing surf. Emma found the threads she wanted, her hands clenched before relaxing, fingers contorting and easing as she made the Gesture, and the Word shaped itself on her tongue.

"*Ex–k'Ae–t!*" As usual, the Word was soundless, filling her, thunder in stormclouds. The curricle jolted, sparks fountaining from clockhorse hooves, and the sudden eerie quiet as wheels and hooves bit nothing but air enfolded them.

Her eyelids fluttered, daylight spearing into her skull, the impression of Mikal standing, reins now loosely held as the clockhorses settled into a jogtrot. Emma's own contorted fingers held finer, invisible threads, snapping and curling, fresh ones sliding into existence as the old tore.

The carriage *flew*.

Up they climbed, lather and sparks dripping, fog closing over Park Crescent below them, its green sickly under the pall. Still rising over Regent's proper, the only sound the curricle's wheels spinning freely and one of the clockhorses snorting, tossing its fine head. From the withers and haunches to the hooves, cogwheels meshed and slid, the pistons in the legs working in a simulacra of a flesh horse's bones, its skeleton sorcerously reinforced and the russet metal melding seamlessly into bay hide lovingly tended by half-lame spine-curled Wilbur, the stable boy, who stammered so badly he could not make himself understood. The scar on his forehead perhaps showed why, but he had a charmed touch with clockhorses. Yet another indenture she was glad to have performed – her one-time kindness reaping a reward out of all proportion. Harthell, her usual coachman, was another – but she had no time to think on her collection of castaways.

For there, drifting as lightly as a soap bubble, the great Collegia stood on empty air. The lattices of support and transferral cradling the massive tiered white-stone edifice were clearly visible to Sight, but to the ordinary it seemed that the Collegia simply . . . floated. It drifted in a slow, majestic pattern above the Park, confined there to keep the Londinium rabble from rioting at the idea that it could fall on their slums and tenements – or vent its waste onto their heads.

Though they merrily shovelled excrement over each other, a sorcerer's dung was another thing entirely. None saw fit to tell them the waste was shunted into the Themis, just like their own.

The horses high-stepped up an invisible grade, turned as Mikal flicked the reins, and the Gates were open. Sharp black stone dully polished and sculpted with flowing fantastical animal shapes, running with bloody-hued charter symbols, the Gates had been the first thing built for the Collegia. They had stood open since the first stone had been laid by Mordred the Black, who had claimed descent from Arthur's left-hand line. Whether that was true, who could say?

The Lost Times were lost for a *reason*. Much as the records of the Age of Flame and the Age of Bronze were only fragmentary, or the records of the time during Cramwelle's Inquisition. Britannia, her physical vessel murdered and the shock of that murder reverberating through the Isle, had surfaced finally in a fresh vessel and halted Cramwelle's violent hatred of his sorcerous betters.

As the historial Lord Bewell had remarked, a little ambition could make even a hedge-charmer dangerous.

The most difficult part of entering the Collegia was landing on the slick marble paving. Even the cracking sound of transferring force away into empty air was to be avoided. Difficult, delicate, dexterous work; clockhorse hooves touched down soft as feathers, the curricle's wheels given a preparatory spin to match speed, and the gradually rising volume of hooves and wheels until every step rang on the cold white stone was a small triumph. The silver rings on Emma's left hand were warm, her attention rushed back firmly into her body and she cautiously opened her eyes.

The heavy veil took some sting from the foggy sunlight, much brighter here above the thicker soup of ground-level fog. Still, she squinted most unbecomingly before she half lidded her eyes languidly as a lady should. The curricle raced up the long circular drive; the massive fountain in the middle of the round garden played a sonorous greeting as multicoloured streams of light and prismatic water laved its surfaces. A half-nude Leda reclined under Jove in the form of a swan, blinding white; she chucked the snake-necked creature under its chin and for a moment the wings moved as her limbs did, dreamily. The light and water caressing them both made it far more indecent than the worst of the gentlemen's flash press.

It was, Emma reflected as Mikal steered the horses past the chill-white, massive Great Staircase, a very good metaphor for sorcerers in general.

The Library's white dome was low compared to the jabbing snowy enamel spires of the rest of the Collegia, but it was still large enough to swallow the Leather Market whole and ask for seconds. Mikal pulled the horses to a stop and a Collegia indentured appeared to take charge of them; her Shield leapt down from the curricle and Emma gathered her skirts.

This should prove interesting.

The Library's dome glowed, stone scraped thin enough to let sunshine through. In that drenching, directionless light, flapping shadows moved. They circled in small flocks, sometimes lighting on the tops of high shelves, other times fluttering toward the gigantic nautilus-curled circulation counter. A vast central well, five storeys of bookshelves rising around it and raying out in long spiralling stacks, was enough to make one dizzy. Balustrades of ivory and mother-of-pearl, the carpeting rich blue; the Library glowed with nacre, the smell of paper mixing with a faint breath of salt and sand. Thin cries could be heard as some of the books fluttered aloft, gaining altitude and swooping with gawky grace.

Mikal followed, perhaps more closely than was strictly necessary. But then, his life was forfeit here. A Shield could not be taken from a Prime's service and put to death, no matter the crime he had committed. The law was very clear on that point – even if the Shield in question had done the unthinkable and murdered his own sorcerer.

No other sorcerer was willing to run the risk of taking him in. None of her fellow Primes – indeed, no sorcerer, and no other person – knew *precisely* what had happened in that small room in the bowels of Crawford's palatial home, because she had steadfastly maintained her silence. As far as she could tell, so had Mikal. Yet the fact of his survival in her service, and Crawford's demise, could not be ignored; it shouted to the heavens what had most likely occurred.

It is you, or the chopping block, he had said, his jaw iron-hard and his eyes glowing venomously. *I prefer you. If you will not take my service, do me the courtesy of killing me yourself. I will let you.*

And Emma had believed him. Her fingers still tingled with the feel of his chest underneath her touch, the rasp of subtle scaling—

Stop it. You are not here to daydream. She stalked for the circulation desk, shaking herself out of memory with a sharp disciplined mental effort. It would be easy to believe Mikal felt . . . what?

Nothing she could trust. It was best to remember that.

Behind the desk, a tangle-haired witch in no-nonsense grey wool glanced up, startled by her approach. Of course, any livre-witch would feel a Prime's approach like a storm bearing down on a small sloop. Especially here at the Collegia, where sorcery vied for air as the most common medium.

This livrewitch was plump, her hazel eyes unfocused, and she swayed slightly as she gripped the desk's edge until she adjusted to the disturbance Emma represented. "Title?" she chirped, in a colourless little voice. Her dishwater hair was a rat's nest, matted locks hanging and others piled high with a collection of bones, small shiny bits of metal, and feathers. "Author? Catalogue number? Cover colour? Subject?"

"*Principia Draconis.*" Emma fought back a curling lip. Witches. Male and female both specialised young, and by the time they reached twenty their brains were capable of holding only their Discipline. Theirs were not the deep Disciplines of the Inexhaustible – fire, water, magnetism, creation, destruction – but the tiny niches. Swallows nesting in a cliffside, and never straying far from their tiny holes.

Do not pity the witches, a teacher had once intoned. *They are not less than sorcerers. They are far happier than you shall ever be – for they lack ambition. They find their joy in their Discipline, not their danger.*

"*Principia Draconis*," the livrewitch repeated, slowly. A shuffling movement went through the flocks of books, shelves moving as the Library sought inside itself. "De Baronis, originally, 1533. Amberforth updated and glossed in 1746; James Wilson in 1801. Eight hundred pages, folio, cover is—"

"Bannon." The sneering behind Emma could only come from one man. "Still bringing trash into hallowed halls, I see."

"Lord Huston." She inclined her head, but did not turn. "Still unacquainted with basic etiquette, I see."

"*Ladies* are due etiquette, Bannon." The Headmaster's cane – an affectation, of course, with its silver mallard's head – hit the carpeting. He must have forgotten he wasn't in one of the stone-floored halls, where the tapping of his progress would send a wave of dread through the sensitised fabric of reality.

Mikal moved, a susurrus of cloth as he faced the Headmaster. Emma kept her gaze on the livrewitch, who was mumbling. At any moment the book would appear, and she could give the Headmaster short shrift before taking herself to a study table to do some quiet digging.

"And the trash seems to have ideas." Mock-surprised. "When *are* you going to take a proper Shield, Bannon? If any will serve with *that* murdering apostate behind you."

"Be careful, little man." Bannon allowed her right toe to lift and tap the carpet precisely *once*. Her skirts would cover it, but she was still annoyed at the movement. He was Prime, yes – but just barely. Had he not been extraordinarily lucky, he would be merely an Adept, or even a Master Sorcerer, since his Examination scores had been dreadful. "I am not a student."

"*A sorcerer who ceases to learn ceases to thrive,*" he intoned piously. "Whatever are you doing *here*, then, if you are no longer learning?"

"The Library is open to every Adept and above, at every hour." It was her turn to sound pious. "Or perhaps you'd forgotten that Law?"

A direct hit. "I forget no Laws," he hissed. "*You* are the one who has a Shield who no doubt murdered his charge. You should hand him over to justice."

Her temper stretched. "If you challenge me for one of my possessions, Huston, I might almost think you've grown tired of breathing."

The Library's rustling silence took on a sonorous, uneasy depth. *I do not have time for a duel today, Alfred, Lord Huston. Take advantage of that.* For a moment she considered how easy it would be to see him as a conspirator and administer appropriate justice.

The thought almost managed to soothe her.

"The *Principia Draconis* is not here." The livrewitch cocked her tangled head, the words a thin reedy murmur as she clasped her hands. Her gaze was already sliding away, uninterested in the drama before her. "It has been borrowed."

"That is quite impossible." Emma's temper rose afresh; she bottled it. Today was already unpleasant, and it was early for her to be so irritated. "It is one of the Great Texts; it is not to leave the Library."

Huston's sneer was absolutely audible. "Oh, the *Principia*? I believe Lord Sellwyth wished to peruse it at leisure; I gave my approval. Since he is such a *special* friend to the Collegia."

For a moment, Emma Bannon literally could not believe her ears. Books fluttered nervously, several taking wing from the carved banisters. Shadows darted, and she turned on her heel, the cameo at her throat warming dangerously. Her skirts belled, and Mikal took a half-step to the side, his broad back tense under green velvet. No blades were visible yet – of course, if he drew, she would be hard pressed to calm the layers of ancient stifling protection meant to safeguard students from misfired lessons.

Even the simplest spell could kill, here. Bloodlust on Collegia grounds carried a heavy price.

Huston, his scarecrow form in an antiquated black suit, collar tied high and snowy cravat under his chin as if Georgus IV was still Britannia's vessel, actually paled and stepped back. Thin strings of bootblack hair crossed his domed cranium, and if Emma had been a devotee of phrenologomancy she might well have decided to examine his skull for an organ of Cowardice and one of Idiocy to boot.

With a hammer, or another suitably blunt bludgeoning tool.

His breeches were spotless, and a perfumed handkerchief frothed in his free hand. The man even wore dandy boots, the toe pointed and heel arched. The clicking of his cane was usually followed by the soft tapping of his heels, a sound that featured in student nightmares. Long bony strangler's fingers, his right hand bearing the heavy carnelian Collegia Seal, spasmed on the silver duck's head.

The light in here was too damnably bright, but it was Emma's stinging eyes that reminded her of her priorities. The veil, thankfully, might hide her expression. "You . . ." She did not cough, but she did pause. "You allowed Llewellyn Gwynnfud to take a Great Text from the Collegia Library? The *Principia Draconis*?" She congratulated herself on only sounding mildly surprised. "When was this? I ask, Lord Huston, only to be quite accurate when I make my report."

"Report?" Now Huston was positively chalky. He would have no idea to whom she would make such a report, but the creeping cowardice of petty officialdom ran to his very marrow. The Seal made a scratching noise, the carnelian shifting from a carving of Pegasus to the double serpents of Mordred's time. It was, she reflected, far too large for his fingers.

"Yes." She also wondered – and not for the first time

– precisely which charm he used to colour his hair. The dual thoughts bled her anger away. A dangerous calm closed over her. "When was it, sir?"

"Well, let's see . . . hmmm . . . that is . . ." He tapped the head of his cane with one manicured index finger. "You know, I cannot quite—"

"*Principia Draconis*. Checked out. A fortnight ago exactly," the livrewitch said dreamily. "The Psychometry books were restless that day. So was the Bestiary section. It took some work to calm them. They are not exercised enough."

Huston's expression was priceless. Emma smoothed her gloves. "Thank you. That will be all. Come, Mikal." Dismissive, she set off for the entrance. *Well. A mostly wasted trip. But now I know you are to be mistrusted to an even greater degree than I did before.*

And that is very valuable knowledge.

Her Shield fell into step behind her. There was a sound from above – a student perhaps, witnessing the exchange. This would be round meat indeed for them. Only the almost randomness of Huston's malignancy made a revolt in the student ranks unlikely. Besides, he largely allowed the professors to do as they pleased, and they liked the power so much they kept him firmly seated at the helm of the Collegia.

Or what he believed was the helm.

"Harlot." Whispered just loud enough to be an insult. "*Whore.*"

It was the oldest insult hurled at a sorceress – or indeed, at any woman who did not do what a small man wished. Did he expect it to sting?

If only you knew, you bastard bureaucrat. Other words rose; she considered each one and decided a lady would not speak them, so *she* certainly would not.

Her back was alive with Mikal's nearness. She swept out of the Library with rushing blood filling her ears. Outside, the sorcerously cleansed air still reeked of Londinium's disease. Nevertheless, she stopped and took a deep breath.

"Prima?" Mikal, his tone promising vengeance, should she want it. She would be well within her rights to call Huston to the duelling ground – but she would have only Mikal and a livrewitch for witnesses. It would not do.

She would merely remember this, as she remembered so much else. A Prime's life was long, and she would see Huston falter one day. "Leave it." She did not have to try very hard to sound weary. "He is of little account. Besides, there is another copy of the *Principia*."

"Indeed? Where?"

"At Childe's. Fetch the curricle."

Chapter Twenty-Three

Better Your Sausage Than Your Life

The mystery of Valentinelli's disappearance was solved in spectacular fashion. At least, Clare decided that the body falling from the rafters was intimately connected to the Neapolitan's vanishing, even as he leapt – in a display of agility surprising even himself – and hit Sigmund squarely, knocking the burly Bavarian and his chair over. A tangle of arms and legs, Sig's wurst and cheese went flying, and the body thudded on to the carpet as the grate exploded with blue flame.

Clare freed himself with a violent, wrenching twist, losing his top hat, and made it up to one knee, his freshly loaded silver-chased pepperbox pistol out. Smoke billowed, and Sigmund had regained his breath, to judge by the volume of curses in German coming from his quarter. Already it was difficult to see, smoke stinging Clare's eyes, and for a terrible moment he was swallowed by the memory of last night's irrationality.

LOGIC! he bellowed inwardly, jerking to the side as something whooshed through the smoke near his head. *Smoke, a body from the ceiling – multiple attackers; the Neapolitan may be injured but I think it unlikely. The smoke is to confuse us.*

The motive was not simply murder, he decided. Which raised some interesting questions he had no time to consider, for there was a movement in the smoke. *Too tall to be the Italian, and moving incautiously. Do something, Clare!*

Sigmund was still cursing.

"*Quiet*, man!" Clare barked, and his free hand closed around one of Sig's spanners, dropped next to the spilled chair. He scooped it up and flung it, calculation flashing just under the surface of his consciousness so quickly he was barely aware of the motion. His aim was true; there was a muffled scream of pain, and Clare dived to the side, fetching up against the Bavarian again. "Stay low," he whispered fiercely, and his busy faculties cross-checked an internal dictionary. "*Unten blieben!*"

"*Ja!*" Sig whispered back, and they set off, crawling, away from the coal grate and its belching black smoke. "*Verdammt sie! Meine Wurst!*"

Better your sausage than your life, man! Clare kept the pistol pointed carefully away. "Crawl! *Kriechen!*"

"I remember my English, *mein Herr!*" Damn the man, he actually sounded offended. "My workshop! What do they do with my workshop?"

I only have three shots. Choose them carefully. "Weapons! Do you have any weapons?"

"I haf—" But whatever Sigmund had remained unsaid, for there was a scream and the sound of clattering metal. "No! *Scheisse,* not my *Spinne*! Bastard!"

Clare got a fistful of Sig's jacket, hauling him back. The Bavarian went down in a heap, another dark shape loomed through the acrid smoke, and Clare's hand jerked at the last moment, sending the shot wide.

"*Idioti*." Valentinelli bent down. His shirt was singed, and there was a spatter of blood on one of his pocked cheeks. "Put that away! Come!"

"What is it?" Clare had a fair idea already, but it certainly never hurt to ask.

"*Alterato*." His ruined face alight, the assassin held a knife with the blade reversed against his forearm. There was a dark stain on his left knee, whether grease or blood Clare did not wish to venture. "To capture, not kill. This way."

Flashboys, perhaps. Come to kidnap me or Sig? We shall find out. "Good show. Sig old man—" A fierce whisper. "Sigmund!"

"Aha!" The Bavarian appeared, crawling with surprising nimbleness for such a bulky man; he had found his wurst. He stuffed the remainder of the sausage in his mouth and scrambled after Clare.

The Neapolitan was a wraith in the rapidly thinning smoke, bent almost double and moving with jerky efficiency. One sleeve of his pale shirt flapped slightly; he cast a look over his shoulder at Clare and vanished again, stepping sideways into the vapour. Clare coughed, spat to the side. Bulky metal shapes loomed. Sigmund cursed again, but very low. A scraping sound – Sig had found a weapon.

Good.

His ears strained, eyes burning from the acrid vapour, his left hand scraping on packed earth and scattered straw as he endeavoured to keep the pistol free in his right, Clare realised he had not been bored *once* since Miss Bannon's appearance. Which was truly marvellous, and a relief for his busy faculties, but he could still wish things were not *quite* so bloody interesting.

And why had he thought of her? The crystalline pendant, snug under his shirt, was oddly cold. Was this a dire enough situation to warrant her attention? Probably not. He wished he had thought to find his hat before setting off at a crawl through Sigmund's workshop—

There was a wet crunching noise, and a soft cry. The smoke, draining in whorls and eddies, had lost none of its terrible stench. He motioned Sigmund aside; a huge metal carapace afforded a slightly safer hiding space. Inside, there was a tangle of sharp poking ends, but Clare pressed back nevertheless, and Sig crowded in beside him.

"*Mein Gott*, what smell!" he whispered, and Clare was forced to agree.

"Sulphur and agatesbreath, I believe." *Coal doesn't burn hot enough to ignite it; how did they? Must experiment later.* He readied the pistol, torn metal jabbing his jacket. "Be still."

More soft, stealthy scrapings. A clatter of metal; Sigmund twitched and breathed a rather filthy imprecation. The smoke became striations, behaving oddly, thick and greasy as it slid questing fingers over a broken clockhorse skeleton. The metal vibrated, resonating to a silent current of bloodlust, and Clare watched as a shape melted into view behind a screen of smoke.

He was Altered, but not a flashboy. Lanky, dark-haired, unshaven in ill-fitting grey worsted, he placed his shoes carefully and edged through the smoky fingers, moving with jerky, oily care. The Alteration wasn't visible, but Clare noted the irregularity under the rough homespun workman's shirt and his gorge rose. Limbs were all very well, but Alteration of the trunk of the body? Not only was it expensive and dangerous, it was simply *wrong*.

Sigmund, thankfully, had frozen. Whether he was immobilised by surprise or Teutonic rage was difficult to tell. Clare raised the pistol, the motion slow and dreamlike. The dry stone in his throat was unwelcome; it took effort to shelve the persistent nagging animal fear of being hunted. His mouth was dry, and his pulse pounded alarmingly. His ears heard each muffled beat, blurring together into a distracting roar.

The Altered stiffened, his head tipping back. Valentinelli's face appeared over his shoulder as his knees slowly buckled; the Neapolitan grabbed a fistful of dark hair and dragged the head back further. A swift jerking motion, then he slit the Altered man's throat. Arterial spray bloomed, smoke flinched away, and the assassin breathed a soft love word as the Altered slumped.

Valentinelli flicked the knife, bent down to wipe it on his victim's clothing. Clare lowered his pistol, silver glinting. His head was full of rushing noise.

Why does this disturb me so?

The Neapolitan's gaze was flat and blank. He looked, for all the world, like a man who was simply performing a mildly disagreeable but not very difficult task. "*Bastarde*," he said, softly. "Not even worth pissing on. Come to take Ludo's job away, eh? Not today. Is safer now," he continued, not even bothering to glance at the two men hiding like children. "Come out, little *polli*. Ludo has made it well again."

Acrid smoke thinned. Clare coughed, finding his eyes welling with hot water and his throat afire. "Sig?" he croaked. "Dreadfully sorry about your workshop."

"*Schweine*." The genius pushed past Clare, brushed himself off. He glared at the dead body, and as the smoke cleared, Clare found other lifeless forms scattered throughout the factory. "My beautiful wurst. And my *Spinne*. I hope she not damaged." He fixed Clare with a beady glare. "So, this is the trouble you bring to Papa Baerbarth, my friend? I find you Prussian capacitors. I help you. They pay for this, the *Schweinhunde*."

"Good show. I say, Valentinelli, very good." Clare emerged from the metal carapace, blinking. "Er, who were they after, do you think?" It was vanishingly unlikely they were here for Sig, but thoroughness demanded he ask. And his nerves required a question answered, *any* question, to steady them.

"Simple." The Neapolitan resheathed the knife. "If they after fat one there, I let them have him."

Clare swallowed. The crystalline pendant had warmed again, no longer a chip of cold metal ice under his shirt. His throat was amazingly dry. He could use even some of Sig's atrocious tea. "I see. Well, I thought as much. Sig, fetch your bag. We're going capacitor-hunting. Where do we start?"

Sigmund took his hat from his round head, dusted it fastidiously, and jammed it back on while setting off for the still smoking grate. "Docks. Always start docks first. Tell me *everything*."

The docks of Londinium seethed under a dome of sulphur-yellow fog. Here, the nerve endings of Empire sizzled with goods crated and bundled in every conceivable way, crawling with hevvy-mancers lifting loads or charming them into balance, sorcery spitting and crackling between the mountains of goods of every stripe, shipwitches wandering among them and laying carpets of charter charms. Tabac, indigo, flour, wine, carpets, chests, tea, coffee, cloth of every colour and description, spread and piled high over miles of timber. More hevvymancers charmed loads off the waiting ships, ship- and saltwitches humming in the rigging and calming restive breezes. The non-sorcerous carters, lifters, haulers, bullies, and half-clad ragged men looking to earn a few coins by shifting and hauling milled, choking the streets; warehouses stood tall and proud with Altered guards – some flashboys, others more serious and soberly modified – watching the crowded streets. No doubt many of them had a thriving trade in embezzlement to pay for their Alterations and the servicing of their metal, too.

They left the brougham and its driver at a nearby livery stable, the driver even more ecstatic that the day's work was proving so easy. Pressing forward on foot, Clare and Sigmund were soon lost in the crowd. Valentinelli drifted in their wake, and such was the confusion and clangour of Threadtwist Dockside that none remarked the blood on his clothes. To be sure, in the yellow glare it could be any dark fluid fouling him. Still, Clare found it difficult to look at the man.

Sigmund, still bemoaning the loss of his breakfast, kept up a steady stream of banter the entire way. Clare confined himself to non-committal responses, sunk in profound contemplation. He'd told the Bavarian the absolute minimum required, and they were now en route to a place where the tracing of a specific shipment of Prussian capacitors could begin. Miss Bannon's papers had included an invoice from a certain Lindorm Import Co., Threadtwist Dock, Londinium – an invoice that, when he had examined it after Miss Bannon's morning departure, had borne surprising fruit: a scrawl under "Rec'd of" he had more than a passing familiarity with.

After all, he had seen it many a time at Yton on Cedric Grayson's papers. The Chancellor of the Exchequer was involved indeed, and Clare could not wait to share the news with Miss Bannon. A dragon's word – he shuddered at the thought of the beast, hurried on – might not be acceptable proof to take Cedric to account, but *this* certainly was. And she had possessed it for who knows how long, without knowing its import.

That was satisfying in and of itself.

Chapter Twenty-Four

Never Aesthetically Lacking

Childe lived on Tithe Street; his wife was in Dublin and happy to remain there with his son. Mrs Childe had probably once thought to domesticate the man, but Primes were not easily tamed, especially one of Dorian's stripe. Still, she was a sorcerer's wife now, and did not want for support. At least Childe took care of his own, even if he also threw guineas over the young panthers of Topley like water. Whether he kept Mrs Childe well supplied because she had borne him a son who showed sorcerous promise, or because he had once cared for her, or because it was the decent thing to do, none could say. Emma was most inclined to believe the first, public opinion the second, and none but the extraordinarily naïve held to the last. A small contingent of fashionable opinion aired the view that since Childe was so busy buggering everything that moved, cash sent to Dublin was merely a means of keeping the woman away from his pleasures so she could tend to his son in magnificent seclusion.

Regardless, the Tithe Street house was magnificent; one of Naish's best, terraced and graceful, it rose for four storeys above the wide avenue, a low stone wall curving around it and containing a froth of gardens generally considered to be some of the finest in Londinium. Mikal paused before the gate as the invisible protections resonated – every knot and twist whispering

Childe's name to the extramundane senses, seashell murmurs of a Prime's disturbance in the fabric of the real.

Childe was at home. The defences swept aside, a not-quite-shimmering curtain, grandly theatrical like all his gestures. Mikal guided the high-stepping clockhorses on to the drive.

Emma's cheeks were damp. Achieving the Collegia grounds was one thing, descending was quite another. She blinked furiously, more tears sliding free. The blasted sun, just like everything else, was conspiring to fray her patience today.

Sometimes she wished her Discipline did not give her such an aversion to the daylight. Never for very long, and never very deeply, for on that path lay a danger she was unwilling to court. *A Prime should never doubt his Discipline*, the saying ran. Still, it would have been bloody lovely to be able to produce a Major Work that did not leave her half blind.

The stairs, a sweep of slick gold-veined marble with knife-sharp edges, marched to a huge crimson door. Only Childe would have such a *vulgar* thing. The urns lumbering up the steps held scarlet poppies, their blowsy heads nodding in unison, strangely bleached by the yellow cast of sunlight filtering through the fog. The air was deadly still, though a few stirrings promised rain later, perhaps at Tideturn. It might wash the filthy smell from the city, though Emma doubted it.

Inside, it was blessedly dimmer, the vast arching foyer was lit only by a few shafts of golden sunlight and several hissing witchballs in cages shaped like half-open amaryllis. Childe's long-suffering butler Mr Herndrop bowed, slightly and correctly, as he took the card from Mikal. His indenture collar was lacklustre, but his florid cheeks and nose more than made up for it. "He is in the front parlour, mum. Had quite a night of it."

It is a wonder he is receiving, then. But Childe very rarely turned *her* away. "Thank you, Herndrop. How is your arthritis?"

His chest puffed a little – not that it needed to; Herndrop possessed under his butler's black a barrel organ of a ribcage. "Tolerable, mum, thank you."

Emma nodded; he did not precede her to the parlour. That could be an indicator either of Childe's esteem for her, or of his incredibly foul mood. Or both. Besides, stationed at the door leaned a Shield of surpassing lankiness, his chestnut curls trimmed close but his moustache particularly fine.

"Lewis." Mikal, quiet and polite.

Lewis merely nodded. A flush had begun on his throat; he swallowed visibly. Few Shields would acknowledge Mikal openly now.

Not unless Emma forced them, and today she did not feel the need.

Emma, her skirts gathered and her stride lengthening, made straight for the door – white-painted, gold leaf trimming its rectangular carvings, the knob a carved crystal skull. *That* was a new addition – previously it had been red curtains and a pasha's fancy beyond. "Good heavens," she remarked, "I almost shudder to think of what's behind the door *this* time."

"Mum." Lewis sounded half strangled, but he reached for the knob anyway. Mikal did *not* let loose an amused half-chuckle, but it was very close.

The door swept open, bright light stung her eyes afresh, but Emma reached up to pull aside her veil. Childe had redecorated in bordello blue, with a French twist, Louis *L'Etat Quatorze* with curlicues, slim-legged tables, ormolu, and overstuffed furniture. Leaning on the mantel was a young man; Emma took him in at a glance and sighed internally. The loud coat, soft white hands, and scented hair all screamed a St Georgeth panther, brought home with Childe's usual utter lack of propriety or even good sense. This particular one had a fresh face still clinging to youth, but the sullen expression – no doubt charming when he was a lad – marred whatever remained of his attractiveness. He gave Emma an insouciant look, curling his lip and his little finger, and she suppressed a flash of irritation.

"*Well!*" Dorian Childe, sleek-haired, heavy-lipped, and one of the more powerful Primes of the Empire, was in a violently patterned green and black kimono, but his toilette was otherwise immaculate. "If it isn't my dearest Emma. Are you here for tea, or is this another of your flying visits?"

Emma gave him her hands, an unwonted smile curving her lips. A tear trickled from the corner of her right eye, and he *tut-tut*ted. "How silly of me. Here, darling—" A Minor Word slid free of his mouth, his lips shaping the sibilants sensually, and the indigo drapes freed themselves from their ropes, falling gracefully across the windows. The witchballs darkened, and the young man at the fireplace shivered. "Is that better? You must have had a morning of it. Come, sit down."

"I am here to plunder your library, Dorian. I see you've redecorated."

"You hate it, I can tell. Not all of us have your restraint, my darling. Still carrying your baggage around, I see." But his bright darted glance at Mikal held no malice. Just predatory interest, and Emma did not miss the reined distaste spreading from her Shield.

"Oh, don't start." Her shoulders relaxed, fractionally. Childe, at least, was a monster whose loyalty was not in question. Rather like a gryphon. "I saw Huston this morning. Do you know what charm he uses to colour his hair?"

"Whatever it is, I am certain it's dreadful. Do come and sit down; the library can wait a few moments while you refresh yourself. Paul, be a dear and fetch some tea. Cook knows what we like."

"I ent yer lady's maid," the panther at the fireplace sneered, but he peeled himself fully upright and slouched towards the door.

"Delicious, isn't he?" Childe stage-whispered. "And so tractable. At least, at this stage."

"You'll get a knife in the ribs one of these days," Emma murmured, as the tractable Paul banged the parlour door shut. "Where are your Shields?"

Childe magnanimously didn't note that said knife would have

to be applied while he was insensible not to earn its wielder a terrible sorcerous death, but the arch of his eyebrows and flare of his nostrils remarked for him. "Oh, around and about. You're a fine one to talk. I could give you Lewis, he's grown quite disapproving. Or even Eli. A lovely young thing like yourself shouldn't be wandering alone."

"Do I want the responsibility of another Shield? They require care and feeding, you know." *Eli. I remember him. Dark, and very quiet. He was with Alice Brightly, but she returned him to the Collegia. If he's returned again, it might be unpleasant.* "You've grown tired of Eli, then?"

"No, he's just so *serene* all the time. It interferes with my jollities. So, darling, my library. What are you after? A little bit of flash? Something no respectable girl should be reading? A novel or two?"

She restrained herself from remarking that she wished she had time to read the novels gathering dust on her nightstand. "Actually, I am after a Great Text. *Pricipia Draconis*. You have, I seem to recall, a rather fine edition."

"And you were at the Collegia earlier. Which means their copy has gone missing. How interesting." Childe's eyes all but sparkled. "My dear, what would you say if I told you that barely a fortnight ago, a dreadful little Master Sorcerer came with a letter from someone very important, asking me ever so nicely if I'd loan out my *Principia*?"

Emma blinked. *I wonder.* "Ah. It wouldn't by any chance be a rather slovenly fellow by the name of Devon, would it?"

"You've been divining, my dear." Childe's interest mounted another notch. "Can you guess who the letter was from?"

Llewellyn? She pretended to think it over, tapping at her lips with a gloved finger. "Hmmm. Would it be, by chance, Gwynnfud? Lord Sellwyth himself?"

"Oh no, darling. No indeed." Childe looked delighted to have feinted so successfully. He actually clapped his well-manicured hands, dropping into a chair as soon as Emma was settled on a settee swathed in gold-embroidered blue silk. "'Twas a wonder of penmanship from a certain Sir Conroy."

Conroy? The Duchess's hangman. The Duchess – the Queen's mother. Oh, dear God. Emma did not sway, though the world rocked slightly underneath her. "The comptroller? What use would he have for it?"

"Her Royal Matronliness herself, the Duchess of Kent, wished to peruse it." Childe positively wriggled with delight. "Oh, I've surprised you. How *delicious*. Tell me, is it high intrigue? Was I right to graciously refuse? I told Devon I couldn't *possibly* loan it, as it is a Great Text, but the Duchess was *more than welcome* to visit, at her convenience, to peruse it. At her leisure, too."

Emma was cold all over now. If she had to reappraise Childe's loyalty, this would be a dire situation indeed. "Did she ever accept your invitation?"

"No. Devon looked like he'd swallowed a stoat. After, of course, it had desperately battled with his hair. I tell you, darling, he could be so fetching if he simply took some care with his appearance."

"Intriguing." The relief of not having to suspect him was only matched in its intensity by fresh alarm. *How far is the Duchess involved? Or is it merely Conroy? Where he is, she isn't far behind, and she would like nothing better than to embarrass the Queen into compliance again.*

"No, he's rather boring, but he'd be decorative." Childe snorted.

"Not to my taste. What *precisely* did Devon say after you denied Her Majesty's darling mother the use of your *Principia*?" A touch of sarcasm here, for she knew it would please him.

So it did. His face lit with an expression of dawning *Schadenfreude*. "It *is* intrigue, then! You are never boring, my dear. He gave me to understand the Duchess would be most piqued at my refusal; I replied that I didn't care a fart in a windstorm – shocking I know, but he annoyed me; don't *laugh* so – if she was piqued or if she sang an entire aria in the water closet. Then the little hedge-charmer had the sheer effrontery to ask if he could *see* the book! I informed him I am not a lending library and the Collegia library is open for Master Sorcerers just as for Primes, though not, of course, at the same *time*." He almost wriggled with delight with the memory of the insult implied to Devon's status. "Did I do right, darling?"

"Oh, absolutely." Emma settled herself more firmly in her chair. "If I ask very nicely, Dorian dear, will you allow me to peruse the *Principia*?"

"My most enchanting Emma, you could set the damn thing on fire page by page in my bedroom while watching me disport with one of those boys you so highly disapprove of. *You*, at least, are never impolite *or* aesthetically lacking." He panto-mimed a yawn. "But first let's have some tea. And really, darling, I was about to return Eli to the Collegia and pick out a more *active* Shield. Do you want him?"

Emma's heart pounded in her ears. Another Shield would not be a bad idea at all, in light of this news. She could not risk returning to the Collegia and publicly taking more of them into service, and Eli would no doubt be glad not to return to the Shields' dormitories in almost disgrace. "Yes." She folded her hands in her lap. "Yes, I rather think I do."

It was, she decided, probably a mercy she could not see Mikal's face.

After a very satisfying cup of tea, Dorian left her in his library, one of the few rooms he had never redone since his father had left him a good address and sorcerous ability but precious little else. Whether the room was left alone because Childe saw no need to alter it, or because he spent very little time among the rare texts he collected so assiduously, was a mystery Emma felt no need to solve.

Two storeys high, the ceiling frescoed with Grecque gods cavorting among pale nymphs, the library was dark heavy wood, comfortable leather furniture that had belonged to Dorian's father, a healthy fire in the grate, maroon drapes pulled against daylight. She breathed in the scent of paper, dust, old leather, smoky sorcery, and her shoulders eased still further. The other Prime was bursting with curiosity, and she had told him as much as she dared. The rumours he would start would be priceless in sowing confusion among her enemies.

At least Mikal waited until they were alone.

"Another Shield, my Prima?"

She turned away from the shelf, the *Principia Draconis* in her arms. It was a leather-bound monstrosity; this edition lacked Wilson's gloss, but she didn't think it would matter much. Wilson had simply cleaned up some of the archaisms. "I think it wise, if the Duchess of Kent and her hangman are involved. And I wondered where our conspirators received their money."

"Can you trust a Shield from *his* service?"

"Childe is loyal." *He has a great deal to lose under the sodomy laws if he dares to be anything less.* "And Eli is capable, from what I recall. Top of his year-class at the Collegia, rather as you were. Did you not recently seek to have me take on the responsibility of more Shields?"

He quieted, but the set of his chin was mulishly defiant. Emma sighed, hauling the book towards her usual table. The thing was as long as her own torso, and beastly heavy. Mikal let her take two steps before arriving to subtract the book from her arms. Surprised by its weight, he exhaled, shifted backwards and turned; she trailed behind, her skirts making a low, sweet sound.

The glow she had felt just before Tideturn, waking in his arms and feeling the rough texture of his skin against her back, was all but gone.

I am Prime, she reminded herself. *It is his duty. And I shall not make the mistake of acting like a silly girl over this.*

And yet. "Mikal—"

"Well enough. As long as he is *capable*." The *Principia* thudded on to a small rosewood table, and she winced.

"That is a Great Text, Shield. Pray do not injure it."

"Certainly. If you will take care not to injure *yourself*."

"I am taking on an additional Shield, Mikal. One who will be glad of my service instead of Childe's, perhaps, and one who may have learned restraint and obedience." She tucked her veil aside, unnecessarily; it was still securely fastened. "Perhaps he can show you the value of such."

"Perhaps." He turned away. "Will he share your bed too, Prima?"

Is that it? For a moment, the silence was full of a resonant un-noise, as if the books had taken a collective breath after witnessing a sharp slap. Heat crawled up Emma's throat, stained her cheeks. Had he just called her a whore, too? From Huston, she had expected it.

I am Prime. Your petty rules do not apply to me.

But it did not salve the sting. Why should she care what a Shield thought?

Because he is not merely a Shield, Emma. He is Mikal, and you are perhaps more grateful to him for saving your life and killing Crawford than you should be.

She composed herself, took a deep breath, and sank into the chair. Her gloved hand passed over the *Principia*'s cover, and the two locks holding the book closed clicked. Green with age, they flew apart as if they had never intended to stay clasped. Sorcerous force rose, Emma's left hand flashing forward to curl around a slippery, not-quite-tangible armoured eel, as the book tested her will. It subsided quickly – after all, like every book, the Great Texts *wanted* to be read.

When she was certain the *Principia* knew who held the reins, she delicately lifted the heavy cover. Thick pages riffled.

"Prima." Mikal sounded oddly breathless. "I am—"

About to apologise? That would imply I have taken insult, and from a Shield, no less. "I have no wish to hear you speak." Her welling eyes fixed themselves on the *Principia*. Ink writhed, and the writing became clear. Serpentine illustrations flowed like water, bordering each page. She leaned closer, and breathed her query across the pages.

"*Vortisssss.*" The name trailed into a hiss, and the *Principia*'s pages riffled more quickly. A hot breeze lifted, touching her hair, fingering the entire library. The curtains rippled, paper on the gigantic desk near the fireplace stirred, the bronze-caged witchballs sizzled and turned bloody. Above the fireplace, a heavy-framed oil painting of Childe's father glowered, and the dark coat the man was encased in was suddenly alive with golden traceries of charter charm.

The pages slowed, the *Principia* humming as it woke fully and sought within itself. Finally they stilled, and Emma leaned slightly back, blinking back hot saltwater. Her throat was full.

The flush of anger and pain turned to ice. A cold metallic finger traced her spine. She had to swallow twice before she could clear her throat, not from hurt, but from another emotion entirely.

Two pages. On the left side, a woodcut of a vast black wyrm, triple-winged and infinite horned, wrapped about a hill with a white tower. On the right, closely packed calligraphy, the ink still remembering the quill that had spread it. The words runnelled together before her will flexed, then cleared. At the top of the page, gold leaf trembled as it shaped a word.

Vortis was merely a use-name. Emma's entire body quivered, and her earrings swung, tapping her cheeks uneasily. The cameo at her throat warmed, and she dimly heard the door open, Mikal saying something. Her well-trained memory dilated, the book speaking to her in its ancient language, her lips moving as the world hushed around her, motes of golden dust hanging suspended and the witchballs pausing in their spluttering hisses.

She was not one for prayer, except the fashionable sort uttered at conventional moments; besides, sorceresses were doubly damned by every church, Roman, Englican, or otherwise. But had she been the pious sort, Emma thought hazily, she might well start praying.

Vortis cruca esth, Mehitabel had hissed.

The *Principia* slammed shut, locks thudding closed. Emma

blinked. Her cheeks were crusted with salt, and her stomach rumbled. How much time had she lost, gazing at the pages, intuition and intellect communing directly with the Text?

Mikal's hand closed around her shoulder. "You are at Childe's, in Tithe Street. It is almost Tideturn." Did he sound ashamed? Did she care?

At the door stood another Shield. Dark-haired, a trifle shorter than Mikal but a little broader in the shoulder, a Bowie knife worn openly at his hip and his eyes closed. His features were even, regular, and as she shuddered, fully waking, his own eyes opened. He shifted forward incrementally, his mouth firmed. He looked just like a quick-fingered Liverpool bravo, though Childe, with his usual irritating attention to detail, had him in a flashy waistcoat over a fine white high-collared shirt. At least his cloth was good, even if the boots looked dreadfully impractical.

For a moment she could not remember who or what she was. It flooded back, and she shuddered again. Mikal's fingers tensed. She did not need the pain to steady herself, though the Duchess of Kent had suddenly become rather a small problem indeed.

Vortis cruca esth.

Or, if you did not speak the wyrm's slow sonorous hiss . . . *Vortigern will rise.*

Chapter Twenty-Five

Throckmorton, I Presume

As chance would have it, Sig's acquaintance Becker had lodgings near Thrushneedle Dock, a mean hole reeking of cabbage and gin but cleaner than one would suppose. There was much cheerful swearing in heavy German, Sigmund slapped the young hevvymancer's back, and glasses of beer were produced.

Becker was lean, in a hevvymancer's traditional red bracers and herringbone wool cap, heavy boots and a wide smile missing his front left canine. Perhaps he hated toothcharmers too, or could not afford one. Clare surmised that most of the young man's money went to his ailing mother in a lumpen shawl, who shuffled between the single cot and the ancient stove, poking at a pot of boiling something and gazing at her only surviving son with weak, misty eyes. The woman spoke no English, but Becker had been born in Londinium, and a good thing it was too. Had he been born in Germany itself, his hevvymancing would be unreliable here, and both of them might starve.

"Lindorm," Becker said, finally, standing because he had pressed Clare to take the only chair. Valentinelli stood by the door, examining his fingernails; the room was far too small for four males and the old woman's skirts. "*Ja*. Only open a fortnight and odd, taking deliveries." His accent was a mixture of his mother tongue and pure dockside nasal, a song of the displaced.

"We wondered. But they paid good bounty on Prussians, so they raked 'em in. No use sitting about when's shill'n to be earned."

"What bounty did they pay?" Clare settled himself carefully. The chair was alarmingly fragile, not to mention fusty, and the floor sloped.

"Two bob apiece, more for more. Heps over at Mockgale, he brought crates o' them, got a pound apiece. That fair made it scruth. Every jack and hevvy scramblin t' sell any bit o'metal an shine could be called Pruss." Becker's face twisted; he removed his cap and scratched along his hairline. "Made out fair m'self, I did. But legal-like."

Oh, certainly. And I am a monkey's waistcoat. "I am quite sure you were entirely legal. So, Lindorm closed after a fortnight and a few days?"

"Aye. 'Twixt one Turn and the next, pop! Gone like a skipper's goodwill. Never quite right, that place. We smells the odd, we do, and there was mancy there. Big, not like a hevvy or a shipwitch. Lord magic, that was. High'n mighty."

"Most curious. Who is buying Prussian capacitors now?"

"Naught. Some gents like to tear their own hair out waiting; some says they're in France somewhere, others say held up in the Low, one or two wot might know says the Pruss factories holdin 'em. Frenchie glassers and Hopkins shinies selling hand over fist now, since Prussians ent to be had."

Clare's eyelids dropped to half-mast; his thin fingers steepled under his proud long nose. Sigmund peered longingly toward the cauldron at the stove; Frau Becker muttered something and waved a wooden spoon as she advanced, menacing.

Sigmund sighed, heavily.

Clare absorbed the implications of young Becker's tale. "Would you happen to know where Lindorm sent the capacitors they had?"

"Oh, 'tis easy, guv." Becker's lean chest puffed, and he stuck his thumbs under his bracers. "Hired a crew of hevvy to charm a load of waggon, drays and all, four days' wages for two day haulin' to St Cat's, in the Shadow. Big warehouse there, black as sin, 'twas."

"Did you take advantage of this easy work?"

"Weren't *nuffink* easy 'bout it, sir. Nags were restless, loads kept slippin', heavy as churchman's purse each crate and bell. Each hevvy *earned* that two pound, sir."

"I see. Well, what particulars can you tell me of the gentlemen engaging your services?"

On this Becker was no fountain of knowledge; the work had simply been available, and he had taken it. By the time Clare had finished questioning and paid the man for his trouble – two guineas, part of the purse thoughtfully supplied by Miss Bannon that very morning against just such an eventuality – he was almost feeling cautiously cheerful. Becker gave one of the coins to his mother, who held it up and bit at it, though she was lacking teeth; the young man assured him that should he ever need a hevvy, Becker was *sienen Mann, ja.*

Outside, the street was still as throbbing-active as ever, carts rumbling by, hevvymancers chanting a song of harsh consonants and sliding nasal vowels. A line of yellow glare fell against the wall opposite, broken only by the low doors of public houses vying for trade, rollicking even at this early hour. A heavy-bearded Jack, fresh from the sea by the roll in his drunken gait, stumbled to a stop and began heaving up a mess of gin and somewhat else, to the amusement of passers-by and the great delight of a pair of ragged, bony curs, who immediately began lapping at the offal.

The Neapolitan, however, was not in the mood for sightseeing. He grabbed Clare's elbow. "Eh, *signor*, you are not planning a visit to *la Torre*?"

"If I must. Into the belly of Hell itself, Mr Valentinelli. Britannia is in need, and this is passing interesting."

"*La strega* said nothing about *la Torre*."

"If you feel yourself incapable, *signor*, by all means depart." Clare jammed his hat more firmly on his head. "Sig! Old man, find us some repast and a decent place to smoke a pipe. I must think."

But Valentinelli gripped his arm even more firmly. "You insult me."

If I had, sir, you would already be attempting to kill me, blood oath or no. "By no means, *signor*. Do you know what the most incredible part of young Becker's tale is?"

The Neapolitan's answering oath expressed that he cared not a whit, and Sigmund's florid face was suddenly drawn and grey as he witnessed this. The worthy Bavarian's hand was hidden in his coat pocket, probably preparatory to bringing forth his trusty clasp knife, and Clare decided he had best smooth the waters. People were so *difficult*.

"The incredible part, sir, is that young Becker is still alive." He met Valentinelli's gaze squarely. "Which means the feared Shadow of the Tower of Londinium is the least of our worries, for our greatest is whoever may be watching a hevvymancer or two, to see if they speak. Or to pay them for reporting any enquiries made about a certain load of goods. Or – and this is the idea I find most unsettling, sir – their plan is so near fruition they care very little about any hound on their trail."

The assassin halted. His pocked face was still and set, but the rigidity of his jaw had eased, and so did his hand upon Clare's arm.

Clare nodded, once. "You see. Very good. Come, my noble Neapolitan. I do need to think, and I'd prefer to do it somewhere a touch more comfortable." He paused. "And perhaps more defensible as well."

The Tower of Londinium was actually a collection of towers, held back from crashing down on the city by the grey arms of the Sorrowswall clutching at each rising spire. The White Tower rose above them all, sorcerously sheathed in glittering pale marble, bloody-hued charter symbols sliding in rivulets down its sides. Traitors met their end here, and those criminals judged too noble to be hanged at a common gaol. The fetid moat ran with murky oilsheen, and under its surface rippled . . . something. Rumour hotly disputed what beast it was, but all agreed it ate the bodies after the beheadings, and the heads sometimes after the showing.

And, occasionally, it took live prey.

But it wasn't the Dweller in the Moat Londinium's masses feared. It was the Shadow.

Sometimes it wreathed the towers, slinking along the walls, slithering down to brush the surface of the moat's oily water. It was not fog, or cloud – it was simply dark dank grey, and it prowled the neighbourhood of the Tower as a silent lumbering beast. Charm and charter did not hold it back – only a Master Sorcerer or above could make it seek elsewhere, by some means they kept hidden behind closed mouths.

Sorcerers disliked the Tower's environs too – the misery and death soaking it, perhaps. The quietest places in Londinium were under the Shadow's heel. Still, there were those who sought it as a sanctuary – those who needed to be certain of the law's reluctance to follow them.

Or those whose Alterations had gone badly. It was against the Tower's walls that the Morloks lived. During the day, one did not need to fear them overmuch.

Fortunately, the Shadow's grey bulk was clinging raggedly to the White Tower as the afternoon's yellow glare wore on. The light through the fog had deepened, the northern quarter of the sky bruising with weather approaching. It might almost, Clare thought, be a relief if rain would sweep in. Except in rainy weather, one could not be so sure of the Shadow's movements.

The warehouse Becker had described on Lower Themis Street, the Sorrowswall visible even over its bulk, was indeed black. Clare studied the structure as Sigmund burped contentedly. Feeding the Bavarian to make up for his thwarted breakfast had also given the mentath an opportunity to collect himself and smoke his pipe, and Valentinelli had applied himself to a quantity of coarse fare at a run-down public house a good distance from Becker's lodging. The dark, crowded interior had not been ideal, but at least Clare had gathered his wits and forced the spectre of agitation threatening his nerves away for a short while. The brougham driver would not approach the Tower this closely, and was left a few streets away, well satisfied with a tot of gin and a generously packed basket of dinner purchased at the pub with more of Miss Bannon's guineas.

The warehouse's stone walls had perhaps once been grey, but a patina of coal dust had packed itself on the rough surfaces. Normally the rain would streak such a building with runnels of acid-eaten paleness, but as Clare gazed, he caught a shimmer in the air around it.

Sorcery.

Valentinelli had either noticed it at the same moment he did, or waited for Clare's expression to change. "*Maleficia.*" His pocked face wadded itself up theatrically. "We wait for *la strega, ci?*"

"Miss Bannon has other difficulties." Clare did not see any reason to tell the assassin of the conclusions he had reached concerning Miss Bannon's likely availability to appear and deal with problems of a sorcerous nature. "Do you think we may enter that building? Is it possible?"

Valentinelli squinted. "*Ci.*" He rubbed at his forearm, meditatively, and Clare deduced there was a knife hidden in his sleeve. "But not for long, eh? Is work of large, very big *stregone*. Very nasty."

"Oh, I thought as much." Clare tapped at his left-hand breeches pocket, almost unaware of the motion. The tiny metal box of coja was safely stowed, and he felt soothed, even if the pendant under his throat was warming alarmingly. "Sig, this may be a bit dodgy. Are you sure you—"

"I go home, *mein Herr*, perhaps they try again? And not so politely." The Bavarian rolled his broad shoulders back in their sockets. "Is very interesting, this business of capacitors."

"Oh, very interesting indeed. Well, gentlemen, no time like the present."

Forcing a door was almost anticlimactic. Valentinelli sniffed, declared the shimmer in the air only dangerous to sorcerers, and stepped through. Two kicks and rotted wood shattered, he peered inside. "Eh. Come."

They plunged into a thick dimness, the dust and the smell of oiled metal mixing with an odd reek. The pendant was red-hot now; logic told Clare it would not burn him, and he kept his hand away from his chest with an effort. Sigmund choked back a series of mighty sneezes, managing to be almost as loud as if he had allowed them free rein. A close, clotted-dark hallway led along the outer wall for ten paces, then abruptly terminated, and the warehouse space bloomed, lit only by a few weak shafts of yellow Londinium glow stabbing down from high, papered holes in the roof.

They stood in serried ranks, each shrouded in canvas, slump-shouldered shapes three times as high as a man and broad as a shay. Two protuberances gleaming of metal peeked out from under each sheet of canvas, and Clare blinked fiercely, deducing. *I wonder—*

But there was no time for wondering. There was a fluttering motion atop one of the mysterious shapes. A small, definite click echoed through the dimness, and an unfamiliar male voice broke the hush.

"Move, and I shoot."

Clare's smile was broad – and, he hoped, invisible in the bad lighting. He lifted his own pistol, and noted, without any surprise at all, that Valentinelli had once again disappeared. "Mr Cecil J. Throckmorton, I presume?"

Chapter Twenty-Six

Introductions Can Wait

The curricle was left at Childe's excellent stable, and Bannon was glad she'd found her fellow Prime in a good mood. For not only did she have another Shield, but Childe had also pressed the use of a smart ivy-coloured landaulet on her; drawn by white and silver clockhorses, it was a darling little vehicle that had an absolutely bone-rattling ride. It mattered little at this speed.

For she had a rather pressing idea that Clare was in some trouble. The Bocannon she had given him was uneasy, scenting harmful sorcery in his vicinity and twitching the fine invisible thread tied to her consciousness. Which meant that, like a dach's-hund down a rathole, Archibald Clare had flushed prey she was interested in and would soon have a snout in dire danger of clawmarks.

Eli drove, and handled the carriage rather well. "Serene" was an understatement – the Shield looked half asleep, and only the grip of his hands on the reins betrayed him as, indeed, alert. His hair combed back from his face in the sulphurous breeze, the air bringing colour to his cheeks, and Mikal on her other side was a red and black thundercloud of tightly leashed frustration.

Serves him right. But she could not fault him overmuch. She was, indeed, a spectacular failure at femininity – except in the area of weakness. For last night had been merely that. Had she been born a man . . .

What? Had you been born a man, you would be Llewellyn. That is what drew you to him, was it not? Deep down, Emma, you do not care.

Then why did she put herself to this trouble?

Enough. Think of what you will do when you reach the man you sent scurrying off with only Valentinelli to protect him. The situation has changed somewhat, even without the addition of a dragon so old he slept even before the Age of Flame. If the Duchess and Conroy have their fingers in this, it is not likely to end well. Victrix will not thank me if I injure – or, God forbid, murder – her mother, even if she hates the woman and Britannia would more than likely approve.

The thin, fine invisible thread twitched again, more definitely this time. Her gloved hand flashed out, and a witchball sizzled into being. Her concentration narrowed as the globe of brilliance sped forward, settling in front of the clockhorses. Stray sparks of sorcery crackled, and traffic on the avenue drew away like water retreating from oil. Eli's chin dipped slightly, a fractional nod, and Emma settled back, impatience thinly controlled as the Shield piloted the juddering vehicle in the witchball's wake. The invisible strand twitched once more, more definitely, and the Bocannon she had given the mentath woke fully.

Clare was indeed in a great deal of trouble. Tideturn was approaching, and traffic was thick. Even with a Shield pressing the horses onwards and a free witchball before them warning all Londinium that a sorcerer was in a hurry, she would likely be too late.

The warehouse slumped under a bruise-ugly yellowgreen sky, banks of opaque fog drawing back as thunder rumbled uneasily. A storm coming up the Themis, perhaps, or a deeper unsettling. The elegant, powerful shell of sorcery laid over the building to disguise it would have been enough to make Emma's gaze simply slide past – if the Bocannon had not already been inside, and had she not been gripping Mikal's arm so tightly her fingers ached.

There!

The witchball sizzled, gathering momentum as Eli hauled back on the reins, Mikal flowing half upright, the veil plastered to Emma's damp face and stormlight prickling her tender eyes. Thunder rattled again, far to the north. The witchball arrowed forward, splashing into the glimmering not-quite-visible shield over the slumping warehouse, and fine silver traceries flashed, digging into the coaldust-sheathed sides. The horses pranced, more sparks snapping, and the landaulet jolted to a stop. Emma was already moving, gathering her skirts, and Mikal had anticipated her. His boots hit the hard-packed dirt, he turned; his hands were at her waist and he lifted her down in one motion.

"Clare!" she snapped. "*Find* him, and protect him!"

A single yellow-fuming glance, and he was gone. One of the smaller warehouse doors had been broken in – Valentinelli, she would lay money on it – and the other Shield was suddenly beside her as she ran breathlessly in Mikal's wake.

The building shuddered as the defences on it woke fully, cracks veining the coaldust casing as she fed more force through the erstwhile witchball. An unsecured globe of sorcerous energy was difficult to control – but it was also plastic, and it reacted to the sudden cramping of the defences with a vengeance. Londinium fog flushed as the sun dipped, another peal of thunder resounded, and the coaldust cracked, shivering away from grey stone just before Mikal nipped smartly through the door in search of Clare.

Emma plunged into a close, stinking passageway, her eyes suddenly relieved of the burden of bright light and picking out details in the flimsy wooden walls. She skidded out into the warehouse itself, her skirts all but snapping as Eli's hand closed around her arm and gave a terrific, shoulder-popping yank.

The Shield pivoted, pulling her to the side as something

crashed into the wooden archway they had just cleared. The earth shook, and Emma groped to find the source of the attack. It was not sorcerous, she realised, just as Eli shoved her aside again and gave a short sharp yell.

What in God's—

It rose from wooden wreckage, gleaming and mechanical, its oddly articulated arms creaking as the man closed in its casing let out a piercing shriek of unholy glee. Emma screamed, terror seizing her, and sorcerous force struck. It was a blind, instinctive assault, force spent recklessly, and it had precious little effect.

The mechanical casing hunched, eerily mimicking the movements of the man inside it. The head was a smooth dome, its shoulders high so it shambled and slouched; its feet were oval cups. Cogs whirred and ground. Oil dripped from shining metal, and the thing screeched like a hound from brimstoned Hell.

The man shook his head, cogs sparking and grinding as the casing's domed top replicated the movement. It looked like a squat, bronze bald frog, especially as the controller sank back and it bent its oversized knees. The arms came up, fuming smoke pouring from the left, and a large hole pointed straight at her.

"*Hiiiiiii!*" The yell came from a human throat, but a grinding rumble swallowed the last of it. A metallic gleam lurched, and Emma's faculties almost deserted her as a second monstrosity shambled forward, its stubby arms rising in a weirdly graceful arc. The first thing's left-hand barrel was knocked skywards, a deafening roar sounded, and a hole opened in the roof. Stormlight poured in, and the sorcerous defences cracked yet further, sagging.

Emma backpedalled blindly, scrambling, her legs tangled in her skirts and her veil torn, her hat knocked askew, curls falling in her face. Eli yanked her again, and her abused shoulder flared with dull red pain. She realised she was screaming, could not help herself. The *thing* was not sorcerous; her mental grasp could not close around it and crush it. It simply shunted the force aside, spending it uselessly, and fresh terror clawed at her vitals.

The right-hand barrel lowered, pointing at her. The man inside the casing laughed, shrilly. There was a flicker of movement, bright knives lifted, and Mikal's feet slipped, seeking vainly for purchase on the thing's domed head. He fell, but twisted catlike in mid-air, and the knives flashed again as he drove both at the chest of the thing's internal rider. They missed, one skittering across the glowing golden disc; it cracked and fizzed, bleeding sparks.

The second metal abomination staggered, its dome head swivelling. But it lurched forward, and knocked aside the second gun just as it spoke.

Confusion. A massive noise, a geyser of dirt and splinters. And something else, invisible threads tightening.

The sorcerer was in the shadows, and she could sense his Shields. She recognised him just as Mikal hit the ground, curling and springing up. She saw messy tangled hair, fingers curled into a half-recognised Gesture, charter symbols spitting venomous crimson as they roiled between his palms.

Kill his Shields. Don't kill him. You need him alive for questioning, and he is only—

But before she could finish the thought, he cast the bolt of crimson charter charm. He could not have expected it to hold her or even damage her, for he immediately lunged backwards – but Eli knocked into her from the side as a flash of gunpowder igniting added to the confusion, driving the breath from her in a sharp huff and killing the chant rising to her lips.

One of the sorcerer's Shields had fired a pistol. And Mikal was otherwise occupied.

Gears screeched, grinding, and the falling-cathedral noise of a sorcerer's death filled the factory. *No! No, don't kill him, I need him for questioning, Mikal!*

Something atop her, pressing down. She struggled, treacherous skirts suddenly chains, her wrists caught in a bruising grip. "*Pax!*" someone yelled in her ear, her head ringing and swimming. "*Pax, Prima!*"

She went limp, ribs flickering as they heaved with deep drilling breaths.

What was that? Dear God, what was that?

Eli rolled aside, and as he pulled her to her feet Emma stared at the slumped mountain of metal. Its chest was empty now, the golden circle dead and cracked, lifeless. Shouts and clashing metal, Mikal's hissing battle cry rising over the din.

The second *thing* clicked, humming as its arms lowered, and Archibald Clare, his lean face alight with glee, hung inside its chest. It replicated his movements uncannily, a glowing golden circle strapped to his chest like a flat witch-ball. The glow threw his features into sharp relief, his hair blew back, and the metal structure around him creaked and shuddered.

The circle of light dimmed. Mikal appeared, glanced at Clare inside the metal abomination, visibly decided he was not a threat, and turned on his heel. Stopped, staring at Emma, whose knees were decidedly *not* performing their function of holding her up with their usual aplomb and reliability. Eli held her arm, not hard but very definitely, bracing her.

The light at Clare's chest snuffed itself. "*Most . . .*" The mentath's speech slurred. "Most intrig— Oh, *hell.*"

Ludovico Valentinelli, singed and bleeding, appeared out of the gloom. A stolid older man with massive side whiskers also appeared, and Emma blinked. *What in God's name just happened here? What are those . . . things?*

"Sig!" Clare sounded drunk, or perhaps so exhausted his lips were numb. "Come . . . damn straps, man. Help me."

"*Ja.*" The stranger, his whiskers half singed as well, climbed *up* the metal man-thing with quick dexterity. He began fiddling with the straps holding Clare inside it, and the mentath sighed wearily, closing his blue eyes.

Emma told herself firmly that now was *not* the time to engage in a screaming fit, or a swoon, though both would indeed be very welcome.

"Are you well?" Mikal was suddenly before her, his face inches from hers. "Prima? *Emma?*"

"Sorcery does not affect it," she managed, in nothing like her usual tone. "Dear gods. Sorcery did not even *touch* it."

That caught Clare's attention. "Rather . . . regrettable . . . side effect." The words slurred together alarmingly. Had the man been at gin? If he had, Emma rather hoped he had saved some. She could do with a tot of something stronger than tea at the moment.

Leather creaked, and the man with side whiskers cursed under his breath. Valentinelli peered up at the twisted ruin of the other metal monster, whistling low and tunelessly.

"Here." Mikal had a flask, held it to her lips. Rum burned; she took a grateful swallow. Her eyes stung, and it was a good thing Tideturn was soon. She had expended a truly ridiculous amount of ætheric charge on the thing, and it had not even affected it.

There were shapes under canvas standing in serried ranks all through the building's maw. They were all roughly the same size and shape as the mechanisterum abominations uncloaked before her. She took another long swallow of fiery liquid; it burned all the way down, and she handed the flask back to Mikal with numb fingers.

And . . . yes, her sensitised eyes pierced the gloom with little trouble. There was a body on the floor. She studied it and breathed a *most* impolite term. "That . . . is Devon. Hugh Devon." She sounded half witless, even to herself. "I needed him for questioning . . . oh, blast and bother and *Hellfire*."

"Rather . . . changes things." Clare almost fell; the side-whiskered stranger braced him, and they negotiated the distance to the ground more gracefully than seemed possible, given Clare's slurring and the portly stranger's girth. "Miss . . . Bannon. We need . . . to talk."

"Well, *rather*." The irritation was a tonic; she braced her fists on her hips and tilted her head. Whoever had been inside the wrecked abomination had made good his escape; *that* was an annoyance as well. "Someone will be along soon to see this mess. I suggest we repair to a far more suitable location. Where on earth is the brougham I engaged to—"

"*Strega*. I take them." Valentinelli did not turn away from the corpse. "What we do with body, eh?"

Clare leaned on his stout friend. The sulphurous glow sliding through the holes in the roof dimmed, and Emma did not like that, despite the comfort it afforded her aching eyes.

"Well, if he was alive I could question him." She tapped one gloved finger against her lips. *I sound as if my nerves are steady. Thank God. Who was in that . . . thing? And Devon, dead.*

"I broke his neck. But his head is still intact." Mikal's tone could best be described as *sullen*.

Well, there is that. "Ah. Yes. I see." She decided. "Very well, bring him. Ludovico, do take Mr Clare and his companion to my home. Formal introductions can wait until we are not *here*. We shall join you soon." She eyed the mentath, who swayed. His colour was *not* good at all, and his thinning hair stood straight up, grimed with soot. "And mind the mentath, he looks a bit—"

Clare's eyes rolled up in his head, and he collapsed. And Emma felt the chill along her fingers and toes that meant the Shadow had taken an interest in proceedings. She did not know how long they had before it arrived and must be dealt with, and she had expended far more force than she wished attacking the metal . . . *thing*.

"Oh, bloody *hell*," she breathed, just as the light failed completely.

Chapter Twenty-Seven

Unpleasant, But Instructive

Clare clasped the crackling brown paper, soaked with vinegar, to his aching head. "Unpleasant," he murmured. "Highly unpleasant. But instructive."

"I am glad to hear your afternoon went so well," Miss Bannon replied. "Mine was equally instructive, and it was very disagreeable dealing with the Shadow near the Tower. But, my dear Mr Clare, please answer me. What in the name of the seven Hells *were* those . . . things? Sorcery does not touch them; this upsets me a *great* deal."

He shifted on the fainting-couch. The sitting room was very comfortable, despite the tension sparking in every corner. "Obviously. I am trying to find a word that would explain them to a layman, but the best I can do is *homunculus* or *golem*. Neither is *precise*, mind you, but—"

"Mr Clare." Quietly, but with great force. "Kindly do not become distracted, sir. I have a dead body in my study that grows no fresher, and I cannot question the man's shade effectively unless and until I have some answers from you." Her tone grew sharper. "And Ludo, darling? *Stop whistling*, or I shall sew your lips together."

Clare peeled open one eye to see Miss Bannon perched on a low stool at his side, high colour in her cheeks and her hair most fetchingly disarranged. Behind her, Sigmund's wide faithful face loomed. The Bavarian was chewing on something that rather startlingly resembled a wurst and a slice of yellow cheese.

"Ah." Clare cleared his throat. "Miss Bannon, may I present to you Mr Sigmund Baerbarth, genius, and my personal friend? Sig, this is Miss Bannon, a most interesting sorceress."

"How do you do," Miss Bannon said over her shoulder, and Sig nodded, swallowing hastily.

"Seer geehrte, Fraulein Bannon."

The sorceress returned her dark gaze to Clare, who had gathered himself sufficiently to face such an examination calmly. The vinegar did not help much. "Pray fetch me some ice and salt, if you would. My head aches abominably."

Bannon glanced over her shoulder again, her jet earrings swinging, and there was a murmur from the door. There seemed a large number of people crowding the sitting room. The rain had started, and its patter against the window panes was an additional irritation. When she again returned her attention to him, her mien had softened.

"You saved my life, Mr Clare." Her childlike face was sombre now. And yes – those were her gloved fingers, delicately holding his free hand. "That *thing* had cannons on its . . . arms, I suppose one would call them. Who was controlling the other one?"

"Hm. Well, yes." An uncomfortable heat mounted in his cheeks. Her little hand was trembling; he could feel it through the kidskin. "Bit of quick thinking, that. It was a mentath. Throckmorton."

"Remarkably spry for a dead man. He escaped. Helped by Mr Devon's Shields, I am told, which is shocking enough. I am *quite* put out that Mr Devon was not captured alive."

"Ah. Well. Miss Bannon, allow me to collect myself for a moment. Then I shall answer your questions. Is there tea?"

"Of course. Shall I fetch you some?"

Well, she is remarkably calm, under the circumstances. "With lemon, please."

The ice arrived in a well-scalded and proof-charmed cloth, and between that and a cuppa he was soon sitting upright, blinking in the rainy failing light. He did not care to know how he had been transported to Miss Bannon's house, other than to be grateful at the occurrence. The splitting pain of strained faculties inside his skull receded bit by bit.

Mikal hovered at Miss Bannon's shoulder as she sipped her own tea, thoughtfully, her little finger raised just so. The Shield's face was a thundercloud, and Clare suspected the reason was the *other* Shield, a dark-haired man who leaned almost somnolent at the mantel. The mystery of where Miss Bannon had acquired *him* could wait, Clare decided as his temples throbbed.

Ludovico Valentinelli, on the far side of the fireplace, was engaged upon cleaning his fingernails with another of his many knives, and glancing curiously at the new Shield. Sig was at the tea table, munching happily. Every so often the Neapolitan would drift to the table and help himself. It was a comfort to see their appetites undiminished, even if they were still soot-stained and faintly wild-eyed.

"Now," Clare said, finally, when he was certain his voice would remain steady. "It is much worse than either of us feared, Miss Bannon. Those things, the *mechanisterum homunculi,* for lack of a better term; Sig would merely call them *mecha*, dear boy that he is – do not run on Alterative sorcery. They can be run directly through the smaller logic engines inside their chest cavities. You will no doubt have noticed the glow at my chest while—"

"Yes. Proceed." One of her hatpins, he saw, had broken. He wondered if she had found the pieces; decided not to think on it too deeply lest overstress fuse his brain into uselessness.

"They *must* be run by a mentath. My current state is the cost of handling such an engine without preparation. The equations are . . . very difficult. But that is not what concerns us." He winced, took another swallow of tea. "Some toast, perhaps?"

"Of course. Mikal, please fetch him a plate." Visibly calmer,

Miss Bannon settled on the cushioned stool. Her skirts were arranged very prettily, Clare noticed.

It was the first time one of these episodes had not ended with her in tatters, he reflected. Doubtless she was glad.

He brought his attention back to the matter at hand. "The larger – the master logic engine, you see, would not be in that warehouse. It is being kept safe elsewhere. The master engine will be the transmitter. Those – the mechanicals you saw – are all *receivers,* with limited capability of being run directly. With a large enough transmitting engine, especially handling the sub-equations in a useful fashion, which is possible with enough power supplied through the core, the mentath wired to the transmitting engine will have control of an army."

Silence.

Miss Bannon had gone quite white. She stared not at him but *through* him, her gaze disconcertingly direct and remote at the same time.

"An army." Very thoughtful, and very soft. She took another sip of tea. "One that does not need food, or rest. One that sorcery does not touch."

"The field generated by the logic engines –"

"– rather makes it difficult for sorcery to penetrate. Yes, Mr Clare. And Mr Throckmorton alive." She continued, pedantically, after a long pause. "I wonder whose corpse was at Grace Street. And what Throckmorton was doing *there* with Devon."

"Standing guard, perhaps? Who would look for a mentath in the Shadow?" He suppressed a shudder at the thought. "I am not quite myself at the moment, Miss Bannon. Pray do not question me too much; it may overtax my faculties and I shall become a brain-melted embarrassment."

A fleeting, half-guilty smile greeted his sally. Mikal appeared, bearing a plate of provender. "Prima?"

"Hm?" She glanced up as Clare started gratefully on his toast.

"I have an idea."

"Yes?"

"I think it would be most instructive to learn the recent movements of a dead Master Sorcerer." The Shield straightened, folding his arms. "One who was running errands for Lord Sellwyth."

Sellwyth? Yes, the dead Prime. Clare winced again. Even such a simple act of memory strained the meat inside his skull most alarmingly.

"Quite." She took another sip of tea. She was still distressingly pale. "I wonder if anyone else has seen Mr Devon of late? Childe said a fortnight or so ago. The last time I saw him was at Tomlinson's. Where he had bungled the traces rather neatly, it now appears." She closed her eyes, gathering herself. When she reopened them, her gaze was very direct – and very, very cold. "Still, a corpse to mislead investigation is not difficult to procure, and the remains at Grace Street were so badly burnt . . . If Throckmorton is alive . . ."

Silence filled the room. Clare hoped she did not require his faculties to see her way through the tangle. He crunched on his toast, relishing the butter and the thick bread.

"I am very interested in Hugh Devon's movements," Miss Bannon continued. "However, following him is a waste of time, since he is dead. If Throckmorton is alive—"

"Cedric Grayson's signature is on the papers you gave me, Miss Bannon. You must not be as familiar with his hand as I am." Clare's attention snagged on a memory, and a braying laugh surprised him. "The sherry was poisoned. How *typical*."

"Sherry?"

That was why it reeked as it did. It was cheap, yes, but also adulterated. "When we visited the Chancellor. At the time I thought the sherry dreadfully cheap, but Cedric's aesthetics are so bad—"

"Poison. I see. A slow-acting one, no doubt, meant to preserve some parts of you."

"Preserve?"

"The other unregistered mentaths were missing their brains

and spinal cords. I rather thought it had something to do with a mad Alterations sorcerer."

"Oh." Clare shuddered. No wonder she had reserved that information. It changed the entire complexion of the affair, but his faculties were too aching and strained to make use of the revelation.

"And the trap in Bedlam," Miss Bannon continued daintily, "was meant to take care of *me*, possibly while I was occupied in ministering to you. Rather tidy. Which brings us to another interesting question."

As long as you do not expect me to answer said query, dear God. "Which is?"

"Where is Lord Sellwyn? If Throckmorton is alive, I find it hard to believe *he* is truly deceased."

Indeed. "Ah. Well. I cannot help you."

"No need." She sipped again, delicately, and he had the sudden fancy that there were very few places Lord Sellwyn would be able to hide once Miss Bannon took a serious interest in finding him. "Tell me, Mr Clare, how long will it take your faculties to recover?"

He cogitated upon this, carefully, wincing. "A few hours, and one of your most excellent dinners, should see me right as rain, Miss Bannon."

"Very well. Concern yourself with restoring said faculties, sir, and I shall speak with you after dinner." She opened her eyes and rose, waving at him abstractedly as he moved as if to rise as well. "No, no, *do* stay seated. You have done very well, Mr Clare. Very well indeed. After dinner, then."

He found his mouth was dry. "Certainly. But Miss Bannon?"

She was already halfway to the door, her teacup handed to Mikal and her stride lengthening, skirts snapping. "Yes?"

"The next time you use me as bait, madam, have the goodness to inform me. I do not mind being dangled on a hook. As a matter of fact, I derive a certain enjoyment from it. But I would rather not endanger my friends."

She paused. "You were not *bait*, Mr Clare. You were more of a dach's-hund, meant to flush the prey."

"Nevertheless."

A single, queenly nod. Did she unknowingly copy that movement from Victrix? Yet another question that could wait until his head ceased its abominable pounding.

"Yes, Mr Clare. You have earned as much. My apologies." And with that, she swept out through the door the new Shield held for her.

The door closed, leaving him with the assassin and Sigmund. Who crunched on something from his plate, licked his fingers, and belched contentedly.

"What a woman," he said, dreamily. "*Ein Eis Madchen*. Archibald, *mein Herr*, I believe I am in love."

The Neapolitan, upon hearing this, laughed fit to choke. Clare simply clasped the water-proofed ice cloth to his head and sighed.

Dinner, though superb, was a somewhat hurried affair.

Miss Bannon, appearing in black silk and even more fantastic jewellery, waited until the vegetable course. "I shall deal with Lord Sellwyth, Grayson, and Throckmorton. You, Mr Clare, shall deal with finding and – should it become necessary – destroying the larger logic engine."

"Splendid." He dabbed his lips with his napkin. Beside him, Valentinelli had dispensed with rudeness for once, and was partaking with exquisite manners. Across from him, Mikal and the new Shield – Eli – set to with a will. On the Neapolitan's other side, Sigmund expressed his admiration for the excellence of the dinner in mumbled German. He seemed supremely unconcerned with any larger questions, such as what his landlady and his apprentice would think of his disappearance and the state of his workshop. He had already dashed off a note for them penny-post, and then put them from his capacious mind, which was already busy worrying at other problems. "How do you propose I do so? I have my ideas, of course –"

"– but you would like to know if I questioned a dead sorcerer's shade, and can shed any light on the situation. I did, Mr Clare, and I can."

Clare noted that the new Shield turned pale and stared at his plate, before shaking his head slightly and renewing his interest in his food. *Interesting*. It was a pleasure to deduce again, without the inside of his skull feeling as if acid had been poured through it. The equations had nearly cracked him, the small logic engine cramming force through his capabilities until his head was a swollen pumpkin ready to burst. He had not felt so skull-tender since his Examination.

The new Shield was a Liverpool boy, dark-haired and not very comfortable in his high-collared coat that almost matched Mikal's. His boots were more impractical than Mikal's – or for that matter, the sorceress's – and Clare thought it likely Miss Bannon had not acquired his services as part of a well-laid plan. Another refugee, perhaps, to add to her household of cast-offs?

Or did Miss Bannon think the dangers of the situation finally required another Shield? Why not more than one, then?

The implications of *that* question were extraordinarily troubling. Just like the implications of the harvesting of other mentaths' nervous organs.

He brought his attention back to the matter at hand. Sometimes, after a violent shock, a mentath's mind wandered down logical byways, taking every route but the one most direct. "Please do."

"My method of procuring the information—"

"Does not trouble me at all, Miss Bannon. I believe I am past being troubled, at least for the next fortnight. After that, we shall see." His digestion, at least, was sound. It was a small mercy. "Nothing you could tell me would discommode me more than this afternoon's adventure."

Her pained half-smile told him she rather doubted it, but was too polite to say as much. "Very well. Mr Devon's shade, when pressed, informed me that the conspiracy is very near fruition.

It appears a single thing is lacking – a shipment of something from Prussia."

"Prussian capacitors, most likely." Clare nodded. "Especially if they intend to have a *single* mentath run the transmitting engine; each one will help with the subsidiary equations. I am not so sure what the nervous organs are for, but no doubt they have some function. The question of just *which* mentath they have to run the damn thing—"

"Is irrelevant at the moment. The Prussian things were delayed due to weather; they are to arrive in Dover tomorrow morning." Miss Bannon was pale again. "You and your companions shall intercept this shipment and do whatever possible to delay and disrupt the part of the conspiracy that hinges on them."

"And you will be occupied with?" Though he already knew, he found he wished to hear her say it. She was, he reflected, a most unusual woman, and it was rather nice to converse with someone who did not require intellectual coddling.

Someone who could *think*.

"It is high time Lord Grayson answered some questions." Level and chill, her gaze focused on the graceful silver epergne. The table's gryphon legs writhed, uneasily, but the snow-white tablecloth was flat and straight. The cadaverous Mr Finch, without asking, brought a decanter and a small glass to Miss Bannon's place; without looking, she accepted the glass and tossed its contents far down her throat with only a small ladylike grimace afterward. "Thank you, Mr Finch. Excuse me, gentlemen, but I require some bolstering. This is an unpleasant business."

"I agree." Clare found himself reaching for his wine glass. *I rather envy her the rum.* But it would dull his faculties, even as it afforded him some relief. A fraction of coja might help, but he could not take that at table. Later, then. "There is something that troubles me, Miss Bannon."

A slight lift of an eyebrow. "And what is that?"

"This is no ordinary conspiracy. What could these persons wish to accomplish with an army, even one so formidable as this? And where has the money to fund such a venture arrived from? This is most remarkable. I am very curious."

The rum seemed to make no impression on her. "There are things it is best for you not to know, Mr Clare. I am sorry."

"Ah. Well." He sipped at his wine. "I work best when I am informed, Miss Bannon. It is very unlikely that whoever wishes to unseat Britannia's current incarnation has merely *one* army or plan at their disposal. Even if that army is one sorcery will not touch."

The table rattled slightly. Even Sigmund looked up, his chewing halted for a moment.

Miss Bannon's childlike face turned even more set. Twin sparks of crimson flashed in her pupils for a few moments, then vanished. "We are not dealing with merely one conspiracy, Mr Clare. We are dealing with an unholy alliance of competing interests, none of whom are being exactly honest with each other. There is at least one party who wishes the destruction of Britannia Herself, one who possibly only wishes the damage of Her current incarnation to make said incarnation amenable to coercion, and a third who wishes to sow as much confusion and chaos as possible in order to impair the Empire in any way they may." Her long jet earrings swung even though she was motionless, and the large black gem on a silver choker about her slim throat flashed with a single white-hot charter symbol for a moment. Her curls stirred, on a slow cool breeze that came from nowhere and ruffled along Clare's own face. "I will allow *none* of this, and I *will* conclude this matter to my satisfaction and in the manner I deem best."

The silence was immense. Every gaze in the room had fastened on her. Ludovico Valentinelli seemed thoughtful, his pocked face open and interested. The Bavarian was still unchewing, his eyes wide like a frightened child's. The new Shield had turned cheesy-pale and laid his fork down. Mikal, on the other hand, simply watched her, and his expression was as unguarded as Clare had ever seen it.

I wonder if she knows what he feels. I wonder if he *does.*

Clare leaned back in his chair. He tented his fingers under his long sensitive nose and studied Miss Bannon's immobility. Finally he had marshalled his thoughts sufficiently to speak. *Be very careful here, Archie old man.*

"Miss Bannon. According to what I have seen so far, the Queen trusts you implicitly. This trust is well placed. You are neither stupid nor irresponsible, and you are, I daresay, one of the finest of Britannia's subjects. Despite the fact that you have suspected me and told me virtually nothing of the contours of this conspiracy, I find that I trust you implicitly as well. I am" – he untangled his fingers, lifted his wineglass – "your servant, madam. I shall do my very best to discharge the duty laid upon me, by God and Her Majesty. Now, do you view the situation as dire enough for us to pass over the sweets, or shall we partake, as this may be the last dinner some of us are fortunate enough to consume?"

Miss Bannon's mouth compressed itself into a thin line, and for a moment he was certain he had said exactly the wrong thing. People were so bloody *difficult*, after all, and she was a woman – they were noted for irrationality, never mind that this sorceress was one of the least irrational creatures he had ever known the pleasure of meeting.

But her mouth relaxed, and a smile like sunrise played over her face. "I believe the situation is dire enough on my account but not so dire on yours, so you and your companions will have to do justice to the sweets for me. I wish to see Lord Grayson as close to Tideturn as possible. Thank you, gentlemen."

She rose, still smiling, and the men leapt to their feet as one. She swept from the dining room, and the Shields hurried in her wake.

The Neapolitan breathed a curse. "Last time *la strega* look like that . . ." He lowered himself back into his chair as Mr Finch reappeared with two footmen bearing the sweets. The butler did not seem at all distressed or surprised to find his mistress had quit the table.

"What happened, the last time Miss Bannon looked like that?" Clare enquired.

Valentinelli allowed the scarred footman to clear his place. "Oh, nothing. Just Ludovico almost hanged, and *il sorcieri* laughing in the dark. *La strega*, the bitch, she save Ludo's life." A single shrug. "Some day I forgive her. But not today."

"Ah." Clare filed this away. Valentinelli's drawer in his mental bureau was almost as interesting as Miss Bannon's, by now.

But not quite. He could still feel her gloved fingers on his hand, trembling. And three separate interlocking interests making this conspiracy an even more troubling – and fascinating – puzzle.

Sig looked mournful. "We finish dinner, *ja*?"

"Indeed." Clare sat, slowly, and Mr Finch poured the sherry. "We finish dinner, dear Sig."

It might indeed be our last one, if what I suspect is true.

Interlude

The Cliffs Will Be No Bar

The rain had stopped as Tideturn swirled through the streets; but with the coming of night the fog resurged. It boiled down to the surface of the streets, and as the brougham thundered along at a steady pace towards the station, its driver occasionally cracking the whip, Clare steepled his fingers again and did his best to tease out the implications bothering him so.

This was difficult for a number of reasons, one of which was Sigmund, who could not or would not cease muttering about his new-found admiration for Miss Bannon. Valentinelli occasionally snorted, but otherwise held his tongue. The carriage roared along, clockwork hooves and the jolting a severe distraction – especially since Clare *had* taken his fraction of coja before setting out. The resultant sharpening of his faculties and dulling of his limitations would have been wonderfully soothing had he been alone.

"Such grace!" Sig muttered. "Baerbarth will be hero, yes! And so will Clare. Good man, Clare."

Dear God, we are possibly about to die, and he cannot stop himself. Leave it be, Clare.

Three players, then – or at least, three players that Miss Bannon was willing to admit to. A dragon, obviously. His reluctance to believe in such beasts had taken rather a shock lately.

Gryphons were all very well, but the wyrms who could halt Time itself, the harbingers of disaster and great concentrators of irrationality, the beasts supposedly responsible for teaching Simon Magister, the great mage who had offered gold to Petrus for God's powers, and been hailed by the surrounding crowds as a greater miracle-worker than a disciple of the Christos . . .

. . . that was a different thing entirely. Although the logic engines created a field of order and reasonableness sorcery would not penetrate, a dragon's irrationality was so vast it might not matter. The other conspirators might hope that it would – the question was, who exactly were those other conspirators? For Clare did not think even *he* could deduce a dragon's motivations.

Except Miss Bannon had already provided them. The destruction of Britannia? Was it even possible to destroy the ruling spirit of the Empire? She was ageless, changeless, accumulating knowledge and power with every vessel's reign. What was the nature of the dragons' quarrel with Her? He could not guess, and shelved the question for later.

Cedric and a sorcerer – Lord Sellwyth. The Earl of Sellwyth, who I do not know nearly enough about. What would tempt Cedric? Power, obviously. And the sorcerer? Power as well. Ambition is a sorcerer's blood, they say.

"A *Hexen*, yes. But that can be overcome, eh, Clare? I will build her something. What do you think *Hexen* want from *mechaniste*? Not my *Spinne*, no. But—"

"I rather think Miss Bannon is not the marrying type, old chap." *Why Prussian capacitors?* he wondered, suddenly. *They are of high quality, yes . . . but for the mecha I saw, not necessary to this degree. Davenports or Hopkins would work just as well, and could be transported with greater chance of secrecy. Why Prussians?*

Ludovico's lip curled. He maintained his silence, however, and Clare was suddenly glad. He longed for a few moments' worth of peace and quiet to follow this chain of logic. "Why

Prussians?" he murmured, staring out of the window at the gaslit fog, dim shapes moving in its depths.

Well, why not? Standardised to make the process of building the mecha easier – and there was another problem, Clare acknowledged. Who had *built* the damn things, including the smaller engines? Two or three mentaths were not capable of such a feat, and Miss Bannon's investigations should have uncovered a factory or two busily churning out the massive things if they were made in Londinium's environs – or even *shipped* to the city from elsewhere, a massive undertaking in and of itself.

Not to mention the . . . parts . . . of unregistered mentaths. Harvested.

Something is very wrong here.

He cast back through memory as Sigmund began meandering on about Miss Bannon's dark eyes again.

Becker. The hevvymancer. Something in that conversation . . .

"Most curious. Who is buying Prussian capacitors now?"

"Naught. Some gents like to tear their own hair out waiting; some says they're in France somewhere, others say held up in the Low, one or two wot might know says the Pruss factories holdin 'em. Frenchie glassers and Hopkins shinies selling hand over fist now, since Prussians ent to be had."

"Aha," he murmured, his fingers tightening against each other. The pleasure of a solution spilled through him, tingling in his nerves.

The second group, of course, would be a domestic party wishing Victrix controlled in some way – she was Britannia incarnate, of course, but while she had been unmarried she had been led by a coterie headed by her mother. The Duchess of Kent was banished to Balgrave Square, of course, and had been since the marriage. The Prince Consort was rumoured to be pressing for a reconciliation between Victrix and her mother, but so far it had come to naught.

The third party in Miss Bannon's allusions? Why, ridiculously simple once he considered it logically. Of course, this line of logic depended on much supposition—

"I shall build her lions!" Sigmund suddenly crowed. "What do you think, Clare? Lions to draw her carriages! Shining brass ones!"

"*Do* be quiet a moment, Sig." Rudely interrupted, Clare frowned. That was the problem with coja. If one was jolted free of the reverie, it was rather difficult to exclude all the endless noise about one and gather the traces again. "I rather think . . ."

"What is it you rather think, *mentale*?" For once, the Neapolitan was not sneering. "I tell you what I am thinking. *La strega* send me with you, she expect bad trouble. Everything to now, *pfft!*" A magnificent gesture of disdain was curtailed by the lack of space inside the brougham. "No, this is where trouble begin. Ludo has sharpened his knives."

"You may very well need them," Clare retorted. Would *none* of them grant him some time to think? "For I believe we may be facing not merely mecha, my dear Neapolitan prince, but perhaps, also, a deeper treachery."

And the white cliffs of Dover will be no bar to it.

Chapter Twenty-Eight

The Unforgivable

The Chancellor would not be at his *official* Londinium residence, of course. His unofficial residence was near Cavendish Square, a bloated and graceless piece of masonry with gardens clutched about it like too-thin skirts at the cold legs of a drab. Stacked precipitously tall and throbbing with sorcerous defences, the place was almost as ugly as the Chancellor's Whitehall offices.

Mikal handed Emma down from the hansom, Eli wide-eyed, for once, behind her. It felt like a lifetime since she had last had a Shield with her in the carriage and another running the rooftop roads.

She waited until the hansom had vanished into the fog before turning to look down the street, feeling Grayson's house pulse like a sore tooth. Along with the showy defences were one or two very effective ones, and if what she suspected she might find inside was indeed there, it was a very cunning and subtle way to camouflage it.

"Prima?" Mikal, carefully.

Tideturn had come and gone. The fog had thickened, venomous yellow with its own dim glow. Emma wondered, sometimes, if the gaslamps fed the fog's eerie foxfire on nights like this. The fog would suck on them like a piglets at a sow's teats, and spread a dilute phosphorescence through its veins.

"I expect this to be unpleasant." The stone at her throat was ice cold, and the rings clasping her fingers were as well. They were curious things, these rings – carved of ebony, silver hammered delicately into them, four rings connected with a bridge of cold haematite across the top pads of her palms. The haematite was carved with a Word, and from it clasping fingers held the ebony loops.

She did not like wearing the gauntlets, for the Word against the skin of her hands was a constant prickling discomfort. And they did not allow her to wear gloves.

Mikal made no reply. Eli shifted his weight, the leather of his boots creaking slightly. "How unpleasant?" he asked, in his light, even tenor.

Childe had perhaps chosen him for his voice. It would be just like the other Prime.

"We will find at least one dead man inside." She wore no shawl, no mantle, and no hat, either. A well-bred woman would not be seen on the street in such a manner.

Then it is as well I am not one, for all I am a lady. Well, mostly a lady.

She was procrastinating.

"Well." Eli absorbed this. "One less to kill, then."

"Not necessarily," she replied, and set her chin. They fell into step slightly behind her as she set off in the direction of the sparking pile of sorcery. "Not necessarily at all."

Fortunately, he did not ask what she meant. Emma was not sure she could have kept the sharp edge of her tongue folded away. She would not waste *that* on a Shield who was only seeking to lighten her mood. Perhaps Childe required banter of him.

And no doubt the exact branch of her Discipline had been a shock to the man.

An iron gate in the low wall surrounding the house was not locked, and Mikal gingerly pushed it open enough to slip through. Eli followed Emma, and gravel crunched underfoot as the circular drive trembled under the pressure of the fog. The gardens were indistinct shadows; the front door atop three worn steps was a monstrosity of steel-bound oak. It was there, before the steps, that Emma's heart thumped twice and turned to cold lead inside her chest.

For the left-hand door was open very slightly.

He was expecting her.

"Mikal?"

"Yes." He was in his accustomed place behind her right shoulder, and her flesh chilled.

For he had broken Devon's neck, keeping the head intact so she could question the man's shade, but robbing the body below it of the shade's control. As if he had anticipated she would wish to speak to the dead sorcerer, and provided the safest means to do so.

Which was . . . interesting.

"He is *mine*. You will confine yourself to the Shields."

"Yes, Prima." As if he did not care.

We shall have a long conversation later, Mikal. But for now . . . "Eli."

"Yes, Prima?"

"Very carefully, open the left-hand door further. *Very* carefully."

There was little need for care, for the heavy oak and iron swung easily and silently. The darkness inside was absolute. The defences shimmering to Sight did not spark or tighten. Emma delicately tweezed them aside, tasting the unphysical traces of the personality behind them.

There was no need; she would recognise his work anywhere. It seemed yet another lifetime ago she had been learning the subtle twists, his habit of disdain, the serpentine shifts of his considerable intellect.

It had perhaps never occurred to him what he had been teaching her with every moment she spent in his presence. The lessons were many and varied. Dutifully, she applied one of them now.

Do not spring a trap until you know exactly its manner and measure, dear Emma. Slightly sarcastic, with the bitter edge; she could almost *hear* him. *But when you know, do it swiftly. So it knows it has been sprung.*

Chin high, she gathered her skirts and strode through the door.

For a moment the darkness stretched, a rippling sheet of black, but the spell was so laughably simple she broke it without even needing Word or charm, simply a flexing of her will. Of course, there could have been a more fiendish and complex spell behind it – but she did not think so.

And she was correct. The foyer was narrow but very high, the grand steps at its back managing to be the most utterly abhorrent piece of internal architecture she'd seen in easily six months. It was as if Grayson actively pursued the ugliest thing possible.

Where would he be? Parlour or bedroom? "Mikal?"

"They do not seek to be quiet," her Shield murmured. He pointed to the side. "There."

Parlour, then. Which meant a number of uncomfortable things.

"No servants to take one's wrap, even," she commented. "Dreadfully rude."

The parlour door's porcelain handle clicked. A slice of ruddy light widened as the flimsy door – painted with overblown cherubs, in a style that had not been fashionable even when it was attempted ten years ago – swung silently open.

Cheap theatrics, my dear. But she continued on, briskly, the two Shields trailing her. Her skirts rustled; there was no need for silence. She stepped over the threshold and on to a hideous but expensive carpet, patterned with blotchy things she supposed were an attempt at flowers.

The furniture was chunky and graceless, but again, very expensive. Someone had the habit of antimacassars and doilies, hand-wrought from the look of them, just the sort of meaningless thrift she would expect from whatever lumpen thing Grayson could induce to marry him. All Grayson's taste and judgement had gone into playing politics, and he was a keen and subtle opponent there.

But now, all his keenness and subtlety was splashed in a sticky red stinking tide across the terrible carpet. The brassy odour of death filled the stifling parlour, and from the least objectionable leather chair by the fireplace, licked by the glow and the furious heat given forth by a merry blaze, Llewellyn Gwynnfud chuckled. His long pale hair was pulled back, and for a dead man, he looked remarkably pleased with himself.

"Punctual to the last, dear Emma." The erstwhile dead Prime lifted a small cut-crystal wine glass of red fluid, and Mikal's sudden tension told her there were other Shields in this room. Hidden, of course, and she wondered if they knew of the fate of Llew's *last* crop of Collegia-trained protectors.

Grayson's twisted, eviscerated body was flung over a brown horsehair sopha, the tangle of his guts steaming. Now, as she spared it a longer glance, she wondered if the Prime had killed his Shields himself.

And if Mehitabel the Black had helped.

"A simulacrum," she replied. "And a fantastic one too, well beyond your power. Did you and your sleeping master truly expect the strike at Bedlam to kill me?"

A swiftly smoothed flash of annoyance crossed his face. Long nose, fleshy lips, his blue eyes a trifle too close together . . . well, he was handsome, Emma allowed, but only until one knew him.

Only until one saw the rot underneath.

"I have no *master*, my dear. One or two of our partners expected you to meet your doom before now, but they don't know you as I do." He twirled the small glass, the viscous fluid in its crystalline bowl making a soft sliding sound under the roar of the fire.

"Oh, you have a master. Not Mehitabel – she couldn't craft a simulacrum that fine, being of the Black Line." She tapped a finger to her lips, not missing Llewellyn's eyelids lowering a fraction. It was as close to a flinch as he would allow himself, facing her on this carefully set stage. "But no worries, I will settle accounts with your *master* soon enough. I have decided to deal with you first."

That produced a snarl, a flash of white teeth. "I'm flattered."

"Not at all. You are, after all, the smaller problem."

Sparks crackled, the breathless tension heightening a fraction. The fire was large, yes – but it was *not* large enough to produce such heat. There was the matter of the fluid in the glass, and the shadows clustering on the walls, any of which might hide a Shield or two. Or half a dozen. The eviscerated body of the Lord Chancellor was worrisome too, and the rest of Grayson's house ticking and groaning as nightfall settled and yellow fog began to press upon it in earnest was not quite as it should be. The sounds were too sharp, too weighty.

In short, Llewellyn Gwynnfud had prepared this for a reason. Emma took a half-step to her left, away from the ruin of Grayson's body. "The Chancellor did not expect this," she observed, as Eli and Mikal moved with her – Mikal soundless and Eli's boots creaking just a fraction.

Llewellyn didn't twitch. Instead, he lifted the cordial glass and stared into its swirl. "You found another Shield. Who did this one kill?"

Indirectly reminding her of Crawford, to see if he could unsettle her. Of course. "Not nearly as many as you have, I would fancy. Your former Shields, all dead and gutsplit in an alley." She indicated Grayson's indecently splayed body with a sudden sharp movement, and was gratified to see Llewellyn flinch. "Just like him. You're exhibiting a pattern, Lord Sellwyth." Her hand dropped. "That's right. *Sellwyth*. Dinas Emrys is part of your family's holdings, isn't it?" A long pause. "I've always wanted to visit it. Perhaps now's the time."

For in the lore of the Age of Flame, the ancient citadel of Dinas Emrys was tangled with the *Pax Draegonir*. It was where simulacra of the wyrms would meet in conclave, in the presence of their sleeping progenitor, the Third Wyrm, the one from who all the wyrmlings now were descended.

The first two Great Wyrms were either dead or sleeping so deeply they might as well be – or so sorcerers hoped. But Vortigern lay just under the surface of the Isle, and his might was such that even Britannia might not quell him.

The other Prime had gone very still. He made a slight *tsk tsk* noise. "You are *so* quick, dear Emma. Listen for a few moments."

"You have my attention." *For now.*

"It's one of your best features, my dear, that quality of wide-eyed listening you sometimes employ." His tongue stole out, wetted his fleshy lips. "A tide is rising." An eyebrow raise robbed the sentence of portentousness, but he was still, Emma thought, serious.

Deadly serious.

He continued, each word careful and soft. "How long will you spend chasing your hobbyhorse of duty, my dear? You are so talented, and lovely besides. I did not like our parting."

You dropped me like a hot stone the instant you thought that French tart would give you an advantage, and I was unwilling to share your bed with another woman. Then there was Crawford, and you did not bother to show your face afterwards. No doubt you were busy with high treason and murder. Emma merely tilted her head slightly. The stone at her throat was still ice cold, quiescent.

"You are here. But you haven't yet attacked me. Which means you need information you think you can force me to provide, or you're intrigued. Most probably the former. But just in case you are intrigued, my dear, how do you like the idea of immortality?"

Oh, Llewellyn. A silly lure, even for you. "Overrated. Primes have such long lives anyway, and any immortality has conditions. Try again, Gwynnfud."

"There is an immortality without conditions."

Ah. "A Philosopher's Stone." *That's what you were offered? Or you have been granted. If it's the latter . . .* "Am I meant to infer that you've been granted a Stone, in reward for services rendered, and *that*, instead of a simulacrum, is to blame for your wonderfully revived state? Oh, Llewellyn. *Really.* I abhor insults to my intellect."

"As soon as Britannia's vessel is breached and our great friend awakened, darling. The wyrms do not throw away a useful advantage."

You would do well to remember that. The heat was mounting, uncomfortably. "A Stone can only be made from a wyrm's heart. Slaying a wyrm brings a curse. Have you forgotten that?"

"Vortis has many children."

Under the close stifling heat, she was cold all through. "And he will slaughter a wyrmchild for *you*. Llewellyn, for God's sake, don't be an idiot."

"Two, actually. Two Stones. One was to be Grayson's. But since he's met with an accident, one will be in my power to give." Another quick wetting of his lips, and Emma's heart gave a shattering leap. "You are the only companion to hold my interest long enough to make such a gift worthwhile. *Think* of it, Emma. You, and me. Doesn't that sound lovely?"

And you have convinced the Duchess of Kent that you will help her coerce her daughter. A pair fit for each other, indeed. "You are," she informed him, "completely mad. I am Britannia's servant. Or have you forgotten?"

"You bow and scrape to that magical whore because you see no advantage elsewhere. Come now, do not play the high-and-mighty with me. I know you, Emma. Inside and out."

He was not precisely wrong. In fact, he was more correct than she cared to acknowledge, and the realisation was a slap of cold water.

"Apparently not." The water became ice, sheathing her. "You think I would betray Britannia for this pack of idiotic promises? I left you, Llewellyn, because you had grown *boring*." She took a deep breath, and uttered the unforgivable. "A Shield is far less trouble, and far more . . . *athletic*, besides."

The colour drained from Lord Sellwyth's cheeks. His eyes flamed, pale blue, and the cordial glass sang a thin note as his fingers tightened.

Almost too easy. Every man has the same sticking point, and it nestles in their breeches.

He gained his feet in a rush, flinging the glass aside. It hit the grate and shattered, the liquid inside blossoming into blue-white flame. Sorcery uncoiled, streaking for her, and Emma batted it aside with contemptuous ease. Part of the ceiling shattered, a flare of sorcerous flame breaking through four storeys and lifting into the fogbound Londinium night. Llewellyn's mouth shaped a Word, torn air suddenly full of choking dust. She was quicker, a half-measure of chant spat between her lips, warm and salt-sweet; it sliced the springing spell in half and knocked the other Prime back into the chair he had just leapt from. The chair skidded back, its legs tearing the hideous carpet, and smashed into the heavy oak wainscoting.

There were clashes of steel and sudden cries, but she ignored them. Llewellyn's Shields, bursting from their cocoons of invisibility, were not her worry. In a Prime's duel, her only concern was the other sorcerer. The Shields were left to make shift for themselves.

And, she thought, as the gauntlets warmed against her hands and Llewellyn rose out of the chair with a sound like a thunderstorm breaking, it was just as well.

For no Prime had ever duelled Lord Sellwyth and won.

Chapter Twenty-Nine

I Find Myself Reluctant to Disappoint

It was just as well he had taken the coja. If he had not, the ride would have been even *more* a nightmare. The knocking of the clocktrain's pistons, steam and charm working together to an infernal rhythm, was enough to drive a mentath's sensitive brain, recently bruised, into a state very near absolute madness. Still, the compartment was adequate, cushioned seats and a window he ensured was firmly shut – for he found he did not wish to see any of the flying cinders trains were famous for.

The difficulty of finding lodgings when they arrived in cold, fogbound Dover was most provoking. Valentinelli was little help, presumably because he cared not a whit where he laid his intriguing head, but Clare required a measure of comfort. There was the question of anonymity, too, but in the end, a respectable hotel was found, a room secured, and Clare gazed out of the window at the pinpricks of yellow gaslight receding down the slope of the town before the Neapolitan, making a spitting noise, shoved him aside and yanked the pineapple-figured curtains closed. Sig, who had napped on the train, took one of the beds, stretched out atop the covers without removing his boots, and was snoring within moments.

"*Porco*," Valentinelli sneered, and took himself to a chair by the coal fire. Clare settled himself in the other chair, propping his feet on an uncomfortably hard hassock covered in the same pineapple fabric as the curtains. The coja still sparked, his faculties honed and extraneous clutter cleared away, every inch of his capability aching to be used.

He tented his fingers below his nose, and shut out the sound of Sig's noisy sleep. Valentinelli watched him, dark eyes half lidded and thoughtful. The lamp on a small table at Clare's elbow gave a warm glow, and the fire was delightful.

The entire jolting, unhappy experience of travel had almost managed to unseat the excellent dinner he'd finished. Miss Bannon's pendant was cold against his chest, and he wondered how the sorceress fared.

Clare closed his eyes.

"Eh, *mentale*." Valentinelli shifted in his chair. "Use the bed, no? I wake you, at time."

"I am quite comfortable, thank you. I wish to think."

"She got you too." The Neapolitan's chuckle was not cheery at all. "*La strega*, she get every one of us."

Clare's irritation mounted. "Unless you have something truly useful to say, *signor*, could you please leave me in peace?"

"Oh, useful." Valentinelli's tone turned dark. "We are *very* useful, *mentale*. She send us off to find a shipment of something. Bait again. Dangle *mentale* and Ludo, see what happens."

"We are not bait," Clare immediately disagreed.

"Oh no?"

"No. As a matter of fact, I believe we are Miss Bannon's last hope."

The Neapolitan was silent.

"Consider this, my noble assassin. We are three men against enemies who wish nothing less than the destruction of Britannia's Empire and quite possibly the murder of Her physical vessel. Given Miss Bannon's attachment to Queen Victrix, what does it tell you that she has left the defence of Her Majesty to *us*? For that is what she has done by sending us here. She is pursuing an enemy *more dangerous*, in her opinion, than rebellion or even assassination. The fact that she has left this part of the prosecution of said conspiracy to us I find outright disturbing in its implications. Also, did you notice the second Shield? You must have, for he was at dinner. For Miss Bannon to engage another of Mikal's type, when by all accounts she has resisted doing so quite strongly, makes me think this situation very dire indeed." He tilted his head slightly, his eyes still closed. The comforting darkness behind his lids held geometric patterns, interlocking vortices of probability and deduction. "Also, she left us at table and quit her home most ostentatiously, drawing off whatever pursuit she could and waving herself before possible attackers like a handkerchief fluttered out of a window. She has given us *every* chance, sir, and furthermore gave her word not to treat me as bait. No, my noble assassin, we are men Miss Bannon is relying upon. And I do not think that lady relies easily."

Silence filled the room to bursting. The quiet had several components – the whisper of the lamp's flame, the coal fire shifting and flaring briefly, a steady dripping outside the window. The fog here was not Londinium's yellow soup, but it still pressed down on the town from white cliff to railway station, muffling the dosshouses and rollicking publics where Jack Tar drank to dry ground. It muffled the sound of clockhorse hooves and rumbling wheels outside the hotel, and it gave even the warm room a dry, bitter scent tinged with salt.

Valentinelli breathed a soft curse in his native tongue.

"Quite," Clare commented, drily. "Now do be still, sir. I must cogitate. For I will be brutally frank: I do not see much hope of us fulfilling the task Miss Bannon has given us, yet I find myself most unwilling to disappoint her."

Not to mention that Londinium – and indeed, all Britannia – would be distinctly uncomfortable for a good long while if Queen Victrix was removed from the living and Britannia searching for another vessel, or if the Queen were unhappy under her mother's control again. *An unhappy vessel means an unhappy Isle*, whether from bad weather, crop failure, or the creeping anomie that would thread through every part of the Empire.

And, dash it all, this entire affair was simply an affront to the tidiness and public order any good subject of Britannia preferred.

Clare settled himself deeper in the chair. His breathing deepened.

There are more logic engines. I must be prepared.

An onlooker would think he slept. But it was a mentath's peculiar doubling he performed, half his faculties engaged upon the riddle of tangling the three parties wishing harm to Britannia in their own brisket; how best to bring this affair to a satisfactory conclusion. The other half, sharpened by coja and shutting out all distractions, embarked on a complicated set of mental exercises. The equations the logic engine had forced him to solve without preparation rested on a series of mental chalkboards, and he set himself to untangling them at leisure and learning the patterns behind their hot white glare.

Motionless, sweat beading on his brow, Clare worked.

He surfaced to the Neapolitan's grip on his arm. "Wake, *mentale*," the assassin whispered. "Ships coming in."

The lamp guttered, throwing shadows over the pineapple-embossed paper. The damn room was a shrine to tropical fruit, Clare thought sourly, and moved very gingerly, stretching his legs. The body sometimes protested after a long period of torpidity. After a few minutes of various stretches, watched by a curious and half-amused Valentinelli, he found his hat and was not surprised to see Sigmund yawning and scratching at his ribs, peering carefully out of the window.

"Too quiet," the Bavarian muttered. "I do not like this."

"Ludo doesn't either." For once, the assassin did not sound sour. "But it could be the tide. Or the fog."

Clare washed his face at the basin, and a quarter-hour

afterwards found all three of them outside in the thick fog, making for the docks. After a brisk walk, there were no more complaints of it being too quiet.

Ports, like Londinium itself, rarely slept, and the infusion of fresh seaswell into a harbour was a potent yeast. Even through the thick white-cotton vapour shouts and curses could be heard, the straining of hawsers and the heave-ho chants of hevvy-mancers. Saltwitches chanted too and wove their fingers in complicated rhythms, drawing the fog aside in braided strands and lighting the ships into port. Shipwitches would be standing at bows, easing the tons of wood and sail safely towards the docks; pilots cursed and spat, hawkers, merchants, and agents rubbed elbows. Bullyboys and Shanghai-men with fresh crops of charmed and coffled Jack Tars waited impatiently – they would be paid a shilling a head, in some cases, less for any with obvious deformities, and the tars would be trapped on a ship as crew for God knew how long. Those with even a small talent for sorcery were safe from the coffles; the tars were those born without. And there were many of them – for what else was a Jack Tar to do when the ship he had been chained aboard was in a foreign port? To sign on a trifle less unwillingly was his only option, either for the pay due at the end of the voyage or for the simple fact that the sea worked its way into a man's blood.

The crowd, in short, was immense, even at this dark and early hour. Some indirect questioning brought the news that the *Srkány*, sailing from Old Emsterdamme, had indeed docked.

As a matter of fact, it had docked last night, and had sailed on the outgoing tide; nobody knew where, and the harbourmaster's office was disinclined to answer such queries. Clare cared little, because Sigmund, with his usual genius for such things, struck up a conversation with a hevvymancer who had helped unload the *Srkány*'s cargo, among which were several crates bound for an estate near Upper Hardres. Heavy crates the hevvy-mancers cursed, for they behaved oddly under the lifting and settling charms.

Clare would hazard a guess that this was the very estate Masters had perfected the core at, never mind that it was a Crown property. Sig paid for the dour-faced hevvy's next pint of ale and they plunged back into the crowd, Clare nervous without good reason. Or, perhaps, the reason had not presented itself yet, struggling to rise from an observation he had not given proper weight to.

When he finally located the source of the unease, it was marked enough to force him to lay hold of Sig's arm and pull the Bavarian into a close, conveniently dark, reeking alley. "Look there," he muttered, and Sigmund knew better than to protest. "And there. What do you see?"

Valentinelli swore, melding with the dimness behind them. Clare was perhaps just the tiniest bit gratified that he had seen them before the Neapolitan.

Across the street, a heavyset man with tremendous sweeping whiskers stepped sideways, as if he did not quite have his land legs yet. His coat was of a cloth not often seen on Britannia's Isle, and his bearing was unmistakably military. He had, so far, wandered once up and down in front of the nameless inn already doing a brisk business in gin and merriment, and he turned to make another pass.

Once Clare's attention had snagged on him, other bits of wrongness blared like trumpets. "The man in grey, across the street. See how he holds his pipe? No Englishman does so. And his boots – Hessians, and shone to a fare-thee-well. Now, look there, chap. Another one, with Hessians and his coat. You'll notice it's turned inside out. There, the two men in the tavern door – the same boots, the same coats. They have sought to disguise themselves, one with a kerchief and another with those dreadful breeches. Look at their whiskers. Not the fashion *this* side of the Channel, dear Sig. What does that tell you?"

The Bavarian spread his hands, waiting for Clare to answer his own rhetorical question.

"Prussians, Sig. Mercenaries, I'd lay ten pound on it. Look

at the way those two hold their hands – they are accustomed to rifles. *That* one is a captain – he subtly presents his chest, so none below him in rank will miss the badge he has been forced to lay aside. And see, that one there? He is watching the street."

"This is Dover," Sigmund said heavily. "Different men from different countries come here, *ja*?"

"Indisputably." Clare frowned. "But there are *two* in the door, another *there* standing watch, and the captain is patrolling. Looking for stragglers, perhaps? Or making certain nobody remarks that the inn there, and probably all the rooms inside it, is full to the brim with Prussian mercenaries. *That* is why Prussian capacitors, and *that* is what else was on the ship. I expected as much."

Valentinelli swore again. "We leave now. *Now.*"

"Quite." Clare jammed his hat more firmly on his head. "We must find horses. I doubt the train runs to Upper Hardres before noon."

Chapter Thirty

Duel and Discipline

The Major Circle about her glowed, quicksilver charter charms inside its double circuit spitting and hissing as Llewellyn threw a Word at her. She batted it aside, her throat swelling with chant, and another hole tore itself in the parlour wall, narrowly missing one of Llewellyn's Shields as the man leapt for Mikal. Who turned, with sweet economy of motion, and drove a knife into his opponent's throat with a sound like an axe buried in seasoned wood.

Her fellow Prime was off balance; she had always been much better at splitting her focus. He was contaminated water, seeping at the borders of her will; she countered with clean lake and ocean, and a Word shaped itself under her chant, blooming hurtful bright as fire burst through the ocean's surface and scorched him. Llewellyn took a half-step back within his own Circle, his pale eyes narrowing, and his answering Word robbed the fire of breath, crushing blackness descending on Emma and *squeezing*.

She had expected that, though – it was one of his favourite tricks. A non-physical shift sideways, her hand flung out, and the curse jetted free of the gauntlets, the charter symbol sleek and deadly as it pierced veils of ætheric protections. Llewellyn almost did not hop aside in time, and his left arm whipped back, blood exploding from his shoulder. He ignored the injury, flicking his right hand forward, force expended recklessly to crack her own protections. Which shimmered, shuddered . . . and held, just barely.

Thick crimson, almost black in the uncertain light, flowed down Llewellyn's arm. His frock coat was going to be absolutely ruined. A sudden burst of amusement threatened to dislodge Emma's grip, but she recognised the attack and let it slide away, her chant taking on the sonorous ripple of a hymn. Llewellyn's face twisted, and she was certain her own countenance was not smooth either.

It is a very good thing I am not a lady. She pressed the attack, her will bearing down, the chant rising in volume as his faltered. The blood painting his sleeve dripped, but too slowly – globules hung in the air below his contorted hand, spinning gently in mid-air. The fine hairs all over Emma's body rose.

Llewellyn's spine twisted. The blood slowed further, and she scented the beginning of a Major Work, hovering on the edge of probability and possibility, its structure a glory of tangled crystal lattices calcifying with pure white-hot iron.

He's using blood to fuel it; be careful, Emma!

If she had not once been so close to Llewellyn, she would not have seen the weakness, carefully protected by a nest of thorn-burning spikes.

Do not hesitate, he had told her, over and over again, his hand on her hip, warm and safe in the nest of whatever bed they were sharing at the moment. *Hesitation in a duel is loss*.

She struck for the raw spike-choked gap, ætheric force turned to a shining-sharp blade that *bent*, a jolt pouring up her arms as her own Work mutated, responding to the shape of his. This was the critical juncture – if she misjudged, the force of her defence would be spent and his attack would strike her head-on.

But she had not misjudged.

Llewellyn's body crumpled, flung back like a rag doll as his own Work detonated beneath him. Broken charter symbols spun, spitting sparks in every shade, and the entire house shuddered on its foundations. The limp form of the other Prime crashed into the fireplace, a jolt of blue flame searing Emma's sensitised eyes, and two of his Shields dropped mid-motion as he shunted the backlash aside, sacrificing them.

That's not a good si—

Mikal screamed, inarticulate rage a bright copper note against the sudden throat-cut quiet. He launched himself at her, both knives out, and Emma's instinctive twitch to protect herself was unnecessary.

For Mikal was not striking at her. Instead, he had read the threat from Llewellyn far more accurately than she had, and reacted more quickly to boot. Frozen, her unneeded defence sparking as the stone at her throat warmed fractionally, Emma could only watch as Mikal flung himself past her –

– and straight into a scythe-storm of sorcery, as Llewellyn's black-shrouded form birthed itself from the ruin of the fireplace. Ætheric blades blossomed in a hurtful black rosette, and blood exploded for the second time as her Shield fell.

"Hold his head up." Emma's hands were slick with hot blood. "There. And *there*." Sorcerous force bled from her fingertips. Her earrings shivered, the charge contained in their long swinging beads delicately spinning down her neck, twining across her collarbones, and draining down her arms as she closed the rip in Mikal's belly.

Mikal's eyelids fluttered. Eli held his shoulders, pale cheeks spattered with blood and other fluids. Emma's concentration did not allow wavering. She smoothed the violated flesh, charter symbols flushing red as they sank into torn meat, the language of Mending forced to obey her foreign lips shaping its syllables. She was not of the White, whose branches of Discipline encouraged healing. She was not even of the Grey, the seekers of Balance. No, Emma's Discipline was deeply of the Black; the primal forces too great to be concerned with small things like ripped-wide skin and muscle.

At this instant, she did not care in the slightest. Mending would *serve* her, she had decided, and there was no room for disobedience. Flesh melded together, the spark of life within it responding with far more strength than she thought possible, and Mikal's eyes opened fully, yellow irises glowing with unholy fire. He cried out, a long, shapeless sound full of thunder, and she sat back on her heels. Plaster and brick dust coated her face – Llewellyn had blasted straight through walls in his hurry to flee her.

And well he should, she thought, grimly. But first things first. She looked up, met Eli's gaze. The younger Shield was wide-eyed and very pale. Childish of him, but she did not have the heart to take him to task. "He shall mend," she said, heavily. "Listen to me very carefully, Shield."

"I hear," Eli answered automatically. He was well trained, she decided, but not particularly imaginative. Mikal's eyes had closed again, and he slumped, bloody but whole, in his brother Shield's arms. Grayson's body was twisted wrack, the sopha it had been flung over smashed to flinders. She could not remember when during the duel *that* had happened.

It did not matter. Mikal was alive, and that had to be enough. Her damnable duty lay heavy on her shoulders.

"Take him to St Jemes Palace. Tell whoever is on guard duty that the Raven has sent you. You will be ushered into a certain personage's presence. Tell that personage that Lord Sellwyth is alive and treacherous. Say, *Dinas Emrys*. Furthermore, tell this personage everything you have witnessed so far, word for word, and Mikal shall add his own observations. Afterwards you are to stay with that personage, and guard that personage *with your very life*. Are my instructions clear, Shield?"

"Very." Eli swallowed hard. His clothes were in a sad, sorry state – all three of them were coated with ground-fine plaster, their faces garishly chalked with the stuff. "Prima, where—"

He sought to *question* her? "Cease your noise. I shall be pursuing Lord Sellwyth." She paused; decided he did, after all, require more explanation. He had only just arrived in the game. "Eli, I am about to open the gates of my Discipline. Keep Mikal here until he has Mended sufficiently to travel to St Jemes." Another pause, this one longer, while she touched the quiescent Shield's cheek. Her fingers left a bloody smear on the fine powdery grit. "I . . . do not wish him to see this. Nor you," she added, belatedly, and stopped herself from continuing. *If he does not reach St Jemes whole, if you somehow damage him on the way, I shall hunt you down. And what I do to Llewellyn shall seem a mercy compared to your own suffering.*

But that was not quite proper. She took her hand away and rose, shedding dust and dirt with the crackle of a cleansing charm.

The trail of destruction punched through walls, the entire house vibrating with the after-effects of a duel. Patches of plaster had turned to glass or smooth iron, chalky and inky feathers flew, irrationality transmuting the prosaic materials of the everyday into something else. Moisture dripped from the ceilings, droplets sliding upwards from the floor in some patches. The force of gravity itself was disturbed, and it would take time for the irrationality to bleed itself away through other sorceries worked in the vicinity.

She stepped through the outer wall, shaking her head slightly as the edges torn in the brick facing shivered. They had transmuted to a long red silken fringe, fluttering even in the still, fog-bound air, touching her cheeks and the backs of her hands with sinister, slippery little kisses.

Llewellyn and his remaining Shields had made for the stables. As Chancellor, Grayson had the right to have his carriage drawn by two gryphons on State occasions, as long as he defrayed the cost of their keep.

And of course, with his Shields, Lord Sellwyth could commandeer said beasts to effect his escape.

I must have frightened him very badly.

They had paused long enough to let the gryphons at the clockhorses. Shreds of horseflesh spattered the wrecked interior of the stable; the hot reek of offal and copper blood filled her nose. Shards of bone littered the floor. Grayson had possessed quite a collection, but every single clockhorse was a mess of bone, metal, and rent meat.

It does not matter, Emma. It is time.

She stood, her fists caught in her tattered skirts. The vision of Mikal's broken body rose before her; she banished it with an effort that caused sweat to spring free. The plaster dust turned to a slick coating, and she fought to contain the force rising in her.

When she had again mastered herself, she gazed about the stable as if seeing it for the first time.

Death is here.

Very well, then. She was of the Endor, and it was high time she reminded Llewellyn Gwynnfud of the fact. Incidentally, if he reached his destination and engaged on what she suspected his next step was, her Queen would be in danger.

Emma Bannon, Sorceress Prime, did not like that idea at all. She inhaled smoothly, disregarding everything about her, turning inward to the locked and barred door of her deepest self.

And her Discipline . . . unfolded.

There was the lesser sorcery, charter and charm of force stored and renewed every Tideturn. Then there was Discipline, the unleashing of power that did not follow the sorcerer's bidding. It simply *was*, working through the gateway suddenly opened for it until the strength of the conduit failed. When the gateway closed, the world was *changed*.

This, then, the danger of sorcery – a losing of oneself.

A fierce hurtful flower blooming in her, its barbs tipped with rotting dust and earth in her mouth. Leprous spots crawled over her skin, the taste of bones and bitter ash. *"Aula naath gig,"* she cried, a Language older even than Mending's mellifluousness, and the chant took shape, tearing itself free of moorings inside her. Sorcery rose, pure and unconstrained.

The bones and meat and metal bedecking the stable's interior . . . twitched.

Chapter Thirty-One

Quarry and Quarry

It was a good thing Miss Bannon had left them a well-filled purse. The price of rented clockhorses to Upper Hardres was ridiculous. Ludovico pointed this out and drove a much harder bargain than Clare thought strictly wise, seeming to enjoy the haggling far more than was prudent. The Neapolitan was called a filthy gipsy, and took pleasure in feeding this impression by ill-timed spitting and insults. Sigmund was, of course, no help – the Bavarian could be cheated from pillar to post, and nearly *was* before the assassin intervened so auspiciously. It took a great deal of patience Clare was not overly supplied with in order to conclude the bargain in a reasonably diplomatic fashion.

Nevertheless, they were saddled by the time dawn broke over Dover's cliffs, and a half-hour later had quit the town's clutching limits.

The ride was a green and grey blur, Clare's attention turned mostly inward, equations filling his mental cauldron near to bursting. The pattern trembled just out of reach. He did not know Throckmorton's work, and there were other influences besides – he had read Roderick Smythe's monograph on logic patterns, but the crop of equations bore as much resemblance to Smythe's examples as a single fingernail gear did to Brocarde's Infinitude Audoricon.

The clutching fog tried to follow them, but five miles out of Dover they burst into watery grey sunlight. The waking world was hushed, even the birds forgetting to greet the sunrise.

Their view was for the most part trammelled by high green hedges on either side, and Valentinelli slumped in his saddle as if he wished he were elsewhere. Sigmund clutched at the reins and looked miserable. Clare would have quite enjoyed himself, if not for the incessant mental work. He was no closer to finding a pattern to the equations when they breasted a rise and looked down on the dual villages of Hardres, Upper and Lower. The estate was on the far side of the Lower town, a haze of coal and other smoke riding under the billows of grey cloud, weather sweeping in visible from a long distance away.

Despite his slouching, Valentinelli was a good horseman, and his bay clockhorse picked up the pace as much as was safe. Hoofbeats pounded steady time, jog-trotting, sometimes reaching a bone-rattling canter when the Neapolitan judged it appropriate. Time pressed down on Clare, ticking – there was only a limited amount of it before they reached the estate, and once there time would weigh on them even more heavily.

They passed a weather-beaten sign, proclaiming *Hardres Quarry Ltd 3mi*, proudly pointing down an overgrown track that had nevertheless seen hard recent use, if the state of the broken and battered herbiage on its floor was any indication. Clare noted this, and his uneasiness mounted. The Sun refused to show His face, and the air was heavy with the fresh greensap scent of rain.

"*Mentale.*" The Neapolitan glanced over his shoulder. "What we likely to find here?"

It was somewhat of a relief to turn his attention from the equations. The array of mental blackboards had changed into a forest of hideously twisted chalk scribbles. "More mecha, certainly," he answered, his faculties directed sluggishly at the new question. "Possibly a mentath to deal with the arranging of the fresh capacitors. What troubles me is that almost certainly we will find a few men in the trade of violence. We are not so very far from Londinium, and if Prussians have arrived in Dover, they have arrived elsewhere as well. Brighton and Hardwitch, of course." *The planning involved is tremendous. But they would not need many – just enough to hold the Palace and Whitehall, as well as the Armory at the foot of the Tower. Much will depend on exactly how they plan to incapacitate Britannia or Her vessel.*

The thought of Britannia incapacitated, or Queen Victrix somehow under duress, gave him a queer feeling in the region of his stomach. It could not have been his last meal, for that had been Miss Bannon's excellent dinner.

Well, if it was the last, at least it was a fine one. And in good company.

"Hmm." Valentinelli grinned, white teeth flashing in his dark face. "I tell you what. I kill mercenaries, you kill the other *mentale*. Simple."

"I cannot kill him until I know more of the plan."

The Neapolitan jerked his head in Sigmund's direction. "Is he any good at the torture, then?"

Sig piped up. "The bastards who broke my *Spinne*, yes, I torture them. Baerbarth shall invent *new* tortures!"

"I should think not, Sig old chap." Clare suppressed a sigh. "Dear heavens. A mentath does not respond to such things as a mercenary would."

Valentinelli's snort was a masterpiece of disdain. "A man feel pain, he answer questions. Especially when Ludo is asking, *mentale*. Never mind. We see when we arrive."

"If you would cease speaking like a bad imitation of a Punchinjude puppet, *signor*, we would deal much more easily with each other." For a moment Clare regretted saying it. His irritation had mounted to a considerable degree. Neither Sig nor the assassin was *logical*. Not like Miss Bannon. Of course, she was not logical either, so—

Wait. His attention snagged on the thought, but he was not given leave to follow it.

"So I should speak the Queen's tongue, should I?" The same clipped, cultured schoolboy tone as before. He sounded thoroughly nettled, and had ceased slumping atop his clockhorse. "If I was not blood-bound, *sir*, you and I would have an accounting."

"I am your man, *signor*," Clare returned rather stiffly. "As soon as this damnable affair is finished. In the meantime, can you *please* not insult me by speaking as if you are a dolt? I have rather a sizeable respect for your intelligence, and I wish not to waste time arguing you into acting as if you possess said intelligence."

Silence, broken only by the thumping of hooves. Clare blinked.

I am very uncomfortable with the idea of Miss Bannon in peril. It is not logical, but . . . oh, good heavens, she is a sorceress! *You are becoming ridiculous, Archibald!*

Valentinelli finally spoke. "It is a habit, sir. I wish everyone, without exception, to underestimate me. It makes my life much easier."

"Everyone? Including Miss Bannon?"

"I think she is the only one who never has." The soft, cultured tone was chilling. "And I hate her for it."

Well. "Ah." What could one say in response? "I should think it would be a comfort."

"A man does not like a woman he cannot surprise, *mentale.*"

Much about you becomes clearer. "I see."

Valentinelli kneed his horse into a canter, and Clare hastened to follow suit. Sigmund groaned, and their destination grew ever closer.

And Clare still had no pattern for the equations.

"There is no one here," Sigmund announced. He was flushed and sweating, his broad face shiny.

Clare hushed him, gazing at the crumbling manor from the shelter of an overgrown hedge.

It was of the flat *chateau* style, a box with a sadly punctured clay-tile roof, the gardens crumbling and overgrown, its windows lackadaisically boarded with worm-eaten wood. Weeds had forced their way up between flagstones, and the whole place had such an obvious aura of disrepair that he was half tempted to agree with Sig's assessment.

But only half.

Valentinelli merely pointed. The weeds were crushed where heavy cart wheels had rolled over them. The trail pointed directly to the three stairs leading to the chateau's fire-scarred front door.

The fire was recent. And chemical in origin, from what I can observe. Which does not bode well.

The Neapolitan cocked his head, his dark eyes taking on a peculiar flat shine.

Clare was suddenly cold, and very glad they had left the horses in a small copse outside the estate's fallen gates. The greenery hiding them seemed a very thin screen indeed.

For there was the sound of scraping metal, gears catching, and fizzing sparks. The manor house shuddered, its stone façade zigzagging with cracks. The earth rumbled, vibrating as if a gigantic beast slumbering in its depths turned over in its sleep.

In a blinding flash, Clare thought of the quarry down the road. *Yes. They would not need to dig far to stay hidden; and no wonder there were cart tracks. Building underground; now why did I not account for such a notion?*

The manor shuddered again, and masonry fell. A cavern tore itself in the front wall, belching steam, smoke, and blue-white arcing electricity. Clare's faculties supplied him with an observation he did not fancy *or* trust. He questioned it from every angle, and it became indisputable. He was not going mad.

A gigantic mechanisterum homunculus had been built *into* the house.

Sigmund's disbelieving laugh was lost in the thundering noise. *"Spinne!"* he yelled. *"Bastards! Schweine!"*

The mecha rose out of the manse, shedding bits of masonry

like rainwater from a duck's back. Clare's busy faculties swallowed every detail they could reach while the thing's legs unfolded, a mad dream of a mechanical spider taking shape before him on a lovely sunny afternoon. The appendages thudded down one at a time, while the cephalothorax and abdomen lifted, gleaming. Prussian capacitors winked in orderly rows along the bottom of its body, a constant whining hum rattling every tooth in Clare's head. The pattern behind the deadlights trembled on the edge of his comprehension. Steel-banded glass jars bubbled with green fluid atop the mecha's back, and in each one floated—

So that is what they needed the brains and spinal cords for. His limbs refused to move, his busy brain straining. *A mentath attempting some form of Alterative sorcery? But how? How is it possible?*

The ground would not cease its rumbling, and Clare's imagination served him a picture of other mecha, built in the depths of an abandoned quarry, golden discs on their chests sparking into life as the workers who built them – and he was suddenly quite sure they had been assembled by *things* very like the metal scarecrows in the Blackwerks' depths – capered with furious mechanical glee, their eyes glowing crimson with mad intelligence.

If a dragon could run the stink and clamour and hellish heat of the Blackwerks, one could easily induce its unsleeping metal minions to build in the dank darkness underground. Another thought turned Clare even colder: perhaps there was more than one of the beasts cooperating in this terrible mockery of the mechanisterum's art.

"*Get down!*" Ludovico yelled, shoving him into Sigmund. They fell in a rattling heap, Clare's hat disappearing into the overgrown shrubbery. The juicy green stink of broken sap-filled branches rose, struggling with the odours of ozone, heated machine oil, scorched metal, and stone dust.

The mecha was immense. *No wonder the equations are so complex. This rather changes things.*

Valentinelli crouched, his hip knocking Sig's shoulder. The Bavarian was pressed into the dirt, and Clare thought perhaps the Neapolitan enjoyed the chance to do so . . . but it did not work. For the gigantic mecha lifting its way up out of the ruins of the manse had some means of detecting them. The eyes on its arachnoid head dripped with diseased golden electricity, and the thing squatted over smoking ruins. Massive clicking noises assaulted the shivering air, and apertures slid open where a living arachnid would have spinnarets. Cannon shapes whirred down into place, and Clare's stomach gave a decidedly uneasy message to the rest of him.

The cannons swivelled, pointing unerringly at Clare and his companions. The Neapolitan cursed –

– and there was a booming so immense it robbed every other sound of consequence as the mecha fired.

Chapter Thirty-Two

Bannon's Ride

White bone, red muscle, dark metal. Stink-steaming hides of several colours twitching, shaking free of offal and straw. The hooves coalesced, metal shards bending as sorcery crackled, sliding up splinters of bone as they fused together to become legs.

Emma Bannon stood, her eyes open but sightless, black from lid to lid. Her outstretched hands were loose and cupped; she leaned forward as if into a heavy wind, but her curls only riffled slightly. Her ragged skirts fluttered, and her pale flesh marked itself with charter charms. The spiked glyphs did not glow.

Not completely. The symbols sliding against the texture of her skin were black as well, their sharp edges fluorescing with traces of eerie green foxfire.

The chant came from her slack mouth, but she was not voicing it. Her lips parted, her tongue still; the words swelled whole from her passive throat. The Language was not Mending or Breaking, not Naming or Binding or Bonding. It was not a Language of the White or the Grey. It was the deepest Black, that tongue, and it was given free rein.

Discipline was not entirely inborn, but it was not entirely chosen, either. Rather, the predisposition and character of witch, charmer, mancer or sorcerer narrowed choices until, in the last year of Collegia schooling, the practitioner arrived at the Discipline that in retrospect seemed a foregone conclusion.

The non-sorcerous feared the Grey and despised the Black, thinking the names meant things they did not. The White was often capable of causing the most harm as it sought to cure, and the Black was the restfulness of night after a hard day's labour – or so its practitioners said.

The White disagreed, vehemently. The Grey kept their own counsel.

And yet, even among the Black, the Endor were . . . well, not feared. But held in caution. Once, one of their kind had brought a shade back to flesh to answer a king, a feat still whispered of with awe.

The haunches built themselves, massive, meat rearranged and muscles attaching to re-fused bone. Clockhorse metal filigreed each bone, ran threadlike through the muscles, and crackled with the same rot-green foxfire as the charter symbols on Emma's skin.

A figure appeared behind her, indistinct through plaster dust and the smokegloss of sorcery. *Two* figures, one leaning heavily on the other, both tall, well-muscled men, picking their way through scattered bricks and the destruction of a sorcerer's passage. One man was dark-eyed. The other's irises burned yellow in the gloom.

Emma's delicate fingers tensed. The chant took on sonorous striking depth. The withers appeared, and the thing was unmistakably a horse, but too big. The stitched-together pieces of horsehide flowed obscenely up its legs, hugging naked iron-filigreed musculature. The neck lifted in a proud curve, the vertebrae knobs of glassy polished bone, lengthening to fine thin short spikes of mane. The tail was a fall of metal-chased hair, and its head was two clockhorse skulls melded together to create a larger, subtly *changed* thing. For it had sharp teeth no horse, Altered or pureflesh, would have, and its bone eyesockets were emptily, terribly dark.

The steed stood very still. A ripple went through it as the hide finished its patchwork. More metal quivered and flung itself from the floor, sorcerously magnetised into plates of armour. A saddle appeared, shaping itself from shredded leather tack.

The amalgamation of flesh, metal, bone, and sorcery became a massive destrier, its shoulders straining as ætherial force struggled to violate Nature. Armoured in metal barding and caparisoned in green and black, a gossamer fabric made of dust and foxfire cloaking the hurtful edges, it stood slump-shouldered and obscene.

The sorceress's fingers flicked. The chant halted, turned on itself inside her throat, and birthed a Word.

"*X——v!*"

It did not echo, but it continued for a long time, a hole torn in the world's fabric, a curtain pulled aside. And something . . . descended.

The *Khloros* lifted its massive head. Leaf-green sparks flamed in its eyesockets. A clashing ran along its length as the armour shifted, settling, under the fabric of dust and æther cloaking it.

Crackling silence. But the Work was not finished, for as the sorceress strode forward, the black gem at her throat gave a burst of radiant spring-green flame as well, scorching eye and mind alike. She leapt, caught the pommel, and her foot found one huge silver-chased stirrup. Light as a leaf she vaulted into the saddle, and as she did, spurs jingled, oddly musical. Her own armour appeared, metal striking her Black-charmed skin and spreading as if liquid, flowing up her legs to make greaves, rising to encase her thighs and torso. Her head tipped back, dark curls tumbling feather-free before the helm grew from spiked shoulders. The green became patterns of charter and charm, flowing through sorcery-blackened metal, and the sharp-scaled gauntlets creaked as her fingers flexed again, their paleness disappearing like birch twigs under a flood of ink.

From the helm's shadowed depths, the Word came again.

"*X——v!*"

The *Khloros*, the Pale Horse, neighed. The sound shattered what little of the stable's interior remained intact, and both onlookers flinched.

"*X——v!*" A final time, the Word resounded, full of the rush and crackle of conflagration.

The *Khloros* shook its spiked mane, and its front hooves lifted. It reared, its rider moving with fluid hurtful grace, melded to its sudden poisonous loveliness. By the time the Word's thunder died, the *Khloros* was an unholy, beautiful thing cloaked in twisting pale green fire. At the heart of every flame was the black between stars, a thin thread of utter negation.

The helm's triple spikes nodded among firefly flickers of stray sorcery. The *Khloros* wheeled, a caracole of exquisite, diseased elegance. Its hooves left frost-scorch on the shivering, unwilling ground. From the darkness under the three spikes came the sorceress's voice, and yet it was not hers. It was the lipless sigh of Life's oldest companion.

"*Death,*" she whispered.

The *Khloros* unleashed itself with a musical clatter of metal against stone, another shattering neigh blowing a hole in the only remaining untouched wall in the stable. It leapt forward in a foaming wave, and the two men had gone to their knees in the ruins. The roof creaked dangerously, but neither moved. The Shields clutched each other like children wakened from a nightmare. One was paper-pale, trembling as if with palsy, and he leaned aside to retch uselessly.

The yellow-eyed Shield swayed. His face was alight.

"Beautiful," Mikal whispered.

In the distance, the screams began.

They rode.

The earth itself repelled the Khloros, *so its hooves struck ash-green sparks from a cushion of screaming air. Its gait flowed, its neck arched and its metallic tail sparking on the wind of its passing. The Rider moved with the massive beast as one, and the breathless screams of Londinium were as music over the drumming hoofbeats.*

For the Rider did not merely call forth the pale horse. The sorcery flowing through her had not reached its high tide yet. With every hoof-fall, the city quaked like a plucked string.

And the dead answered.

They rose from their graves, gossamer shades with wide-stretched rictus grins. The Khloros could not step above ground uncontaminated by Death; few places were closed to it. Sanctified ground was no bar to it, for the dead were part and parcel of the hallowing.

This was what caused the screaming. As the Pale Horse cantered, its Rider staring straight ahead under her triple-peaked helm, the dead within sound of their passing rose like veils. The stronger among the deceased, newly woken or newly buried, ran like dogs or rode horses of their own, spectral rotting things with soft pads instead of hooves.

For as long as there was Londinium, there were equines to serve, to labour . . . and to die.

The living cowered and fled, though the dead shied away from their warm breathing fear. Some few claimed to have seen the face of the Rider, but they all agreed it was a man. Those whose gaze did pierce the deep shadows of the helm stayed silent, for they recognised the white-cheeked, burning-eyed woman they glimpsed. The silent ones were those whose candles were already flickering, and within a week those few had been laid to rest in cold earth.

To the west the Dead Hunt rode, a freezing wind tearing shutters from stone houses, shattering windows, bursting chimneys and grinding cobblestones and brick facing in weird lattice patterns. The West End, the homes of the rich and influential, cowered under the lash of the Eternal. There were those on Picksdowne who claimed to see the insubstantial dead rising from the street itself, and the clapperless, immense Black Bell hung in the Tower tolled once, sharply, the Shadow lifting its malformed head and staring with eyes like two flat silver coins. The dome of ætheric protection cupping the Palace of St Jemes lit like a white-hot bonfire, sensing something dreadful afoot.

The Rider cut through one corner of Hidepark, and for months afterward there was a black scar in the lush greenery near the Cumber Gate, one the quality affected not to see as they drove past on their daily promenades.

Then she turned, sharply, to the north, wheeling as a giant bird will. None but the tide of half-seen crystalline shades following her witnessed the helmed head lift, as if she studied the heavens, searching for . . . what? What could such a being be chasing, on such a night?

Whatever it was, she found it. For sudden tension bloomed in the Rider's figure, and her scaled gauntlets tightened on the reins. The Khloros's massive head rose, too, as if it could taste the spectral traces of a traitor's passage against the velvet-yellow clouds reflecting Londinium's nightly glow. The pale horse champed, and its hoofbeats took on new urgency.

A final Word broke free of the Rider's throat. It was feathered with diamond ice, a weightless sound, and the dead flowed forward, streaming around the Khloros. The Rider shimmered as if under cold heavy oil, fog flash-freezing and scattering sparks of foxfire sorcery. The Pale Horse's hooves hit a billowing cushion of vapour, and its bulk heaved up with a gasping-fish leap.

Khloros and Rider flew, on a white-billowing cloud of the dead. Their melting shadow touched the earth below, terribly black and crisp though there was precious little light to cast it. A withering stole through the dark hole of that shadow, and as they flew, the living in houses underneath cowered without knowing quite why.

It was over two hundred miles to Dinas Emrys, and the Rider

had to reach it by dawn. As long as the strength holding the
ætheric conduit open held, the Khloros would bear her.

Following a gryphon-borne traitor, Death flew from Londinium.

Chapter Thirty-Three

Man Only Dies Once

Ears ringing, blood slicking his face, Clare staggered upright. *That is precisely the problem with cannon. Difficult to aim, especially when firing from a suspended carriage.* He shook his head, and Valentinelli was suddenly before him, crouching and bloody. The man's thin-lipped mouth moved, his dark hair half singed and wildly disarranged. Clare blinked, realising he was deaf.

Temporarily, or . . .

As if in response, the world poured into his ears once more. A sudden overwhelming welter of noise scored through his tender skull, threatening to turn his brain into thin gargling soup. His knees hit the smoking dirt, and Sigmund appeared, a thread of bright blood sliding down his filthy, soot-stained face.

Clare strained to deduce, but his faculties would not obey. The coja, false friend, had turned on him. Whatever bolt the immense arachnid mecha had fired at them was no help either.

The bolt. Electrical in some fashion? The mecha was swimming in electrical force; the capacitors are maintaining at a high rate. The core! Masters's core!

The thought was driftwood to a drowning man. He clung to it, his mental grasp tightening with the strength of desperation.

A shifting stream of values! That's it!

For a blinding moment he saw it all – the Blackwerks, where every difference was a *range*, not an orderly single value. The trouble was not irrationality. Rather, it was rationality not wide enough to contain what it saw.

The world is wider, Horatio, than is dreamed of in your philosophy.

The pressure in his skull eased all at once. Marvellous relief, sensory information behaving as it should now, and he opened his eyes to find the Neapolitan's pox-scarred face above his. He had fallen; the assassin had caught him, and even now held him. The ground was charred, soot rising in fine dancing black flakes, the hedges blackened and crisped, peeled back in a perfect circle that had *just* missed them. Had Valentinelli not knocked them aside and held Sigmund down, all three of them might have been caught in the blast, instead of on its smoke-crisped margin.

The earth was quiet now, settling itself after a violation. The only hint of thunder was far in the distance, and one could not be sure it was not merely one's nerves echoing after a sustained assault.

Calculate the stride length. The arachnid will have to pace slowly for the smaller mecha, but they will not grow tired. Sub-equations in the core will take care of that – how is it speaking to the receivers? An invisible signal, bringing it into range – pure electricity? No, and not magnetism either. Perhaps some blend of the two? How? Is it sorcery? No, the logic engine will not allow for that; the brains in the casks atop it must not be Altered then. I must have more data.

Valentinelli's mouth was still moving. Sigmund nodded, leaned down –

– and slapped Clare. Not lightly, either, his work-hardened palm cracking against Clare's cheek.

The shock snapped Clare's head aside, and he thudded back into his body with a sound akin to a carriage wheel jolting through a pothole. "Thank you," he gasped. "Dear heavens, *that* was uncomfortable."

The Neapolitan relaxed slightly. He swore in Italian, more as a means of expressing his happiness than anything else. Clare blinked and found his body would obey him, gained his feet with Valentinelli's help, and spotted his hat among some smoking shrubbery.

"*Spinne!*" Sigmund crowed. "Did you see that, Archie? Bastards built a *Spinne*! And what a beautiful beast. We hunt them down, *ja*? Hunt them and see how they made the *fräulein Spinne*!"

Bending over to retrieve his hat was problematic, but Clare managed it, and turned to survey the smoking pile of rubbish that had once been a reasonably nice, if somewhat decrepit, manor house. "Indubitably."

"*La strega* do not pay enough for this," the assassin muttered darkly. "That *thing*. *Diavolo*." And, of all things, the assassin crossed himself in the manner of the Papists.

"Twenty guineas," Clare reminded him, a trifle more jollily than he felt. "And you said you'd take on the Devil himself, my princely friend."

"Twenty guinea is *not* enough." The man's accent had settled into what Clare suspected might be his true voice – clipped and cultured, but with the song of his native tongue rubbing under unmusical Queen's Britannic. "That was not a cannonball, *signor*."

"Nor was it a kiss on the cheek." Clare jammed his hat atop his head. The reek of singed hair, singed greenery, boiled rock, and dust was immense. If Valentinelli knew he was missing his eyebrows, he gave no sign of it – and Clare wondered if he might be missing his own. "Come, gentlemen. We must find the horses, if they have not bolted. We have work to do."

"Wait. That – that *thing*." Valentinelli's hands were tense and his clothing still steamed. His coat was sadly the worse for wear, and his dark hair was scorched as well. All in all, they were a rather sorry and raffish bunch by now. "How you plan on stopping it? What it *doing*, eh, *signor*? And what you propose *we* do?"

Sig stared in the direction the vast mecha had gone, his broad rough hands working on empty air as if he had the builder of such a contraption by the throat.

Clare took stock of himself, patting his pockets. His pistol had not discharged, thank goodness. His watch was still in its accustomed place, and he drew it forth, noted the time, and wound it, a soothingly habitual set of motions. "First we find the horses." He replaced the watch and pulled his cuffs down, brushed at his frock coat. He stamped, doing what he could to rid his boots of dust and char. Miss Bannon's money was still secure. "Then we visit the quarry three miles from here. If luck is on our side, there will be a mecha there we can steal, for the range of values will no doubt have excluded some of those built." He paused. "If not, we shall think of something. Then we hie ourselves to Londinium and do our best to nip a rebellion in the bud."

There were Altered guards at the quarry's mouth, but Valentinelli left Clare and Sig in a shaded dell and disappeared around the bend in the cart track. He reappeared a few minutes later, wiping one of his dark-bladed knives on a torn rag he dropped without further ado in the dust. Clare did not overly examine the traces of crimson on it; it was enough to deduce the provenance – the shirt the Neapolitan had torn it from as soon as the owner had ceased breathing.

Mercifully, the corpses lay with their faces turned away from the entrance, their necks crooked oddly. Their Alterations were only hinted at – deformed ribs and too-thick legs insinuating changes to the human body that might sicken Clare, did he not have other things to focus on.

"Kielstone," he murmured. It *was* an underground quarry. Kiel could be cut in any direction, unlike slate, and it ran in odd veins, twisting and looping underground. It also was mildly resistant to sorcery, meaning it had to be extracted by hand. Even traces of kiel would camouflage the mechas nicely, before their logic engines turned on.

The entry was a cavern of pitch black, even under the strengthening daylight. The clouds were thinning, and it might turn into a beautiful Kentish spring day before long. The mecha would glitter under the sun as they strode toward Londinium.

Were there other quarries in the districts around the ancient city just waiting to birth a stream of metal monsters? Very likely. How many?

More than will be comfortable, Clare. Concern yourself with the task at hand.

"Archie." Sigmund had gone rather pale under his mask of soot. "In *there*?"

"Come now, Sig. You're a lion for Miss Bannon, aren't you? See there." Clare pointed. "We shall find lanthorns, no doubt. Or glowrock. Signor Valentinelli, if you would be so kind."

In short order they had glowrocks caged in steel, the surfaces of the stones dark and oil-slick as they absorbed sunlight. They seemed well charged, but just to be safe Valentinelli also found a lanthorn with a trimmed wick and plenty of oil. Clare thought to ask if the man had lucifers about him, but the gleam in the Neapolitan's dark eyes told him such a question was foolish.

They penetrated the cavern's black mouth. Twenty paces in it was dim enough that the glowrocks began to shimmer. The floor was stone, scarred and worn smooth, implements stacked against the walls – picks and shovels, rope, kegs of various sizes, scrap lumber, a small pile of miner's hats, candleholders. Fifty paces, and they walked in tiny spheres of silver glow, blackness pressing down all around. A hundred paces brought them to a junction. The main passageway continued down, terminating in what had to be some sort of caged hoist-lift; a much narrower passage veered sharply off to the right.

Valentinelli was a scarred caricature, glowrock light disappearing into his pupils and the pits on his soot-streaked face. "*Signor?*"

Clare swallowed drily, pointed at the smaller passage. "That one."

"How would they . . ." Sig coughed. "No, of course. That is for supplies. *This* is for people."

Pleased, Clare made a noise of assent. Valentinelli handed his glowrock cage over and edged into the small passageway. If there were more guards below, he did not wish to be blinded. It was a good idea. But they did not have to go far. The narrower passageway terminated at a wooden platform. Two frail guard-rails over a pitch-black pit, with the wooden struts of a ladder showing.

"Oh, *Scheisse*." Sig's voice struck the edges of the pit, and a faint echo drifted back up.

"Cheer up, Sig. Man only dies once, you know."

Valentinelli's humourless snigger echoed as well. "In that case, *signor*, you go first." But he shouldered the mentath aside with a small spitting sound of annoyance, grabbing the third glowrock cage and producing a handkerchief. In a trice the cage was tied to his torn waistcoat, and he tested the ladder with commendable aplomb. "Safe enough. Twenty guinea, *definitely* not enough."

The climb down was more arduous mentally than physically. Sig, sweating and muttering awful imprecations under his breath, nearly wrenched one of the ladders free, he trembled so violently. Every twenty feet or so the ladder would end, resting on a trigged platform of warped wood. The glowrocks' shimmer intensified as they descended, and Clare was seeking to calculate just what sort of foul air they might encounter in the depths when Valentinelli hopped off the ladder and on to solid ground. The Neapolitan sighed, a not-quite-whistle, and lifted his glow-rock cage.

A vast chamber tunnelled out of rock greeted them. It was mostly empty, but the scuffs on the dusty, dirt-grimed floor were fresh. To Clare's left, the other half of the large hoist-lift rested in a carven hollow. The sides and floor of the cavern were unnaturally smooth, almost glassy. The cavern's roof was ribbed like a cathedral's vault, but the ribs were odd. Almost . . . organic.

Where did the workers who built this all vanish to? For a moment he had an odd mental vision of them seeping through the cracks in the floor, metal become liquid and returning to earth's embrace. He shook it away, annoyed at the fancy.

Sig let out a bark of relief when his boots touched firm ground. Great pearls of sweat cut tracks through the ash on his face. "Archie. I hate you."

"Ha!" Clare's cry of triumph shattered the stillness.

Scattered on the floor of the cavern were a few bipedal mecha of the sort they had seen in the warehouse near the Tower. They slumped, curiously lonely, and from the way they all faced toward the deepest darkness at the back of the cavern, Clare could imagine the serried ranks that must have stood here before awakening to the invisible call.

"Ha!" he repeated, and actually bounced up on his toes. "As I suspected! Some of them did not receive that call, Sig. You and I are going to mechanister them, and then we will take them to Londinium." The only response his revelation garnered was frank, open-mouthed stares from his companions. "Don't you see? We will have mecha of our own!"

"Mad," Valentinelli muttered. "You are *mad*."

Sigmund, on the other hand, stared for a few more moments. Then a smile spread over his broad face. *"Du prächtiger Bastard!"* He clapped Clare on the shoulder hard enough to stagger the mentath. "Only if I take it to workshop after. *Ja?*"

"Sig, old man, if we make this work, you will have a multiplicity of mecha carcasses to pick over at your leisure. We haven't much time; let us see what they have left us."

Chapter Thirty-Four

Always the Bloody Way

The first thread of grey on the eastern horizon was a silver ribbon under a heavy door of ink. It whipped the *Khloros* into a frenzy of speed, the countryside below running like a sheet of black oil on a wet plate. The Rider leaned forward, spiked helm nodding and armoured shoulders shaking with effort. The door of her Discipline was closing, and she could not stop it.

The tide of the dead who rode with her foamed in the dark-clouded sky, a crystal tracery of flung sea-waves. Under the shadow of *Khloros* and Rider they rose like smoke from grave-yards and ditches, fields and rivers, and joined the procession. The things they rode were vaguely horselike, or they ran in empty air, spirits whole as they had been while living or terribly disfigured as they had been at life's ending. The drowned and the murdered, the beaten and the lost, the starved and the glut-tonous, they ran in the *Khloros*'s wake.

This was why Endor was held in caution. Who could trust a man or woman who held congress with such a crowd? Or a Prime who could bring the *Khloros* to a night's unlife?

The Pale Horse arrowed down. The silvery ribbon in the east became fringes of grey. It lashed sensitive flanks, scored smoking weals in piebald, stitched-together horseflesh. The armoured barding sought to protect the sorcerous skin underneath.

It does not matter. The journey is at an end.

With the thought, consciousness returned to the Rider. For a moment she hesitated, trembling, on the threshold, nameless and irresolute. It seemed an eternity she had been riding, following the scentless trail of treachery borne on gryphon wings. Did he know she followed? Quite possibly; she was loud enough to be heard counties away.

Between one heartbeat and the next she was through the door, the memory of being merely a cup to pour meaning into mercifully evaporating. Even a sorcerer's finely tuned mind could not stand such a violation. Best it were forgotten, and soon.

A white sword coalesced at the eastern horizon. The grey light intensified, and the sound of waves crashed back and forth. *Khloros*, understanding her human need, intensified its speed again. It was graceful even in its desperate shambling, its armour and barding and flesh, bones and metal unravelling into pure æther. It burst into colour – the page written upon, the pallid light broken into its constituent parts.

The crystal wave clustered around the Rider, dead hands outstretched and fingers turned to vapour.

She fell.

Sunlight. Warm as oil against her cheeks, striking her sensitised eyes even through protective lids. She lay on chill dampness, various bits digging into her back and hair and skirts. She did not dare open her eyes, simply lay where she was for a few breaths, taking in everything she could of the space around her.

Morning chill, a damp saltbreath of the sea a distance away, flat metal tang of riverwater closer. The sunshine came in dappled patterns – she was under leaves. A faint breeze rattled them. What was that sound? It was not waves or the groaning crash of rent earth. It was not the hoofbeats of *Khloros*, and it was most *definitely* not her own voice.

Cries. The clacking of razor beaks, a voice raised high and furious in sonorous chant. A shuddering ran through the damp, hard ground underneath her.

What?

Sense returned. Every inch and particle of her savagely abused body hurt. To open the door to Discipline was never undertaken lightly. Things could happen to those whose will was not honed, and Discipline took a hard toll on the body as well as the mind. Emma Bannon sat up, blinking furiously, and found herself in a ragged ruin of a dress, her corset stays snapped and dark curls knocked loose, the morning dew gilding bracken and bramble. To her left a rocky hill rose, choked with vines. It was from the top of that hill that the sounds were pouring, screeches and nasty grindings.

She staggered upright, tearing herself free of clutching greenery. Her knees threatened to give; she silently cursed at them. That gave them some starch, but only *some*. Her rings ran with sparkling light – Tideturn had come while she lay senseless, and she carried a full charge of sorcerous force. It stung, like the touch of sun on already reddened skin.

She took stock. All in all, she was reasonably whole. The black stone at her throat was ice cold, her rings on numb fingers sparked with charter symbols, and her earrings quivered against her neck, brushing dew-damp skin. If she did not take pneumonia from lying on the cold ground for however long, it would be a miracle.

That's Llewellyn up there. She shook herself, cast about for a path. None was apparent.

Oh, isn't that always the bloody way. Where am I? God alone knows where, with a mad Prime above and the fate of Britannia at stake, and not even a goat track in sight.

"Bloody f—king *hell*," she muttered, and other words more improper, as she turned in a full circle. The clashing and scraping and cawing above her was mounting in intensity.

Well. There is nothing for it, then.

She waded through the bramble to the base of the hill, set her hands to the rough grey stone poking out through moss and vine, and began to climb.

Chapter Thirty-Five

Don't Touch the Contacts

Sigmund swore, hit the mecha's froglike head twice with the spanner. The resounding clashes filled the cavern. The glowrocks were dimming. "There. Try now."

Really? Banging it with a spanner? Sigmund, I am disappointed in you. Clare, strapped into the mecha's chest, sighed and shook the jolting out of his bones. Each time Sig banged on something, he was half afraid he would end up skullsplit, sagging in the mecha's straps and buckles.

He curled his fists around the handles, turning his wrists just slightly so the metal plating had full contact with his skin. "I don't think it's going to—"

Golden glow burst from the circle over his chest. The small logic engine sputtered, and Clare was so surprised he almost sent the mecha tumbling over backwards. Ratcheting echoed, capacitors hummed. Clare's concentration narrowed. The equations ran smoothly, ticking below the surface of his conscious mind, as tingling ripples slid up his arms.

Ha!

He had solved the equations. It was now close to child's play to bend the mecha to his will. It took two steps forward, obedient instead of fighting him, and one impossibility followed another.

Around the cavern, humming clangour rose. Golden discs,

hanging slackly in the chests of the slumped mecha, flashed blue-white. *Aha! The variance, that's why they're responding to this one. Must be a redundancy built into their capacitation metrics. There's bound to be several that weren't within the large engine's tolerances but are within mine. Drop in the bucket, but still jolly good.*

"Clare?" Valentinelli sounded nervous.

"It's all right," he called. The words echoed internally, feedback mounting, but he dumped the superfluous noise with a repeating equation. Once one had the trick of it, surprisingly easy. "Climb into a mecha, but don't touch the contacts!"

Valentinelli's reply was unrepeatable, and Clare laughed. The fierce white-hot joy of logic took him, a razor-edged glow. "*Onward!*" he yelled, as the mechanisterum homunculi began to stamp. "*Onward to Londinium! But don't touch the bloody contacts!*"

To run with iron pistons for legs and a burning globe of logic for a pumping heart, faster than a thoroughbred or a sporty carriage, faster even than a railcar. To watch Londinium grow on the horizon, under a pall of smoke rising into the sky like a column of God's guidance, while metal legs tirelessly carried one forward.

This was joy.

Sigmund whooped almost the entire way, drunk with the exhilaration of speed. Valentinelli, his pocked face set and alarmingly pale, hung in the straps, jounced about like a Red Indusan papoose. The assassin had spent the last hour desperately seeking to avoid touching *anything*, not just the contacts.

Clare, overjoyed by the wind in his face and the logic humming through his bones, found himself laughing again.

They were half a mile from Londinium when it suddenly became more difficult to move. The equations tangled, snarling against each other, and sweat sprang on Clare's brow as he fought air gone suddenly glass-hard.

Oh no you don't.

The will pressing down on them was immense, and backed by a much larger logic engine, one powered by a core far more powerful than the tiny one at Clare's chest. But that much strength was clumsy, and created so much interference it was relatively easy to divert the force of its attack.

He had wondered if the mecha he had control of would respond to the larger logic engine's soundless call once they were awake. It appeared they would not – unless the mentath controlling the spider solved the riddle of the variances.

Clare devoutly hoped he would not.

And now the other mentath knew he was here. Clare's attention became fully occupied, his small band of a dozen mecha slowing, Sig finally catching the idea that something was amiss.

Carry that over, dump the quad, string those together, there's the weakness, let it replicate, aha! Eat that fine dinner, sir!

Were Clare to explain this battle, he would liken it to a game of chess – except with a dozen boards, each board in five dimensions, and each player with as many pieces as he could mentally support without fusing his brain into a useless heap of porridge.

There was, unfortunately, no time for comparison or explanation. He pushed the dozen mecha forward, a tiny piece of grit edging under Londinium's shell, metal creaking as he leaned forward, his body tensing inside the straps. Gears whined and ratcheted, fountains of sparks showering the paving of Kent Road.

Shimmering curtains of equations spun and parted, the world merely interlocking fields of force and reaction. For a moment the whole of the city spread below him, nodes and intersections, and he saw the thrust of the other mentath's attack.

St Jemes's Park lay littered with smoking mecha corpses. But there was an endless array of them, pressing north towards the Palace. Further clusters about Whithall and the Tower, and Clare had to decide which he was to strike for.

Save Victrix. Nothing else matters.

It was as if Miss Bannon stood at his ear, whispering. The pendant she had given him was quiescent, neither hot nor cold – of course, the field of an active logic engine would interfere with it somewhat. But ever afterwards, Clare thought it very likely that some quirk of Nature had spoken across time and space, telling him *exactly* what Emma Bannon would say. Perhaps it was only his deductive capability.

He did not think so.

The decision was already made. He quickly made the calculations, turning several of the necessary routines over to the logic engines and smaller subroutines to the glowing Prussian capacitors – their route was now fixed, pedestrians and carriages to be avoided if at all possible, the mecha not carrying himself and his companions striding ahead as pawns. Greenwitch Road, taking care to stay as far away from the edge of the Wark as was possible, then a cut through St Georgus Road; the Westminstre Bridge would be under attack but he would perhaps strike the invaders where they thought it least possible. If he could win the other side of the bridge, there was the battle at Whitehall to skirt and the park to traverse, then the Palace.

"Britannia!" he yelled, and the mecha screeched in reply, a hellish cacophony. "*God and Her Majesty!*" And the mecha leapt forward, just as the other mentath, its core-bloated intellect no longer resembling anything human, realised the small insect buzzing at the southeastron edge of Londinium was not smashed, and gathered itself to smite again.

"*Use the cannon!*" Clare bellowed, but Valentinelli had already – much to Clare's relief – decided that such an operation would be advisable. In any case, the cry was lost in the hullabaloo. Metal shrieked, groaning, and the peculiar discharge of the mechas' cannon – bolts of hot energy, crackling and spitting as they cleaved violated air – did not help matters. Valentinelli had torn the leather straps holding the contacts free of his mecha, as had Sigmund at some point in their wild career across

Londinium. The risk of one of the metal discs inside the leather helmets touching their skin and inducing fatal feedback was too immense.

Especially as the mecha were jolting as they fired. Clare had eight remaining out of a dozen; four had been left at Westminstre – one a shattered hulk, the other three under the control of some doughty Coldwater Guards in their soot-stained, tattered crimson uniforms who had been sent to hold the Bridge against this menace. Good lads, they had ripped the contact helmets free and taken the controls of the mecha in stride.

The Bridge had been littered with bodies and the smoking remains of shattered mecha, some with intact golden cores glittering. Many of the bodies were sorcerers or witches and their Shields; since charm and spell would not work, their only alternative had been to stand and die.

The Park was a wasteland of scorch and metal, trees stripped of their leaves and blasted, the lake boiling from the weird crackling cannon bolts. Clare stopped, wheeling; his fellow mecha did the same.

Wait. They are attacking Buckingham, not St Jemes. That must *be where the Queen is.*

Which was a more defensible palace, to be sure, but it rather altered *his* plans. There was no time to explain; Clare urged the mecha forward, taking over subsidiary control from his companions. The earth quaked as their cuplike feet drummed, mud and metal shards flying. Smoke wrung tears from his stinging eyes, a minor irritant. The other mentath, behind his massive logic engine, had ceased seeking to swat at Clare as if he were a horsefly. Instead, the stirred-hive mass of mecha were running together like sharp metal raindrops on a window pane. Clare could *feel* them, a painful abscess beneath the skin of Londinium. The city quivered, a patient under the tooth-charmer's touch.

Force of numbers would drown what a battering of logic could not. The other mentath's intellect was a smeared explosion of living light, diseased and overgrown, swelling hot and painful in the mindscape of the glowing engines.

Mud sucked at the cuplike feet, the Park thrashed out of all recognition. The Palace lifted its brownstone shoulders, shattered windows gaping and bits of its masonry crumbling as the huge arachnoid mecha squatted, its spinneret cannon ready to fire. Squealing wraithlike howls, the ghost-snarled brains trapped in their sloshing jars atop the spider bubbling and struggling for release, their screams a chorus of the damned as the other mentath used them ruthlessly to amplify his own force.

"ONWARD!" Clare roared, releasing Sig and Valentinelli's mecha. It wasn't quite proper to force them into the charge, and in any case, he had more than enough to do with his remaining five passengerless mecha so near the immense core and engine burning in the arachnid's abdomen. Capacitors glowing, its eight feet stamping in turn, the gigantic thing braced itself as the spinneret cannon began to glow. The Other – for so Clare had christened the opposing mentath – woke to the danger a fraction of a second too late, and Clare's five mecha hurled themselves on the massive arachnid with futile, fiery abandon. Metal tore, screaming, Prussian capacitors shattering and overloaded cores howling at the abuse, and the Other engaged Clare with a burst of pure logic.

Chapter Thirty-Six

An Awakening

It was not the weakness in her limbs, Emma decided. The ground itself was quivering steadily, like a pudding's surface when the dish is jostled. Which was disconcerting, yes, but not *nearly* as disconcerting as the sounds from above.

Clacking razor beaks, the tearing-metal and crunching-bone cries of gryphons, hoarse male shouts, and a swelling sorcerous chant that ripped at her ears and non-physical senses. It was a complex, multilayered chant, a prepared Work of the sort that took months if not years to build. Consonants strained against long whistle-punctuated vowels and strange clicking noises, as if the peculiar personal language of the sorcerer had been married to an older, lipless, scaled tongue of dry fire and sun-basking slowness.

An Awakening chant, of course. She hauled herself up grimly, boots slipping on dew-wet rocks, vines tearing under her hands. The trick, she had discovered, was to push as hard as she could with her legs, silently cursing the extraneous material of her skirts. A minor charm to keep the skin on her hands from becoming flayed helped, but her arms shook with exhaustion, her fingers cramping and her neck afire with pain. *The dragon. Hurry, Emma.*

It was a surprise to reach the top of the rocky, almost vertical slope. She hauled herself up as if topping an orchard wall in the days of her Collegia girlhood, and lay full-length and gasping for a moment, protected by a screen of heavy-leafed bushes.

Shadows wheeled overhead, their wings spread. She blinked, sunlight drawing hot water from her unprotected eyes. The shapes were massive, graceful and fluid in the air, afire with jewel-toned brilliance.

Gryphons. One, two, good heavens, six, seven – Grayson did not have this many!

It did not matter. She rolled to her side, peering through the screen of brush. Exactly *nothing* would be achieved if she rushed into this. The chant was rising towards consummation, its broken rhythm knitting itself together, and she blinked back more swelling water, seeking to make sense of what she saw.

Lord Grayson's gryphon carriage lay smashed against the foot of an ancient, ruined, moss-cloaked tower. The hill shuddered, the tower flexing as if its mortar were some heavy elastic substance. A milky dome of sorcerous energy shimmered around an indistinct figure, whose posture was nevertheless instantly recognisable: Llewellyn Gwynnfud, Earl of Sellwyth, his pale hair crackling with sorcerous energy and his hands making short stabbing gestures and long passes as the passages of his memorised chant demanded. A prepared Work this long and involved required such a mnemonic dance, breath and movement serving to remind the vocal chords of their next assay.

She recognised the tower, too. *Dinas Emrys. That's where I am. Very well.*

The Prime's five remaining Shields were spread out in a loose semicircle, fending off angry gryphons. Three of the gryphons – two tawny, one black – bore shattered leather and wooden bits, the traces they had used to pull the dead Chancellor's chariot broken and useless, dragging them down. The remaining four lion-birds were slightly smaller, their plumage not as glossy. Wild, she realised with a shock.

The gryphons are loyal to Britannia; they must guess his aim. This is bloody good luck.

Two bodies – masses of fur and blood-matted feathers – lay on the stony ground. The Shields had managed to kill two lion-birds; or perhaps that black one had been lost in the chariot crash.

Emma forced herself to stillness. She breathed deeply, listening to the chant, judging the structure of the sorcerous dome protecting Llewellyn. The surface of the hill rippled, in a fashion that would make her ill if she thought too deeply on it, so she put it from her mind and concentrated.

You are alone, and the gryphons will kill you as likely as Llew; their hunger for sorcerer flesh is immense and they are angry. Then there are the Shields; of course they will view me as a threat. That they are occupied does not mean they cannot spare a moment to slay me.

Her fingers plucked at her skirts, thoughtfully. They felt something hard, plunged into the pocket, and brought forth Ludovico's dull-bladed knife. Mikal had found a leather sheath for it, and she had tucked it away, not trusting that the Neapolitan would not find some way of reacquiring it if it were not on her person. She had never underestimated the man, and she devoutly hoped she never would.

Already sensitised. Ah. The stone at her throat chilled further, ice banding her neck and her fingers aching as if she had stepped outside on a winter's day.

She drew the wicked, black-bladed thing from its dark home, tucked the sheath back in her skirt pocket, and worked her ragged left sleeve up. Braced herself and made a fist, then drew the razor edge lightly over the back of her forearm.

Blood sprang up in a bright line. A hiss escaped her taut lips. The knife vibrated hungrily, its dulled blade drinking in sorcerous force and the energy of spilled blood. The ground below pitched, a wave of fluid motion unreeling from the tower's flexing spike. Rock crumbled, and she was almost thrown over the edge of the hill. She jerked forward, the sound of her crashing progress through the bushes lost in a swelling cacophony. The chant swelled afresh, becoming something akin to Mehitabel the Black's long, slow metal-tearing hiss, and the gryphons redoubled their efforts. One of the Shields – a slim, tensile blond man – was distracted by her sudden appearance, and there was a tawny blur as one of the chariot gryphons darted forward, beak and claws striking with terrible finality. Human flesh tore like paper under iron spikes.

Emma ran, every step a jolt of silver-nailed pain up her legs, jarring her back, twisting her neck. The knife, held low, keened hungrily. She bolted for the space left by the Shield's death, and a shadow drifted over her as one of the wild gryphons dived.

Rolling. Razor claws kissing her tangled hair, shearing a few dark curls free. She spat a Word, sorcery striking snake-quick, and the gryphon screamed as it tumbled away, a spray of bright-red blood hanging in trembling, crystalline air. Gained her feet in a lunge, the Collegia's dancing lessons springing back to life in her abused muscles, and the shimmering globe over Llewellyn tensed, preparing itself for a sorcerous strike. The Shields cried out just as the other Prime's chant rose to a deafening roar, sliding towards a massive organ-noise of grinding conclusion. The tower flexed still further, and it was *not* her imagination – the masonry was running like water, shaping itself as one nail of a gigantic claw tensed.

For Vortigern is the Great Dragon, the Colourless One, the *Principia* had whispered, *and the Isle rides upon his back. When he wakes, half the Isle will crumble and Eire become a smoking wasteland. When Vortigern rises, Britannia dies.*

But not, she thought grimly, while Emma Bannon still breathed.

She went to her knees, skirts shredding against jagged rock, gryphons screeching and one of the Shields screaming a filthy word that did not surprise her one bit. Her left hand flashed out, the bright weak dart of sorcery spattering against the globe-shield. But that was merely a distraction. The Shield nearest her bolted in her direction, his broad hand reaching for her left wrist – but it was her *right* hand he should have worried about. It flicked forward, the motion unreeling from her hip just as Jourdain had taught her.

Even in death, her former Shields served her well. The memory of Jourdain's patience was a sting, there and gone, and she realised how much she missed them all.

The knife flashed, blood-sorcery on its blade shredding away as it passed through the globe-shield. The shield flushed red, but the knife itself, freed from its cage of ætheric energy, flew true, its dull blade eating a dart of spring sunlight . . .

. . . and buried itself to the hilt in Llewellyn Gwynfudd's back.

Chapter Thirty-Seven

Hardly Bad Company

I know you, Clare realised, as his mecha landed with bone-rattling force. The arachnid screeched, one of its massive legs twisted and hanging by a thread of metal. That thread was massive in its own right, but the gigantic mecha listed, its mass knocked off balance. Two of Clare's subordinate mecha tore at the Prussian capacitors lining its abdomen, glass shattering and bolts of energy sparking as they arced.

Sig's mecha crouched on the steps of the Palace below, its cannon crackling as he sought to hold back the tide of frog-headed, slump-shouldered mecha controlled by the Other. The Queen's and Queen's Life Guard – Beefeaters, Coldwater, and other regiments, scarlet and blue flashing through the smoke and dirt – was behind him, firing rifles in blocks and chipping away at the oncoming wall of metal. No few among them were sharpshooters, and the Bavarian had marshalled them to shoot at the golden discs; if the core was shattered, the mecha would engage in a jerky tarantella before it died, smashing its fellows before sinking to the ground in a crackling, dangerous mass of sharp quivering metal.

Valentinelli's mecha dangled, a mess of metal and glass, from the thread holding the almost severed leg. He could not see if the Neapolitan still lived, and in any case, it was academic.

Archibald Clare had tribulations of his own.

The arachnid heaved, and one of Clare's mecha flew, describing a graceful arc before crashing like a falling star in the mess of the Park, a geyser of mud vomiting up from its impact.

This is not going well.

His own mecha, its cannon twisted into broken spars serving as grappling hooks, wheezed upright. He had been seeking to climb the leg in front of him and get to where he suspected the Other crouched inside the arachnid, contacts clasped to his own head, battering at Clare with streams of cold logic. If Clare could just get *close* enough, there was a chance of wresting control of the larger logic engine away from the Other. Who was, he realised, Cecil Throckmorton, still not dead, forcing the brains of other mentaths to obey him, and still utterly bloody insane.

The oncoming horde of mecha could not be stopped, though Sig and the Guards were valiant indeed. There were simply too many, and Throckmorton's core was too vast.

Clare tensed every muscle, the mecha around him wheezing and grinding as its tired gears responded. *What am I planning? This is insanity. It is illogical. It is suicide.*

It didn't matter.

Clare leapt, the mecha leaping with him. Shredded metal punched into the arachnid's leg; he pumped his arms, seeking to climb. Gears ground even further, pistons popping, the core at his chest furiously hot, shreds of his mecha falling in a silvery rain. Machines did not become tired, but Clare could swear the metal exoskeleton was exhausted. Shearing, fracturing, the rain of silvery bits intensified as capacitors bled away force, the equations multiplying so rapidly his faculties strained at the corners, seeking to juggle them all and push the Other away. It was a doomed battle, and when the core at his chest shattered Clare fell, narrowly missing spearing himself on spikes of discarded steel and glass. The force of the fall drove his breath out in a long howl, his head cracking against the paving.

It was a sheer, illogical miracle he didn't split his bloody skull.

The shock of the core's shattering caught up with him, drawing up his arms and legs in seizure. Hands on him, dragging, the smoke of rifle fire acrid, stinging his throat as he struggled to force air into his recalcitrant lungs. Equations spun inside his head, dancing, flailing like the thing above him.

He went rigid as they dragged him, staring at the massive bulk above him as it yawed, sharply, a ship sailing on thin legs. One leg spasmed, clipping the roof of the Palace, and stone shattered. There was an insect crawling on the vast shining carapace, a thin shadow against the glow of capacitors. Dust choked the daylight, but Clare squinted. He thought he saw—

"*Retreat!*" a familiar voice was yelling, a battlefield roar that would have done a Teuton berserker proud. Sigmund's mecha was a smoking hulk, and it was two of the Guards – hard-faced country boys, one from Dorset if his nose was any indication – dragging Clare along. He tried to make his legs work, but could not. They might as well have been insensate meat, for all his straining will could move them.

"*Inside!*" someone else yelled. "*Here they come! MOVE!*"

That was a familiar voice as well, and as Clare was hauled through the Palace's door like a sack of potatoes he wondered just what Mikal was doing here.

A deep, appalling cry rose from among the attacking mecha. "*Prussians!*" Mikal cried, as Sigmund cursed in German. "*Fall back! Brace the doors! Move, you whoresons!*"

Well, at least Miss Bannon comes by her language honestly. Clare's eyelids fluttered. Sig bent over him, something damp and cold swiping at Clare's forehead. It was a handkerchief, dipped in God knew what. *Prussians. The mercenaries. They must be very sure of overrunning us. And yes, mecha are not useful inside the Palace. Some part of the conspiracy wants Victrix captured alive, or proof of her death. A mecha cannot report on its victims as a man may.*

"Mentath." Mikal, hoarse and very close. "Why am I not surprised? And . . . where is the assassin?"

"Big *Spinne* outside," Sigmund gasped, for Clare's mouth wouldn't open. "Dead, maybe. *Wer weiss?*"

Now Clare could see the Shield. Grey-cheeked, blood-soaked, his yellow eyes glowing furiously, the man looked positively lethal. Behind him, Eli conferred with a captain in the Guards, glancing every so often at the straining iron-bound door.

"That won't hold for long," Mikal said grimly. "Bring him. Your Majesty?"

And, impossibility of impossibilities, Queen Victrix came into sight, her wan face smudged with masonry dust and terribly weary. An ageless shadow in her dark gaze was Britannia, the ruling spirit's attention turned elsewhere despite the threat to its vessel. "I must reach the Throne."

"Indeed." Mikal did not flinch as a stunning impact hit the door. Several of the Guards were still scurrying to shore its heavy oak with anything that could be moved, including chunks of fallen stone. "Come, then. Eli!"

"What next?" The other Shield looked grimly amused. Half his face was painted bright red with blood, but at least he had found better boots. He was alight with fierce joy, no measure of sleepiness remaining, and Clare found the iron bands constricting his lungs easing.

Sig walloped him on the back hard enough to crack a rib or two. Clare coughed, choked, and almost spewed on the Queen's dust-choked skirts. She did not notice, following Eli out of sight, and Mikal glanced down at Clare.

"Well done, mentath. One of the Guards will find you a weapon. We make our stand before the Throne."

Oh. Clare fought down the retching. "Yes." He coughed, violently, turned his head to the side and spat as Sig hauled him up and Clare found that yes, indeed, his legs would carry him. Shakily and uncertainly, but better than not. "Quite. God and Her Majesty, sir. Miss Bannon?"

"Elsewhere." Mikal turned on his heel and strode after the Queen. Sig clapped him on the back again, but more gently, thank God.

"Archie, *mein Herr*." The Bavarian shook his filthy, bald-shining head. "You are crazy, *mein Freund. Du bist ein Bastard verrückt.*"

Clare coughed again, leaning on Sig's broad shoulder. "Likewise, Siggy. Likewise." *If I must die, this is hardly bad company.*

At his throat, the Bocannon turned to a spot of crystalline ice, and the skin around it began to tingle.

Chapter Thirty-Eight

A Life's Work

The globe of protective sorcery shattered, sharp darts of ætheric energy slicing trembling air. Emma skidded to a stop as Llewellyn staggered, the chant faltering. She intended to reach for the hilt, wrench it free, and stab him *again,* and *again,* as many times as it took to make him cease.

She did not have the chance.

A long trailing scream behind her, a wet crunching. One more Shield had fallen. She snapped a glance over her shoulder – the two surviving Shields were fully occupied now keeping the gryphons from their throats. The lion-birds darted in, the smaller wild ones swooping down in tightening circles. There were too many of them; even a Shield of Mikal's calibre would not keep that feathered tide back.

Britannia's steeds would not cease until this threat was contained and their furious hunger sated.

But Emma's immediate concern was the Sorcerer Prime collapsing to his knees before the tower. An altar – a plain slab of stone – glowed before him with hurtful dull-red ætheric charge, buckled and cracked. He struggled to hold the chant, but a gap of a single note opened and became an abyss, the complex interlocking parts shredding and peeling away.

Her throat closed. A moment's regret flashed through her

– with Sight, she could see the towering cathedral of the spell, beautiful in its wholeness for a single instant before cracks of negation raced up its walls and exploded through its windows, twisting and warping the flawless work of a Prime at his best.

A life's work. How long had Llewellyn been planning this?

Questions could wait. She reached for the knife again, but the Prime pitched violently backwards, his body lashed by stray sorcery escaping his control. It descended upon him, his flesh jerking, force a physical body was not meant to bear searching for an outlet and grinding the cohesion of muscle and blood away.

It was not a pleasant death. It replicated the dragon-fuelled simulacrum in Bedlam, shredding him to a rag of shattered bone and blood-painted meat, his eyeballs popping and his hair smoking as the spell, cheated, took its revenge. The knife fell free, chiming on rock; she bent reflexively to retrieve it, her fingers clamping on its slippery hilt. Something else rolled loose too, and her free hand scooped it up with no direction on her part, tucking it into her skirt pocket.

Oh, Llew.

The tower dropped back into its accustomed shape with a subliminal *thud*. No longer a single claw of a massive reptilian limb, it was now merely a shattered pile of masonry and moss, leaning as if into a heavy wind.

Shadows wheeled overhead as the gryphons dived, screaming triumphantly, and Emma turned away from the body on its carpet of boiling blood, her hand lifting to shield her face.

The ground settled as well. Vortigern, the colourless dragon, the Third Wyrm and mighty forefather of all the Timeless children still awake in the world, sank into slumber again, the Isle on his back pulled tight like a green and grey counterpane, upon which mites scattered and pursued their little loves and vendettas.

And Emma Bannon, Sorceress Prime, wept.

The silence was as massive as the cacophony beforehand had been, and she lifted her head, wiping her cheeks.

Most of the gryphons had settled into feeding at the fallen Shields and the three lion-bird corpses. The ripping and gurgling sounds were enough to unsettle even *her* stomach. No doubt even Clare's excellent digestion would have difficulty with this.

Clare. She swallowed, hard, invisible threads twitching faintly. Londinium was a fair ways away. She had ridden *Khloros* to bloody *Wales*, of all places.

One of the gryphons mantled, hopping a little closer. It was edging away from the carrion and eyeing her sidelong, its gold-ringed pupil holding a small, perfect image of a very tired sorceress armed with a toothpick.

Oh dear. Emma swallowed again, drily.

The gryphon's indigo-dyed tongue flicked as its beak opened. It was the remaining black from the carriage, its glossy feathers throwing back the morning sun with a blue-underlit vengeance.

"*Vortigern*," it whistled. "Vortigern still sleeps, sorceress."

That was the whole point of this exercise, was it not? And now I have other matters to attend to. The hilt, slippery with blood and her sweat, was pulsing-warm in her clenched fist. "Yes."

"We are *hungry*." Its beak clacked.

"You have the dead to feast upon," she pointed out. "And Vortigern sleeps."

In other words, *I have done you a favour. I am loyal to Britannia, as you are.* Or, more plainly, *Please don't eat me.*

It actually laughed at her. Its claws flexed, and the reek of blood and split bowel tore at Emma's nose. Blood could drive the beasts into a frenzy—

The invisible threads tied to a pendant twitched again. For such a movement to reach her *here* meant Clare was in dire trouble indeed.

"I am sorry," she told the gryphon, and her grip on the knife shifted. The stone at her throat, frost-cold, became a spot of ice so fierce it burned, and she knew a charter symbol would be rising through its depths, shimmering and taking form in tangled lines of golden ætheric force.

The beast laughed again, its haunches rising slightly as it prepared to spring. Its feathers ruffled, and its pupil was so dark, the gold of its iris so bright. "So am I, Sorceress. But *we are hungry.*"

Force uncoiled inside her. She was exhausted, mental and emotional muscles strained from the opening of her Discipline. Her sorcerous Will was strong, yes, but the toll of ætheric force channelled through her physical body dragged her down. It would slow her, just at the moment she needed speed and strength most.

I am not ready to die. She knew it did not matter. Death was here all the same, the payment demanded by *Khloros*. Death was inevitable.

Her fingers tightened on the knife's hilt. Inevitable as well was Emma Bannon's refusal to die quietly.

Even for Victrix.

The gryphon sprang.

Chapter Thirty-Nine

Who Dies Next?

The inner courtyard of the Palace, choked with drifts of dust and quaking underfoot, opened around them. The front door had broken, and the brown-jacketed Prussian mercenaries with their white armbands poured through, firing as they advanced. Many of the Guard fell, buying time for Victrix to flee through the halls. All that remained was to cross the courtyard and gain the relative safety of the Throne Hall.

Though how that great glass-roofed hall could shelter them was somewhat fuzzy to Clare. He suspected he was not thinking clearly.

Clare limped along, Sigmund hauling him, the vast shadow of the arachnid mecha stagger-thrashing above. Stone crumbled, the centuries of building and replacement work smashed in a moment. Something was wrong – the arachnid reeled drunkenly, shattering glass from its capacitors falling like daggers.

Victrix stumbled. Mikal and Eli all but carried her, one on either side, and the Guard fanned out. Rifleshot popped on the stones around them – the Prussians had gained height and were firing from the windows. The door to the Throne Hall had never seemed so far away.

They plunged into dust-swirling darkness just as a massive

grinding thud smashed in the courtyard. A gigantic warm hand lifted Clare and flung him; he landed with a crunch and briefly lost consciousness. He surfaced in a soupy daze, carried between Sig and a bleeding, husky Guard with a bandaged head and a limp, who nevertheless moved with admirable speed. Breaking glass tinkled sweetly overhead, and the Bocannon at his chest was a fiery cicatrice.

Shouts. Confusion. Mikal's hoarse hissing battle cry. Queen Victrix screamed, a note of frustration and terror as mercenaries poured in through the side doors.

Clare lifted his head. He blinked, dazed. There was another giant impact, and he realised he'd been half-conscious for too long. They were surrounded, Mikal and Eli flanking the Queen, whose young face was pale, one cheek terribly bruised and her dark hair falling in ragged strands.

Miss Bannon looks much better dishevelled, he thought, and the illogical nature of the reflection shocked him far more than the queer swimming sensation all through his limbs.

Sig had a pistol from somewhere. He was grim and pale, covered in dust and soot, and his mouth pulled down at both corners. A jab of regret stabbed Clare's chest. He should not have drawn his friend into this.

They were all about to die. Except possibly Victrix, whose face aged in a split second, Britannia resurfacing from wherever Her attention had been drawn, alert to the threat to Her vessel.

More shattering glass. The ground quaked violently, almost throwing Clare from his feet.

Then they descended.

The glass fell in sheets. The ancient roof of the Throne Room bucked, snapped, and fell, the shards – some as long as a man's body – miraculously avoiding the knot of Guards, Shields, and mentath-and-genius. The sound was immense, titanic, the grinding of ice floes, as if the earth itself had gone mad and sought to rid itself of humanity.

The gryphon was massive, and black. Its eyes were holes of

runnelling unholy red flame. Driven into the top of its sleek skull was a fiery red nail, a star of hurtful brilliance.

Perched on its back was a battered, wan, half-clothed Miss Bannon. Her dress had been ripped to tatters and her hair was an outrageous mess stiff with dirt, sticks, feathers, and matted blood. Bruising ran over every inch of flesh he could see, and the other shadows were more gryphons, breaking through the roof as Miss Bannon slid from the beast's back. The red flame winked out, and the deadwinged beast slumped to the strewn floor. It twisted, shrivelling, dust racing through its feathers and eating at its glossy hide.

The dead gryphon collapsed. Miss Bannon bent, wrenching the nail from its head.

It was a knife, and it dripped with crackling red as she turned. The Prussian mob drew back, the feathers in their hats nodding as her gaze raked them, slow and terrible.

"*Gryphons*," Britannia whispered, through the Queen's mouth. The single word was horrifying, as cold and ageless as the Themis itself, a welter of power and command.

Miss Bannon nodded, once. She did not sway, her back iron-rigid, but something was wrong. She held herself oddly, and her gaze was terrifyingly blank. Clare groped to think of just what was amiss.

The sorceress looked . . . as if she had forgotten her very *self*.

"Who dies next?" she murmered, very clearly, the words dropping into a sudden rustling silence as gryphons drifted down to land, their claws digging into stone and fallen timber, making slight scratching noises against steel. "*Who?*"

The first Prussian screamed.

After that, the gryphons feasted. But Clare gratefully closed his eyes, finally able to cease deducing. The inside of his skull felt scraped clean and queerly *open*. For once, he did not want to see.

The sounds were bad enough.

Chapter Forty

The Need Was Dire

Britannia's vessel halted a fair distance away. "Emma?" Abruptly, Victrix sounded very young. Perhaps it was all the dust in the air. Or perhaps it was the ringing in Emma's ears.

She suspected she would pay for this episode very soon, and in bloody coin.

The gryphons pressed forward. They had made short work of the brown-coated mercenaries, and in the courtyard was a vast wreck of metal and glass she had only indirectly glimpsed as she struggled to keep the brain-stabbed gryphon in the air. It seemed Clare and company had endured their own travails.

"Your Majesty." She swayed, and suddenly Mikal was at her side. His fingers closed around her arm, and she leaned into that support, too exhausted to be grateful. She felt nothing but a vast drowning weariness. "I murdered one of your steeds, Britannia. You may punish me as you see fit. However, before you do, I beg leave to report that the Earl of Sellwyth is dead and Vortigern still sleeps. Your steeds had most of the stopping of Lord Sellwyth. I did not serve them well."

The body of the black gryphon – the knife, driven with exactitude into the tiny space between the back of the skull and the top vertebrae – bubbled as it rotted swiftly, the stresses endured by its physical fabric as she forced it to fly for

Londinium with its fellows in hot pursuit unravelling it.

The gryphons would not be able to eat their brother, and that was the worst that could befall one of their number.

They would not forgive her for this.

"Lord Sellwyth." The Queen's face was bruised, but granite-hard. Britannia settled fully into Her vessel and regarded Emma with bright eyes, glowing dust over a river of ancient power. "He sought to awaken Vortigern."

I am not certain he was the only one who sought to do so. I do know he almost succeeded. "I caught him at Dinas Emrys. Which is, I believe, part of his family's ancestral holdings." She fought to stay conscious, heard the queer flatness of her tone. Eli appeared on her other side, looking sadly the worse for wear. "I beg your pardon for the method of my return, but the need was dire."

Where is Clare? She glanced at Mikal, who stared at Britannia, a muscle flicking in his jaw. *I do not like that I cannot see him. And Ludovico, where is he?* The knife in her right hand dangled; she could not make her fingers unlock from the hilt.

A Word to steal the gryphon's breath, another Word to snap iron bands about its wings, and she had driven the knife into its brain and uttered the third Word, the most terrible and scorching one of all, expending so much of her stored sorcerous force she almost lost consciousness, holding grimly on to one single thought. *Londinium. Find the Queen.*

And the dead body had obeyed the Endor in her. It had *flown.*

"So it was. We shall inform you of any punishment later." The Queen nodded, slowly. "We do not think it will be too severe."

"*Blasphemy!*" one of the gryphons howled. They rustled, pressing close, and Mikal tensed next to Emma. She leaned into him even further, for her legs were failing her and even the dim, dust-choked light in the Hall was too scorch-bright for her sensitised eyes. "*She robbed the dead!*"

I did so much more than that. The beasts will not forgive this, and their memory is long. "Mikal." Her heart stuttered, her body finally rebelling against the demands she had placed upon it. "*Mikal.*"

He bent his head slightly, his eyes never leaving the Queen. "Emma."

He would kill Britannia Herself, did he judge Her a threat to me. The realisation, quiet but thunderous, loosed the last shackle of her will.

"I have been cruel to you." The whisper was so faint, she doubted he heard her. "I should not have . . . Forgive me."

"There is no—" he began, but darkness swallowed Emma whole.

Chapter Forty-One

Amenable to Control

"And this is the killer of that gigantic *thing*." Victrix inclined her head. "We are grateful, Mr Valentinelli. You performed a great service to Britannia."

The Neapolitan swept a painful, creaky bow. Both his eyes were swollen nearly shut, half his hair singed off, and his face was such a mass of cuts and welts it was difficult to see the pox scars. His clothes were in ribbons, and one of his boots was nothing more than a band of leather about his ankle and calf, the rest of it cut away and the stocking underneath filthy and draggled. "It is nothing, *maestra*. Valentinelli is at your service."

Clare's neck ached. The tension would not leave him. "Cecil Throckmorton. He was mad, Your Majesty, but he was also *used*."

"Used by whom?" The Queen half turned, pacing away, and Clare forced his legs to work. He and Sigmund held each other like a pair of drunks.

The smaller gryphons took wing, their shadows pouring over the glass- and rubble-strewn floor. The sound was immense, a vault filled with brushing feathers. The dust was settling.

Clare suppressed a sigh. But this was *important*; he must make the Queen understand. "There were three parts to this conspiracy. Miss Bannon dealt with those who wished Britannia and the Isle erased from existence; she judged that the larger threat. One part of the conspiracy simply wished Britannia inconvenienced, however they could effect that – I would look to the Prussian ambassador, who will no doubt deny everything, since they were mercenaries and, by very dint of that, expendable. The third part of the conspiracy troubles me most, Your Majesty. It wished *you*, personally, Britannia's current vessel, under control."

"Control." Victrix paused for a moment. Her shoulders came up, and she stalked for the high-backed Throne, the Stone of Scorn underneath its front northern leg shimmering soft silver as she approached. The Throne itself, undamaged, gleamed with precious stones.

It looked, Clare decided, dashed uncomfortable. But Victrix climbed the seven steps, turned sharply so her dust-laden skirts swirled, and sat. Sigmund might have gone up the steps as well, but Clare dug his heels in, and was strong enough to make him stop.

Victrix propped one elbow on the Throne's northern arm, rested her chin upon her hand. The Guards searching through the rubble for wounded compatriots were hushed, muttering among themselves. Men moaned in pain or shock. The Queen closed her eyes, and Clare could have sworn he felt the entire Isle shiver once as Britannia, enthroned, turned Her attention inward.

"And do you think," the Queen finally said, "that Britannia is amenable to *control*?"

"Not Britannia," he corrected, a trifle pedantic. "*Victrix*, Your Majesty. Wounded, frightened, faced with three conspiracies working in tandem? Your Majesty might well rely on . . . improper advice." Then he shut his mouth, almost . . . yes, almost *afraid* he had said too much.

"Well said, sir." Britannia sighed, Her chin sinking on to Her hand as if it weighed far more than it should. "Yet, as long as

We possess subjects of such courage and loyalty as yourself, We shall not worry overmuch."

"Miss Bannon deserves the credit, Your Majesty." He sounded stiff even to himself, but it was merely the agony of exhaustion weighing him down. Staying upright and speaking consumed a great deal of his attention.

A ghost of amusement passed over Britannia's closed, somnolent face. "No doubt she would lay it at your door."

"She is too kind."

"Not at all, mentath. We think it best you leave now. Our Consort approaches, and We wish a private word with him."

Clare thought of protesting. Valentinelli gripped his free arm, though, and it occurred to him that discretion was perhaps wiser than anything he might say, however well founded the chain of logic that led to his suspicions. "Yes, mum. I mean, Your Majesty. By your leave." *Oh, what* is *the proper etiquette for taking leave of one's sovereign in these circumstances?*

"Mentath. Mr Clare." Britannia's eyes half opened, and the aged face rising underneath Victrix's young countenance sent a most illogical shiver down Clare's spine. Her eyes were indigo from lid to lid, small sparks like stars floating over depths he found he did not wish to examine too closely. What would it be like to clasp such a being in one's arms?

No, he did not envy the Consort. Not at all. "Yes, Your Majesty?"

"Make certain Miss Bannon may find you and your companions. We shall wish to reward you, when We have sorted this unpleasantness through." Her eyelids fell again, and Clare heard the drumming of approaching feet, shouts, and crunching of glass.

What *did* one say in this exotic situation? "Yes. Er, thank you, Your Majesty."

Sig tugged him in one direction, Valentinelli in another. They finally decided on a course, Clare's head hanging so low he did not see anything but his own filthy boots dragged over rubble and dust. When he passed into a soup of half-consciousness, it was welcome, his overstrained faculties deciding they required a retreat from recent events. He heartily agreed.

The last thing he heard was Sig's muttering, and Valentinelli's non-committal grunts in reply.

"Just one," the Bavarian kept repeating. "You hear me, *Italiensch*? One mecha. We drag it to workshop. I feed you wurst. You help me."

Chapter Forty-Two

A Most Logical Sorceress

Emma slept for two and a half days, not even waking when Tideturn flushed her with sorcerous force. She finally surfaced to greet a fine clear Thursday dawn, spring sunlight piercing the haze of Londinium and the reek of the city cheerfully pungent, stray breaths of it creeping even into her dressing room.

The servants were slightly nervous, unused to seeing her in such a terrible state. Battered and tattered, of course, but even her corset stays had been broken, and she winced at the thought of the flesh she had shown. A hot bath, Isobel and Catherine's attentions, and a good dose of Severine's fussing brought her to feeling almost human again. *Chocolat* and croissants did *not* satisfy; her mirror informed her she was unbecomingly gaunt, even if the bruises had largely faded. She rang for Mr Finch as soon as was decently possible, and told him to send out for the broadsheets. Which arrived, ink still venomously wet, as she descended to a hearty breakfast.

Cook, it seemed, had missed her as well.

The story bruited about in the press was an Alteration experiment gone terribly wrong. It satisfied most and left the rest with a clear warning not to speak of their uncertainties. Emma found herself licking her fingers free of jam and contemplating another platter of bangers when the breakfast room door flew open and Mikal appeared.

He was just the same, from buttoned-up coat to flaming yellow eyes. Behind him, Eli ducked his dark head. They had evidently been at practice; the fume of recent exertion hung on them both. It was a relief to see Eli in proper boots; Mr Finch was a wonder.

Her heart leapt behind its cage of ribs and stays; the weight in her skirt pocket seemed twice as heavy. She ignored both sensations, though Mikal's gaze almost caused a guilty flush to rise up her throat.

"Good morning, Shields," she greeted them. "If you have not breakfasted, please do so. But I warn you, should you come between me and those bangers, I shall be *quite* vexed." She touched her skirt pocket, took her hand away with an effort. "Mikal. What news?"

"A pouch sent from the Palace, daily visits from the mentath enquiring after your health. He is due again for tea today. Valentinelli is still trailing him, despite being paid." Mikal filled himself a plate and glanced at Eli. "Eli finds your service most exciting."

"Too exciting?" She tried not to appear amused, suspected she failed.

"No, mum." The other Shield eyed the ravaged breakfast table. It was a relief to be in the presence of those who understood a sorcerer's hunger after such events. "Rather a change, that's all. Proud to be here."

Well, that's good. "Should you change your mind, Shield, do feel free to say so. I keep none in my service who would prefer to be elsewhere. Mikal, about Ludovico—"

"I gave him fifty guineas, Prima. Considering that he performed extraordinarily, killed Mr Throckmorton, and brought down a rather large mecha almost by himself. Would you care to hear of it now? Clare has given me the particulars."

She settled herself more firmly in the chair. "Certainly. Eli, before you eat, please fetch the pouch from the Palace. No doubt it is in my library . . .?"

"Of course." He was gone in a flash, closing the door quietly.

Mikal did not look at her. He settled in his customary seat, his plate before him just so.

Emma waited. Silence stretched between them. The lump in her pocket was an accusing weight.

He toyed with his fork, long, oddly delicate fingers running over its silver curves. Still did not look at her.

You will not make this easy. "Thank you."

"No thanks are—"

"Accept my thanks, Shield."

That brought his hot yellow gaze up to hers. "Only your thanks?"

Unbecoming heat finally rose in her cheeks. "At the breakfast table, yes."

"And otherwise?"

Otherwise? I do as I please, Shield. But let us speak of the main thing. "Sellwyth could have killed you."

"And he almost killed you. Do you think I do not *know*? It does not *matter*, Emma. I am your Shield. That is *final*, so whatever game you are pursuing, cease."

A faint smile touched her lips. "Did you just give me an order?"

"If you are testing to see if I am *serious*, if I can be *trusted*—"

I do not forget the sound Crawford made when you choked the life out of him. But you did so for me.

Even a Shield may be, in the end, merely a man. Yet I am grateful for it. "I misjudged you once, Mikal. Never again."

"Are you so certain?" A spark in his gaze, one she found she rather liked.

"Eat your breakfast." She snapped a broadsheet open and examined it critically. "But leave those bangers alone. Else I *will* be vexed, Shield."

"God save us all from that," he muttered. But he was smiling, she saw as she peeked over the edge of the broadsheet. A curious lightness began in the region of Emma's chest. She disciplined it, and returned to her work.

The solarium was drenched in golden late-afternoon light, the charter symbols wedded to the glass cooling the sun's glare enough to be pleasant. The plants sang in their climate globes, and Emma poured the tea. The wicker tables and chairs glowed, each edge clean and bright.

When she had handed the teacup over, she produced the parchment, rolled tightly and bound with red wax. "Your licence is reinstated. You are commissioned as one of the Queen's Own; also, you are to be knighted. Congratulations."

The mentath's long, mournful face pinkened slightly as he accepted the scroll, but he still looked grave. "There are still unanswered questions, Miss Bannon."

And you do not like unanswered questions. "Chief among them is the identity of Grayson's paymaster. Though he was Chancellor of the Exchequer, and had access to a variety of funds." Emma nodded, her curls brushing her cheeks. It was bloody *luxurious* to sit and have a quiet cuppa, and to wear an afternoon dress that had not been torn by some unpleasantness. "Suffice to say, there are personages we may not move directly against, no matter *how* high we may temporarily be in royal esteem. However, we have stung their fingers mightily, and now I may watch them. Which will be all the more easy, given recent events."

"Ah yes, your creation as Countess Sellwyth. Congratulations to *you*."

Britannia has her own strange sense of justice, and She wishes Dinas Emrys watched. "That was not what I was referring to." She indicated the tiers of dainties. *And I do not want your nimble brain worrying at the question of who crafted the simulacrum in Bedlam. Even if it is a question that probably will not interest you, it is too dangerous for you to pursue.* "Please. You look rather not your usual self, Mr Clare."

He set to with a will. Apparently his digestion was still excellent. "There is something else that troubles me. Sellwyth's family held that place for generations. What made him think *now* was the proper time to unleash its, erm, occupant?"

They offered him something his ambition could not refuse. Emma shrugged. *And now I am left wondering what* my *ambition cannot refuse. We are alike, Llew and I, more than even he suspected.* "Who can tell? He was Throckmorton's paymaster, that much is certain; the mentath kept that secret very well. Pity Valentinelli killed him, though I understand it was necessary. Was he truly bollixing about with Alterative sorcery, I wonder?"

Clare looked a trifle uncomfortable for a few moments. "Mad. He was utterly mad. Throckmorton, I mean. Oh. Mr Baerbarth sends his regards, by the way. He was quite put out that he could not examine one of the mecha at leisure."

"Perhaps something can be arranged." The core and the large logic engine, of course, had been moved in secret. It was only a matter of time before someone else created something similar, and Emma half suspected Clare's first project as one of the Queen's commissioned geniuses would have something to do with preparing the Empire for such an eventuality.

"He would be most pleased. Also, Signor Valentinelli—"

"Will cease following you very soon; if he visits tomorrow, I may release the binding on him."

"Well, that's just the thing." Clare pinkened again. "He extends his regrets, but says he wishes no such thing. He rather likes the excitement, you see, though I've told him a mentath's life is usually deadly boring. He says he has grown too old for his usual line of work, and I apparently need some looking after. He sounds like an old maiden aunt, frankly, and the sooner you send him on his merry way the better."

"Ah." Her mouth wanted to twitch. *Oh, Ludo. You have ideas, I see.* "Well. He did seem to have taken a liking to you." She took a mannerly sip of tea, finding it had cooled most agreeably. The savouries looked very appetising indeed, and she was hungry again. It would take time to regain the lost weight.

"You mean, each time he threatens to duel me after your spell is taken off is a mark of affection? He is quite fond of that threat."

"He must enjoy your company." *And that bears watching too.* "How very droll."

The conversation turned to other things, and Clare did his best to observe the pleasantries. It irked him, though, and she could see the irritation rising in him. After another cup and a few pastries he began the process of taking his leave. He had a question of research waiting for him at his lodgings, and regretted leaving her so soon, et cetera, et cetera.

It was no surprise, though she did feel a slight sting.

Emma rose, and offered her hand. "Mr Clare. *Do* be reasonable. You have endured much in the service of Britannia, and I thank you for your courage and the care you have shown for the Empire's interests. You are under no social obligation to me. I know how sorcery . . . discommodes you."

He took her hand, pumped it twice. He was outright crimson now. "Not the case," he mumbled, swallowed visibly. "Not the case at all. Miss Bannon, you are . . . You are a . . ."

She waited, patiently. He did not turn loose her hand. There were many words he could choose. *Sorceress. Bitch. Whore. Managing female.*

He finally found one that suited him, drew himself up. "You, Miss Bannon, are a very *logical* sorceress."

Her jaw threatened to drop. Of all the epithets flung at her, she had never experienced *that* one. A second, very queer lightness began in the region of Emma's chest. "Thank you."

He nodded, dropped her hand as if it had burned him, and turned to leave.

"Mr Clare."

He stopped next to a false orange tree. The climate globe

around it jangled sweetly. His thinning hair did not disguise the way the skin over his pate was even more deeply crimson.

Thankfully, she had a gift she could offer to match his own. "I trust your digestion is still sound?"

"As a bell, madam." He did not turn to face her.

Emma took a deep breath. "May I invite you to dinner? Perhaps on Sunday? You may bring Ludovico, and Mr Baerbarth. If they wish to attend." *If they wish to avail themselves of my table without absolutely being required to do so. Odd. This is the first time* that *has occurred.*

Clare turned, retraced his steps, grabbed her hand, and pumped it furiously. "I say! Of course! Honoured to. *Honoured.* Sig will be beside himself."

"Sunday, then. Shall we say six? I dine early."

"Certainly!" And after a few more furious pumps of her hand, he was gone. She closed her eyes, tracing his progress through the house. Mr Finch let him out of the front door, and by the time Clare reached the laurel hedge he was whistling.

She brought her attention back to the sunroom. Mikal would be along at any moment. Her hand had slid into her skirt pocket, and she drew forth the stone that had fallen from Llewellyn's body. It had been on her nightstand when she awoke.

Had Mikal placed it there? Did he have any idea what it was?

It was deep red, flat on one side and curved on the other. Smooth and glassy, and when she tilted it, it throbbed. A pulse too deep for the stone's shallowness, a slow, steady beat.

Like a dragon's heart, perchance.

Two stones, and he was reserving one? One stone gifted to him in advance, one later? Or there was only one stone to begin with, and he was paid at the beginning? But how could they be certain he would do what they wished? And who among the wyrms would have slain one of their own young for this?

Who crafted that simulacrum in Bedlam?

She cupped the stone in her gloved hands. Its pulse slowed as it basked, drinking in the sunlight.

The gryphons were at his body. And should I visit Dinas Emrys now, I would find nothing but anonymous bones. Still . . . it troubles me.

Llewellyn Gwynnfud had always troubled her.

It was difficult to undo her bodice, but she managed. She slid the stone against the bare skin of her chest, tucking it securely under the top edge of her corset. Uncomfortable, but only temporary.

You are right, Mr Clare. There are quite a few unanswered questions.

She breathed out a long, slow, single sorcerous Word.

There was a melting sensation over her heart as the Philosopher's Stone sank into her skin. A flush of warmth tingled through every particle of her flesh. Her head tipped back, and the solarium dimmed. The rush of flame in her veins was a welcoming heat, gentle and inviting.

In the end, she decided, it mattered little. She was Prime and in the service of Britannia, and if another wyrm raised its head, she would crush it underfoot.

Smiling, Emma Bannon set her bodice to rights, and decided on another cup of tea.

Rankes of those Sorcerousse

(taken from the Domesnight List)

Minor: Charter[1] (lightfinger, bakewell)
    Charmer (hedgecharmer, charing-charmer)
    Mancer (hevvymancer, pickmancer)
    Skellewreyn (not used past 1715[2])

    Commons: Witch[3]

---

1 The ability to draw a simple charter-symbol in charming is available even to the non-sorcerous. Those of very faint talent may perform the simplest of charter-symbols as long as said symbols are "married" to a physical item. A charmer must be able to hold a charter-symbol in free air for at least a few moments in order to be apprenticed; it is legal to indenture charters but not charmers or above.

2 The last Skellewreyn, the famous and rebellious Agnes Nice, was hung in 1712 in Hardwitch. Afterward, Skellewreyn – too much talent to be a mancer and not enough to be a properly-Disciplined witch, driven mad and physically twisted by their sorcery – did not appear, or if they did, they kept to certain shadows. Some of the Morloks are rumored to be of their ilk.

Major: Sorcerer
            Master Sorcerer
            Adeptus
            Prime

---

3 Witches are held to be Common, since their Discipline fills their entire brain with no room left for the "splitting" of focus a Sorcerer or above must perform. A Sorcerer may perform a Greater Work without losing track of one's whereabouts; a Master Sorcerer or Adeptus may move physically while performing a Greater Work, and of course a Prime may successfully assay more than one Greater Work at once.

. . . it is not required to possess a mentath's faculties in order to Observe, and to reap the benefits of said observation. Indeed, many mentaths are singularly unconcerned with any event or thing outside their chosen field of study, while a rich treasure trove of wondrous variety unreels before their very noses. A mere observer skilled in the science of Deduction may surprise even a mentath, and has the added benefit of a great deal of practical knowledge and foresight ever at hand. The faculty of Observation lies within each man competent enough, and taught to, read; it may be strengthened with practice, and indeed grows ever stronger the more one exercizes it.

If Observation is the foundation all Deduction is built upon, then the quality of Decision is the mortar holding fast the stones. Tiny details may be important, but it is of greatest necessitude to decide which details bear weight and which are chaff. Perfect, unclouded decision upon details is the purview of the Divine, and man's angelic faculties, wonderful as they are, are merely a wretched imitation. Even that wretchedness can be useful, much as the example of Vice's ultimate end may serve to keep Virtue from the wide and easy path to Ruin.

Much as Time seeks to bring down every building, and Vice seeks to bring down every Virtue, the treacherous Assumption *ever seeks to intrude a detail's importance wrongly into Deduction. A proper Assumption may save a great deal of time and trouble, but an improper Assumption is a foul stinking beast, ever ready to founder the ship of Logic upon the rocks of Inaccuracy.*

Fortunately, the weapons of Reason and Observation do much to overthrow the false faces of Assumption. The decision to carefully and thoroughly question each Assumption as if it is a criminal, or a fool who does not differentiate Fact from Fancy, will serve each person seeking to strengthen his habit of Deduction faithfully. As the organs of Reason and Observation strengthen, the art of quickly finding the correct details becomes natural.

We shall start with a series of Exercizes to strengthen the faculty of Observation any Reader assaying this humble work possesses. These Exercizes are to be done daily, upon waking and retiring, and at diverse points through the Reader's daily work as opportunity permits . . .

— From the Preface, *The Art and Science of Deduction*, Mr Archibald Clare

extras

about the author

Lilith Saintcrow was born in New Mexico, bounced around the world as an Air Force brat, and fell in love with writing when she was ten years old. She currently lives in Vancouver, Washington. Visit her website at www.lilithsaintcrow.com

Find out more about Lilith Saintcrow and other Orbit authors by registering for the free monthly newsletter at www.orbitbooks.net

interview

The Iron Wyrm Affair is your first experience with writing steampunk. How was it compared to writing your previous books?
To be honest, I didn't think it was "steampunk" when I was writing it. I tend to view steampunk more as an aesthetic than as a genre. For me it was a variety of alt-history mixed with urban fantasy. It was incredibly fun to write, and just happened naturally once the initial image – of Archibald Clare in his study, dishevelled and bored almost to literal death – came to me. From there it was a race to uncover things as the characters did. I literally did not know what would happen next until Bannon's Ride, near the end of the book.

Where did the inspiration for *The Iron Wyrm Affair* come from? Were the Sherlock Holmes books a big influence?
I loved Sherlock Holmes and Encyclopedia Brown as a child. The idea that the power of observation could be used like that . . . it was like a superpower ordinary people could polish. Also, when the recent *Sherlock Holmes* movie hit theatres, there were a couple scenes that were just such fun, so tongue-in-cheek, that they really fired my imagination.

There is a wonderful spark between Emma Bannon and Mikal. An unusual choice since Clare is the other point of view. Why choose Mikal over Clare for the love interest?

My goodness, Clare would *not* be attracted to Emma. Plus, he's a mentath. Logic machines are hard to live with, as are Prime sorceresses. Initially, Mikal wasn't even a love interest, and I hesitate to say he's one now. He was simply an almost-socially-acceptable way for Miss Bannon to relieve, shall we say, a little pressure. He and Miss Bannon have a relationship more founded on mutual respect and a variety of trust than anything else.

Clare, on the other hand, wouldn't know what to do if he did have tender feelings for *anyone*, let alone Miss Bannon.

When did you come up with the idea of jewels and jewellery as a source of power?

Jewellery has always been a source of power and fascination. It's very human to adorn oneself, and have that adornment carry power and significance. I realised about halfway through the book that Miss Bannon's jewellery was a character in its own right, and during revision had to go back and write out every set she wore. It was almost like dress-up.

Emma Bannon is such a fascinating character. So tough . . . and yet so proper at times. Where did you get the inspiration for her?

Her influences are manifold, from Kage Baker's Edward Bell-Fairfax (probably the biggest one) to Rudyard Kipling's Kim, as well as *Jane Eyre* and a huge, choking load of Charles Dickens. I wondered what a woman, especially a woman who had escaped the confines of a lower class, would do with the phenomenal power of a Prime. There was also a very interesting tension in her character – Miss Bannon is, after all, expected to act in certain ways because she is a woman, and sometimes she doesn't. There's always a price to pay for that. It would be anachronistic to have it otherwise. The arrogance and willpower of a Sorcerer Prime and the powerful social strictures of gentility and gender roles make for interesting complexity.

What is next for Bannon and Clare?
Right now I'm hard at work on *The Red Plague Affair*, which starts with a cardiac arrest and goes on to involve plague pits, treachery and Dr Vance, Archibald Clare's nemesis and most treasured opponent. It should be a lot of fun.

if you enjoyed
THE IRON WYRM AFFAIR

look out for

GOD SAVE THE QUEEN

by

Kate Locke

Chapter 1
Pomegranates Full and Fine

London, 175 years into the reign of Her Ensanguined Majesty Queen Victoria

I *hate* goblins.

And when I say hate, I mean they bloody terrify me. I'd rather French-kiss a human with a mouth full of silver fillings than pick my way through the debris and rubble that used to be Down Street station, searching for the entrance to the plague den.

It was eerily quiet underground. The bustle of cobbleside was little more than a distant clatter down here. The roll of carriages, the clack of horse hooves from the Mayfair traffic was faint, occasionally completely drowned out by the roar of ancient locomotives raging through the subterranean tunnels carrying a barrage of smells in their bone-jangling wake.

Dirt. Decay. Stone. Blood.

I picked my way around a discarded shopping trolley, and tried to avoid looking at a large paw print in the dust. One of them had been here recently – the drops of blood surrounding the print were still fresh enough for me to smell the coppery tang. Human.

As I descended the stairs to platform level, my palms skimmed over the remaining chipped and pitted cream and maroon tiles that covered the walls – a grim reminder that this . . . *mausoleum* was once a thriving hub of urban transportation.

The light of my torch caught an entire set of paw prints, and the jagged pits at the end where claws had dug into the steps. I swallowed, throat dry.

Of course they ventured up this far – the busted sconces were proof. They couldn't always sit around and wait for some stupid human to come to them – they had to hunt. Still, the sight of those prints and the lingering scent of human blood made my chest tight.

I wasn't a coward. My being here was proof of that – and perhaps proof positive of my lack of intelligence. Everyone – aristocrat, half-blood and human – was afraid of goblins. You'd be mental not to be. They were fast and ferocious and didn't seem to have any sense of morality holding them back. If aristos were fully plagued, then goblins were overly so, though such a thing wasn't really possible. Technically they were aristocrats, but no one would ever dare call them such. To do so was as much an insult to them as to aristos. They were mutations, and terribly proud of it.

Images flashed in my head, memories that played out like disjointed snippets from a film: fur, gnashing fangs, yellow eyes – and blood. That was all I remembered of the day I was attacked by a gob right here in this very station. My history class from the Academy had come here on a field trip. The gobs stayed away from us because of the treaty. At least they were *supposed* to stay away, but one didn't listen, and it picked me.

If it hadn't been for Church, I would have died that day. That was when I realised goblins weren't stories told to children to make us behave. It was also the day I realised that if I didn't do everything in my ability to prove them wrong, people would think I was defective somehow – weak – because a goblin tried to take me.

I hadn't set foot in Down Street station since then. If it weren't for my sister Dede's disappearance I wouldn't have gone down there at all. Avery and Val thought I was overreacting. Dede had taken off on us before, so it was hardly shocking that she wasn't answering her rotary or that the message box on said gadget was full. But in the past she had called me to let me know she was safe. She always called *me*.

I had exhausted every other avenue. It was as though Dede had fallen off the face of the earth. I was desperate, and there was only one option left – goblins. Gobs knew everything that happened in London, despite rarely venturing above ground. Somehow they had found a way to spy on the entire city, and no one seemed to know just what that was. I reckon anyone who had the bollocks to ask didn't live long enough to share it with the rest of us.

It was dark, not because the city didn't run electric lines down here any more – they did – but because the lights had been smashed. The beam from my small hand-held torch caught the grimy glitter of the remains of at least half a dozen bulbs on the ground amongst the refuse.

The bones of a human hand lay surrounded by the shards, cupping the jagged edges in a dull, dry palm.

I reached for the .50 British Bulldog normally holstered snugly against my ribs, but it wasn't there. I'd left it at home. Walking into the plague den with a firearm was considered an act of aggression unless one was there on the official – which I wasn't. Aggression was the last thing – next to fear – you wanted to show in front of one goblin, let alone an entire plague. It was like wearing a sign reading dinner around your neck.

It didn't matter that I had plagued blood as well. I was only a half-blood, the result of a vampire aristocrat – the term that had come to be synonymous with someone of noble descent who was also plagued – and a human courtesan doing the hot and sweaty. Science considered goblins the ultimate birth defect, but in reality they were the result of gene snobbery. The Prometheus protein in vamps – caused by centuries of Black Plague exposure – didn't play well with the mutation that caused others to become weres. If the proteins from both species mixed the outcome was a goblin, though some had been born to parents with the same strain. Hell, there were even two documented cases of goblins being born to human parents both of whom carried dormant plagued genes, but that was very rare, as goblins sometimes tried to eat their way out of the womb. No human could survive that.

In fact, no one had much of a chance of surviving a goblin attack. And that was why I had my lonsdaelite dagger tucked into a secret sheath inside my corset. Harder than diamond and easily concealed, it was my "go to" weapon of choice. It was sharp, light and didn't set off machines designed to detect metal or catch the attention of beings with a keen enough sense of smell to sniff out things like blades and pistols.

The dagger was also one of the few things my mother had left me when she . . . went away.

I wound my way down the staircase to the abandoned platform. It was warm, the air heavy with humidity and neglect, stinking of machine and decay. As easy as it was to access the tunnels, I wasn't surprised to note that mine were the only humanoid prints to be seen in the layers of dust. Back in 1932, a bunch of humans had used this very station to invade and burn Mayfair – *the* aristo neighbourhood – during the Great Insurrection. Their intent had been to destroy the aristocracy, or at least cripple it, and take control of the Kingdom. The history books say that fewer than half of those humans who went into Down Street station made it out alive.

Maybe goblins were useful after all.

I hopped off the platform on to the track, watching my step so I didn't trip over anything – like a body. They hadn't ripped up the line because there weren't any crews mental enough to brave becoming goblin chow, no matter how good the pay. The light of my torch caught a rough hole in the wall just up ahead. I crouched down, back to the wall as I eased closer. The scent of old blood clung to the dust and brick. This had to be the door to the plague den.

Turn around. Don't do this.

Gritting my teeth against the trembling in my veins, I slipped my left leg, followed by my torso and finally my right half, through the hole. When I straightened, I found myself standing on a narrow landing at the top of a long, steep set of rough-hewn stairs that led deeper into the dark. Water dripped from a rusty pipe near my head, dampening the stone.

As I descended the stairs – my heart hammering, sweat beading around my hairline – I caught a whiff of that particular perfume that could only be described as goblinesque; fur, smoke and earth. It could have been vaguely comforting if it hadn't scared the shit out of me.

I reached the bottom. In the beam from my torch I could see bits of broken pottery scattered across the scarred and pitted stone floor. Similar pieces were embedded in the wall. Probably Roman, but my knowledge of history was sadly lacking. The goblins had been doing a bit of housekeeping – there were fresh bricks mortared into parts of the wall, and someone had created a fresco near the ancient archway. I could be wrong, but it looked as though it had been painted in blood.

Cobbleside the sun was long set, but there were street lights, moonlight. Down here it was almost pitch black except for the dim torches flickering on the rough walls. My night vision was perfect, but I didn't want to think about what might happen if some devilish goblin decided to play hide and seek in the dark.

I tried not to imagine what that one would have done to me.

I took a breath and ducked through the archway into the main vestibule of the plague's lair. There were more sconces in here, so I tucked my hand torch into the leather bag slung across my torso. My surroundings were deceptively cosy and welcoming, as though any moment someone might press a pint into my hand or ask me to dance.

I'll say this about the nasty little bastards – they knew how to throw a party. Music flowed through the catacombs from some unknown source – a lively fiddle accompanied by a piano.

Conversation and raucous laughter – both of which sounded a lot like barking – filled the fusty air. Probably a hundred goblins were gathered in this open area, dancing, talking and drinking. They were doing other things as well, but I tried to ignore them. It wouldn't do for me to start screaming.

A few of them looked at me with curiosity in their piercing yellow eyes, turning their heads as they caught my scent. I tensed, waiting for an attack, but it didn't come. It wouldn't either, not when I was so close to an exit, and they were curious to find out what could have brought a halvie this far into their territory.

Goblins looked a lot like werewolves, only shorter and smaller – wiry. They were bipedal, but could run on all fours if the occasion called for additional speed. Their faces were a disconcerting mix of canine and humanoid, but their teeth were all predator – exactly what you might expect from a walking nightmare.

I'd made it maybe another four strides into this bustling netherworld when one of the creatures stuck a tray of produce in my face, trying to entice me to eat. Grapes the size of walnuts, bruise-purple and glistening in the torchlight, were thrust beneath my nose. Pomegranates the colour of blood, bleeding sweet-tart juice, filled the platter as well, and apples – pale flesh glistening with a delicate blush. There were more, but those were the ones that tempted me the most. I could almost taste them, feel the syrup running down my chin. Berry-stained fingers clutched and pinched at me, smearing sticky delight on my skin and clothes as I pressed forward.

"Eat, pretty," rasped the vaguely soft cruel voice. "Just a taste. A wee little nibble for our sweet lady."

Our? Not bloody fucking likely. I couldn't tell if my tormentor was male or female. The body hair didn't help either. It was effective camouflage unless you happened upon a male goblin in an amorous state. Generally they tried to affect some kind of identity for themselves – a little vanity so non-goblins could tell them apart. This one had both of its ears pierced several times, delicate chains weaving in and out of the holes like golden stitches.

I shook my head, but didn't open my mouth to vocalise my refusal. An open mouth was an invitation to a goblin to stick something in it. If you were lucky, it was only food, but once you tasted their poison you were lost. Goblins were known for their drugs – mostly their opium. They enticed weak humans with a cheap and euphoric high, and the promise of more. Goblins didn't want human money as payment. They wanted information. They wanted flesh. There were already several customers providing entertainment for tonight's bash. I pushed away whatever pity I felt for them – everyone knew what happened when you trafficked with goblins.

I pushed through the crowd, moving deeper into the lair despite every instinct I possessed telling me to run. I was looking for one goblin in particular and I was not going to leave without seeing him. Besides, running would get me chased. Chased would get me eaten.

As I walked, I tried not to pay too much attention to what was going on in the shadows around me. I'd seen a lot of horrible things in my two and twenty years, but the sight of hueys – humans – gorging themselves on fruit, seeds and pulp in their hair and smeared over their dirty naked skin, shook me. Maybe it was the fact that pomegranate flesh looked just like that – flesh – between stained teeth. Or maybe it was the wild delirium in their eyes as goblins ran greedy hands over their sticky bodies.

It was like a scene out of Christina Rossetti's poem, but nothing so lyrical. Mothers knew to keep their children at home after dark, lest they go missing, fated to end up as goblin food – or worse, a goblin's slave.

A sweet, earthy smoke hung heavy in the air, reminding me of decaying flowers. It brushed pleasantly against my mind, but was burned away by my metabolism before it could have any real effect. I brushed a platter of cherries, held by strong paw-like hands, aside despite the watering of my mouth. I knew they'd split between my teeth with a firm, juicy pop, spilling tart, delicious juice down my dry throat. Accepting hospitality might mean I'd be expected to pay for it later, and I wasn't about to end up in the plague's debt.Thankfully I quickly spotted the goblin I was looking for. He sat on a dais near the back of the hall, on a throne made entirely from human bones. If I had to guess, I'd say this is what happened to several of the humans who braved this place during the Great Insurrection. Skulls served as finials high on either side of his head. Another set formed armrests over which each of his furry hands curved.

But this goblin would have stood out without the throne, and the obvious deference with which the other freaks treated him. He was tall for a gob – probably my height when standing – and his shoulders were broad, his canine teeth large and sharp. The firelight made his fur look like warm caramel spotted with chocolate. One of his dog-like ears was torn and chewed-looking, the edges scarred. He was missing an eye as well, the thin line of the closed lid almost indistinguishable in the fur of his face. Hard to believe there was anything aristocratic about him, yet he could be the son of a duke, or even the Prince of Wales. His mother would have to be of rank as well. Did they ever wonder what had become of their monstrous child?

While thousands of humans died with every incarnation of the plague – which loves this country like a mother loves her child – aristocrats survived. Not only survived, they evolved. In England the plague-born Prometheus protein led to vampirism, in Scotland it caused lycanthropy.

It also occasionally affected someone who wasn't considered upper class. Historically, members of the aristocracy had never been very good at keeping it in their pants. Indiscretions with human carriers resulted in the first halvie births, and launched the careers of generations of breeding courtesans.

Occasionally some seemingly normal human woman gave birth to a half or fully plagued infant. These children were often murdered by their parents, or shipped off to orphanages where they shunned and mistreated. That was prior to 1932's rebellion. Now, such cruelties were prevented by the Pax – Pax Yersenia, which dictated that each human donated a sample of DNA at birth. This could help prevent human carriers from intermarrying. It also provided families and special housing for unwanted plagued children.

By the time Victoria, our first fully plagued monarch – King George III had shown vampiric traits – ascended the throne, other aristocrats across Britain and Europe had revealed their true natures as well. Vampires thrived in the more temperate climes like France and Spain, weres in Russia and other eastern countries. Some places had a mix of the two, as did Asia and Australia. Those who remained in Canada and the Americas had gone on to become socialites and film stars.

But they were never safe, no matter where they were. Humans accounted for ninety-two per cent of aristocratic and halvie deaths. Haemophilia, suicide and accidents made up for the remaining eight. There were no recorded goblin deaths at human hands – not even during the Insurrection.

I approached the battle-scarred goblin with caution. The flickering torches made it hard to tell, but I think recognition flashed in his one yellow eye. He sniffed the air as I approached. I curtsied, playing to his vanity.

"A Vardan get," he said, in a voice that was surprisingly low and articulate for a goblin. "Here on the official?"

Half-bloods took the title of their sire as their surname. The Duke of Vardan was my father. "Nothing official, my lord. I'm here because the goblin prince knows everything that happens in London."

"True," he replied with a slow nod. Despite my flattery he was still looking at me like he expected me to do or say something. "But there is a price. What do you offer your prince, pretty get?"

The only prince I claimed was Albert, God rest his soul, and perhaps Bertie, the Prince of Wales. This mangy monster was not *my* prince. Was I wasn't stupid enough to tell him that? Hell, no.

I reached into the leather satchel I'd brought with me, pulled out the clear plastic bag with a lump of blood-soaked butcher's paper inside and offered it to the goblin. He snatched it from me with eager hands that were just a titch too long and dexterous to be paws, tossed the plastic on the floor and tore open the paper. A whine of delight slipped from his throat when he saw what I'd brought. Around us other goblins raised their muzzles and made similar noises, but no one dared approach.

I looked away as the prince brought the gory mass to his muzzle and took an enthusiastic bite. I made my mind blank, refusing to think of what the meat was, what it had been. My only solace was that it had already been dead when I bought it. The blood might smell good, but I couldn't imagine eating anything that . . . awful . . . terrible . . . *raw*.

The goblin gave a little shudder of delight as he chewed and rewrapped his treat for later. A long pink tongue slipped out to lick his muzzle clean. "Proper tribute. Honours her prince. I will tell the lady what I know. Ask, pretty, ask."

The rest of the goblins drifted away from us, save for one little gob who came and sat at the prince's furry feet and stared at me with open curiosity. I was very much aware that every goblin who wasn't preoccupied with human playthings watched me closely. I was relatively safe now, having paid my tribute to their prince. So long as I behaved myself and didn't offend anyone, I'd make it out of here alive. Probably.